Barbie ™

3 in 1

'COND.

PAPERCUT Z ™

NEW YORK

MORE GREAT GRAPHIC NOVEL SERIES AVAILABLE FROM PAPERCUTZ

THREE SMURFS GRAPHIC NOVELS BY Peyo IN ONE
the SMURFS
3 in 1
THE PURPLE SMURFS
THE SMURFS AND THE MAGIC FLUTE
THE SMURF KING
PAPERCUTZ

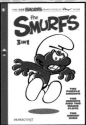

THE SMURFS 3 IN 1 #1

TROLLS
3 GRAPHIC NOVELS IN 1
PAPERCUTZ

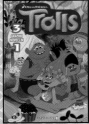

TROLLS 3 IN 1

Thea Stilton
3 in 1
3 Graphic Novels in 1
The Secret of Whale Island
Revenge of the Lizard Club
The Treasure of the Viking Ship
PAPERCUTZ

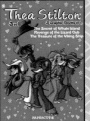

THEA STILTON 3 IN 1 #1

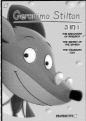

Geronimo Stilton
3 IN 1
THE DISCOVERY OF AMERICA
THE SECRET OF THE SPHINX
THE COLISEUM CON
PAPERCUTZ

GERONIMO STILTON 3 IN 1 #1

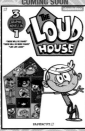

COMING SOON

nickelodeon
3 GRAPHIC NOVELS IN 1
THE LOUD HOUSE
PAPERCUTZ

THE LOUD HOUSE 3 IN 1 #1

geeky f@b 5
It's Not Rocket Science
PAPERCUTZ

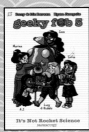

GEEKY F@B 5 #1

DINOSAUR EXPLORERS
PREHISTORIC PIONEERS

DINOSAUR EXPLORERS #1

sea creatures
in their own words
PAPERCUTZ

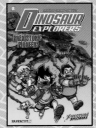

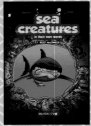

SEA CREATURES #1

MANOSAURS
WALK LIKE A MANOSAUR!
PAPERCUTZ

MANOSAURS #1

Susan Schade
Jon Buller
Scarlett
Star on the Run
PAPERCUTZ

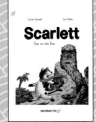

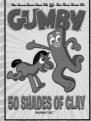

SCARLETT

ANNE of GREEN BAGELS
Susan Schade
Jon Buller
PAPERCUTZ

ANNE OF GREEN BAGELS #1

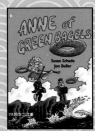

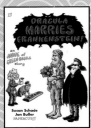

DRACULA MARRIES FRANKENSTEIN!
an ANNE of GREEN BAGELS story
Susan Schade
Jon Buller
PAPERCUTZ

DRACULA MARRIES FRANKENSTEIN!

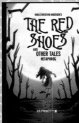

HANS CHRISTIAN ANDERSEN'S
THE RED SHOES
AND OTHER TALES
METAPHROG
PAPERCUTZ

THE RED SHOES

HANS CHRISTIAN ANDERSEN'S
The Little Mermaid
METAPHROG
PAPERCUTZ

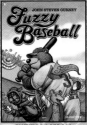

THE LITTLE MERMAID

JOHN STEVEN GURNEY
Fuzzy Baseball

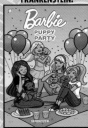

FUZZY BASEBALL

HOTEL TRANSYLVANIA
KAKIELAND KATASTROPHE
PAPERCUTZ

HOTEL TRANSYLVANIA #1

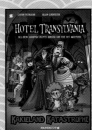

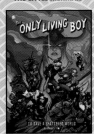

Barbie
PUPPY PARTY
PAPERCUTZ

BARBIE PUPPY PARTY #1

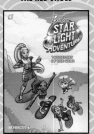

Barbie
STAR LIGHT ADVENTURE
THE SECRET OF THE GEMS
PAPERCUTZ

BARBIE STARLIGHT ADVENTURE #1

THE ONLY LIVING BOY
TO SAVE A SHATTERED WORLD

THE ONLY LIVING BOY #5

GUMBY
50 SHADES OF CLAY
PAPERCUTZ

GUMBY #1

THE SMURFS 3 in 1, TROLLS 3 in 1, BARBIE 3 in 1, GERONIMO STILTON 3 in 1, THE LOUD HOUSE 3 in 1, SCARLETT and ANNE OF GREEN BAGELS graphic novels are available for $14.99 each in paperback only. THE ONLY LIVING BOY and GUMBY graphic novels are available for $8.99 each in paperback, and $13.99 each in hardcover. DINOSAUR EXPLORERS graphic novels are available for $12.99 each in paperback and $16.99 each in hardcover. SEA CREATURES graphic novels are available for $10.99 each in hardcover only. FUZZY BASEBALL graphic novels are available for $9.99 each in paperback only. DRACULA MARRIES FRANKENSTEIN! graphic novels are available for $12.99 each in paperback only. BARBIE, HOTEL TRANSYLVANIA #1 and MANOSAURS graphic novels are available for $7.99 each in paperback and $12.99 each in hardcover. GEEKY FAB 5, THE RED SHOES and THE LITTLE MERMAID graphic novels are available for $12.99 each in hardcover only.

Available from booksellers everywhere. You can also order online from www.papercutz.com. Or call 1-800-886-1223, Monday through Friday, 9-5 EST. MC, Visa and AmEx accepted. To order by mail, please add $5.00 for postage and handling for first book ordered, $1.00 for each additional book and make check payable to NBM Publishing. Send to Papercutz, 160 Broadway, Suite 700, East Wing, New York, NY 10038.

THE SMURFS, TROLLS, BARBIE, GERONIMO STILTON, THE LOUD HOUSE, GEEKY FAB 5, DINOSAUR EXPLORERS, SEA CREATURES, MANOSAURS, SCARLETT, ANNE OF GREEN BAGELS, DRACULA MARRIES FRANKENSTEIN!, THE RED SHOES, THE LITTLE MERMAID, FUZZY BASEBALL, HOTEL TRANSYLVANIA, THE ONLY LIVING BOY, and GUMBY graphic novels are also available wherever e-books are sold.

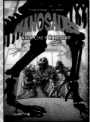

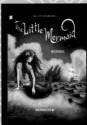

Table of Contents

Barbie 3 in 1

Barbie "Fashion Superstar"

SARAH KUHN — Writer
ALITHA MARTINEZ — Artist
MATT HERMS — Pin up Colorist
LAURIE E. SMITH — Colorist
JANICE CHIANG — Letterer
DAWN GUZZO — Original Design/Production
BETHANY BRYAN — Original Editor

Barbie "Big Dreams Best Friends"

SARAH KUHN — Writer
YISHAN LI — Artist
ALITHA MARTINEZ — Cover
LAURIE E. SMITH — Colorist
JANICE CHIANG — Letterer
DAWN GUZZO — Original Production
MARIAH McCOURT — Original Editor

 "Need for Speed"

TINI HOWARD — Writer
JULES RIVERA — Artist
LAURIE E. SMITH — Colorist (cover)
RONDA PATTISON — Colorist
JANICE CHIANG — Letterer
GRACE ILORI — Original Production
MARIAH McCOURT — Original Editor

Special Thanks to Bethany Bryan, Beth Scorzato, Ryan Ferguson, Debra Moscow Zakarin, Kristine Lombardi, Sammie Suchland, Stuart Smith, Charnita Belcher, Nicole Corse, Karen Painter

JAYJAY JACKSON — Design and Production
JEFF WHITMAN — Assistant Managing Editor
GRANT FREDERICK — Editorial Intern
JIM SALICRUP
Editor-in-Chief

PB ISBN: 978-1-5458-0165-9

Papercutz books may be purchased for business or promotional use. For information on bulk purchases please contact Macmillan Corporate and Premium Sales Department at (800) 221-7945 x5442.

Printed in China
December 2018

Distributed by Macmillan
First Printing

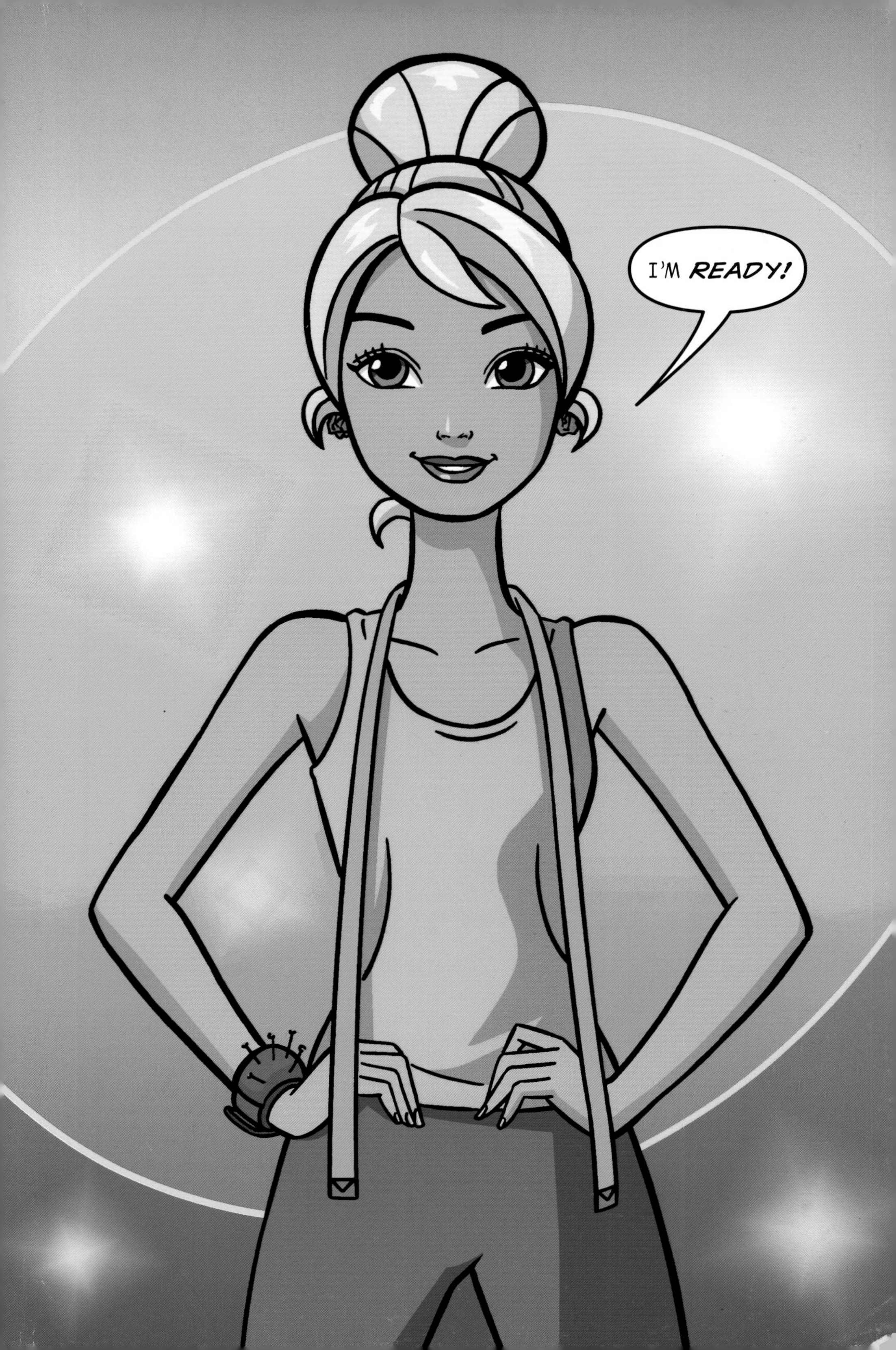
I'M *READY!*

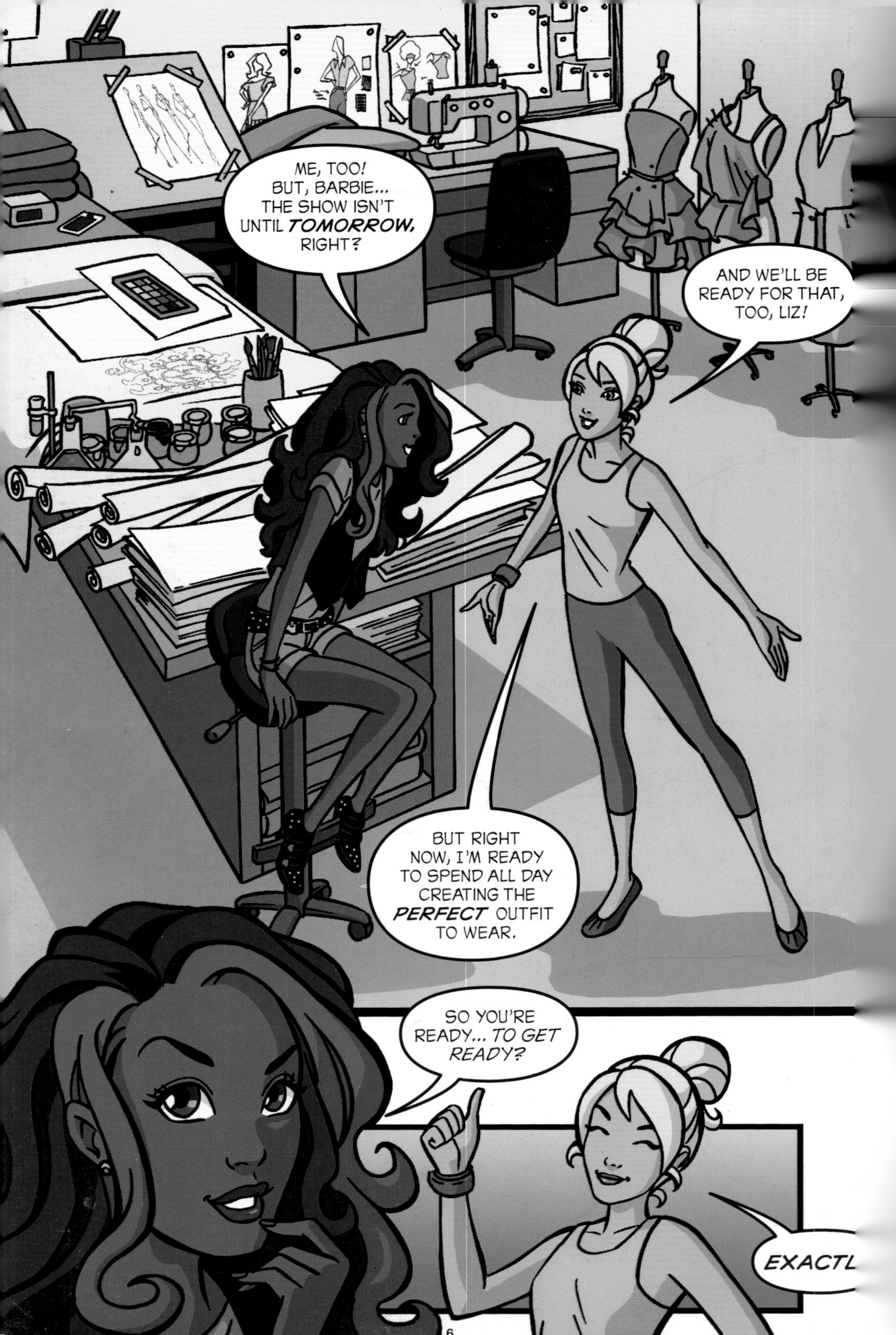
ME, TOO! BUT, BARBIE... THE SHOW ISN'T UNTIL *TOMORROW,* RIGHT?
AND WE'LL BE READY FOR THAT, TOO, LIZ!
BUT RIGHT NOW, I'M READY TO SPEND ALL DAY CREATING THE *PERFECT* OUTFIT TO WEAR.
SO YOU'RE READY... *TO GET READY?*
EXACTL

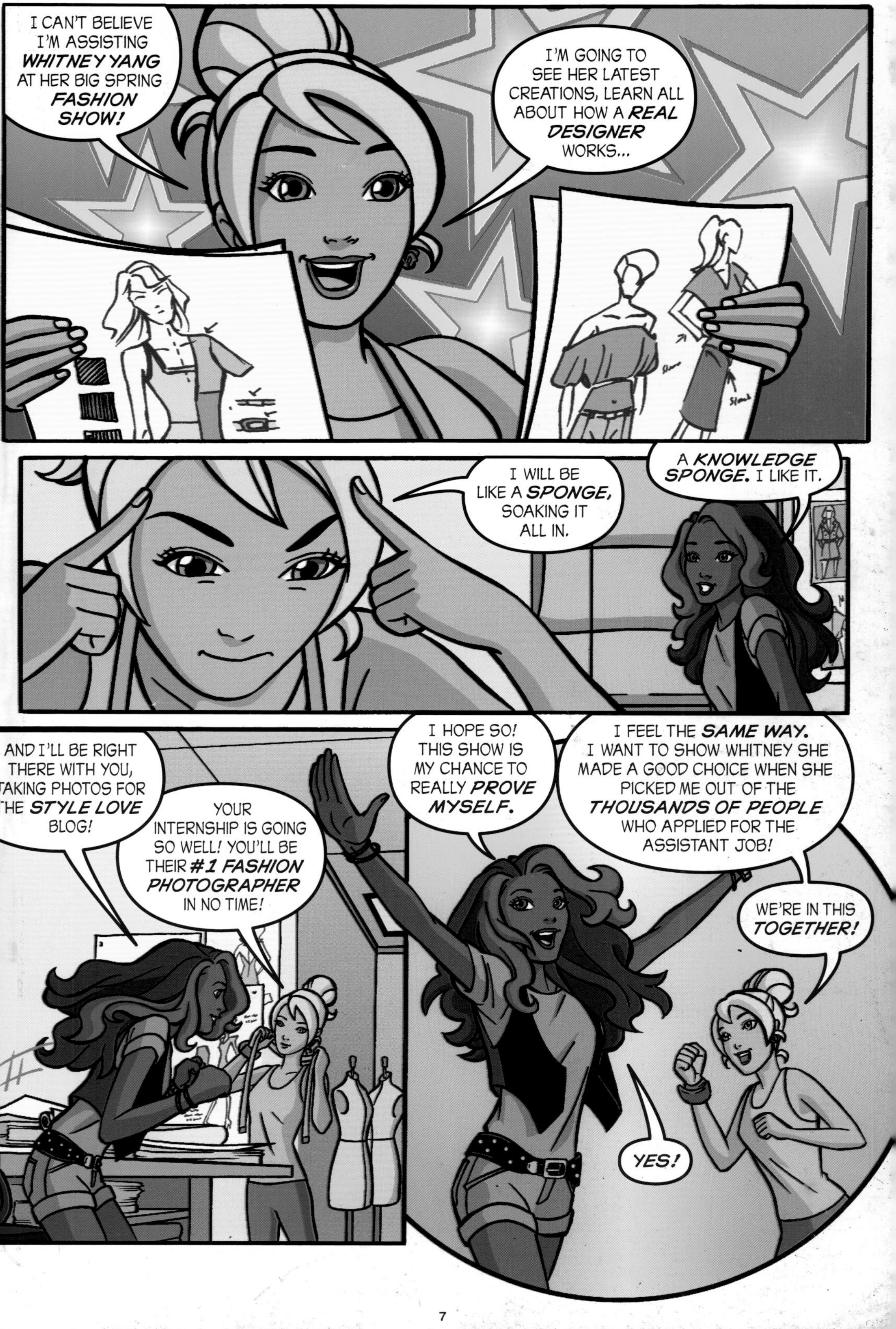

I CAN'T BELIEVE I'M ASSISTING *WHITNEY YANG* AT HER BIG SPRING *FASHION SHOW!*
I'M GOING TO SEE HER LATEST CREATIONS, LEARN ALL ABOUT HOW A *REAL DESIGNER* WORKS...
I WILL BE LIKE A *SPONGE,* SOAKING IT ALL IN.
A *KNOWLEDGE SPONGE.* I LIKE IT.
AND I'LL BE RIGHT THERE WITH YOU, TAKING PHOTOS FOR THE *STYLE LOVE* BLOG!
YOUR INTERNSHIP IS GOING SO WELL! YOU'LL BE THEIR *#1 FASHION PHOTOGRAPHER* IN NO TIME!
I HOPE SO! THIS SHOW IS MY CHANCE TO REALLY *PROVE MYSELF.*
I FEEL THE *SAME WAY.* I WANT TO SHOW WHITNEY SHE MADE A GOOD CHOICE WHEN SHE PICKED ME OUT OF THE *THOUSANDS OF PEOPLE* WHO APPLIED FOR THE ASSISTANT JOB!
WE'RE IN THIS *TOGETHER!*
YES!

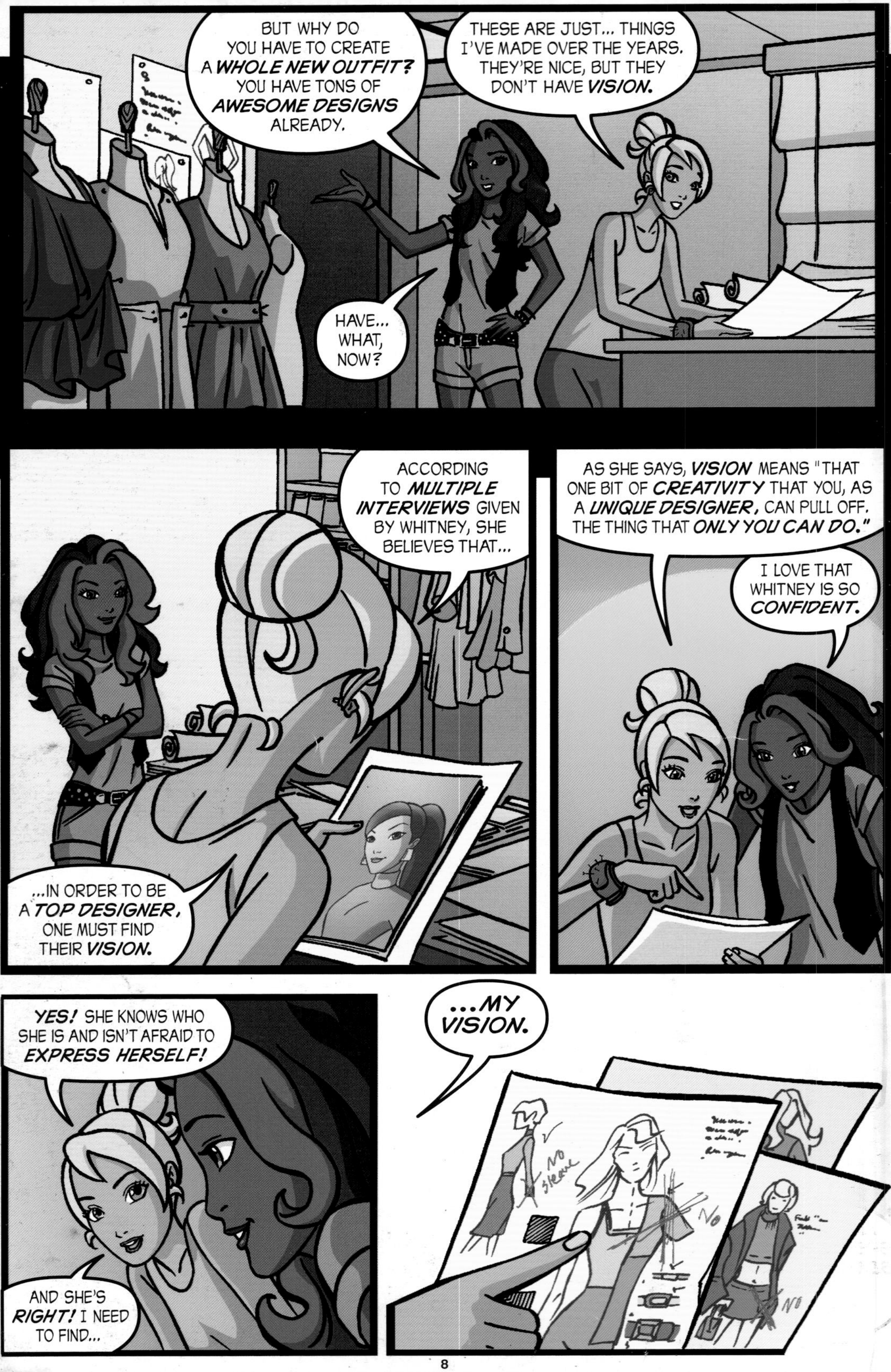

BUT WHY DO YOU HAVE TO CREATE A WHOLE NEW OUTFIT? YOU HAVE TONS OF AWESOME DESIGNS ALREADY.
THESE ARE JUST... THINGS I'VE MADE OVER THE YEARS. THEY'RE NICE, BUT THEY DON'T HAVE VISION.
HAVE... WHAT, NOW?
ACCORDING TO MULTIPLE INTERVIEWS GIVEN BY WHITNEY, SHE BELIEVES THAT...
...IN ORDER TO BE A TOP DESIGNER, ONE MUST FIND THEIR VISION.
AS SHE SAYS, VISION MEANS "THAT ONE BIT OF CREATIVITY THAT YOU, AS A UNIQUE DESIGNER, CAN PULL OFF. THE THING THAT ONLY YOU CAN DO."
I LOVE THAT WHITNEY IS SO CONFIDENT.
YES! SHE KNOWS WHO SHE IS AND ISN'T AFRAID TO EXPRESS HERSELF!
AND SHE'S RIGHT! I NEED TO FIND...
...MY VISION.
NO SLEEVE
NO
NO

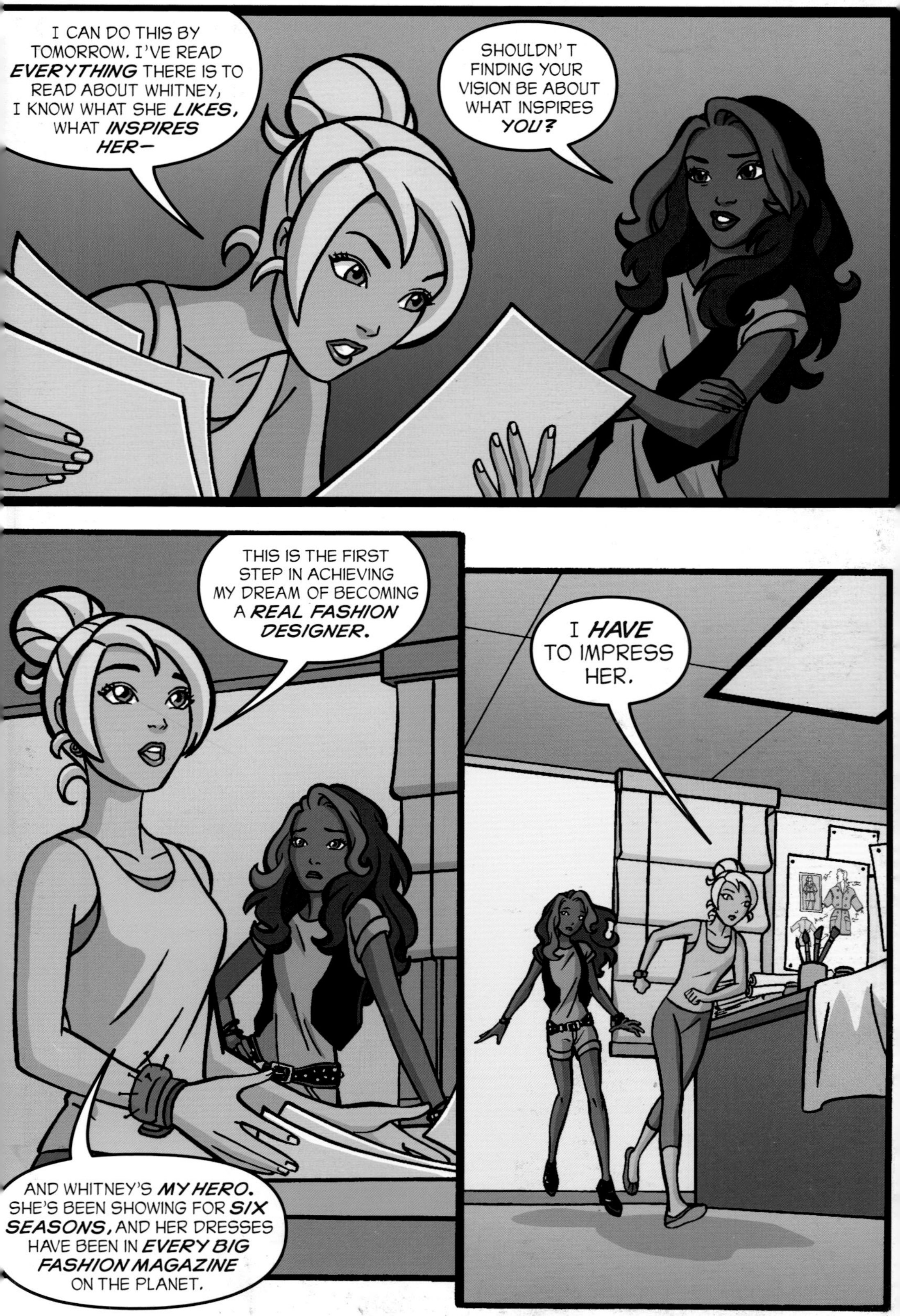
I CAN DO THIS BY TOMORROW. I'VE READ EVERYTHING THERE IS TO READ ABOUT WHITNEY, I KNOW WHAT SHE LIKES, WHAT INSPIRES HER—
SHOULDN'T FINDING YOUR VISION BE ABOUT WHAT INSPIRES YOU?
THIS IS THE FIRST STEP IN ACHIEVING MY DREAM OF BECOMING A REAL FASHION DESIGNER.
AND WHITNEY'S MY HERO. SHE'S BEEN SHOWING FOR SIX SEASONS, AND HER DRESSES HAVE BEEN IN EVERY BIG FASHION MAGAZINE ON THE PLANET.
I HAVE TO IMPRESS HER.

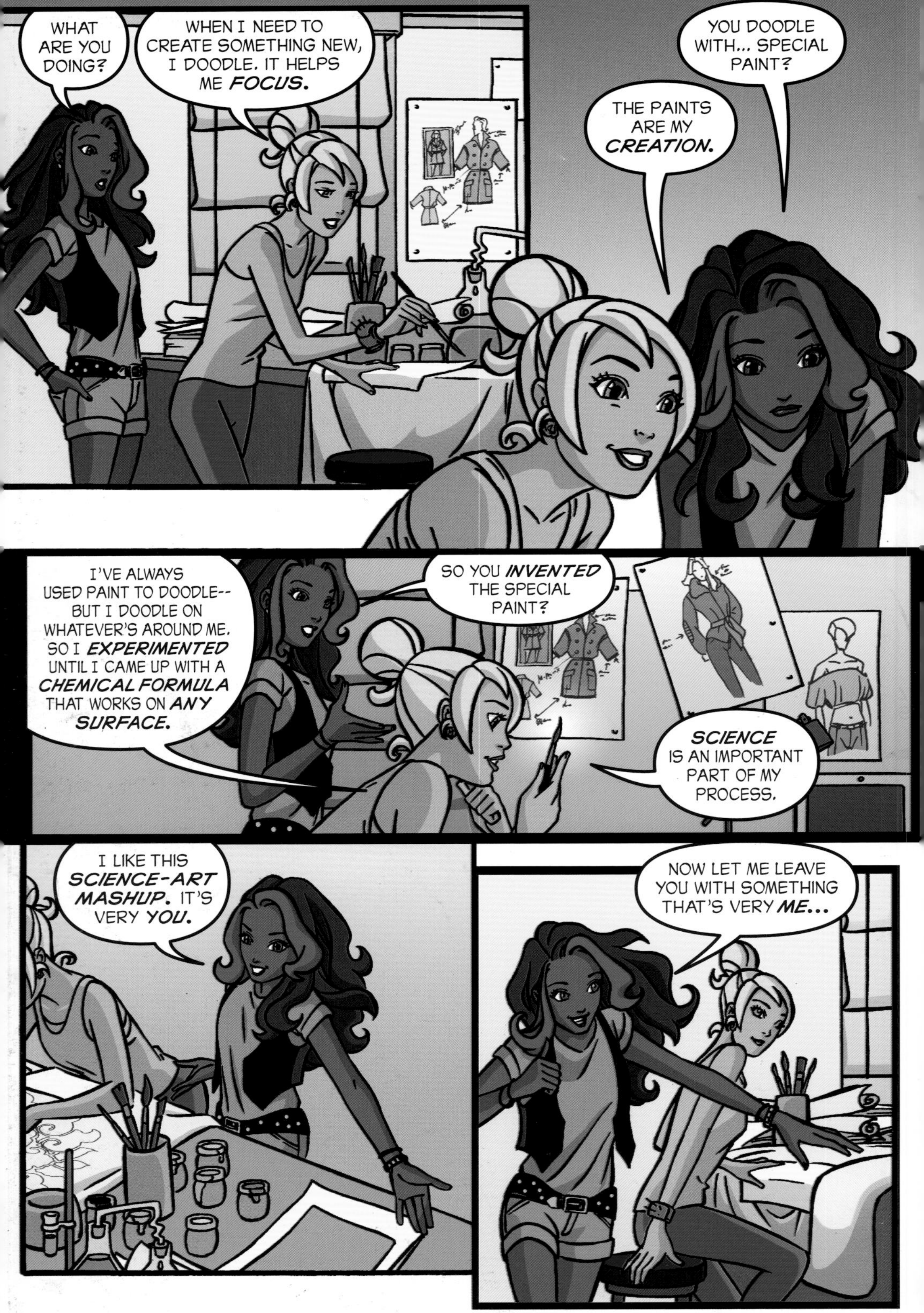
WHAT ARE YOU DOING?
WHEN I NEED TO CREATE SOMETHING NEW, I DOODLE. IT HELPS ME FOCUS.
YOU DOODLE WITH... SPECIAL PAINT?
THE PAINTS ARE MY CREATION.
I'VE ALWAYS USED PAINT TO DOODLE-- BUT I DOODLE ON WHATEVER'S AROUND ME. SO I EXPERIMENTED UNTIL I CAME UP WITH A CHEMICAL FORMULA THAT WORKS ON ANY SURFACE.
SO YOU INVENTED THE SPECIAL PAINT?
SCIENCE IS AN IMPORTANT PART OF MY PROCESS.
I LIKE THIS SCIENCE-ART MASHUP. IT'S VERY YOU.
NOW LET ME LEAVE YOU WITH SOMETHING THAT'S VERY ME...

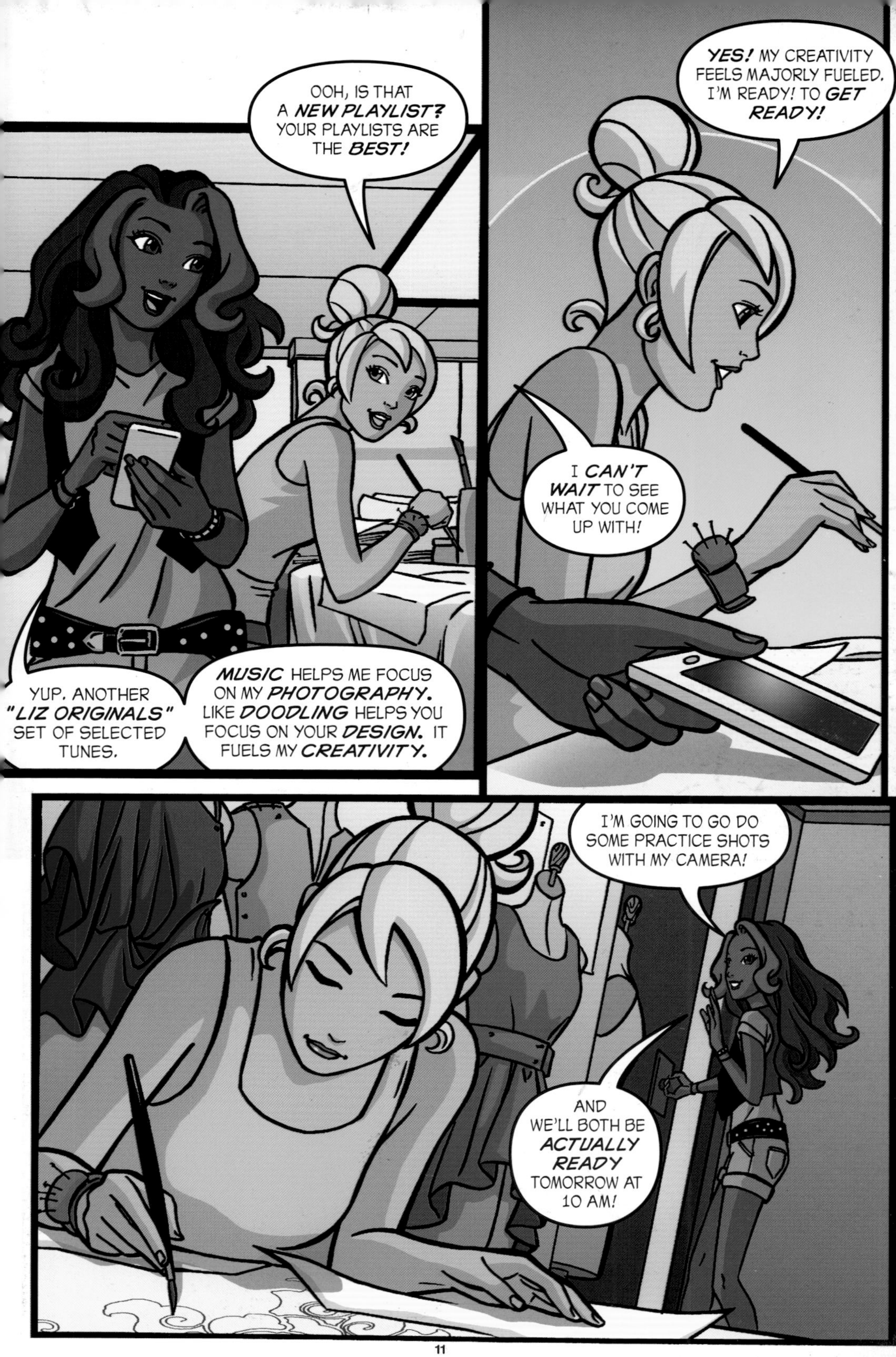
OOH, IS THAT A NEW PLAYLIST? YOUR PLAYLISTS ARE THE BEST!
YUP. ANOTHER "LIZ ORIGINALS" SET OF SELECTED TUNES.
MUSIC HELPS ME FOCUS ON MY PHOTOGRAPHY. LIKE DOODLING HELPS YOU FOCUS ON YOUR DESIGN. IT FUELS MY CREATIVITY.
YES! MY CREATIVITY FEELS MAJORLY FUELED. I'M READY! TO GET READY!
I CAN'T WAIT TO SEE WHAT YOU COME UP WITH!
I'M GOING TO GO DO SOME PRACTICE SHOTS WITH MY CAMERA!
AND WE'LL BOTH BE ACTUALLY READY TOMORROW AT 10 AM!

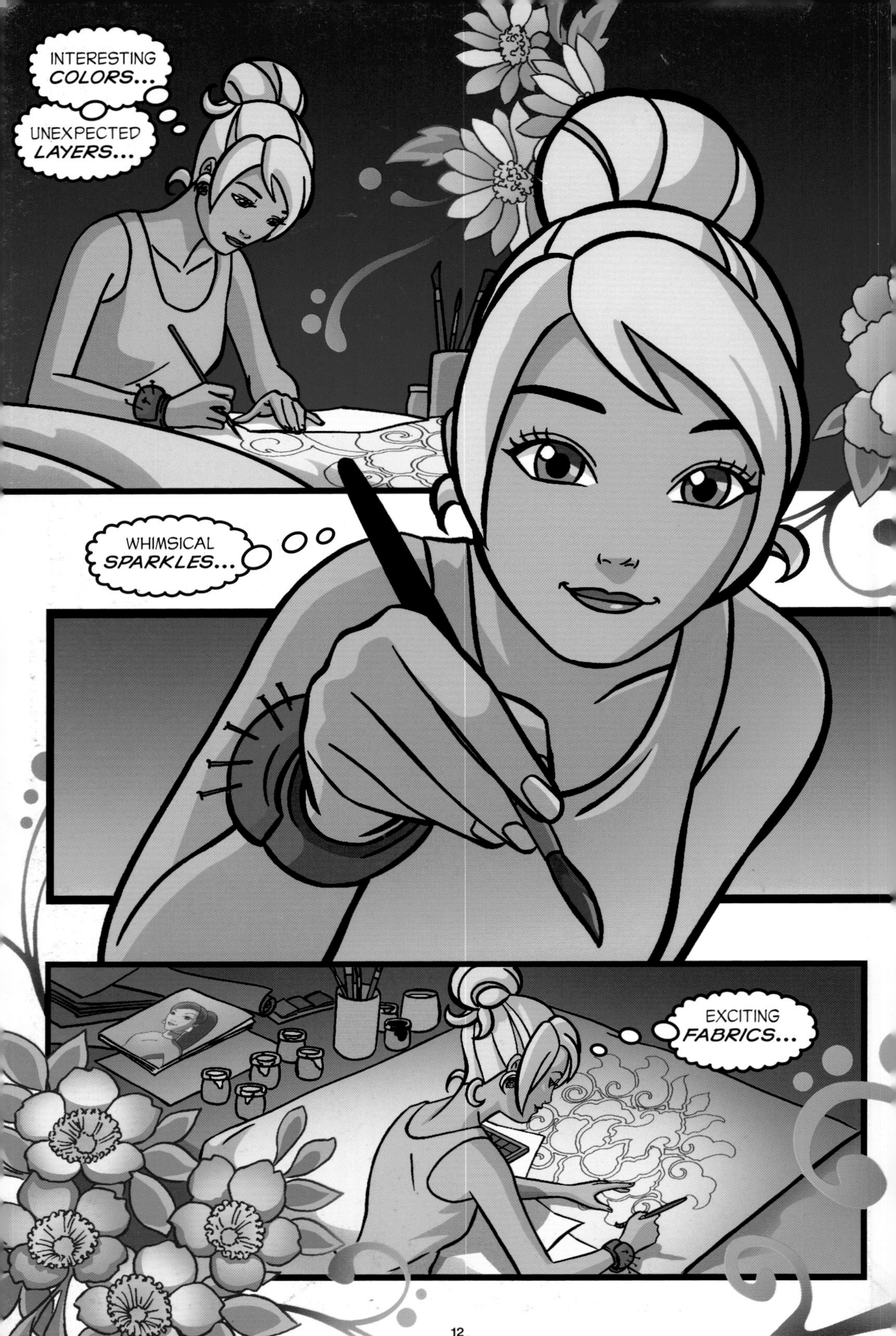
INTERESTING COLORS...
UNEXPECTED LAYERS...
WHIMSICAL SPARKLES...
EXCITING FABRICS...

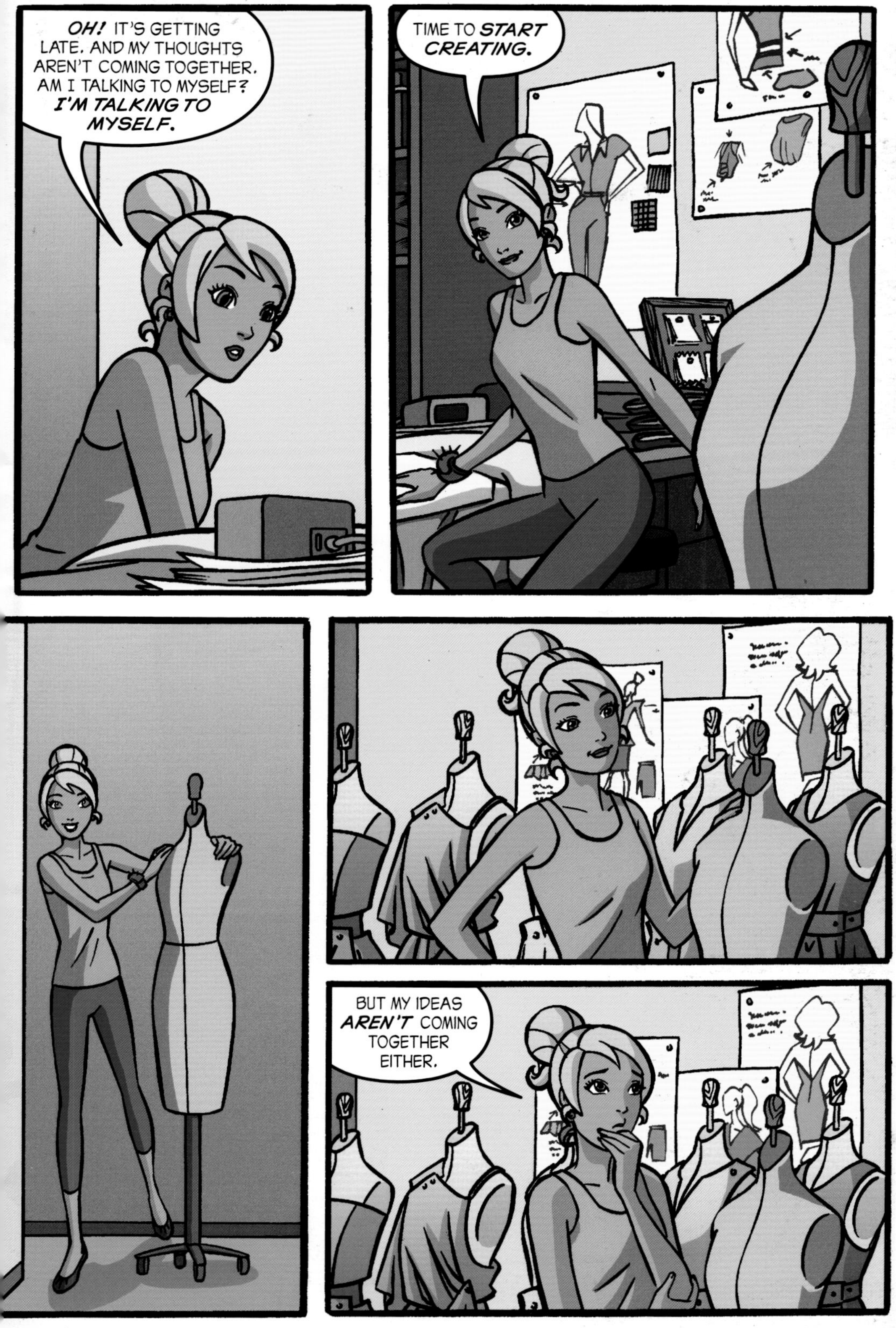
OH! IT'S GETTING LATE. AND MY THOUGHTS AREN'T COMING TOGETHER. AM I TALKING TO MYSELF? I'M TALKING TO MYSELF.
TIME TO START CREATING.
BUT MY IDEAS AREN'T COMING TOGETHER EITHER.

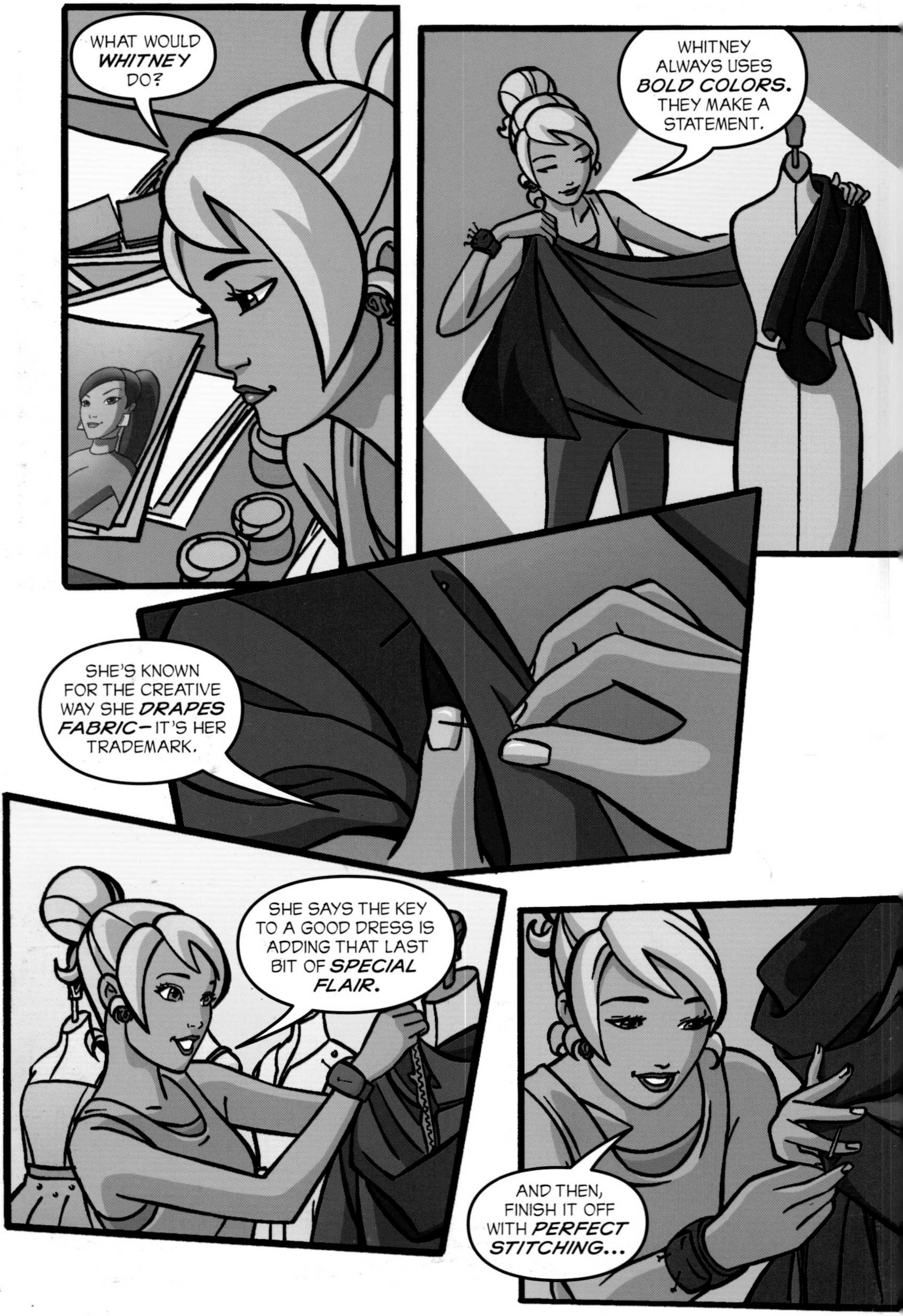
WHAT WOULD WHITNEY DO?
WHITNEY ALWAYS USES BOLD COLORS. THEY MAKE A STATEMENT.
SHE'S KNOWN FOR THE CREATIVE WAY SHE DRAPES FABRIC— IT'S HER TRADEMARK.
SHE SAYS THE KEY TO A GOOD DRESS IS ADDING THAT LAST BIT OF SPECIAL FLAIR.
AND THEN, FINISH IT OFF WITH PERFECT STITCHING...

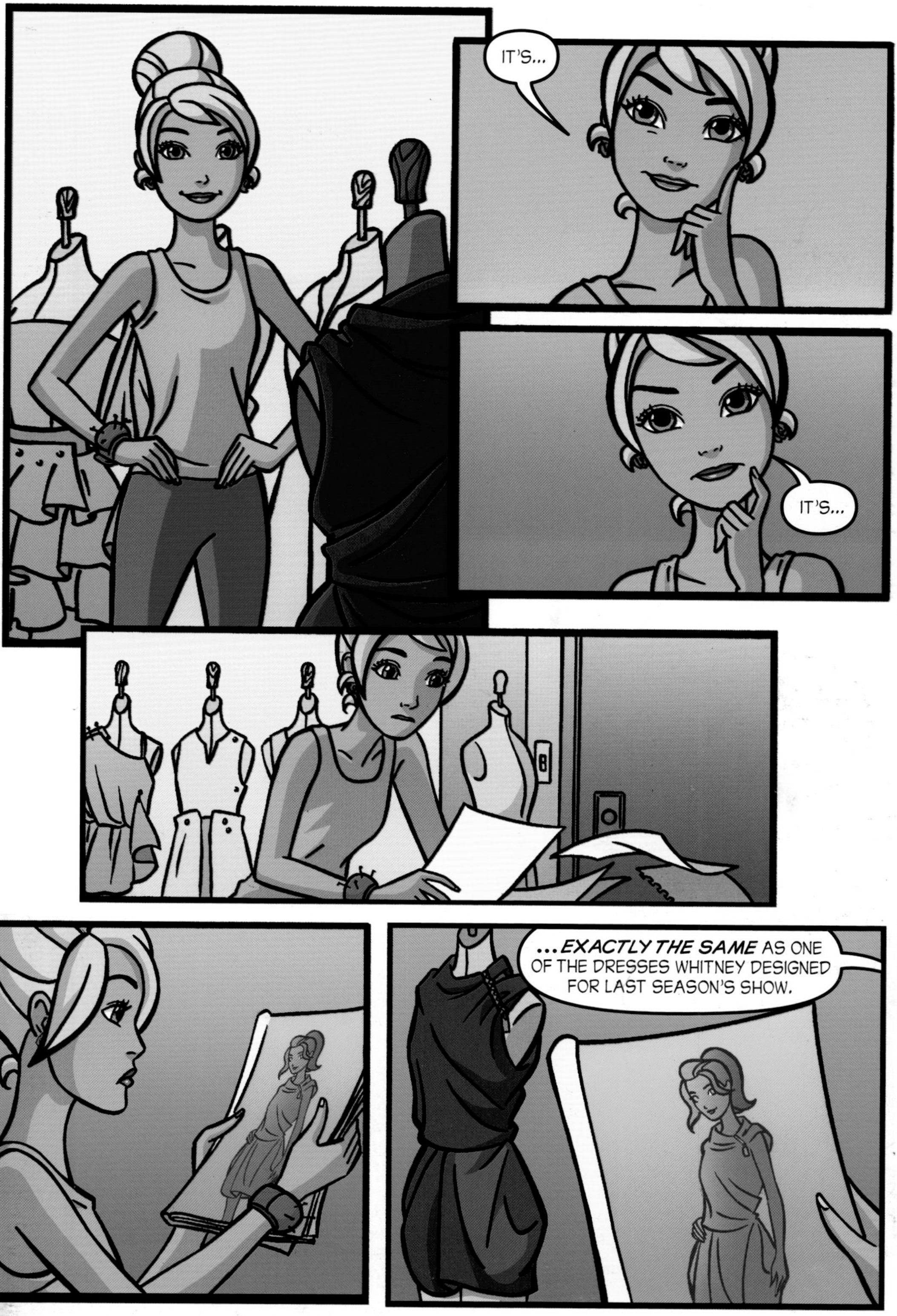
IT'S...
IT'S...
...*EXACTLY THE SAME* AS ONE OF THE DRESSES WHITNEY DESIGNED FOR LAST SEASON'S SHOW.

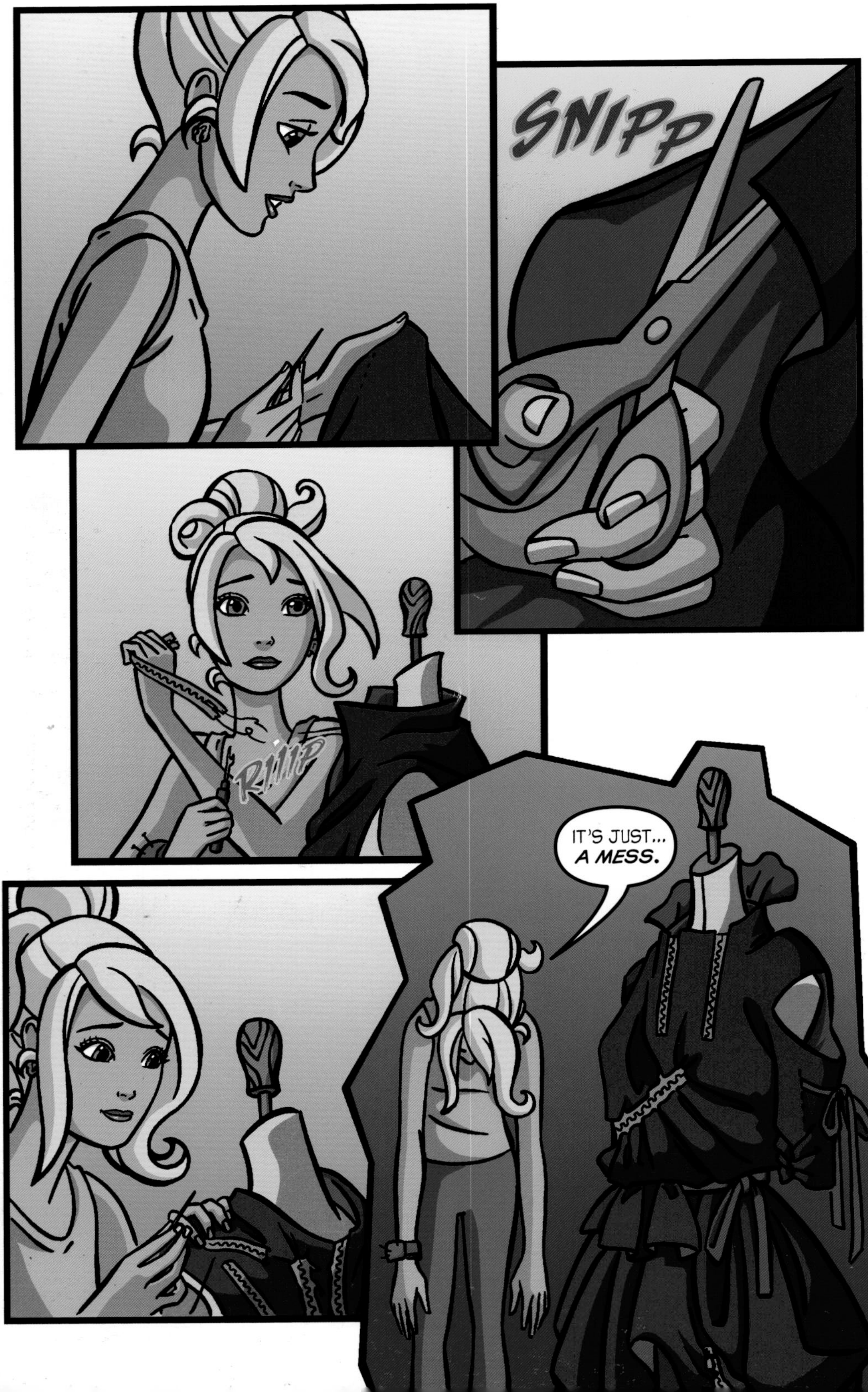
SNIPP
RIIIIP
IT'S JUST... A MESS.

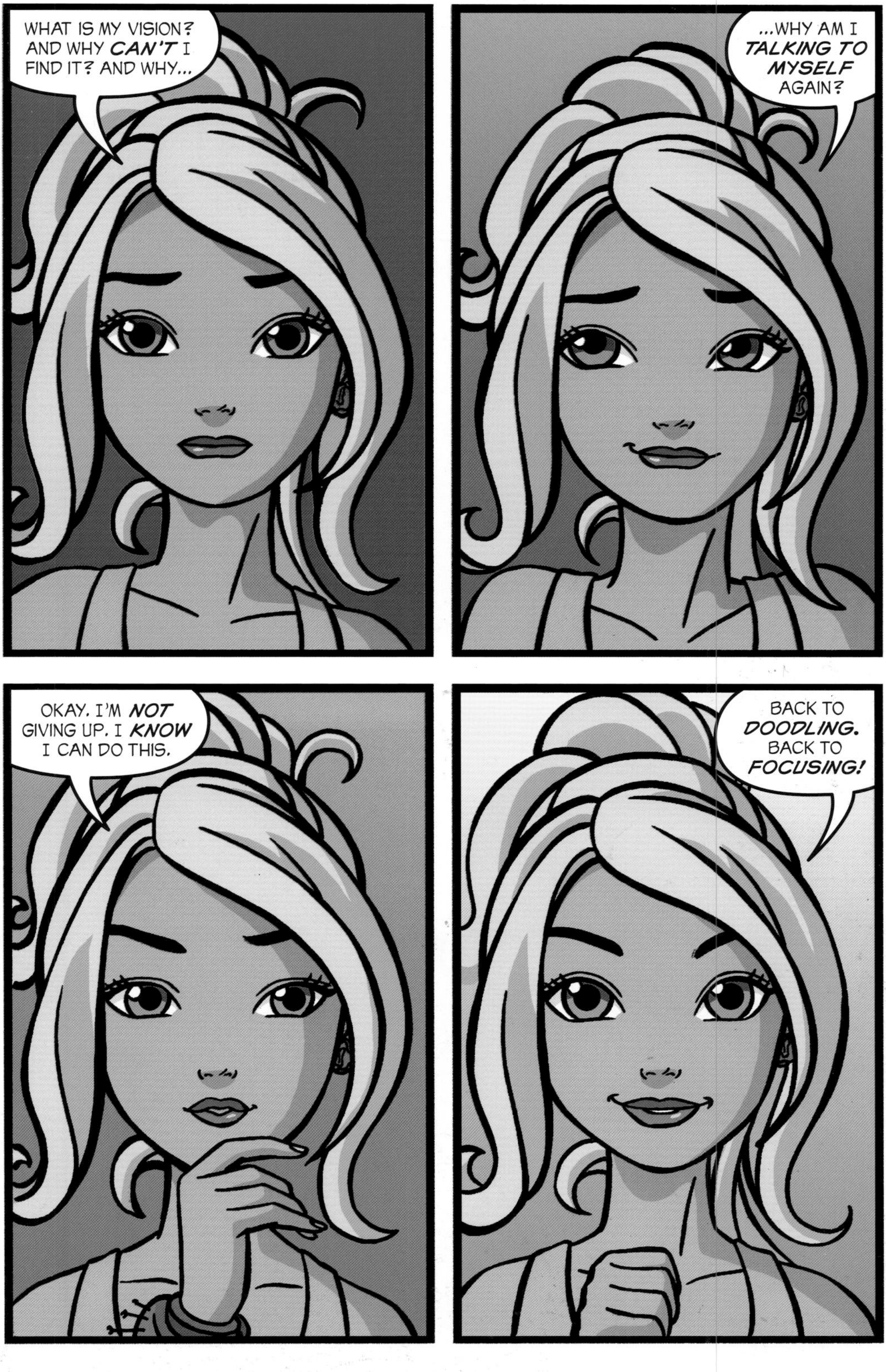
WHAT IS MY VISION? AND WHY CAN'T I FIND IT? AND WHY...
...WHY AM I TALKING TO MYSELF AGAIN?
OKAY. I'M NOT GIVING UP. I KNOW I CAN DO THIS.
BACK TO DOODLING. BACK TO FOCUSING!

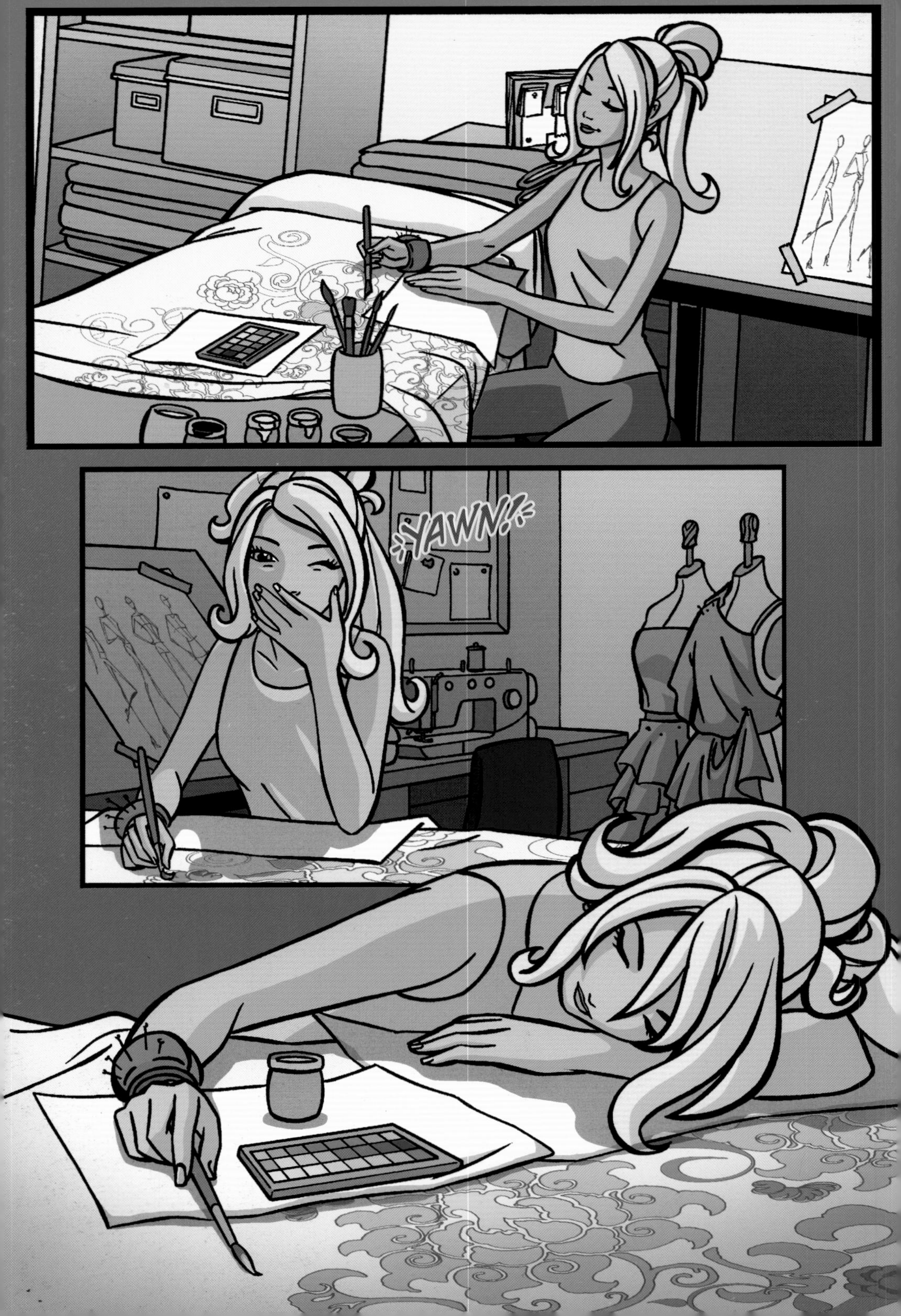
YAWN!

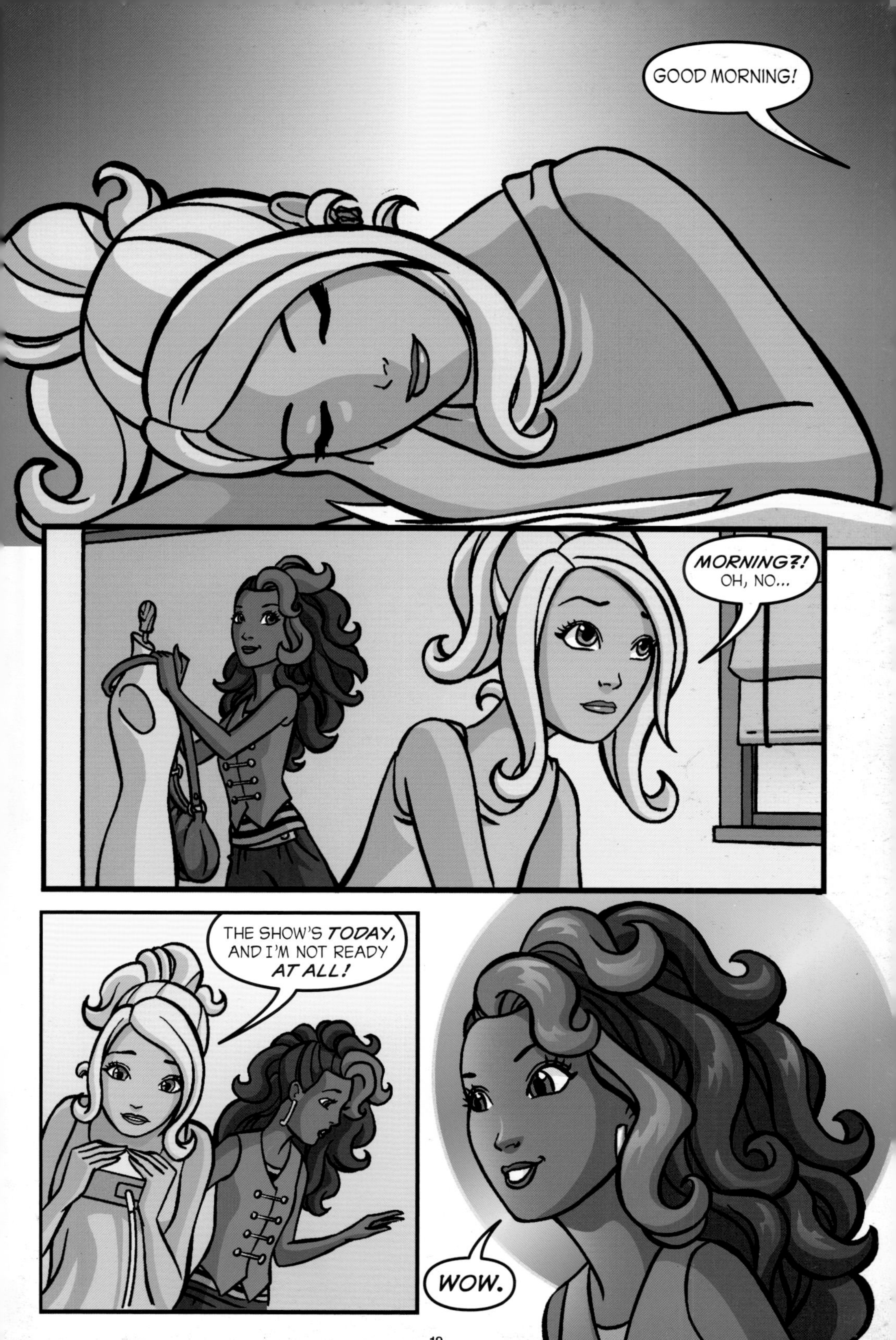
GOOD MORNING!
MORNING?! OH, NO...
THE SHOW'S TODAY, AND I'M NOT READY AT ALL!
WOW.

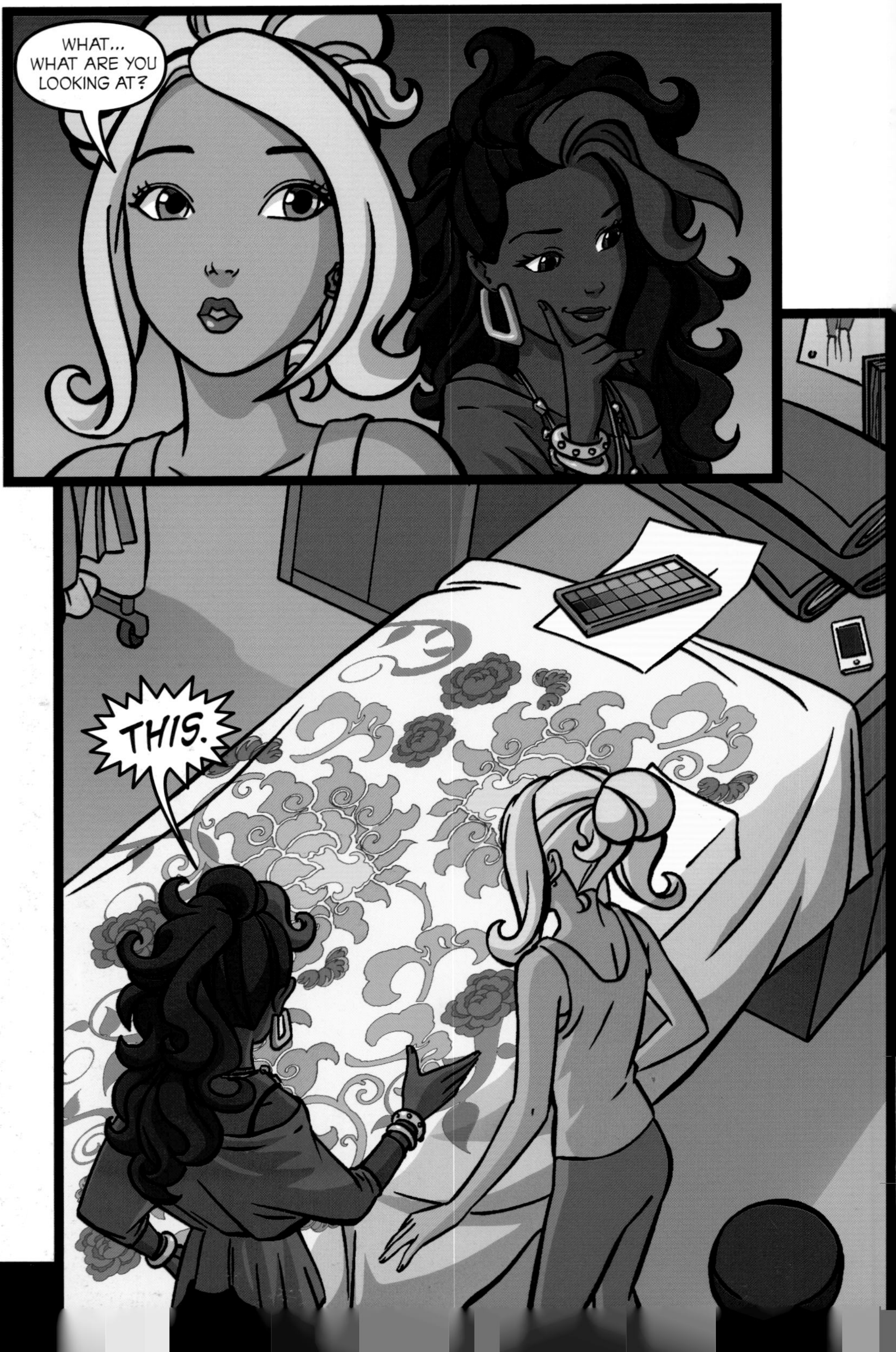
WHAT...
WHAT ARE YOU
LOOKING AT?
THIS.

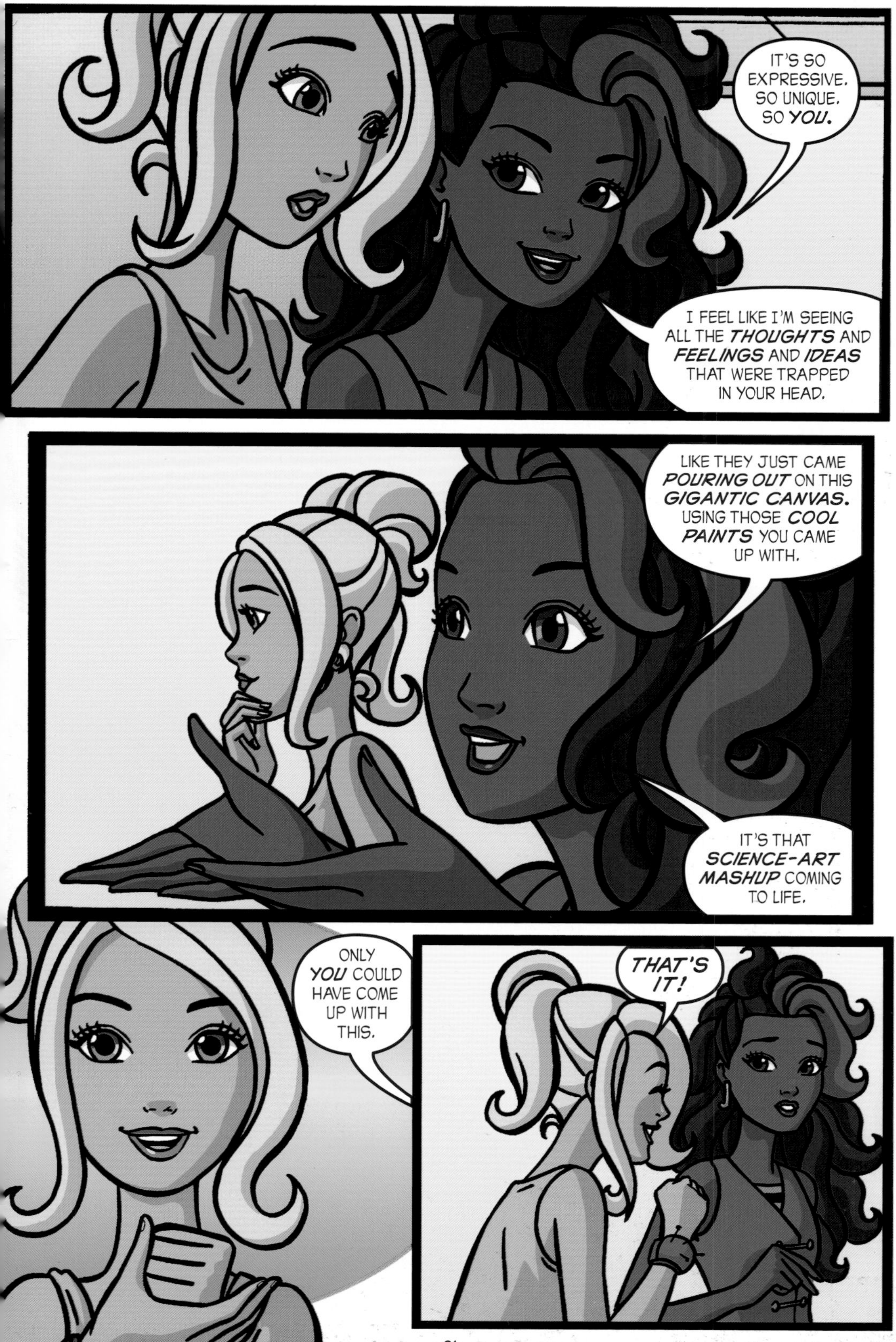
IT'S SO EXPRESSIVE. SO UNIQUE. SO *YOU.*
I FEEL LIKE I'M SEEING ALL THE *THOUGHTS* AND *FEELINGS* AND *IDEAS* THAT WERE TRAPPED IN YOUR HEAD.
LIKE THEY JUST CAME *POURING OUT* ON THIS *GIGANTIC CANVAS.* USING THOSE *COOL PAINTS* YOU CAME UP WITH.
IT'S THAT *SCIENCE-ART MASHUP* COMING TO LIFE.
ONLY *YOU* COULD HAVE COME UP WITH THIS.
THAT'S IT!

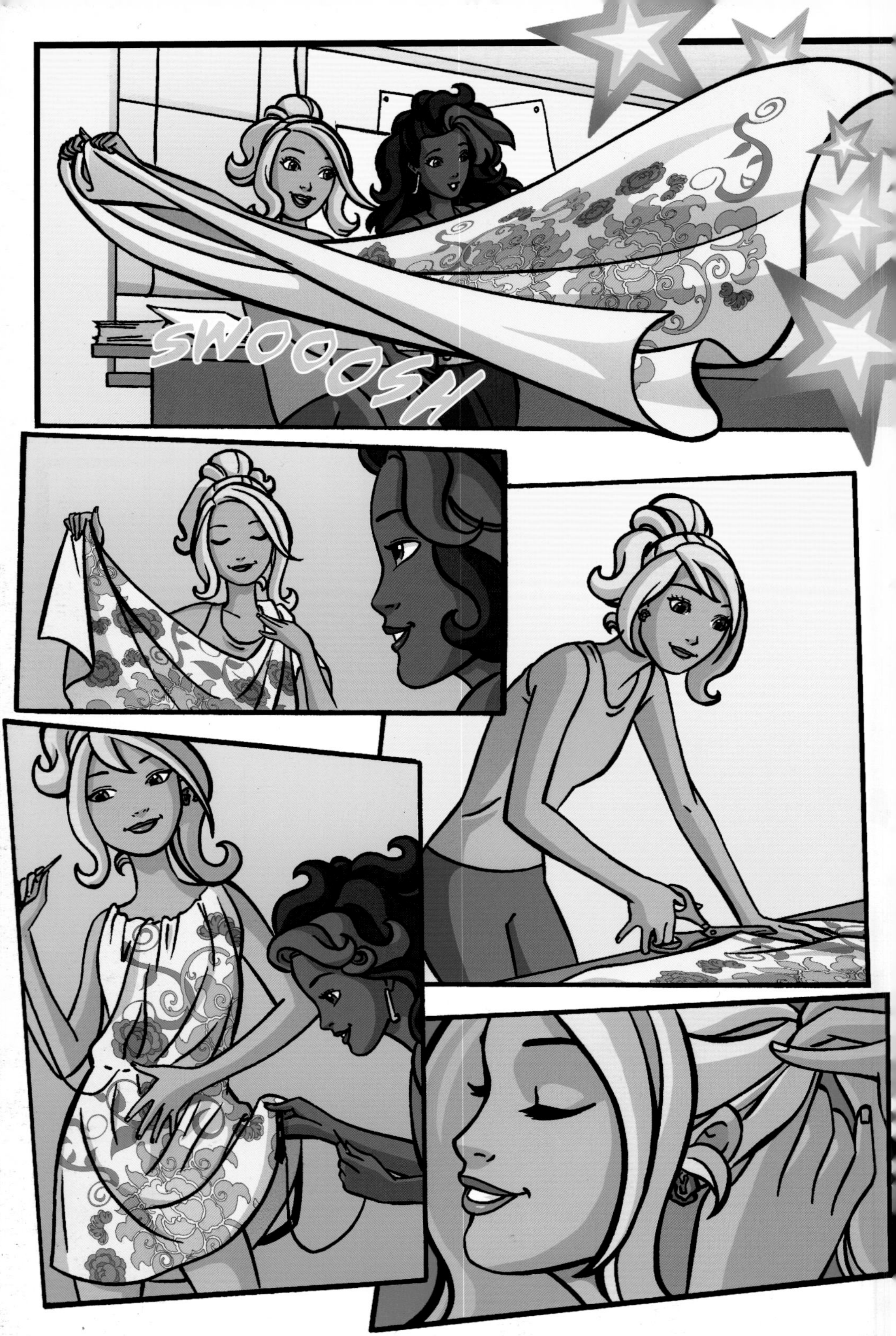
SWOOOSH

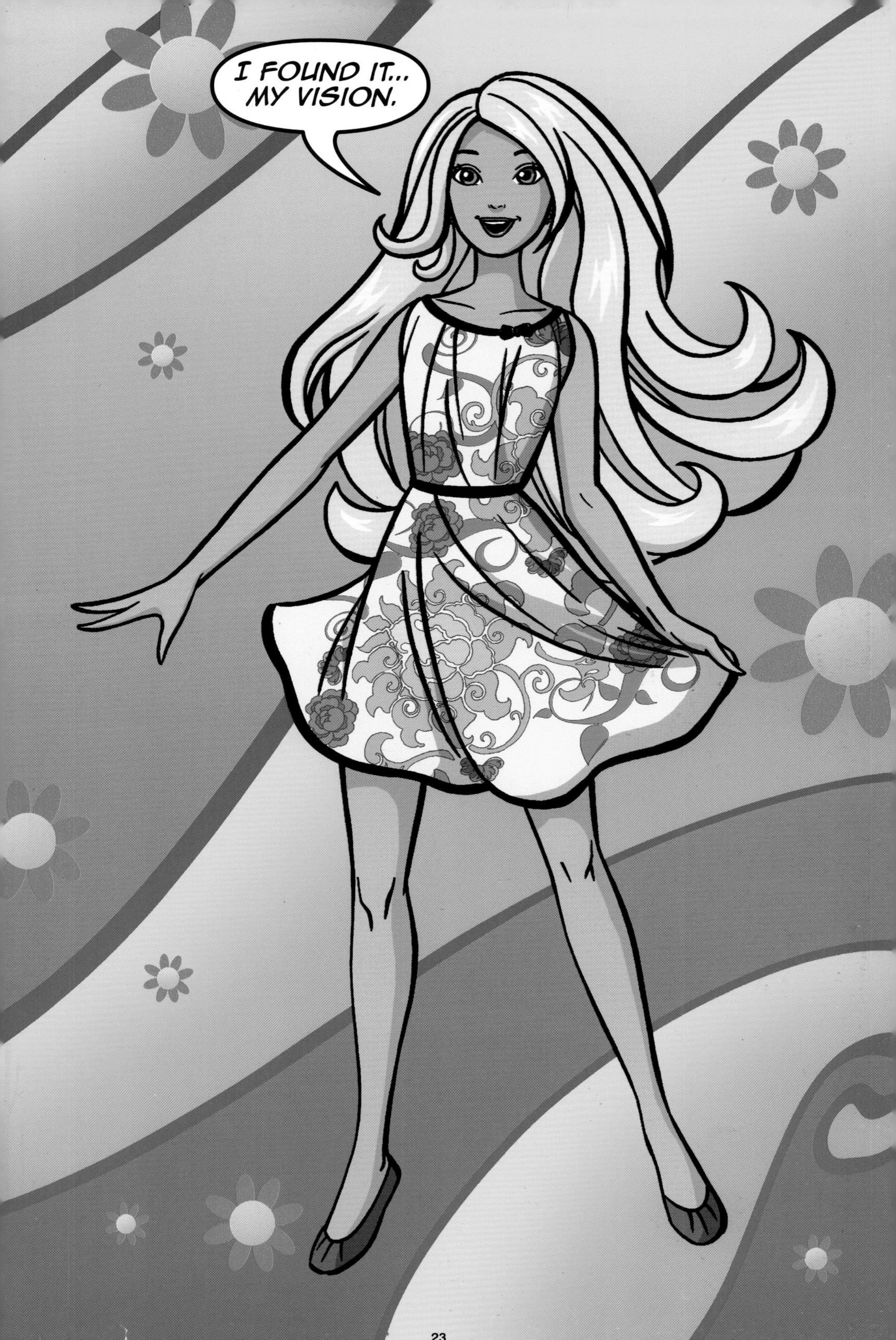
I FOUND IT... MY VISION.

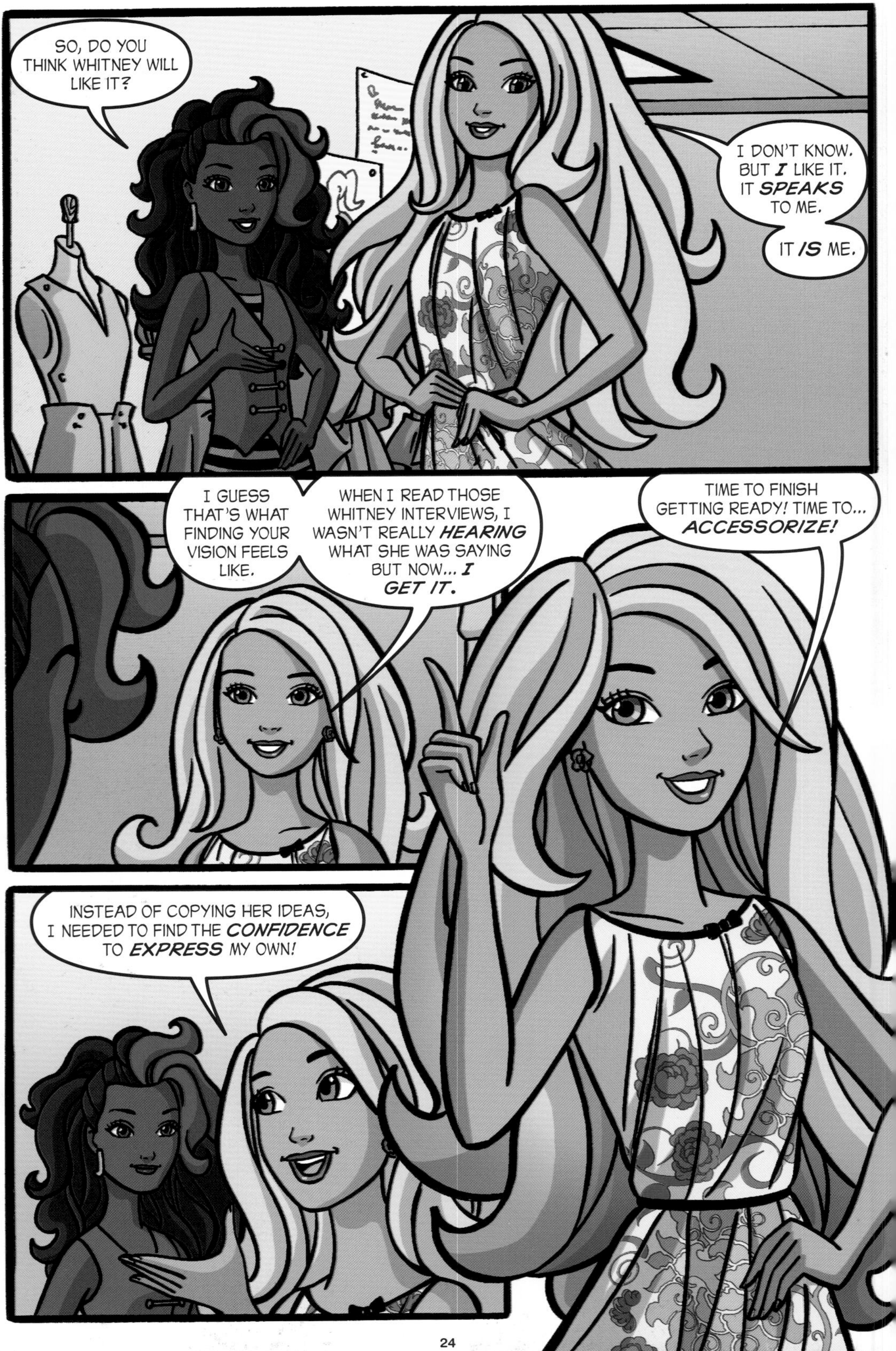
SO, DO YOU THINK WHITNEY WILL LIKE IT?
I DON'T KNOW. BUT I LIKE IT. IT SPEAKS TO ME.
IT IS ME.
I GUESS THAT'S WHAT FINDING YOUR VISION FEELS LIKE.
WHEN I READ THOSE WHITNEY INTERVIEWS, I WASN'T REALLY HEARING WHAT SHE WAS SAYING BUT NOW... I GET IT.
TIME TO FINISH GETTING READY! TIME TO... ACCESSORIZE!
INSTEAD OF COPYING HER IDEAS, I NEEDED TO FIND THE CONFIDENCE TO EXPRESS MY OWN!

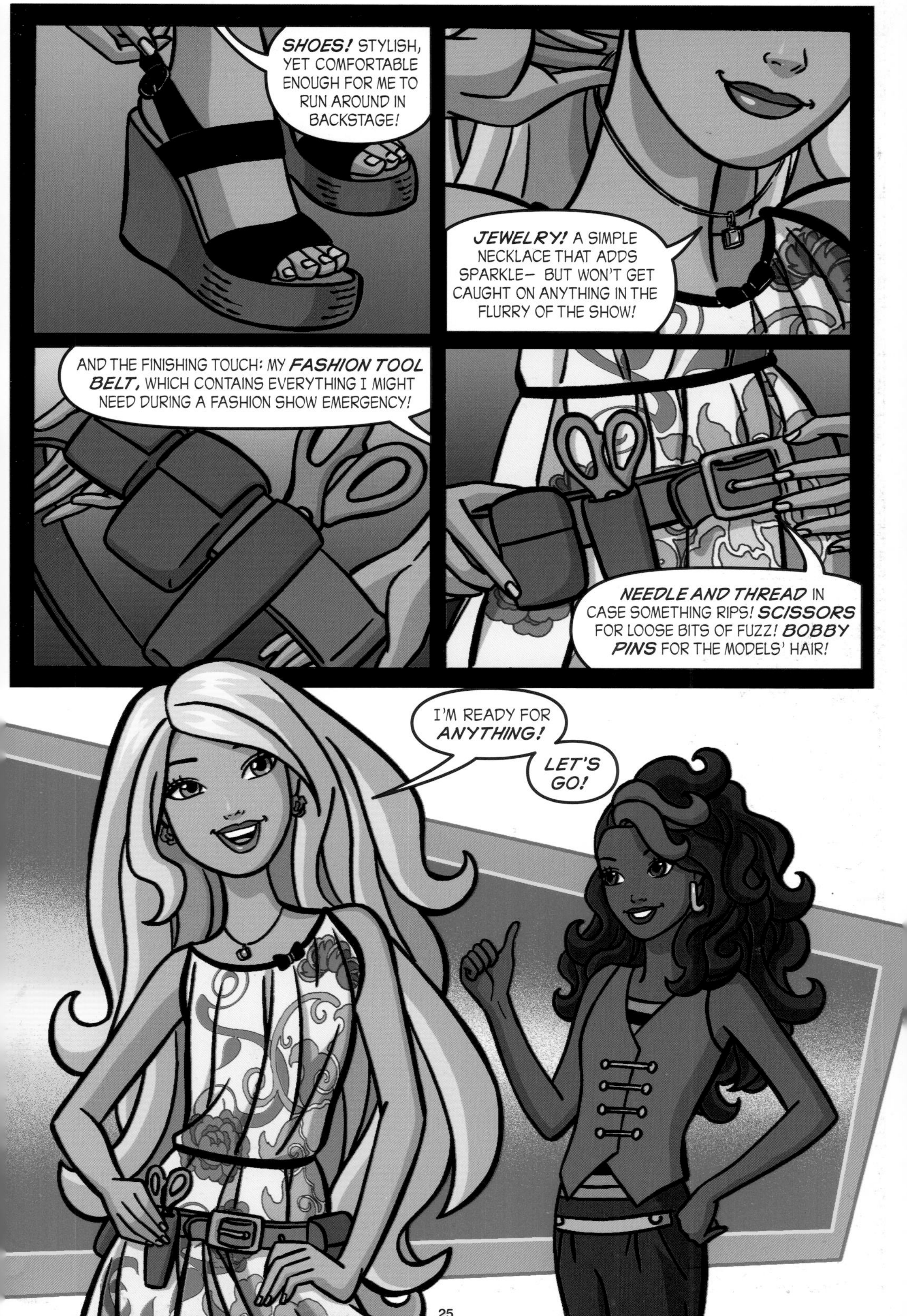
SHOES! STYLISH, YET COMFORTABLE ENOUGH FOR ME TO RUN AROUND IN BACKSTAGE!
JEWELRY! A SIMPLE NECKLACE THAT ADDS SPARKLE– BUT WON'T GET CAUGHT ON ANYTHING IN THE FLURRY OF THE SHOW!
AND THE FINISHING TOUCH: MY FASHION TOOL BELT, WHICH CONTAINS EVERYTHING I MIGHT NEED DURING A FASHION SHOW EMERGENCY!
NEEDLE AND THREAD IN CASE SOMETHING RIPS! SCISSORS FOR LOOSE BITS OF FUZZ! BOBBY PINS FOR THE MODELS' HAIR!
I'M READY FOR ANYTHING!
LET'S GO!

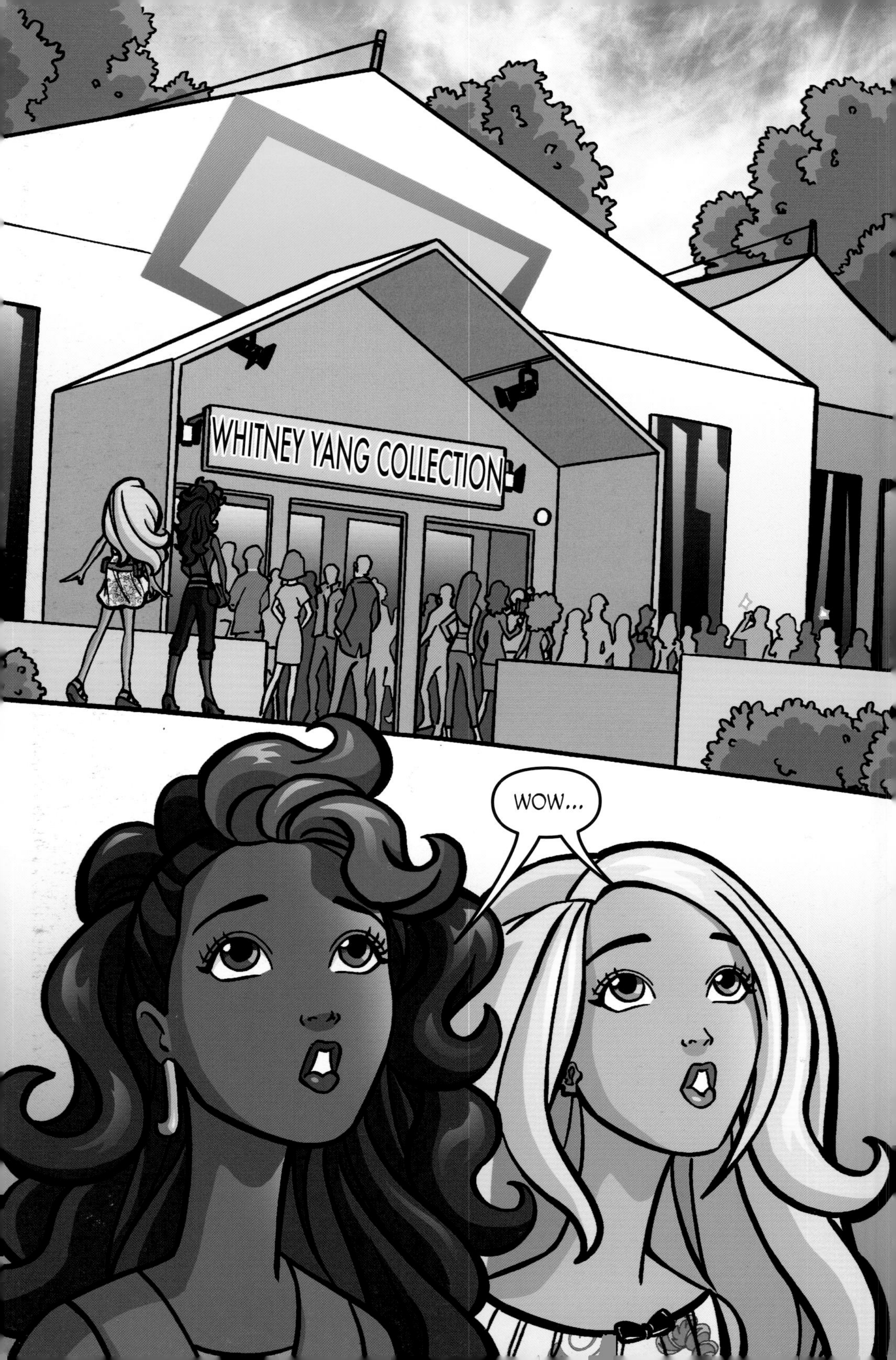
WHITNEY YANG COLLECTION
WOW...

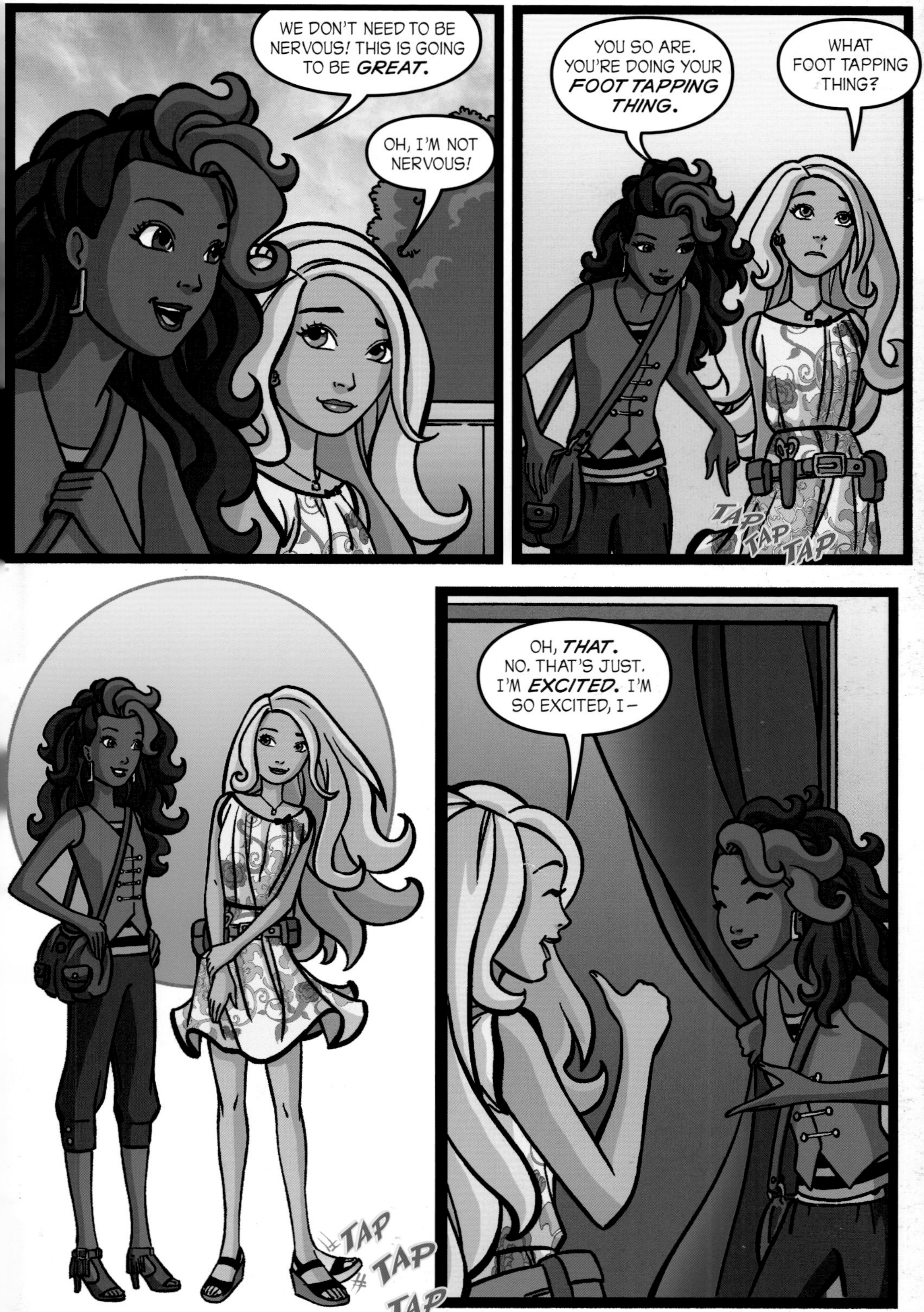
WE DON'T NEED TO BE NERVOUS! THIS IS GOING TO BE *GREAT*.
OH, I'M NOT NERVOUS!
YOU SO ARE. YOU'RE DOING YOUR *FOOT TAPPING THING*.
WHAT FOOT TAPPING THING?
TAP TAP TAP
TAP TAP TAP
OH, *THAT*. NO. THAT'S JUST. I'M *EXCITED*. I'M SO EXCITED, I—

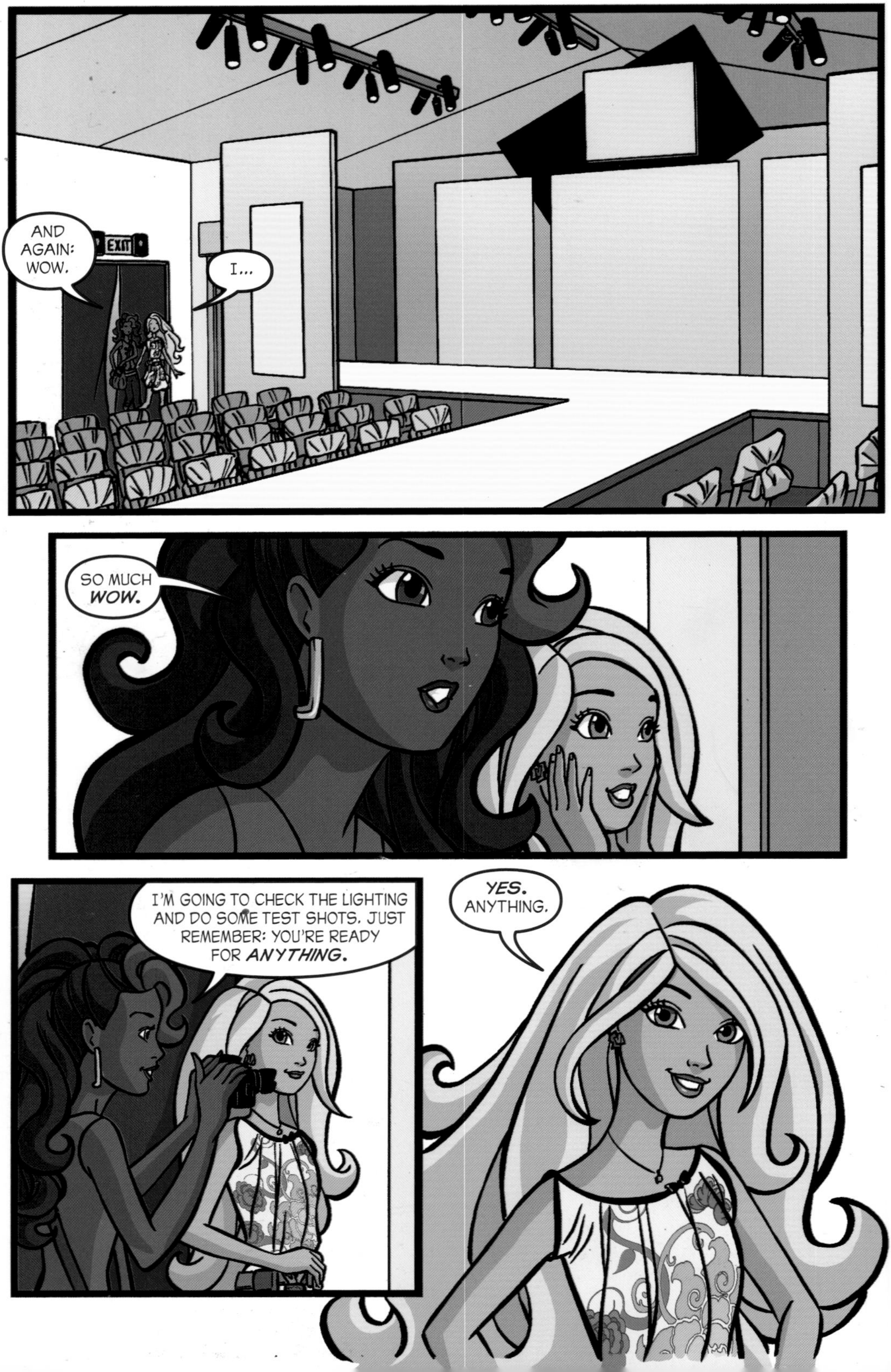
AND AGAIN: WOW.
EXIT
I...
SO MUCH *WOW.*
I'M GOING TO CHECK THE LIGHTING AND DO SOME TEST SHOTS. JUST REMEMBER: YOU'RE READY FOR *ANYTHING.*
YES. ANYTHING.

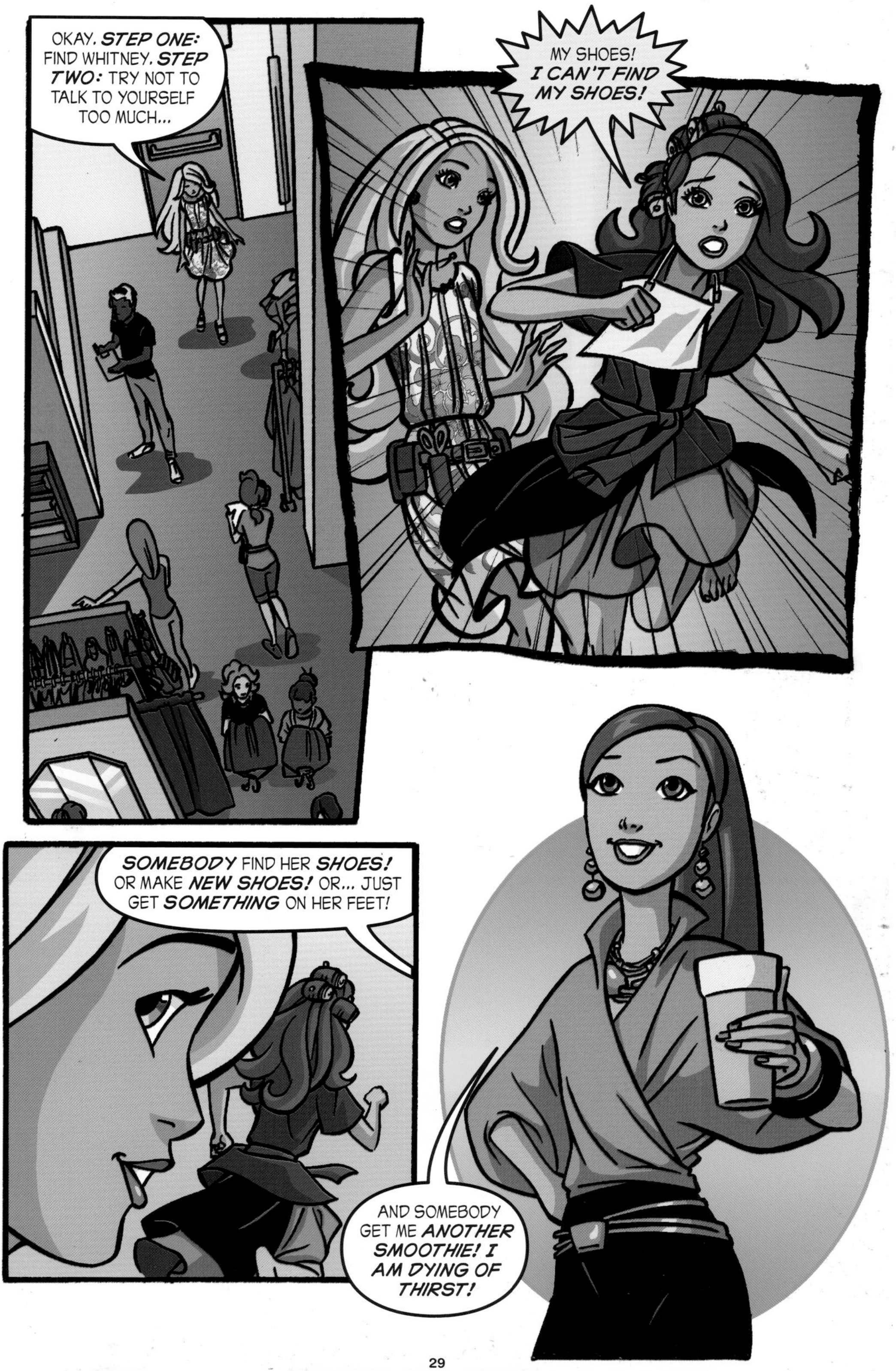
OKAY. STEP ONE: FIND WHITNEY. STEP TWO: TRY NOT TO TALK TO YOURSELF TOO MUCH...
MY SHOES! I CAN'T FIND MY SHOES!
SOMEBODY FIND HER SHOES! OR MAKE NEW SHOES! OR... JUST GET SOMETHING ON HER FEET!
AND SOMEBODY GET ME ANOTHER SMOOTHIE! I AM DYING OF THIRST!

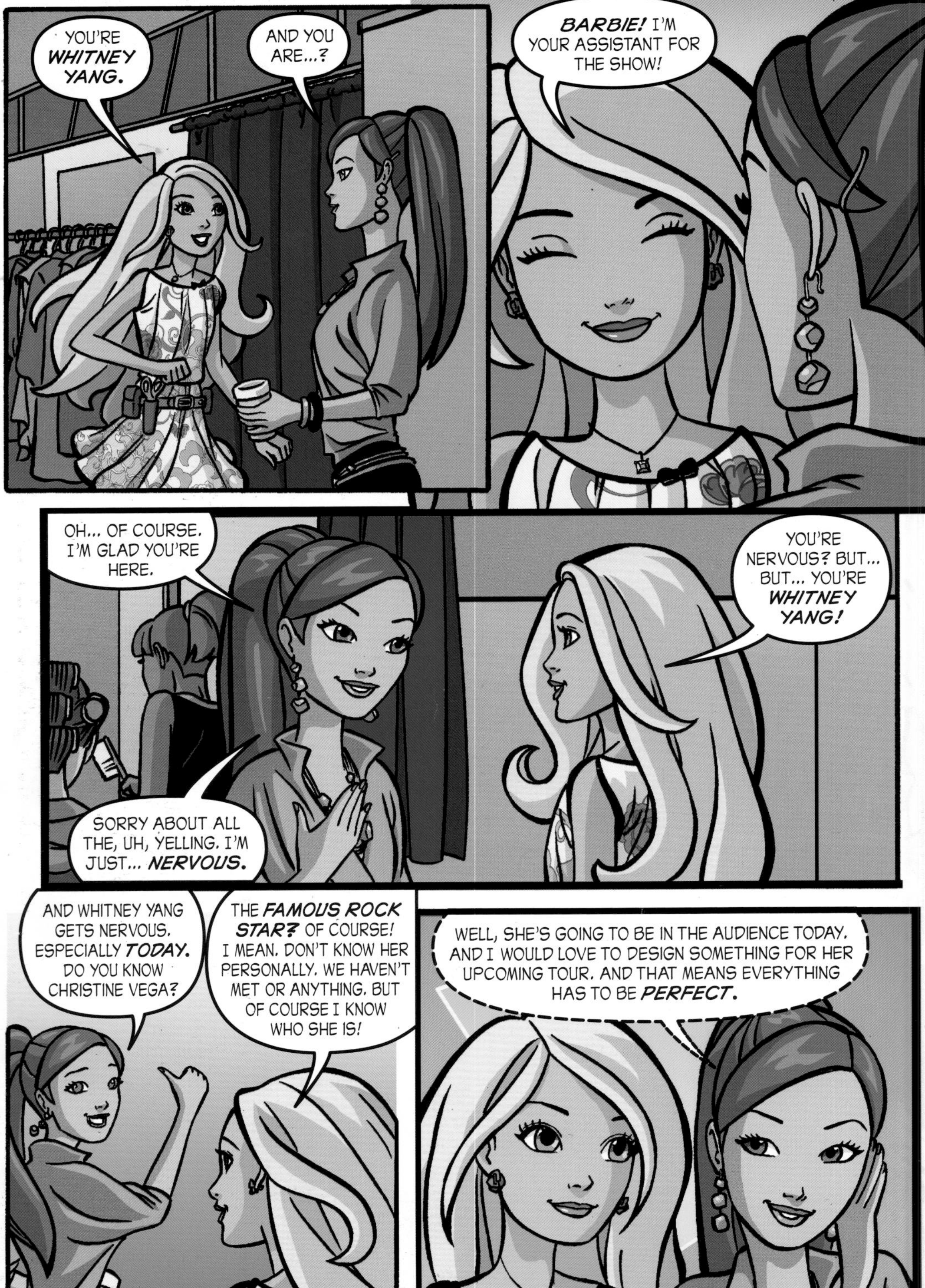
YOU'RE *WHITNEY YANG.*
AND YOU ARE...?
BARBIE! I'M YOUR ASSISTANT FOR THE SHOW!
OH... OF COURSE. I'M GLAD YOU'RE HERE.
SORRY ABOUT ALL THE, UH, YELLING. I'M JUST... *NERVOUS.*
YOU'RE NERVOUS? BUT... BUT... YOU'RE *WHITNEY YANG!*
AND WHITNEY YANG GETS NERVOUS. ESPECIALLY *TODAY.* DO YOU KNOW CHRISTINE VEGA?
THE *FAMOUS ROCK STAR?* OF COURSE! I MEAN, DON'T KNOW HER PERSONALLY, WE HAVEN'T MET OR ANYTHING, BUT OF COURSE I KNOW WHO SHE IS!
WELL, SHE'S GOING TO BE IN THE AUDIENCE TODAY, AND I WOULD LOVE TO DESIGN SOMETHING FOR HER UPCOMING TOUR. AND THAT MEANS EVERYTHING HAS TO BE *PERFECT.*

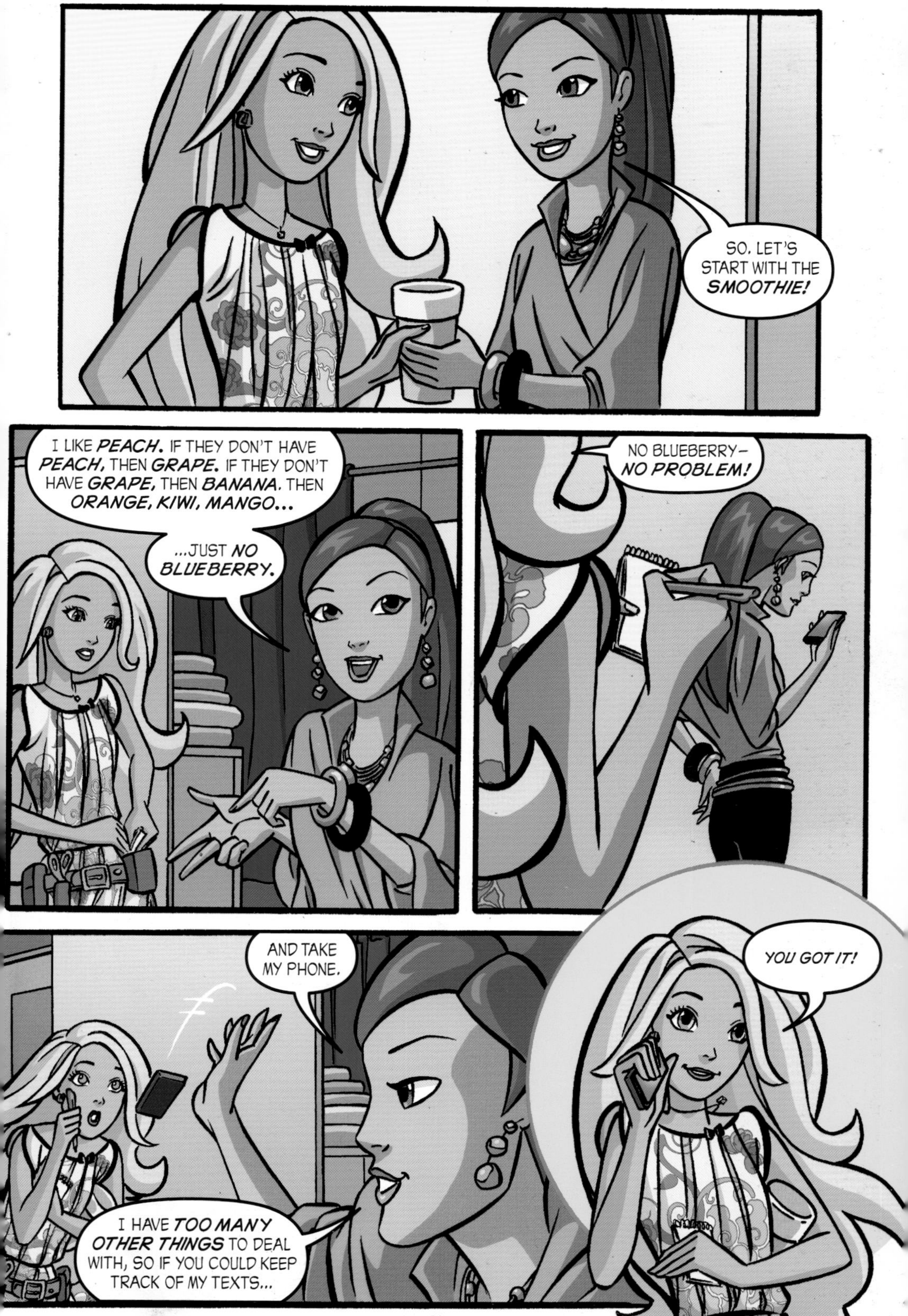
SO, LET'S START WITH THE SMOOTHIE!
I LIKE PEACH. IF THEY DON'T HAVE PEACH, THEN GRAPE. IF THEY DON'T HAVE GRAPE, THEN BANANA. THEN ORANGE, KIWI, MANGO...
...JUST NO BLUEBERRY.
NO BLUEBERRY— NO PROBLEM!
AND TAKE MY PHONE.
I HAVE TOO MANY OTHER THINGS TO DEAL WITH, SO IF YOU COULD KEEP TRACK OF MY TEXTS...
YOU GOT IT!

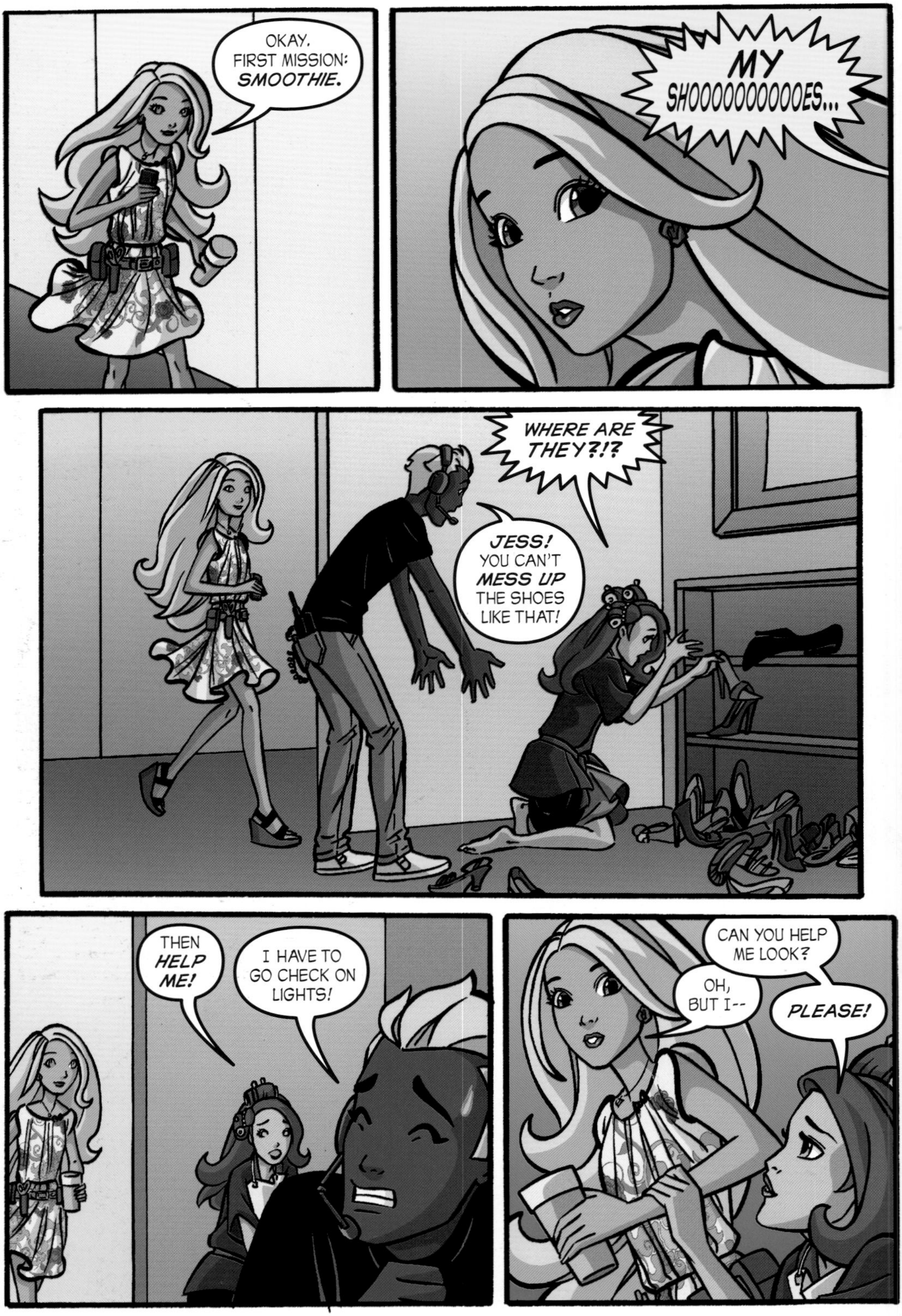
OKAY. FIRST MISSION: SMOOTHIE.
MY SHOOOOOOOOOOES...
WHERE ARE THEY?!?
JESS! YOU CAN'T MESS UP THE SHOES LIKE THAT!
THEN HELP ME!
I HAVE TO GO CHECK ON LIGHTS!
CAN YOU HELP ME LOOK?
OH, BUT I--
PLEASE!

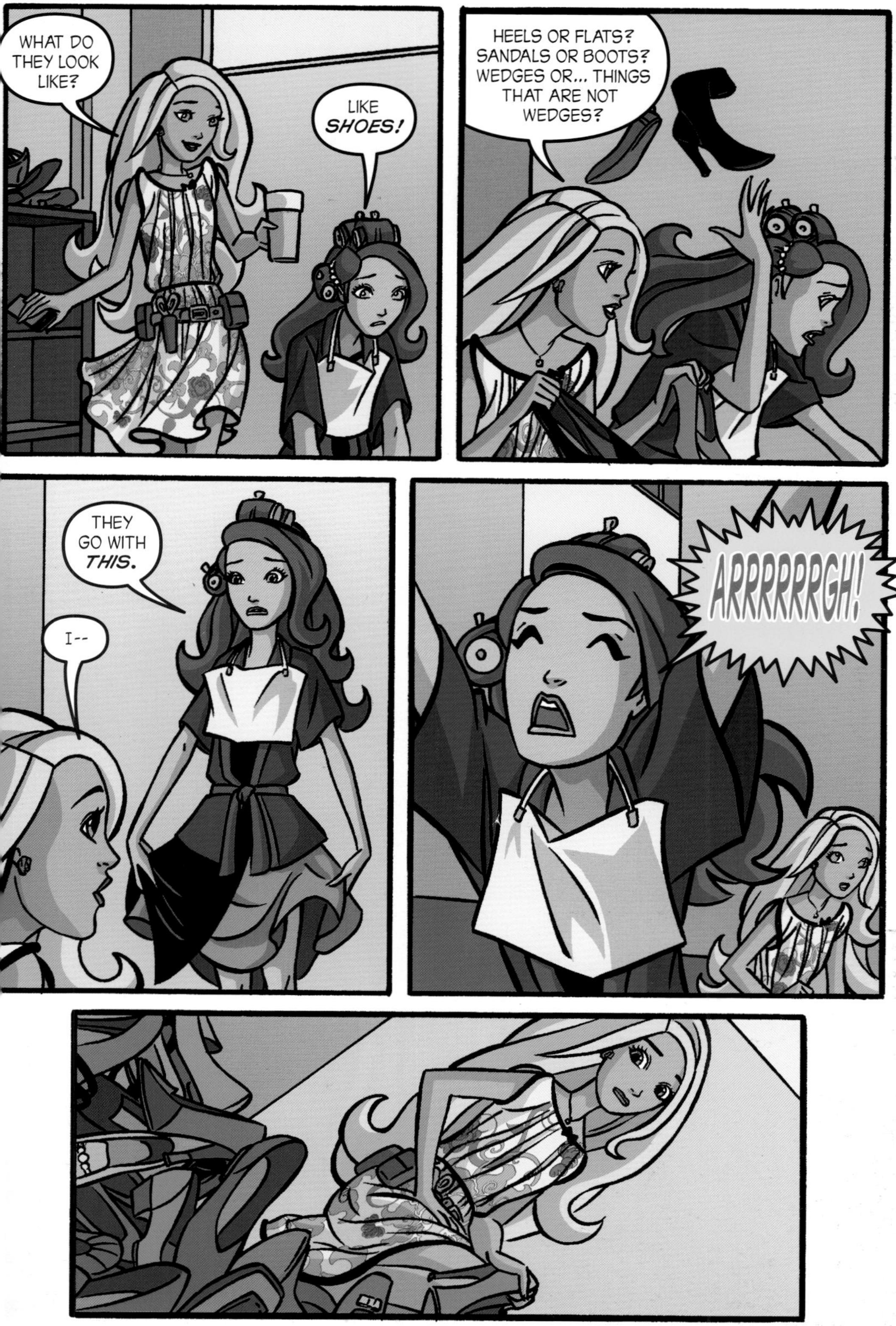
WHAT DO THEY LOOK LIKE?
LIKE *SHOES!*
HEELS OR FLATS? SANDALS OR BOOTS? WEDGES OR... THINGS THAT ARE NOT WEDGES?
THEY GO WITH *THIS*.
I--
ARRRRRRGH!

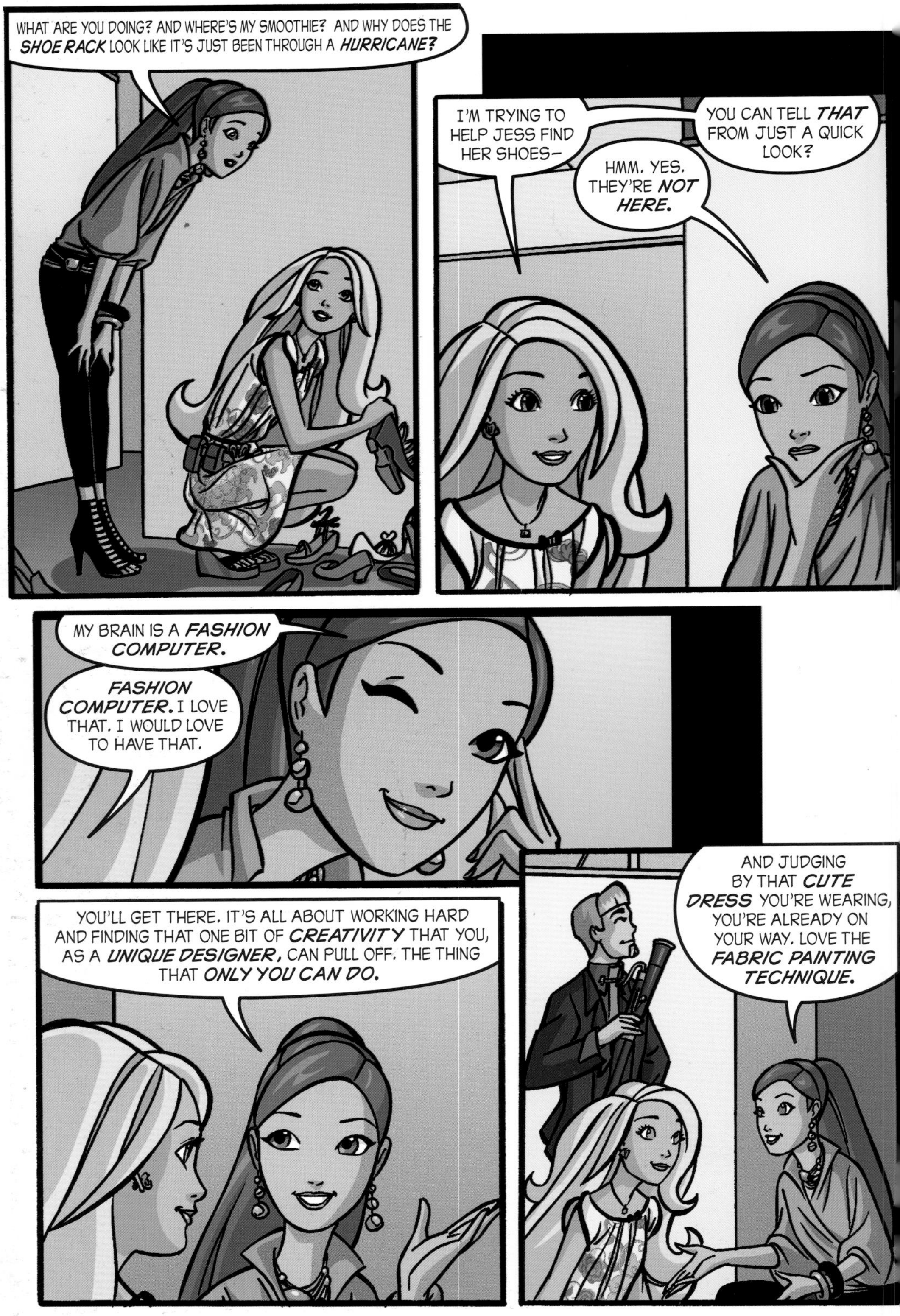
WHAT ARE YOU DOING? AND WHERE'S MY SMOOTHIE? AND WHY DOES THE SHOE RACK LOOK LIKE IT'S JUST BEEN THROUGH A HURRICANE?
I'M TRYING TO HELP JESS FIND HER SHOES—
HMM. YES. THEY'RE NOT HERE.
YOU CAN TELL THAT FROM JUST A QUICK LOOK?
MY BRAIN IS A FASHION COMPUTER.
FASHION COMPUTER. I LOVE THAT. I WOULD LOVE TO HAVE THAT.
YOU'LL GET THERE. IT'S ALL ABOUT WORKING HARD AND FINDING THAT ONE BIT OF CREATIVITY THAT YOU, AS A UNIQUE DESIGNER, CAN PULL OFF. THE THING THAT ONLY YOU CAN DO.
AND JUDGING BY THAT CUTE DRESS YOU'RE WEARING, YOU'RE ALREADY ON YOUR WAY. LOVE THE FABRIC PAINTING TECHNIQUE.

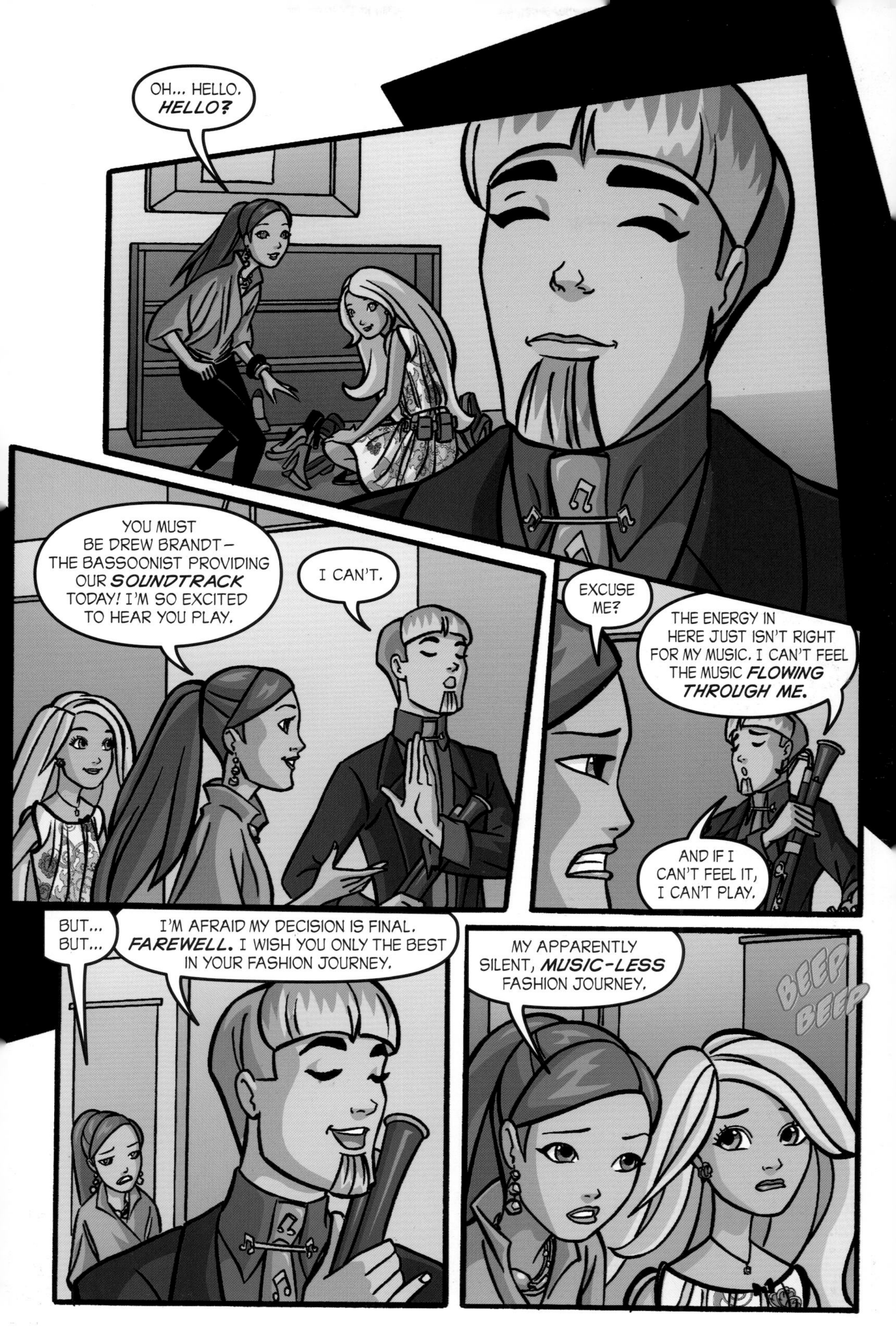
OH... HELLO. HELLO?
YOU MUST BE DREW BRANDT— THE BASSOONIST PROVIDING OUR SOUNDTRACK TODAY! I'M SO EXCITED TO HEAR YOU PLAY.
I CAN'T.
EXCUSE ME?
THE ENERGY IN HERE JUST ISN'T RIGHT FOR MY MUSIC. I CAN'T FEEL THE MUSIC FLOWING THROUGH ME.
AND IF I CAN'T FEEL IT, I CAN'T PLAY.
BUT... BUT...
I'M AFRAID MY DECISION IS FINAL. FAREWELL. I WISH YOU ONLY THE BEST IN YOUR FASHION JOURNEY.
MY APPARENTLY SILENT, MUSIC-LESS FASHION JOURNEY.
BEEP BEEP

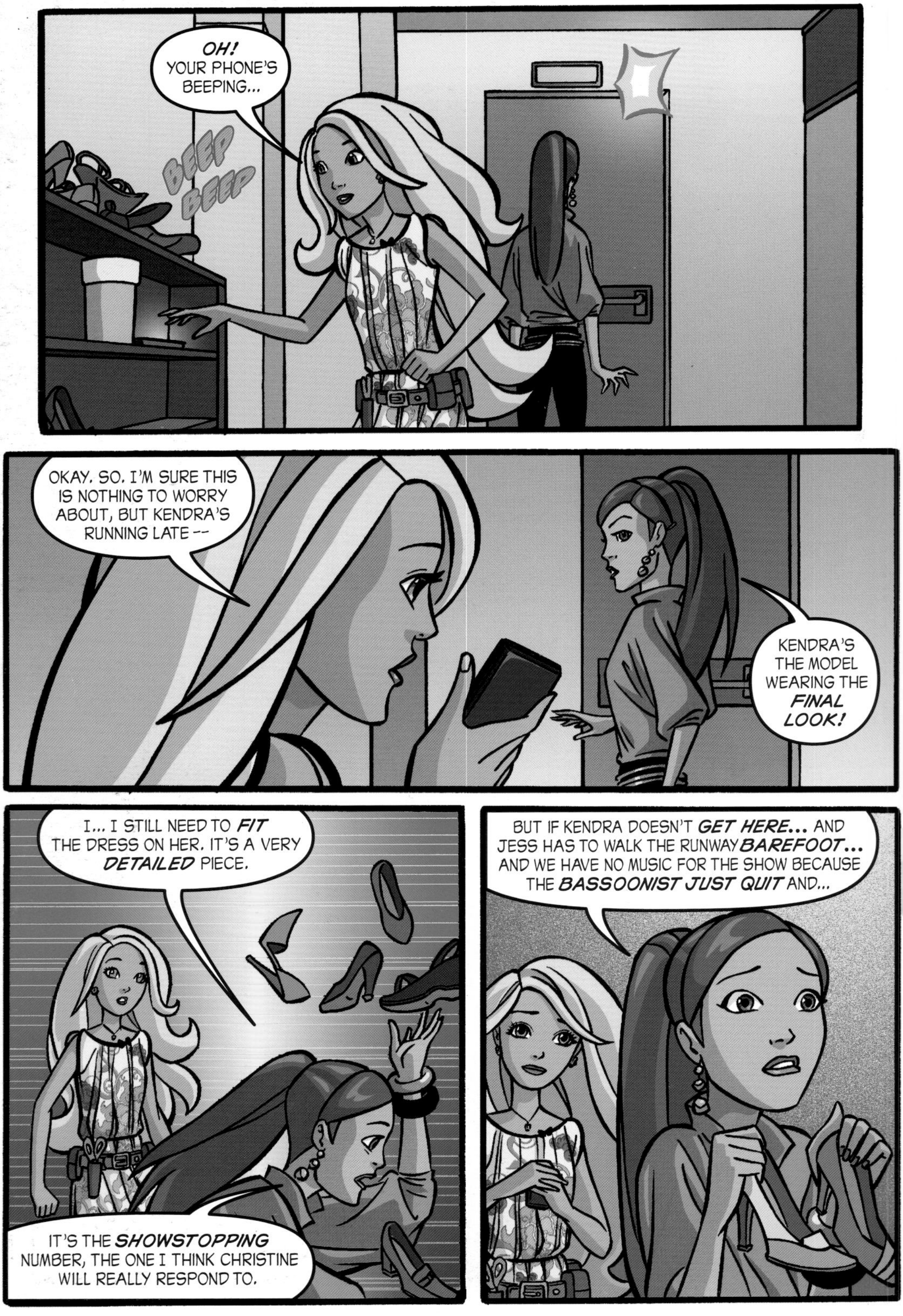
OH! YOUR PHONE'S BEEPING...
BEEP BEEP
OKAY. SO. I'M SURE THIS IS NOTHING TO WORRY ABOUT, BUT KENDRA'S RUNNING LATE --
KENDRA'S THE MODEL WEARING THE *FINAL LOOK!*
I... I STILL NEED TO *FIT* THE DRESS ON HER. IT'S A VERY *DETAILED* PIECE.
IT'S THE *SHOWSTOPPING* NUMBER, THE ONE I THINK CHRISTINE WILL REALLY RESPOND TO.
BUT IF KENDRA DOESN'T *GET HERE...* AND JESS HAS TO WALK THE RUNWAY *BAREFOOT...* AND WE HAVE NO MUSIC FOR THE SHOW BECAUSE THE *BASSOONIST JUST QUIT* AND...

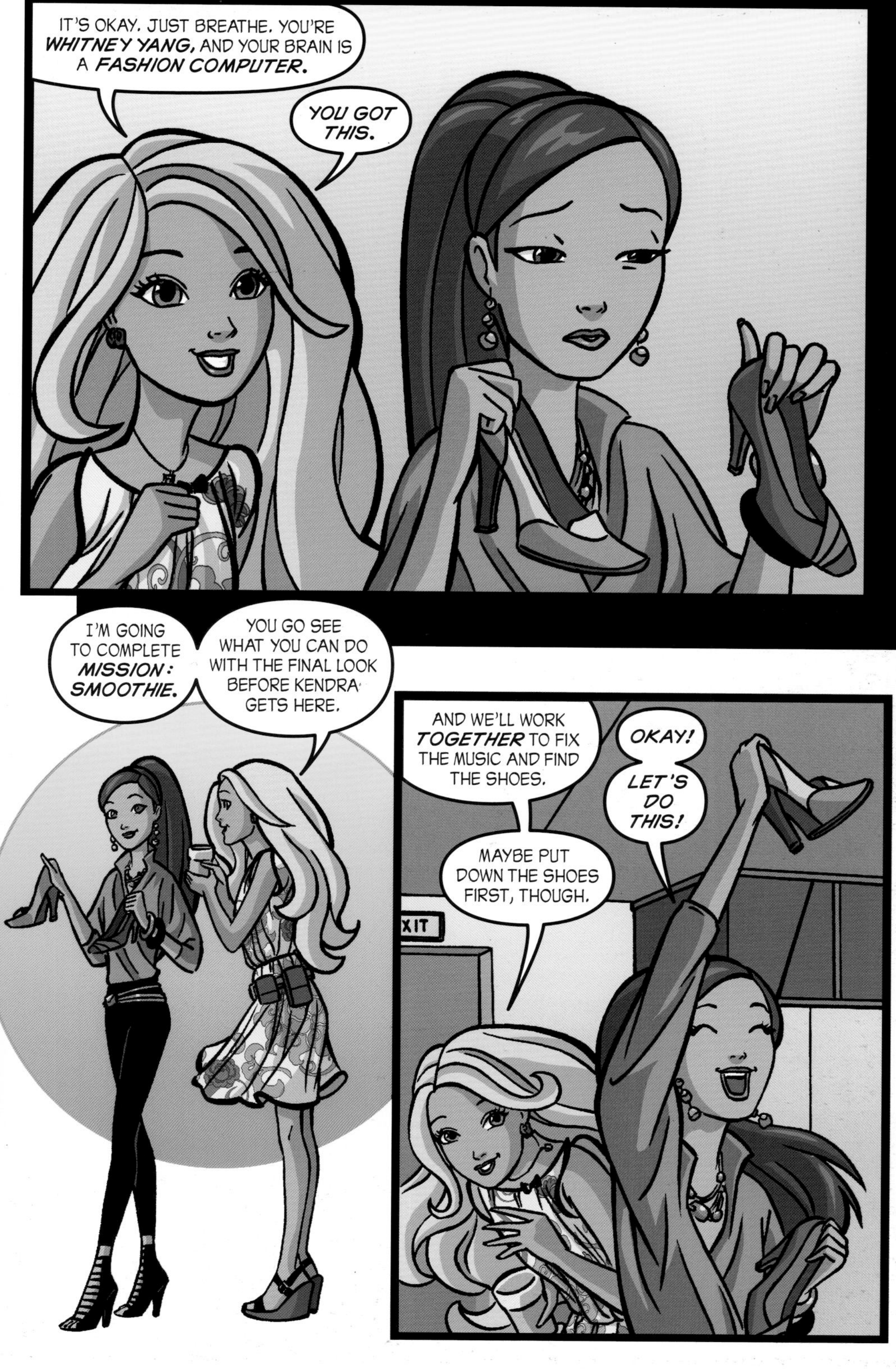
IT'S OKAY. JUST BREATHE. YOU'RE WHITNEY YANG, AND YOUR BRAIN IS A FASHION COMPUTER.
YOU GOT THIS.
I'M GOING TO COMPLETE MISSION: SMOOTHIE.
YOU GO SEE WHAT YOU CAN DO WITH THE FINAL LOOK BEFORE KENDRA GETS HERE.
AND WE'LL WORK TOGETHER TO FIX THE MUSIC AND FIND THE SHOES.
OKAY!
LET'S DO THIS!
MAYBE PUT DOWN THE SHOES FIRST, THOUGH.
XIT

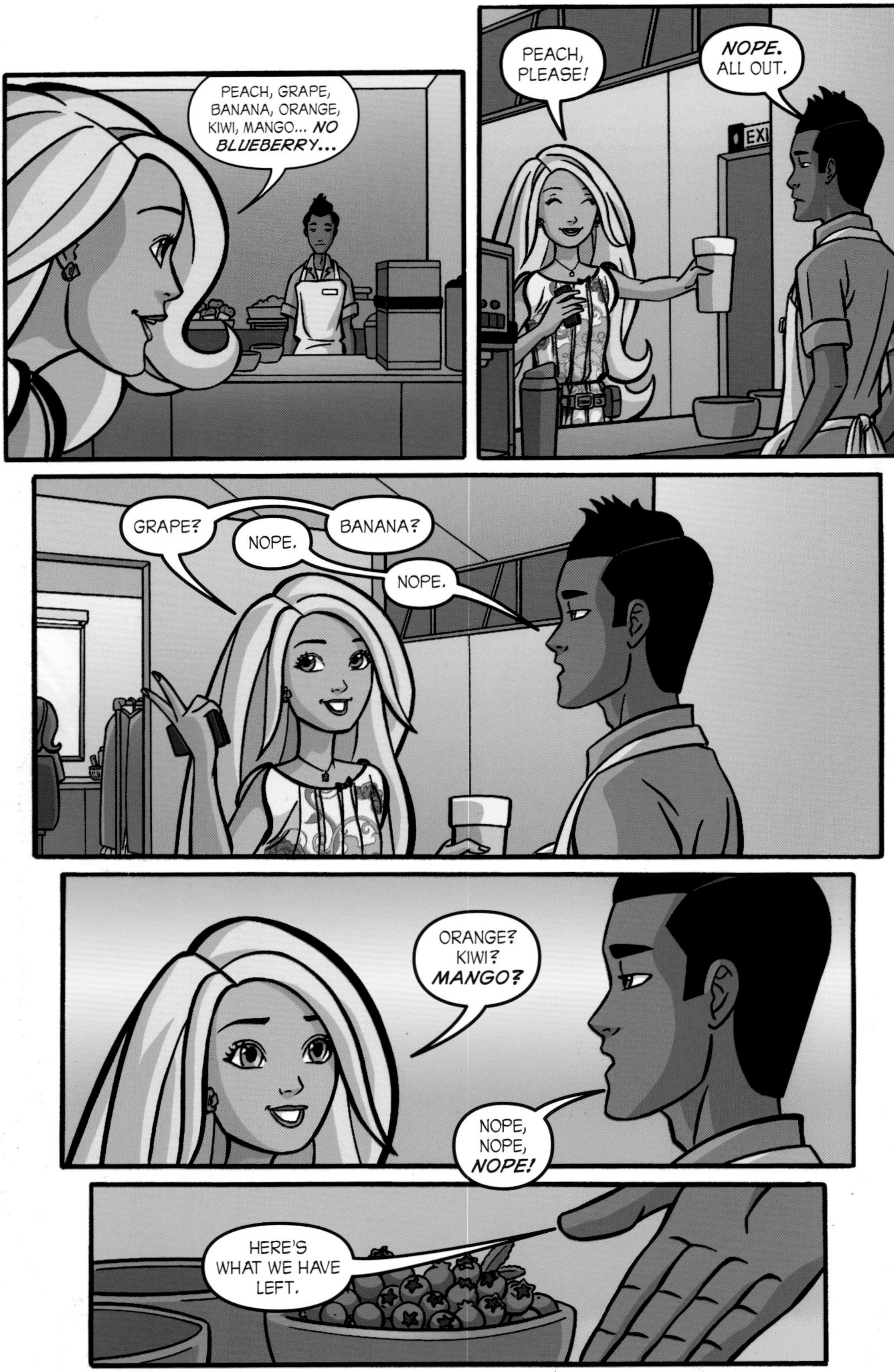
PEACH, GRAPE, BANANA, ORANGE, KIWI, MANGO... NO BLUEBERRY...
PEACH, PLEASE!
NOPE. ALL OUT.
EXI
GRAPE?
NOPE.
BANANA?
NOPE.
ORANGE? KIWI? MANGO?
NOPE, NOPE, NOPE!
HERE'S WHAT WE HAVE LEFT.

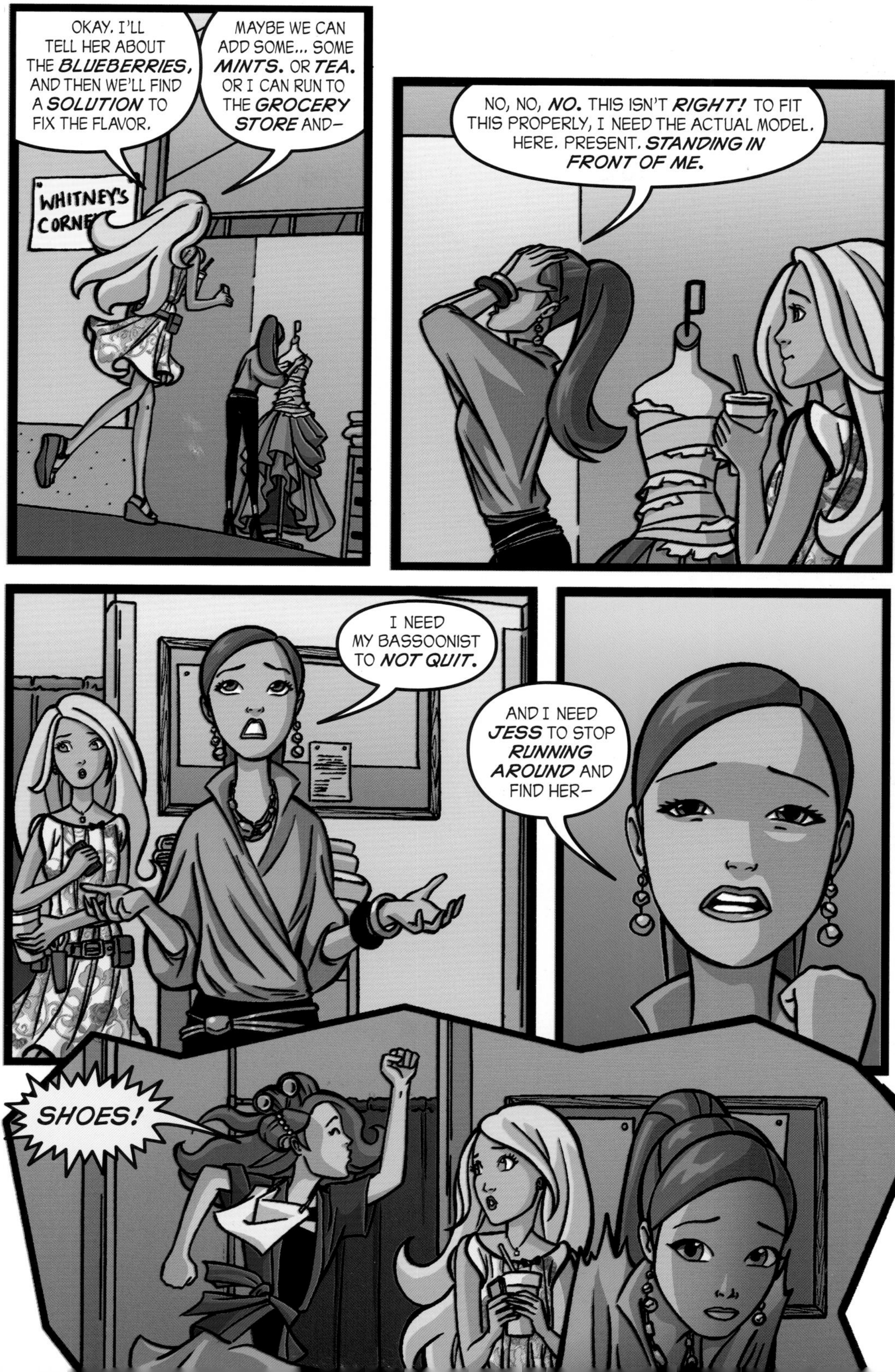
OKAY. I'LL TELL HER ABOUT THE BLUEBERRIES, AND THEN WE'LL FIND A SOLUTION TO FIX THE FLAVOR.
MAYBE WE CAN ADD SOME... SOME MINTS. OR TEA. OR I CAN RUN TO THE GROCERY STORE AND–
WHITNEY'S CORNE
NO, NO, NO. THIS ISN'T RIGHT! TO FIT THIS PROPERLY, I NEED THE ACTUAL MODEL. HERE. PRESENT. STANDING IN FRONT OF ME.
I NEED MY BASSOONIST TO NOT QUIT.
AND I NEED JESS TO STOP RUNNING AROUND AND FIND HER–
SHOES!

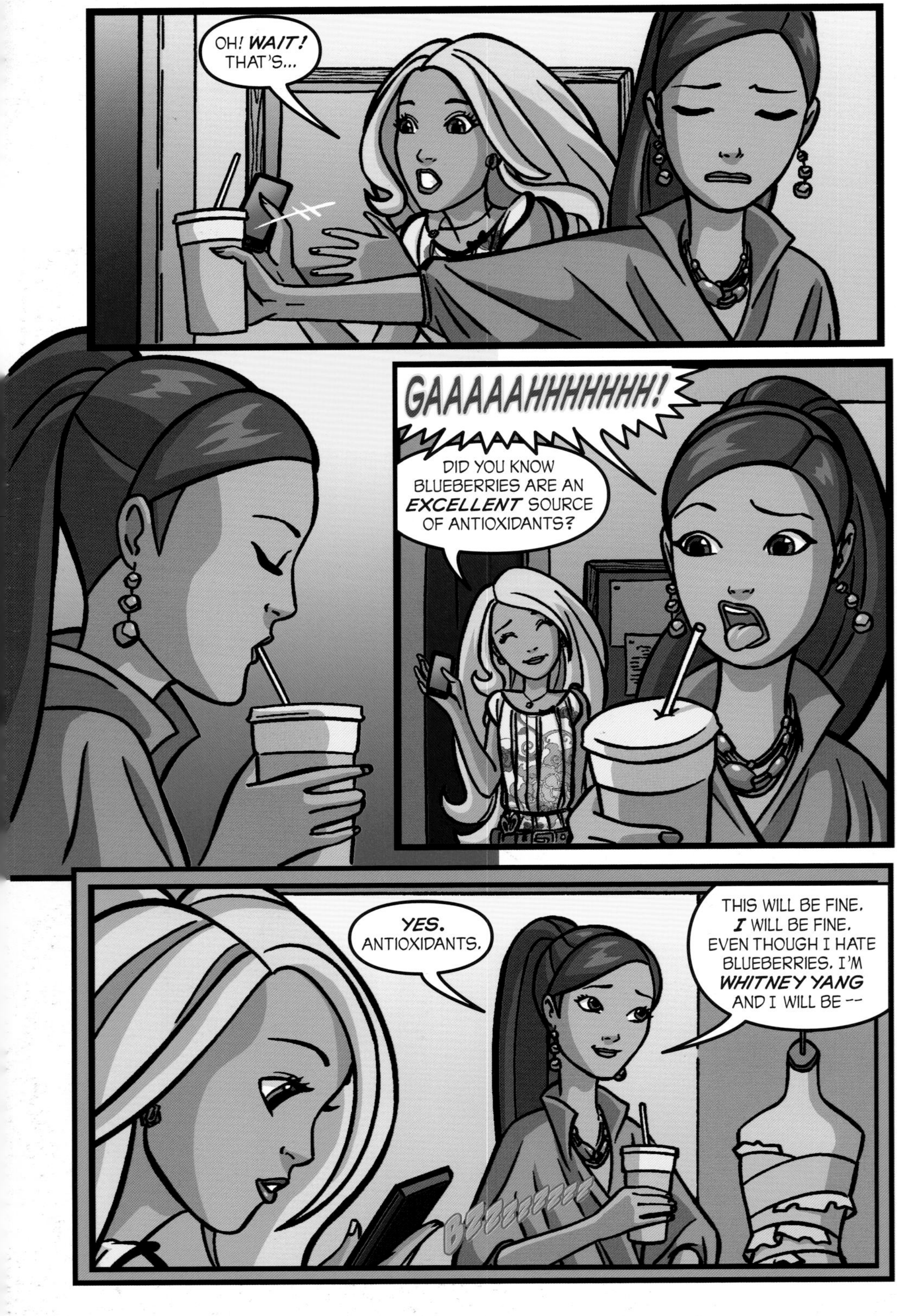
OH! *WAIT!* THAT'S...
GAAAAAHHHHHHH!
DID YOU KNOW BLUEBERRIES ARE AN *EXCELLENT* SOURCE OF ANTIOXIDANTS?
YES. ANTIOXIDANTS.
THIS WILL BE FINE. *I* WILL BE FINE. EVEN THOUGH I HATE BLUEBERRIES. I'M *WHITNEY YANG* AND I WILL BE --
BZZZZZZZ

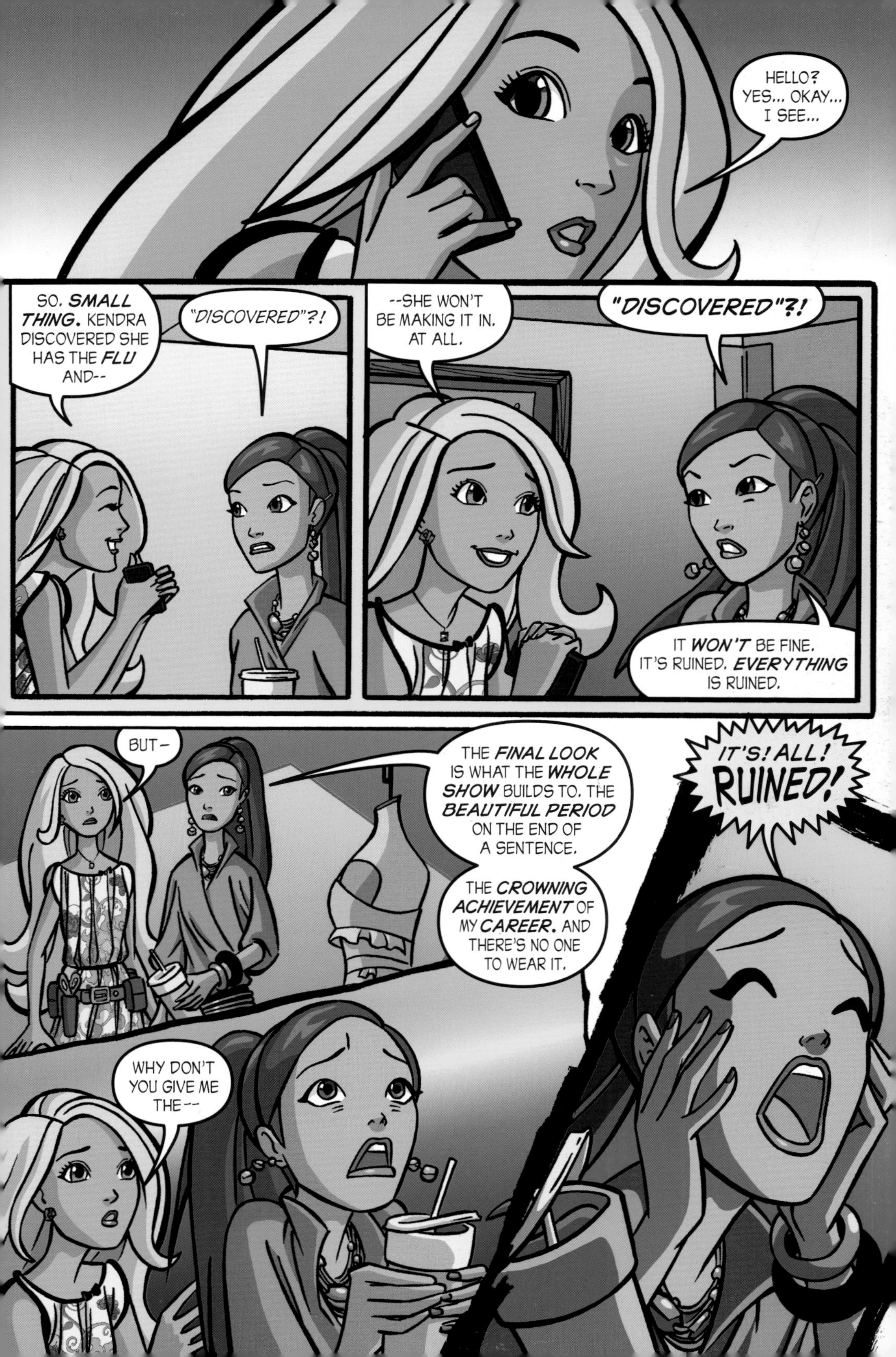
HELLO? YES... OKAY... I SEE...
SO. SMALL THING. KENDRA DISCOVERED SHE HAS THE FLU AND--
"DISCOVERED"?!
--SHE WON'T BE MAKING IT IN. AT ALL.
"DISCOVERED"?!
IT WON'T BE FINE. IT'S RUINED. EVERYTHING IS RUINED.
BUT–
THE FINAL LOOK IS WHAT THE WHOLE SHOW BUILDS TO. THE BEAUTIFUL PERIOD ON THE END OF A SENTENCE.
THE CROWNING ACHIEVEMENT OF MY CAREER. AND THERE'S NO ONE TO WEAR IT.
IT'S! ALL! RUINED!
WHY DON'T YOU GIVE ME THE--

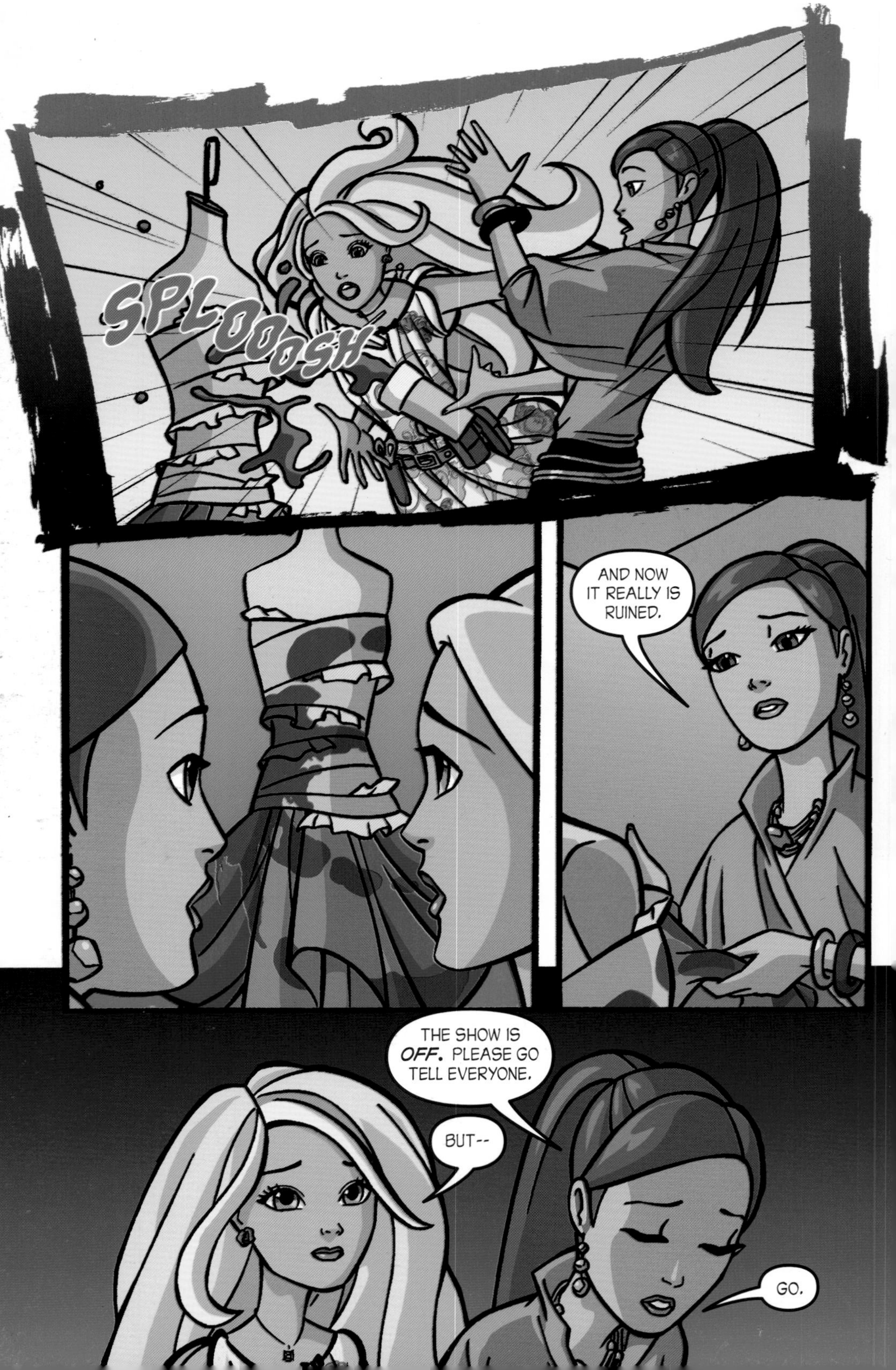
SPLOOOOSH
AND NOW IT REALLY IS RUINED.
THE SHOW IS *OFF.* PLEASE GO TELL EVERYONE.
BUT--
GO.

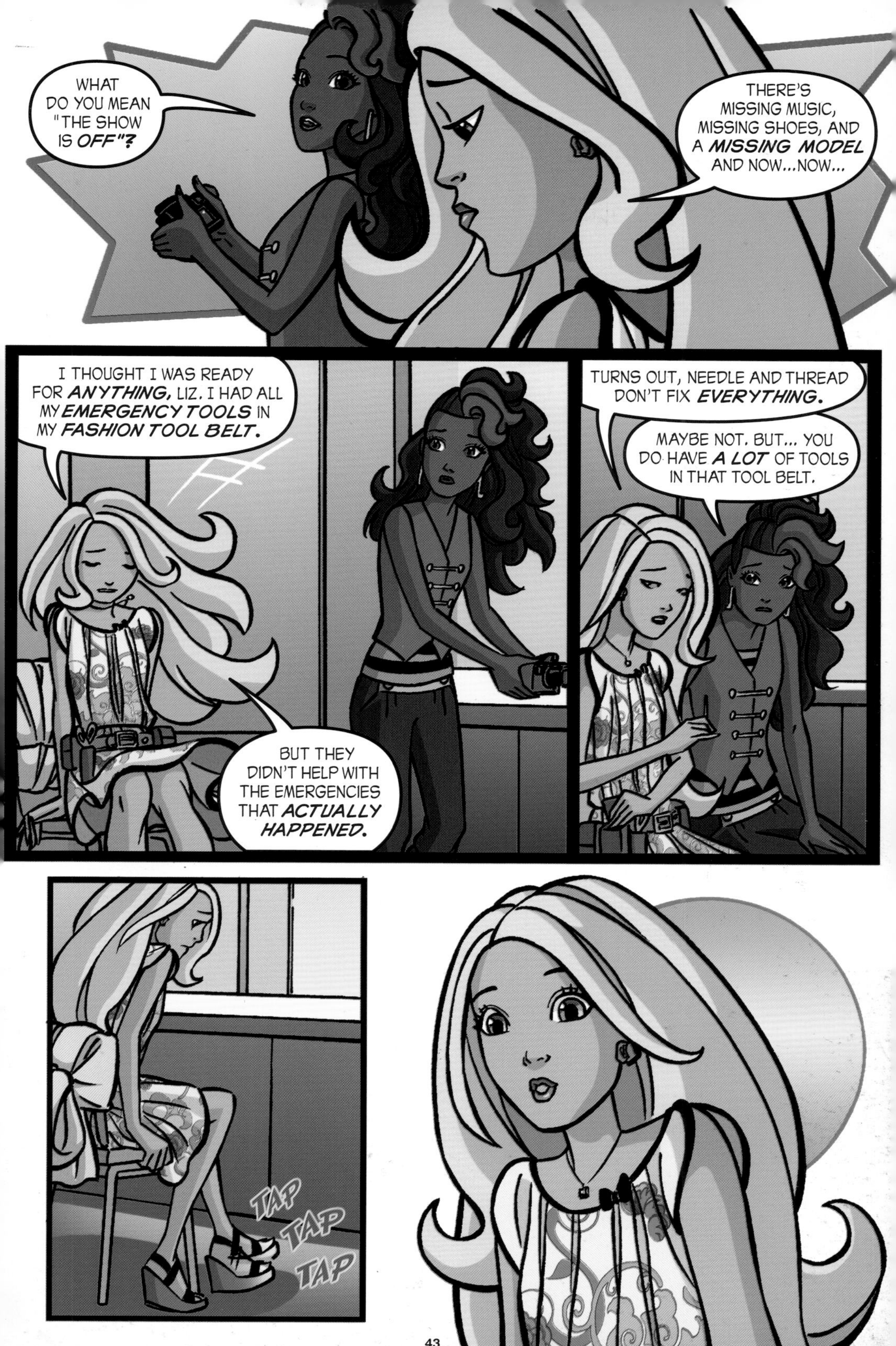
WHAT DO YOU MEAN "THE SHOW IS *OFF*"?
THERE'S MISSING MUSIC, MISSING SHOES, AND A *MISSING MODEL* AND NOW...NOW...
I THOUGHT I WAS READY FOR *ANYTHING,* LIZ. I HAD ALL MY *EMERGENCY TOOLS* IN MY *FASHION TOOL BELT.*
BUT THEY DIDN'T HELP WITH THE EMERGENCIES THAT *ACTUALLY HAPPENED.*
TURNS OUT, NEEDLE AND THREAD DON'T FIX *EVERYTHING.*
MAYBE NOT. BUT... YOU DO HAVE *A LOT* OF TOOLS IN THAT TOOL BELT.
TAP
TAP
TAP

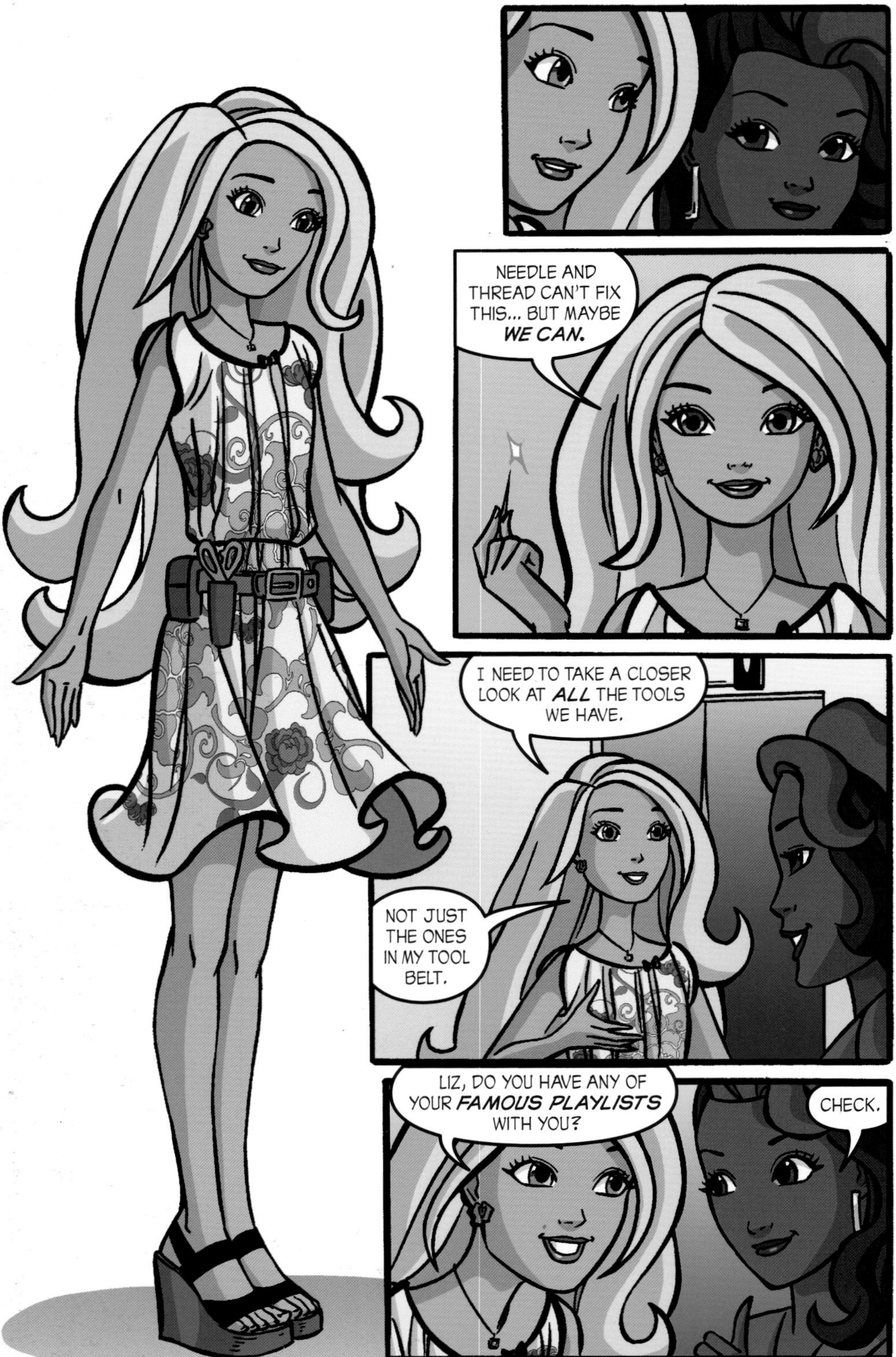
NEEDLE AND THREAD CAN'T FIX THIS... BUT MAYBE **WE CAN.**
I NEED TO TAKE A CLOSER LOOK AT **ALL** THE TOOLS WE HAVE.
NOT JUST THE ONES IN MY TOOL BELT.
LIZ, DO YOU HAVE ANY OF YOUR **FAMOUS PLAYLISTS** WITH YOU?
CHECK.

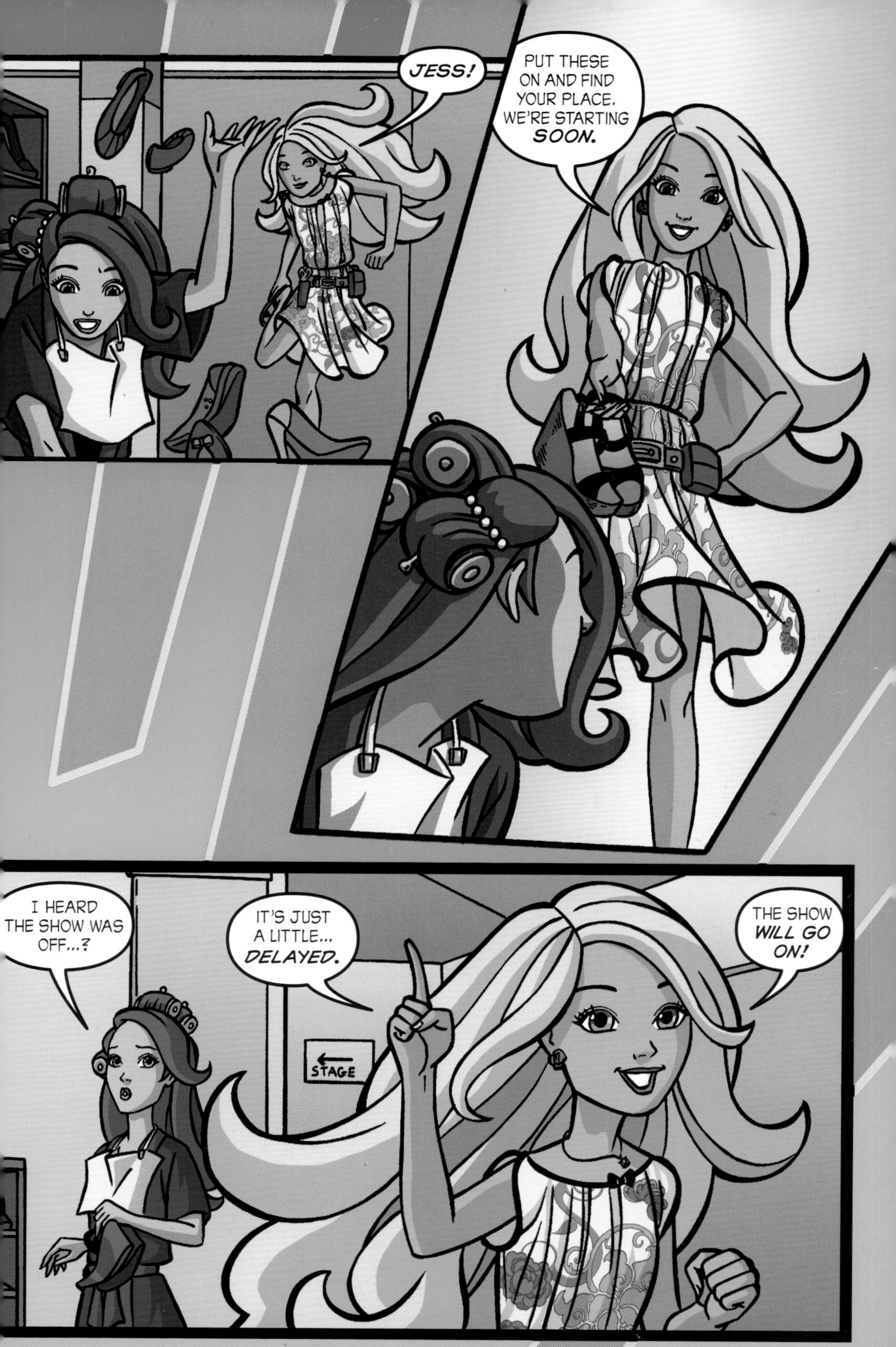
JESS!
PUT THESE ON AND FIND YOUR PLACE. WE'RE STARTING SOON.
I HEARD THE SHOW WAS OFF...?
IT'S JUST A LITTLE... DELAYED.
STAGE
THE SHOW WILL GO ON!

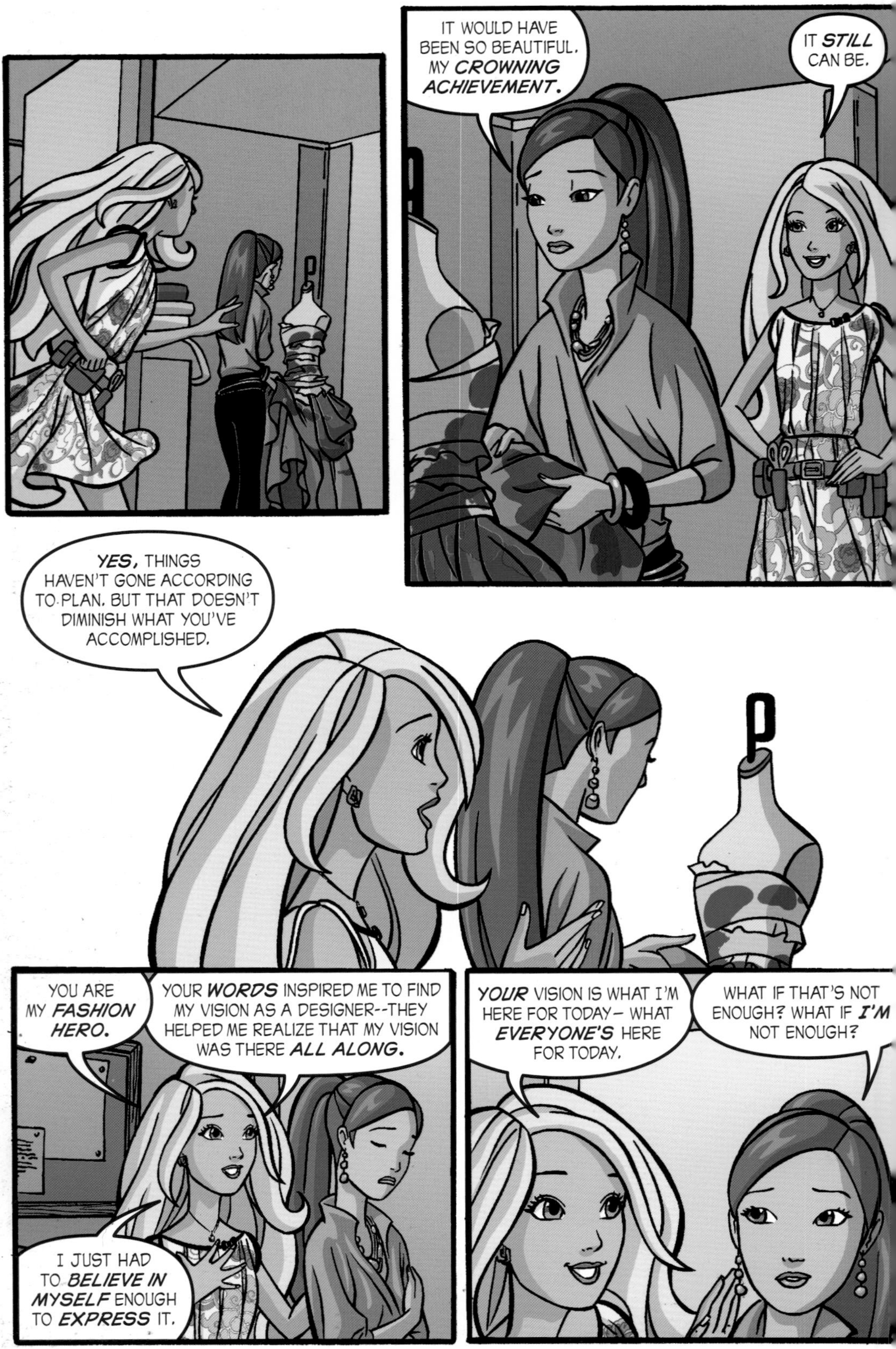
IT WOULD HAVE BEEN SO BEAUTIFUL. MY CROWNING ACHIEVEMENT.
IT STILL CAN BE.
YES, THINGS HAVEN'T GONE ACCORDING TO PLAN. BUT THAT DOESN'T DIMINISH WHAT YOU'VE ACCOMPLISHED.
YOU ARE MY FASHION HERO.
YOUR WORDS INSPIRED ME TO FIND MY VISION AS A DESIGNER--THEY HELPED ME REALIZE THAT MY VISION WAS THERE ALL ALONG.
I JUST HAD TO BELIEVE IN MYSELF ENOUGH TO EXPRESS IT.
YOUR VISION IS WHAT I'M HERE FOR TODAY– WHAT EVERYONE'S HERE FOR TODAY.
WHAT IF THAT'S NOT ENOUGH? WHAT IF I'M NOT ENOUGH?

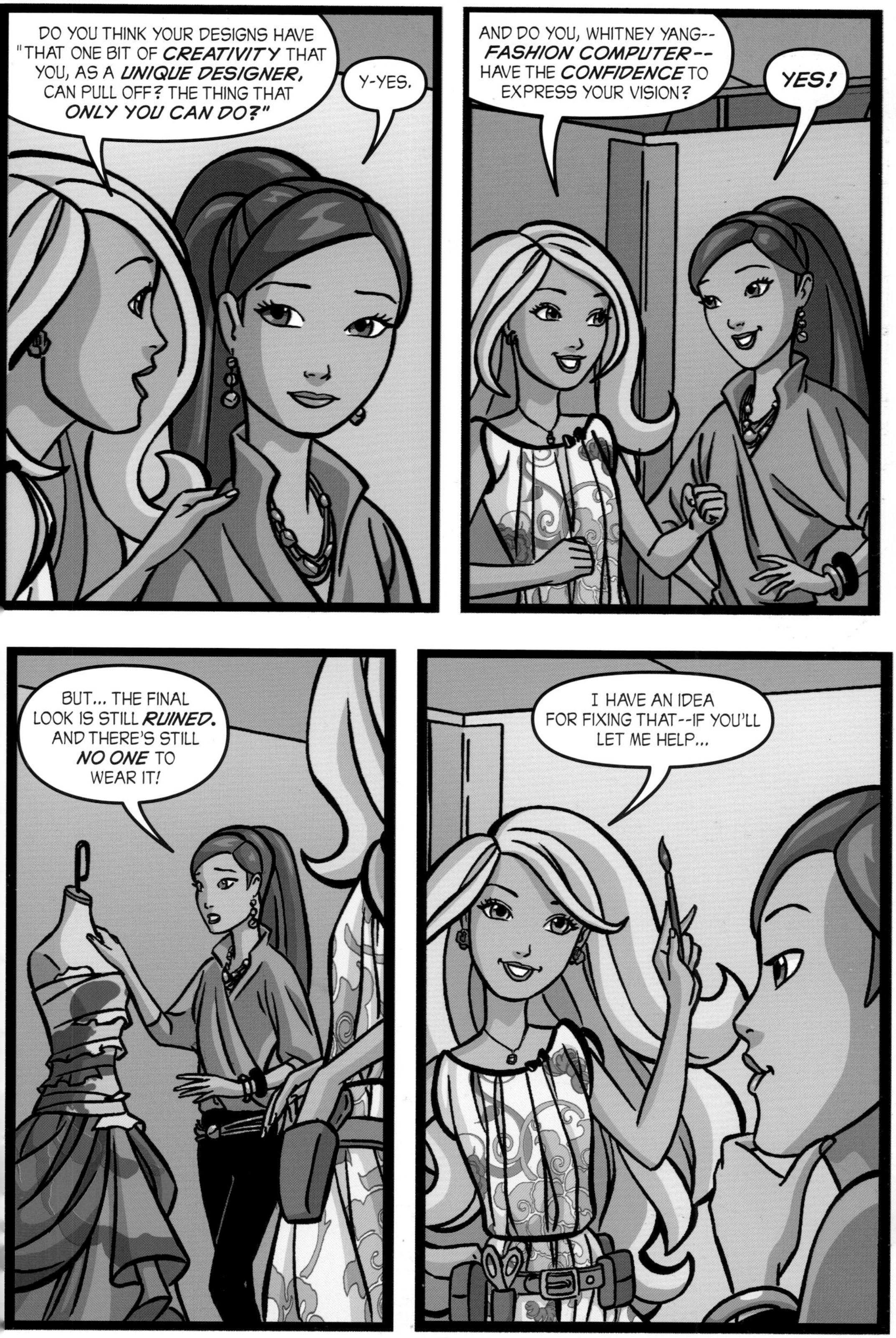
DO YOU THINK YOUR DESIGNS HAVE "THAT ONE BIT OF CREATIVITY THAT YOU, AS A UNIQUE DESIGNER, CAN PULL OFF? THE THING THAT ONLY YOU CAN DO?"
Y-YES.
AND DO YOU, WHITNEY YANG-- FASHION COMPUTER-- HAVE THE CONFIDENCE TO EXPRESS YOUR VISION?
YES!
BUT... THE FINAL LOOK IS STILL RUINED. AND THERE'S STILL NO ONE TO WEAR IT!
I HAVE AN IDEA FOR FIXING THAT--IF YOU'LL LET ME HELP...

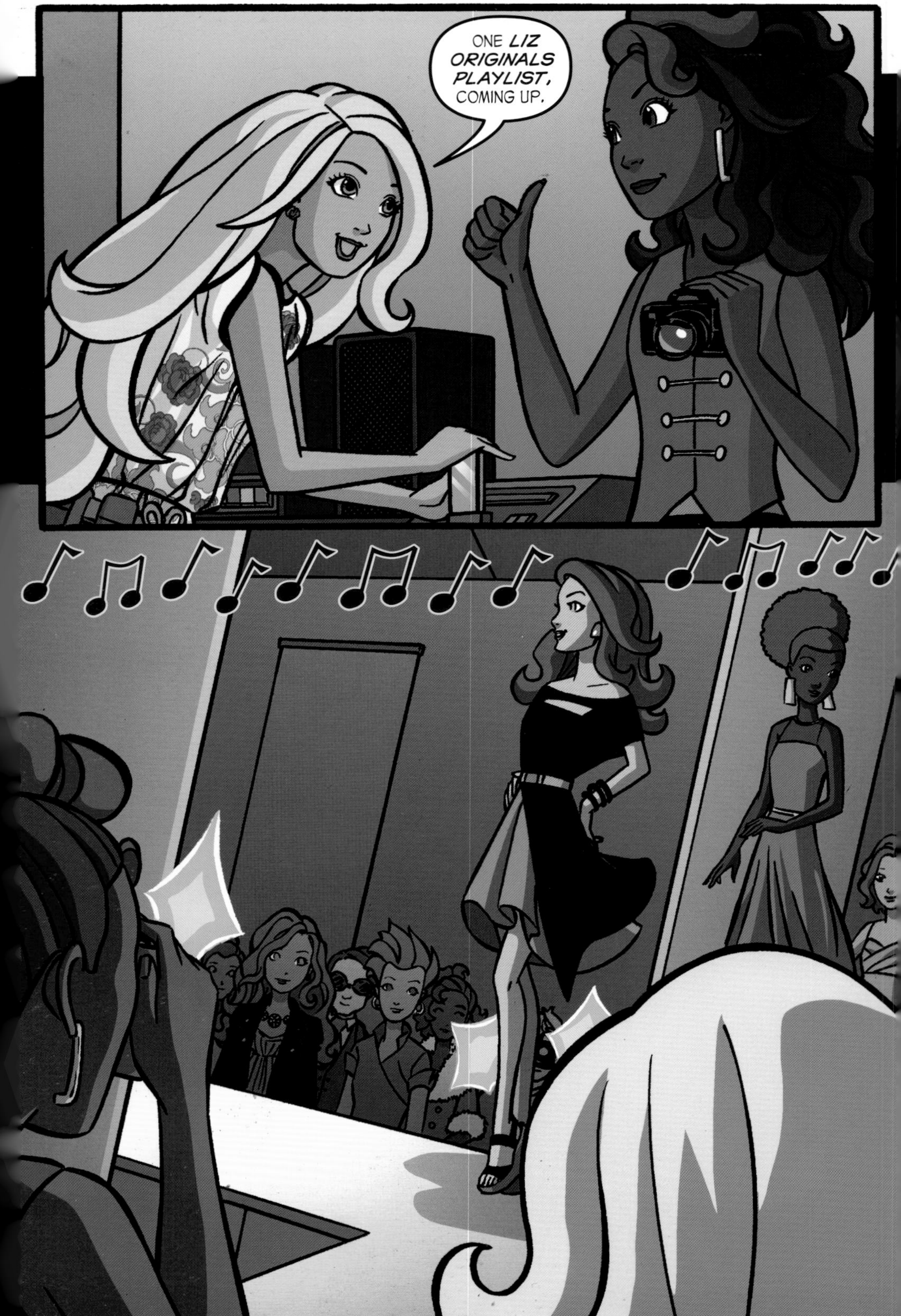
ONE LIZ ORIGINALS PLAYLIST, COMING UP.

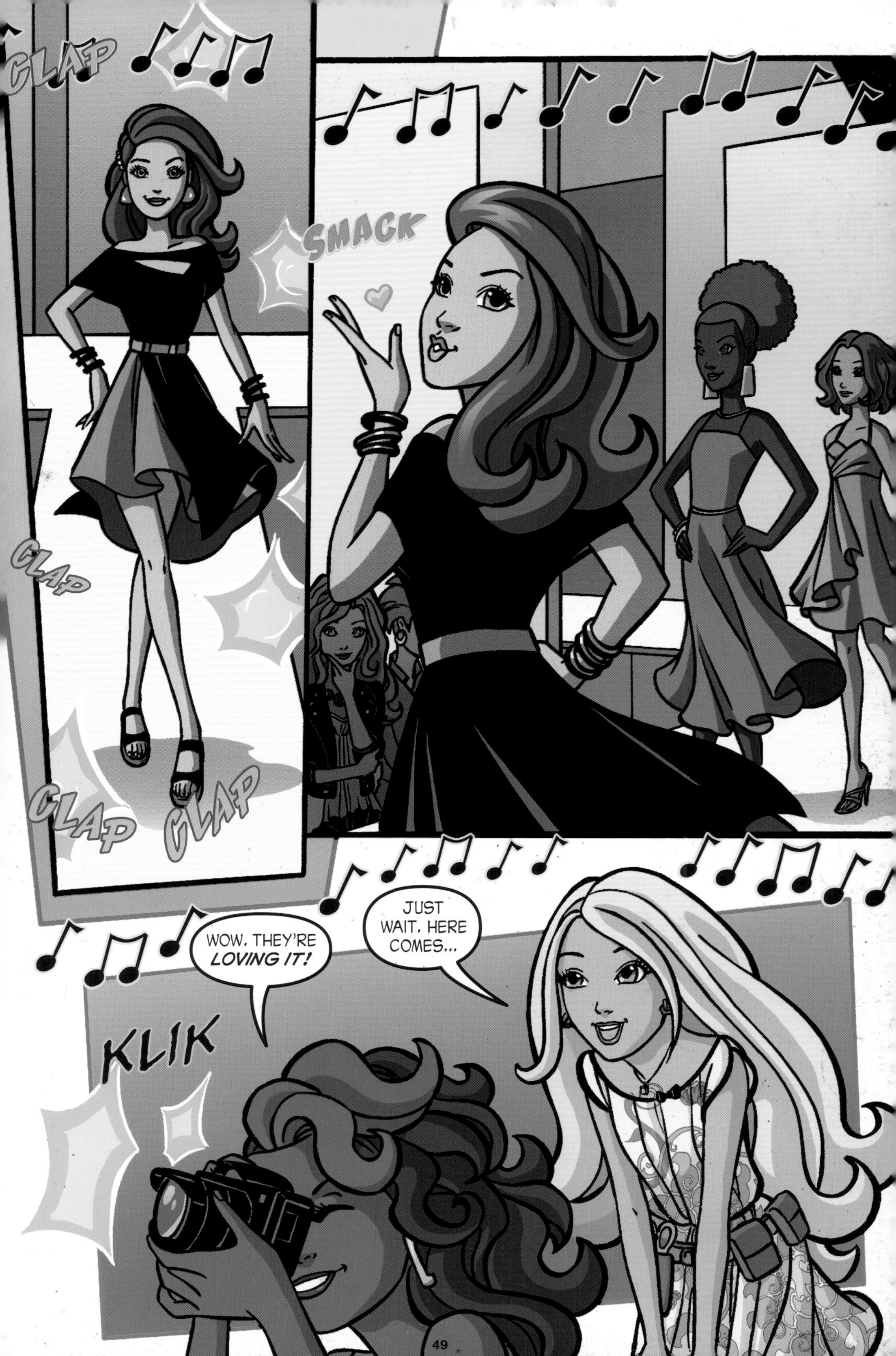
CLAP
CLAP
CLAP
CLAP
SMACK
WOW. THEY'RE *LOVING IT!*
JUST WAIT. HERE COMES...
KLIK

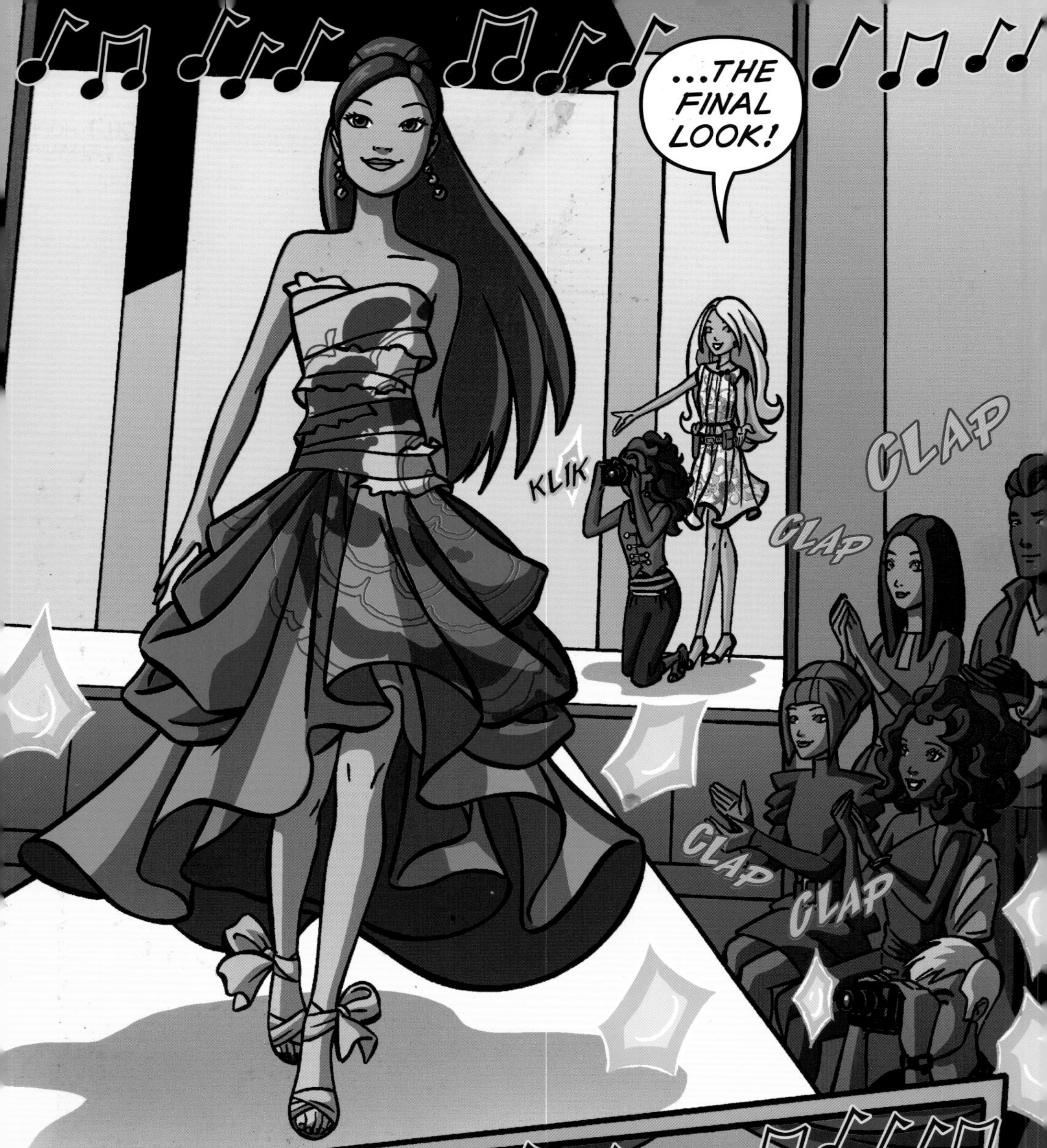
...THE FINAL LOOK!
KLIK
CLAP
CLAP
CLAP
CLAP

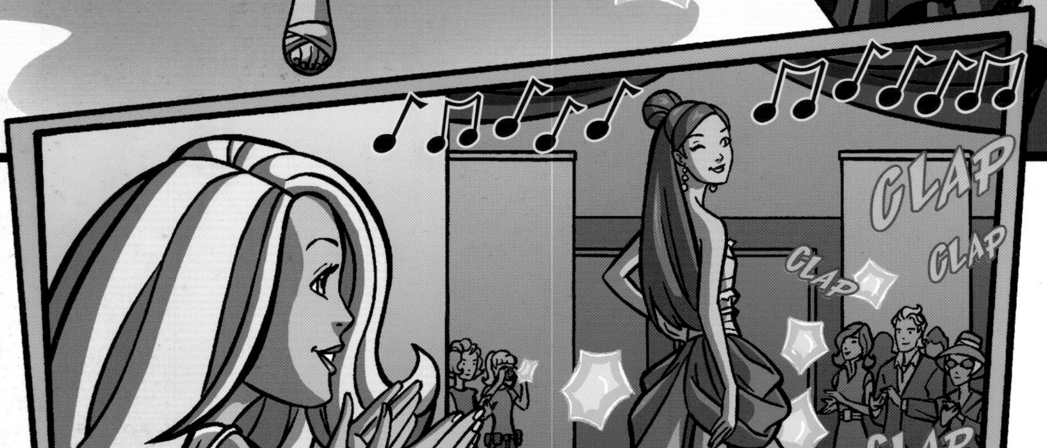
CLAP
CLAP
CLAP
CLAP

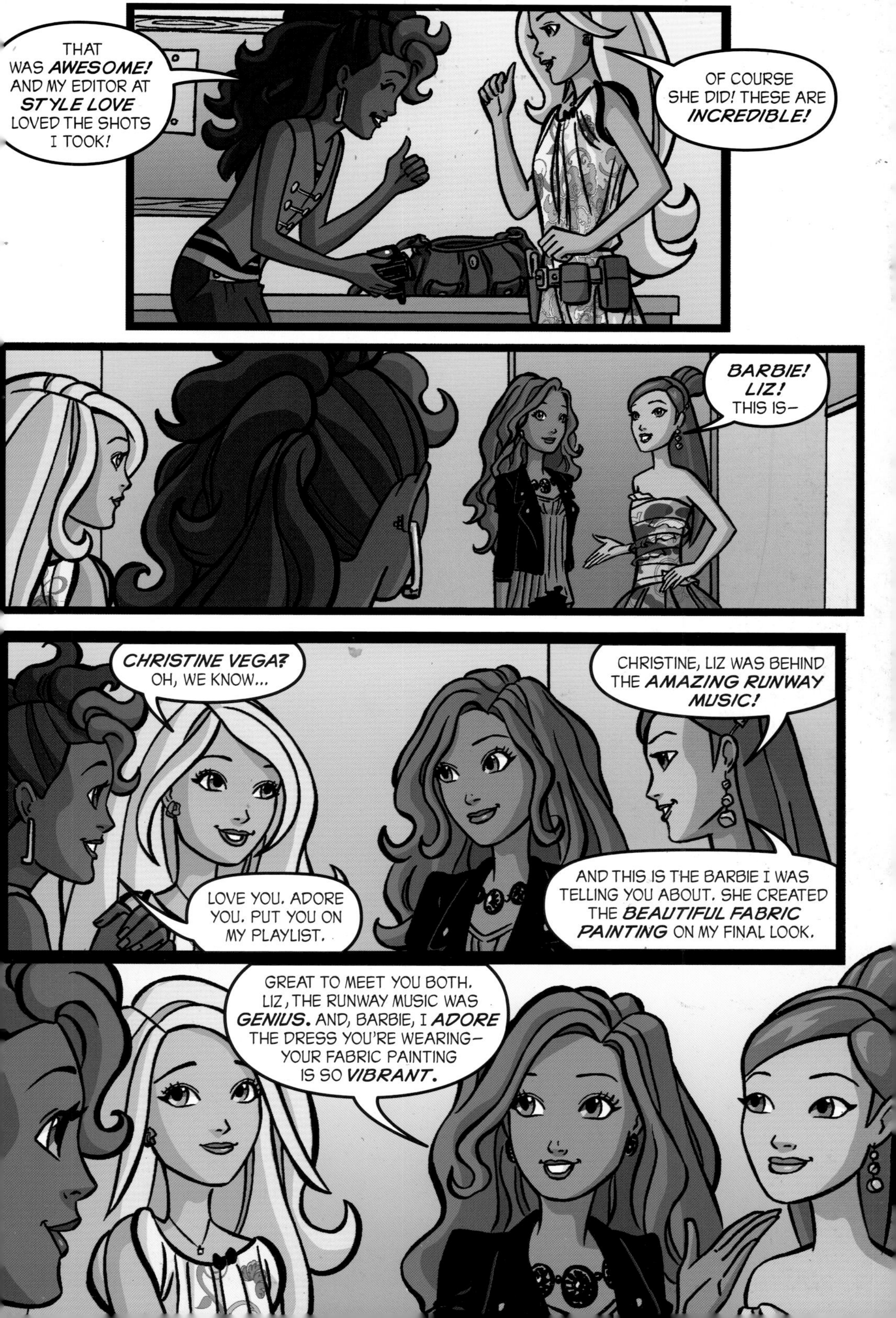
THAT WAS AWESOME! AND MY EDITOR AT STYLE LOVE LOVED THE SHOTS I TOOK!
OF COURSE SHE DID! THESE ARE INCREDIBLE!
BARBIE! LIZ! THIS IS–
CHRISTINE VEGA? OH, WE KNOW...
LOVE YOU. ADORE YOU. PUT YOU ON MY PLAYLIST.
CHRISTINE, LIZ WAS BEHIND THE AMAZING RUNWAY MUSIC!
AND THIS IS THE BARBIE I WAS TELLING YOU ABOUT. SHE CREATED THE BEAUTIFUL FABRIC PAINTING ON MY FINAL LOOK.
GREAT TO MEET YOU BOTH. LIZ, THE RUNWAY MUSIC WAS GENIUS. AND, BARBIE, I ADORE THE DRESS YOU'RE WEARING– YOUR FABRIC PAINTING IS SO VIBRANT.

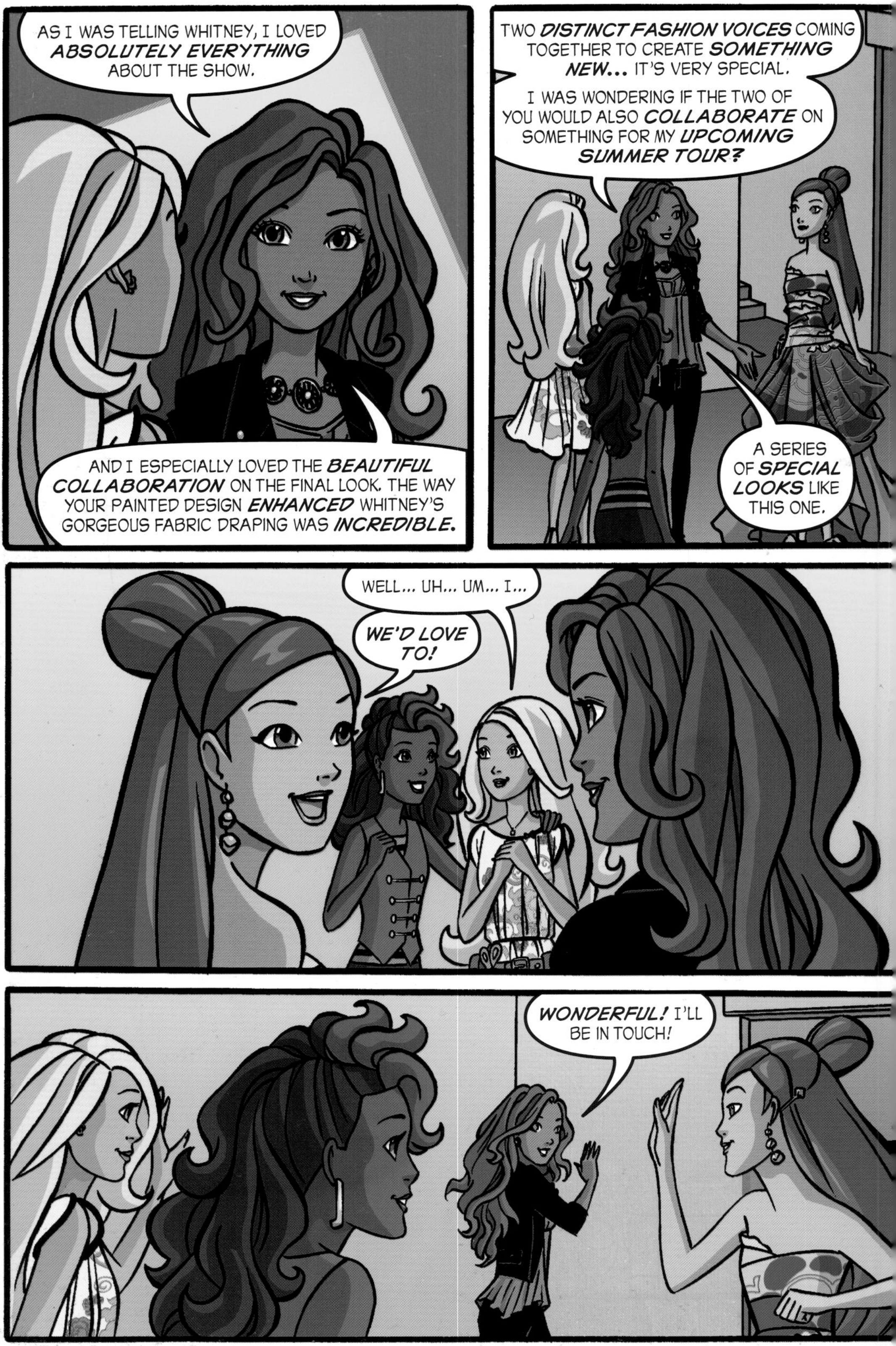
AS I WAS TELLING WHITNEY, I LOVED ABSOLUTELY EVERYTHING ABOUT THE SHOW.
AND I ESPECIALLY LOVED THE BEAUTIFUL COLLABORATION ON THE FINAL LOOK. THE WAY YOUR PAINTED DESIGN ENHANCED WHITNEY'S GORGEOUS FABRIC DRAPING WAS INCREDIBLE.
TWO DISTINCT FASHION VOICES COMING TOGETHER TO CREATE SOMETHING NEW... IT'S VERY SPECIAL.
I WAS WONDERING IF THE TWO OF YOU WOULD ALSO COLLABORATE ON SOMETHING FOR MY UPCOMING SUMMER TOUR?
A SERIES OF SPECIAL LOOKS LIKE THIS ONE.
WELL... UH... UM... I...
WE'D LOVE TO!
WONDERFUL! I'LL BE IN TOUCH!

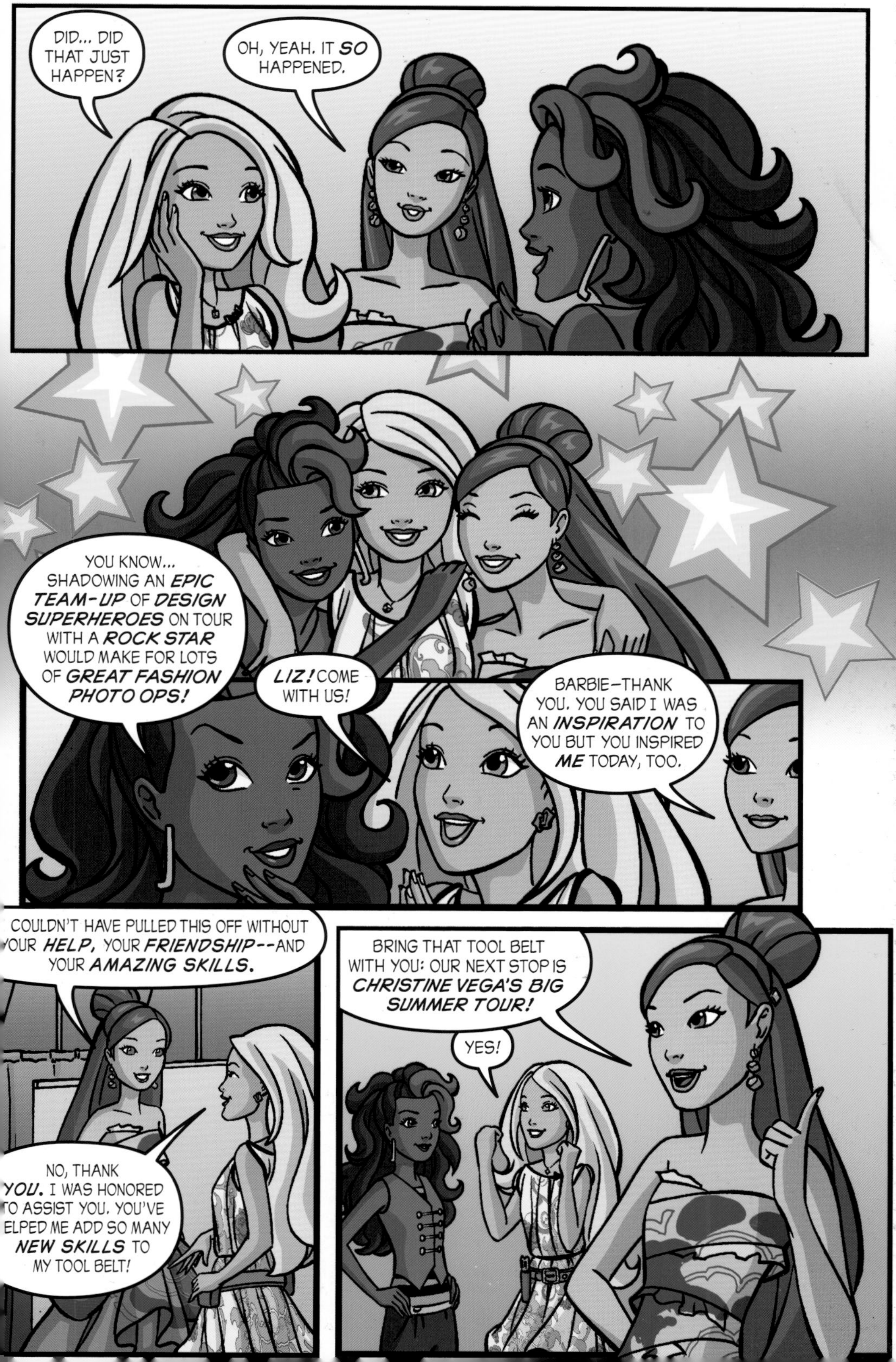

DID... DID THAT JUST HAPPEN?
OH, YEAH. IT SO HAPPENED.
YOU KNOW... SHADOWING AN EPIC TEAM-UP OF DESIGN SUPERHEROES ON TOUR WITH A ROCK STAR WOULD MAKE FOR LOTS OF GREAT FASHION PHOTO OPS!
LIZ! COME WITH US!
BARBIE—THANK YOU. YOU SAID I WAS AN INSPIRATION TO YOU BUT YOU INSPIRED ME TODAY, TOO.
COULDN'T HAVE PULLED THIS OFF WITHOUT YOUR HELP, YOUR FRIENDSHIP--AND YOUR AMAZING SKILLS.
NO, THANK YOU. I WAS HONORED TO ASSIST YOU. YOU'VE ELPED ME ADD SO MANY NEW SKILLS TO MY TOOL BELT!
BRING THAT TOOL BELT WITH YOU: OUR NEXT STOP IS CHRISTINE VEGA'S BIG SUMMER TOUR!
YES!

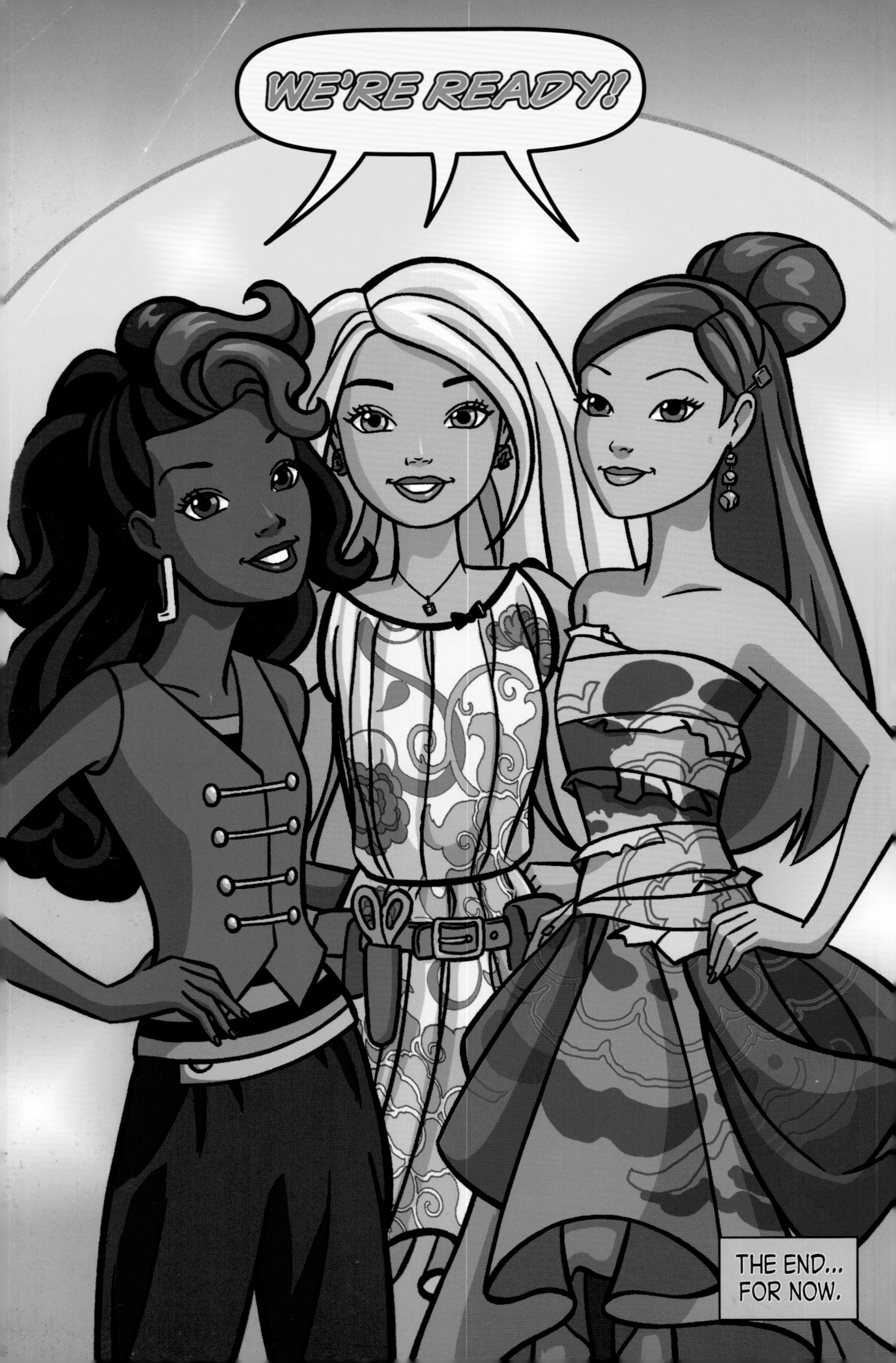
WE'RE READY!
THE END...
FOR NOW.

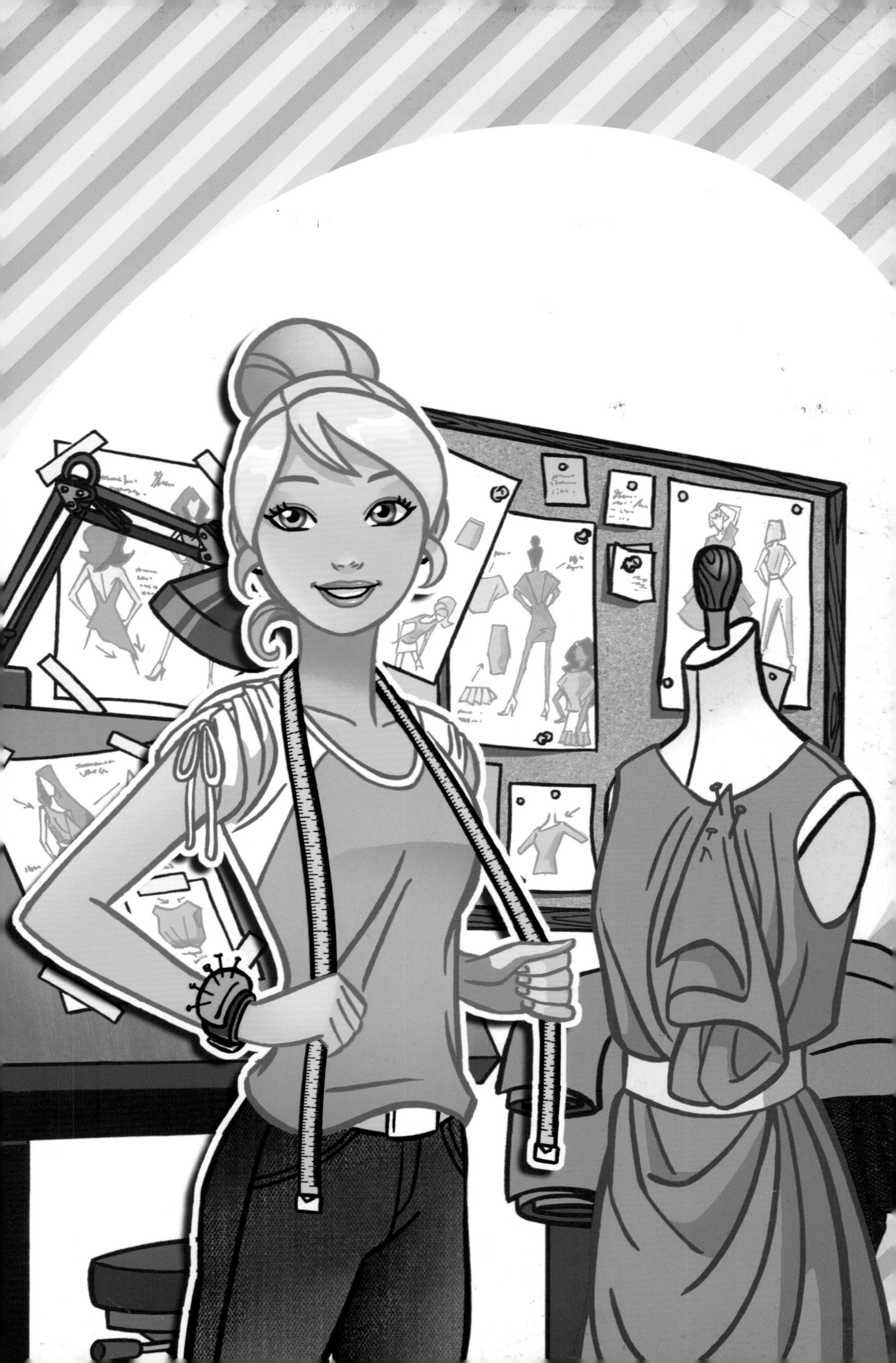

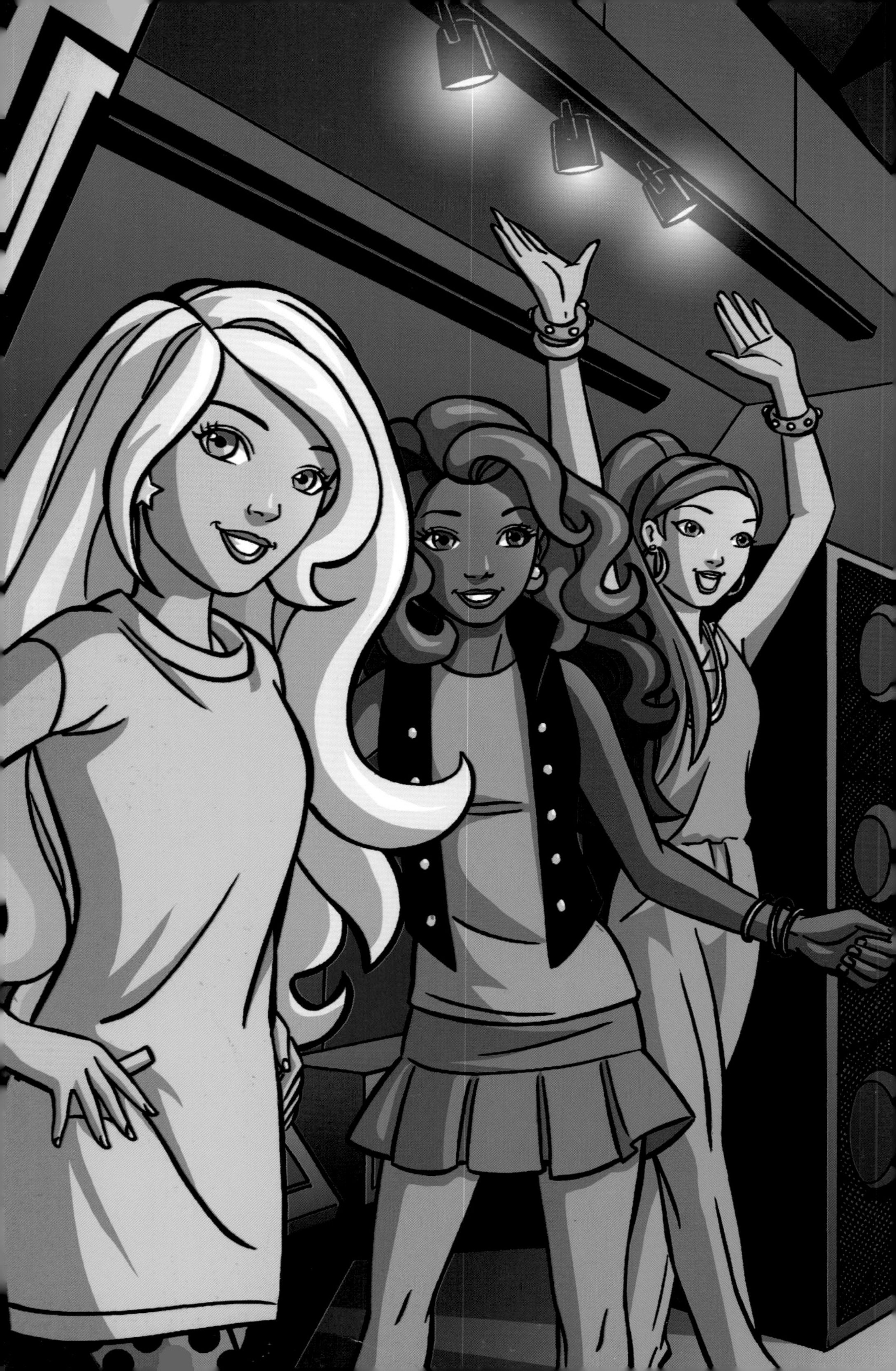

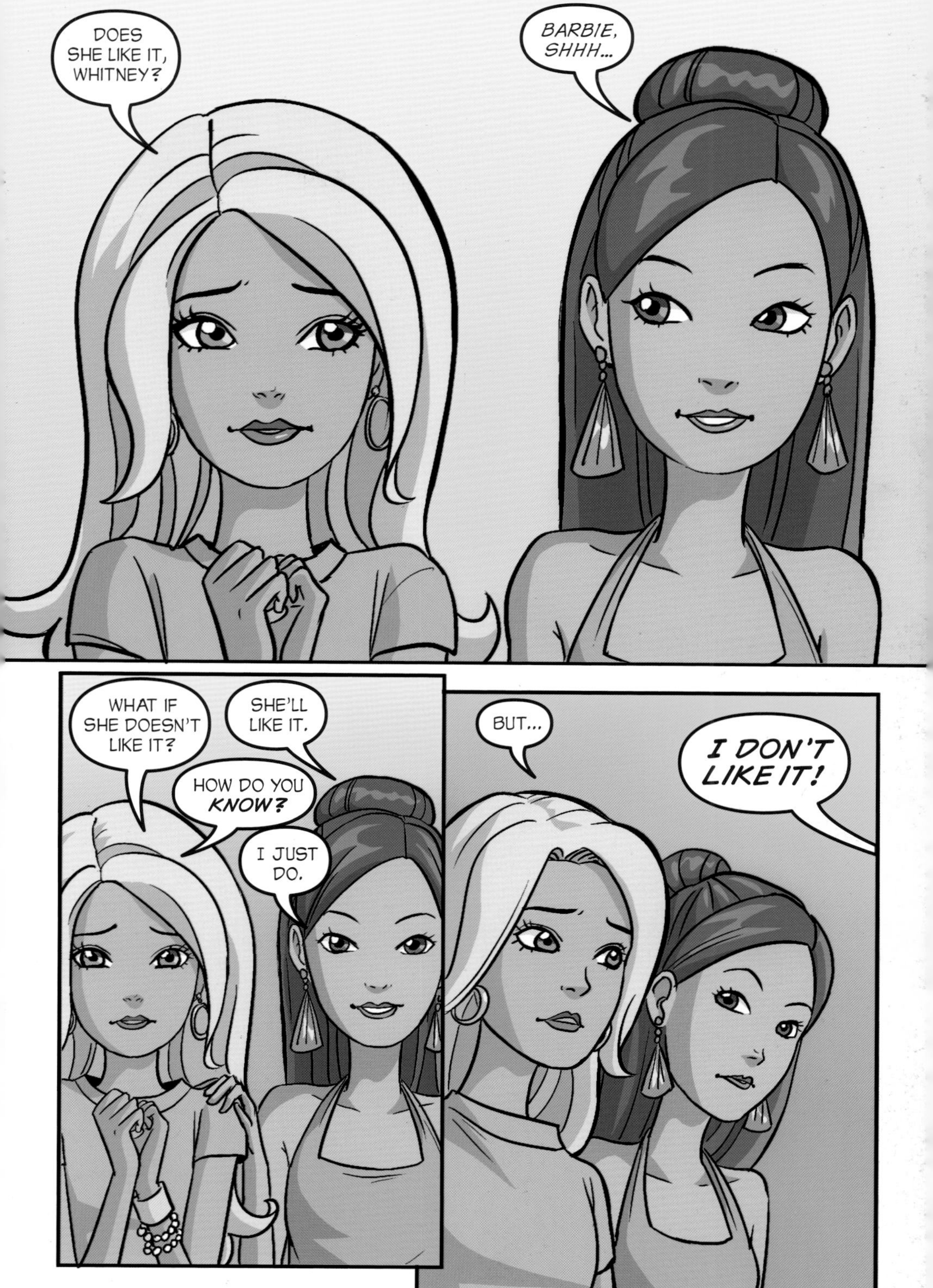
DOES SHE LIKE IT, WHITNEY?
BARBIE, SHHH...
WHAT IF SHE DOESN'T LIKE IT?
SHE'LL LIKE IT.
HOW DO YOU KNOW?
I JUST DO.
BUT...
I DON'T LIKE IT!

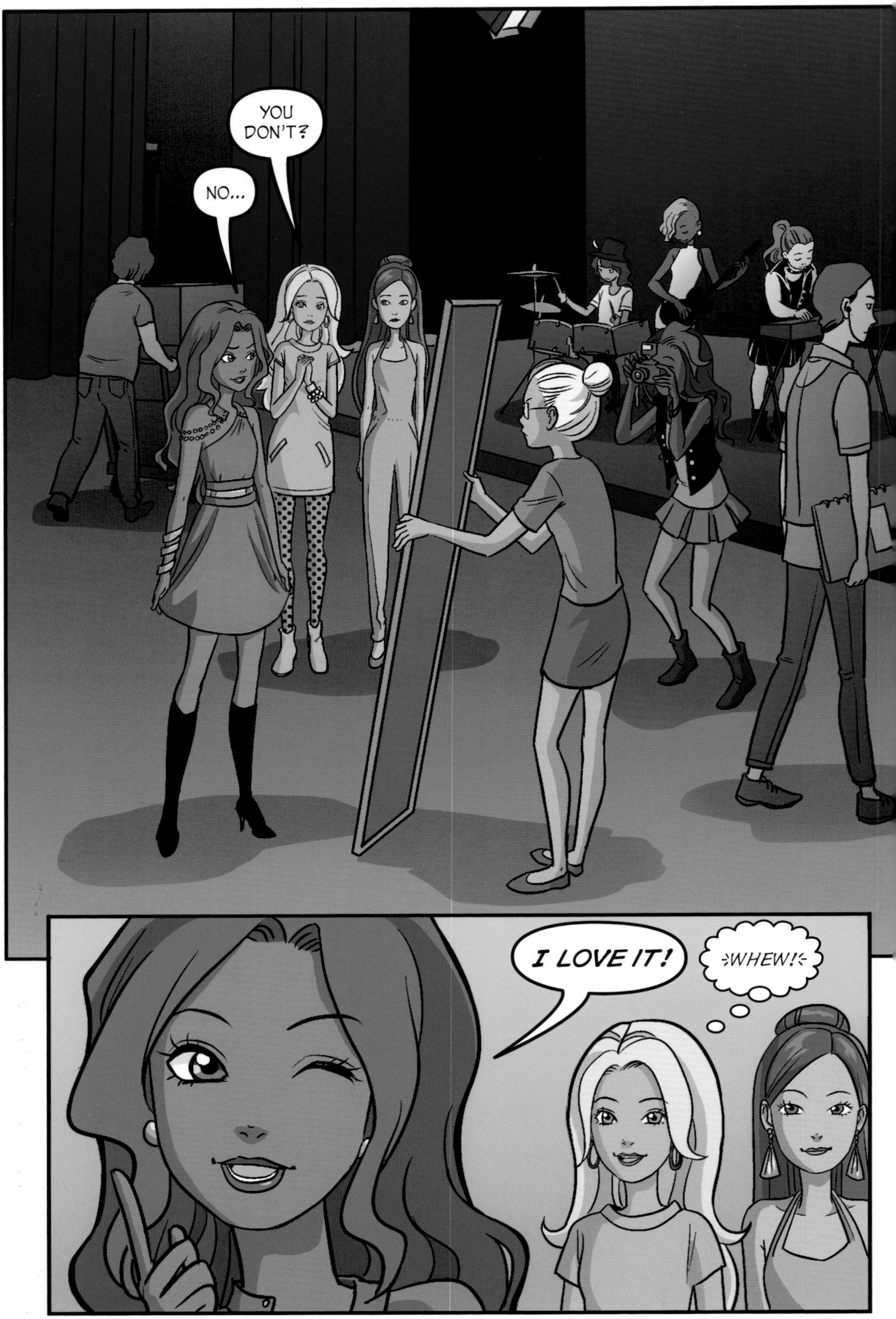
YOU DON'T?
NO...
I LOVE IT!
WHEW!

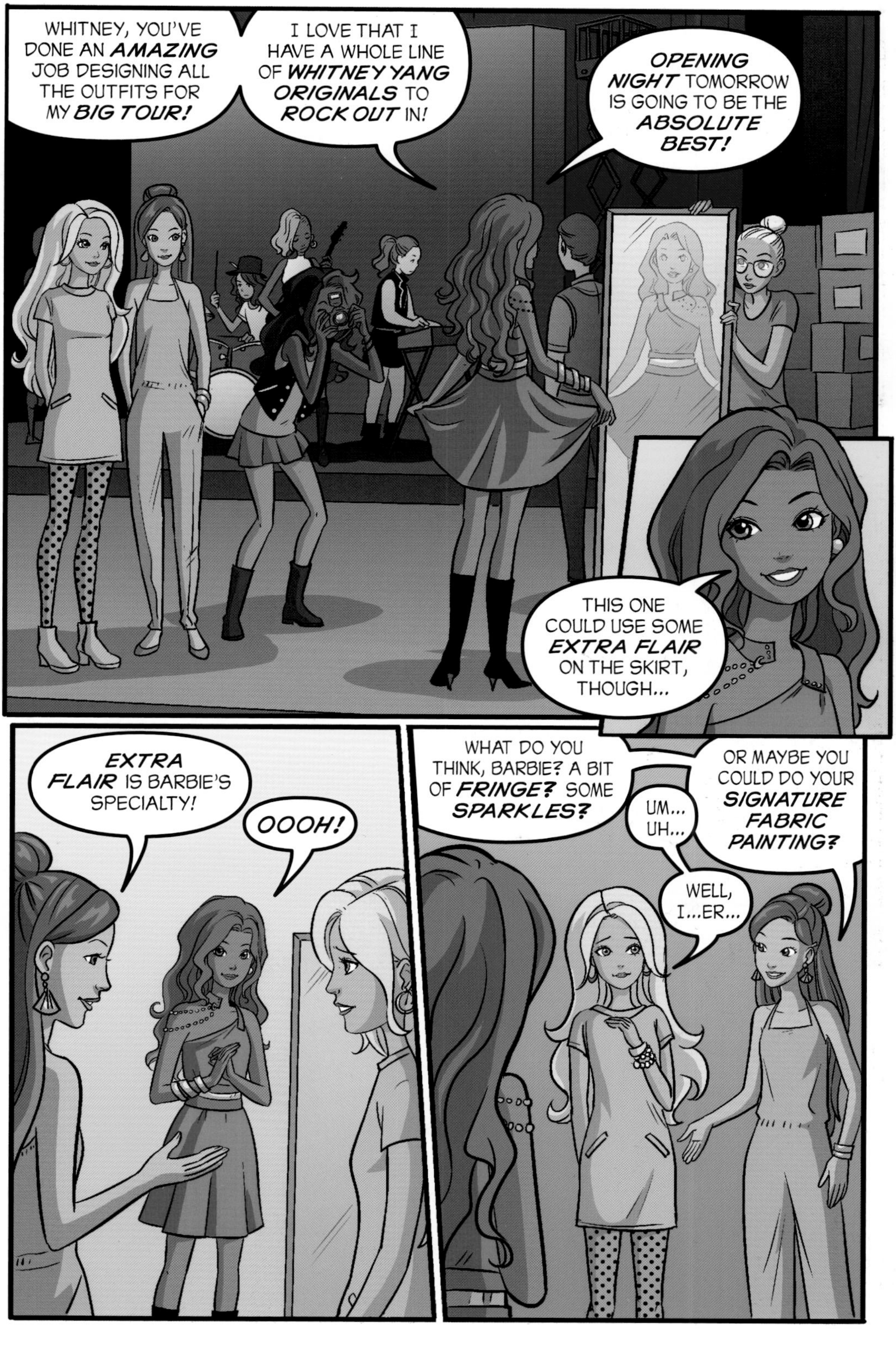
WHITNEY, YOU'VE DONE AN AMAZING JOB DESIGNING ALL THE OUTFITS FOR MY BIG TOUR!
I LOVE THAT I HAVE A WHOLE LINE OF WHITNEY YANG ORIGINALS TO ROCK OUT IN!
OPENING NIGHT TOMORROW IS GOING TO BE THE ABSOLUTE BEST!
THIS ONE COULD USE SOME EXTRA FLAIR ON THE SKIRT, THOUGH...
EXTRA FLAIR IS BARBIE'S SPECIALTY!
OOOH!
WHAT DO YOU THINK, BARBIE? A BIT OF FRINGE? SOME SPARKLES?
UM... UH...
OR MAYBE YOU COULD DO YOUR SIGNATURE FABRIC PAINTING?
WELL, I...ER...

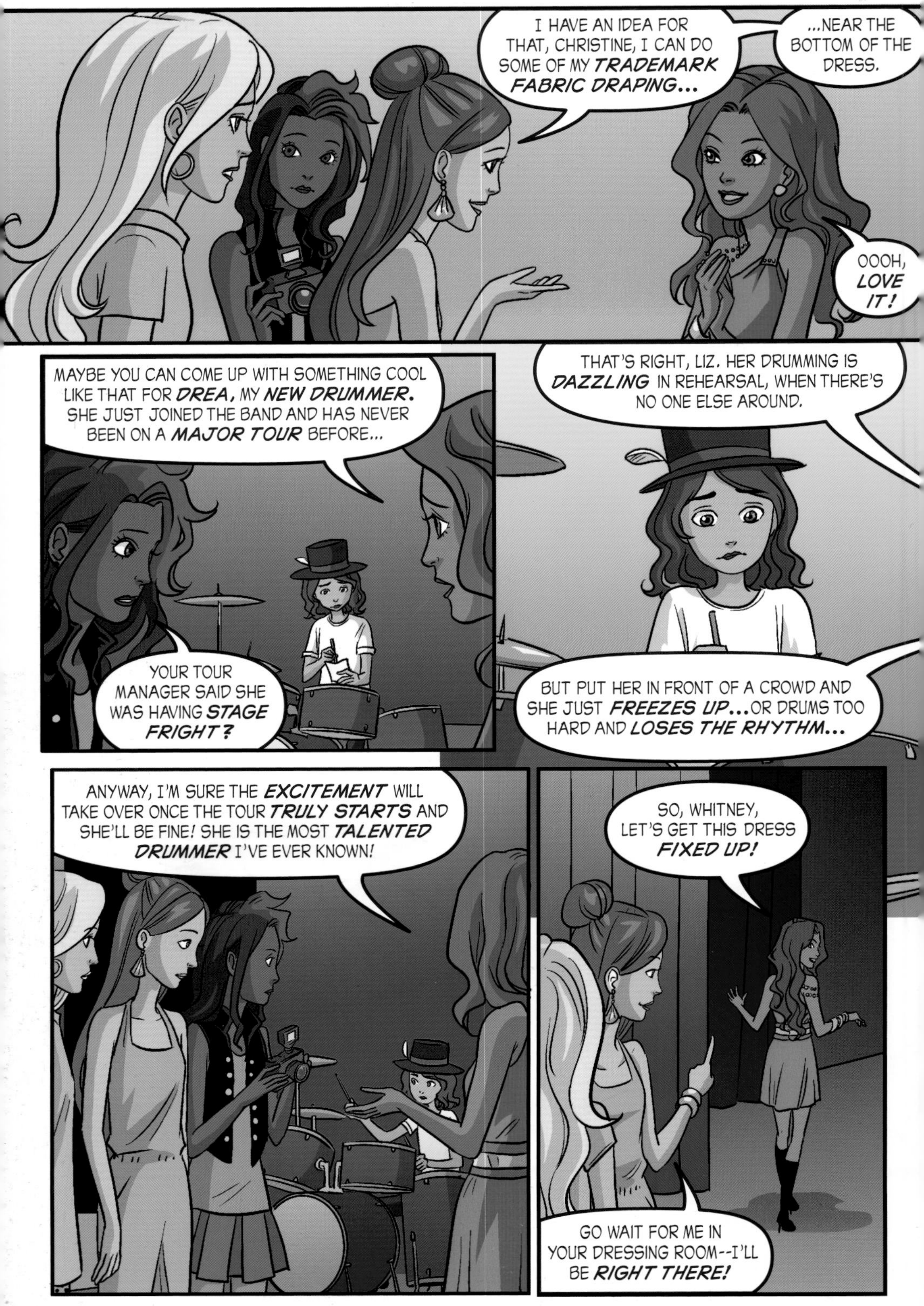
I HAVE AN IDEA FOR THAT, CHRISTINE, I CAN DO SOME OF MY TRADEMARK FABRIC DRAPING...
...NEAR THE BOTTOM OF THE DRESS.
OOOH, LOVE IT!
MAYBE YOU CAN COME UP WITH SOMETHING COOL LIKE THAT FOR DREA, MY NEW DRUMMER. SHE JUST JOINED THE BAND AND HAS NEVER BEEN ON A MAJOR TOUR BEFORE...
YOUR TOUR MANAGER SAID SHE WAS HAVING STAGE FRIGHT?
THAT'S RIGHT, LIZ. HER DRUMMING IS DAZZLING IN REHEARSAL, WHEN THERE'S NO ONE ELSE AROUND.
BUT PUT HER IN FRONT OF A CROWD AND SHE JUST FREEZES UP...OR DRUMS TOO HARD AND LOSES THE RHYTHM...
ANYWAY, I'M SURE THE EXCITEMENT WILL TAKE OVER ONCE THE TOUR TRULY STARTS AND SHE'LL BE FINE! SHE IS THE MOST TALENTED DRUMMER I'VE EVER KNOWN!
SO, WHITNEY, LET'S GET THIS DRESS FIXED UP!
GO WAIT FOR ME IN YOUR DRESSING ROOM--I'LL BE RIGHT THERE!

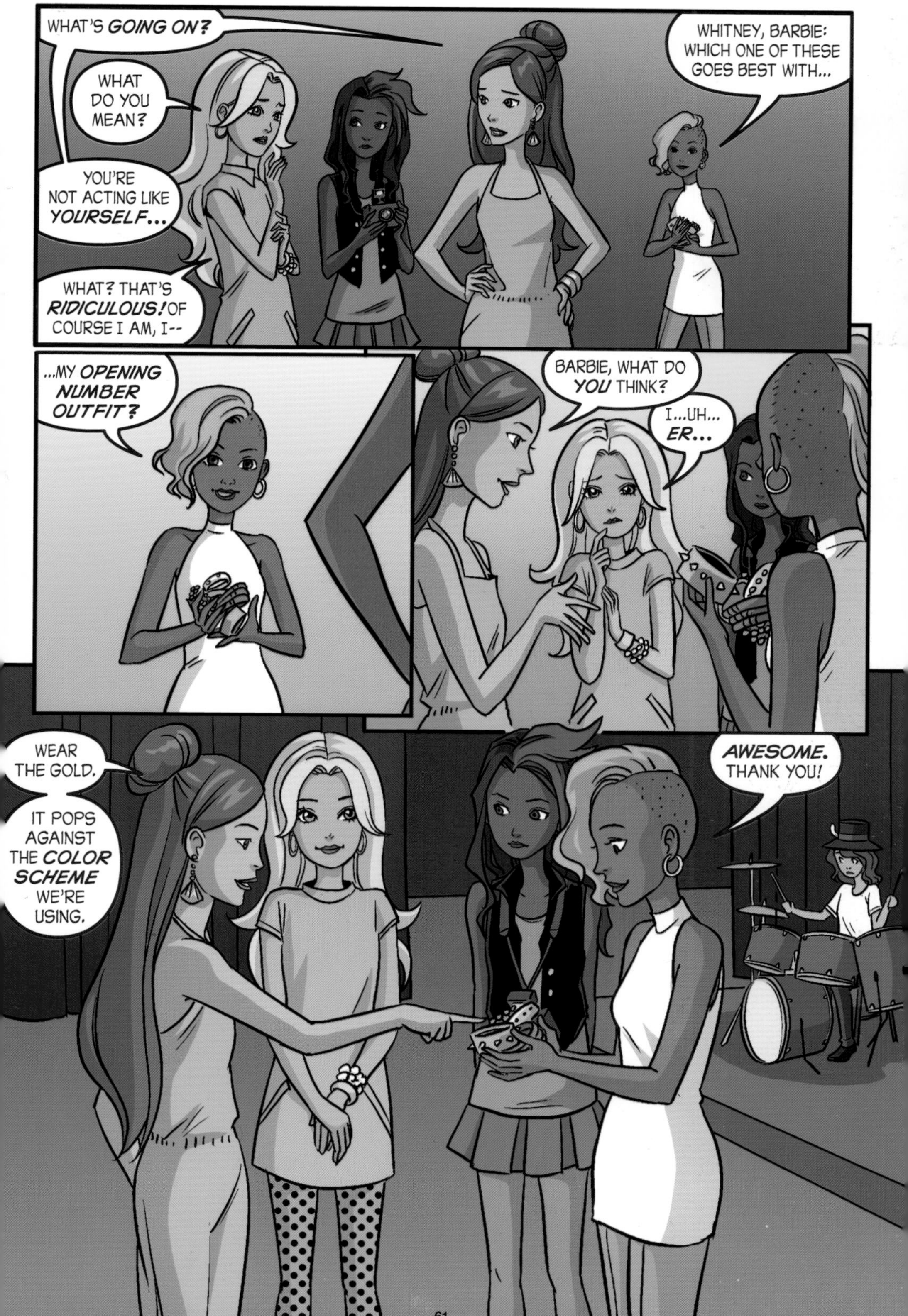
WHAT'S GOING ON?
WHAT DO YOU MEAN?
YOU'RE NOT ACTING LIKE YOURSELF...
WHAT? THAT'S RIDICULOUS! OF COURSE I AM, I--
WHITNEY, BARBIE: WHICH ONE OF THESE GOES BEST WITH...
...MY OPENING NUMBER OUTFIT?
BARBIE, WHAT DO YOU THINK?
I...UH... ER...
WEAR THE GOLD.
IT POPS AGAINST THE COLOR SCHEME WE'RE USING.
AWESOME. THANK YOU!

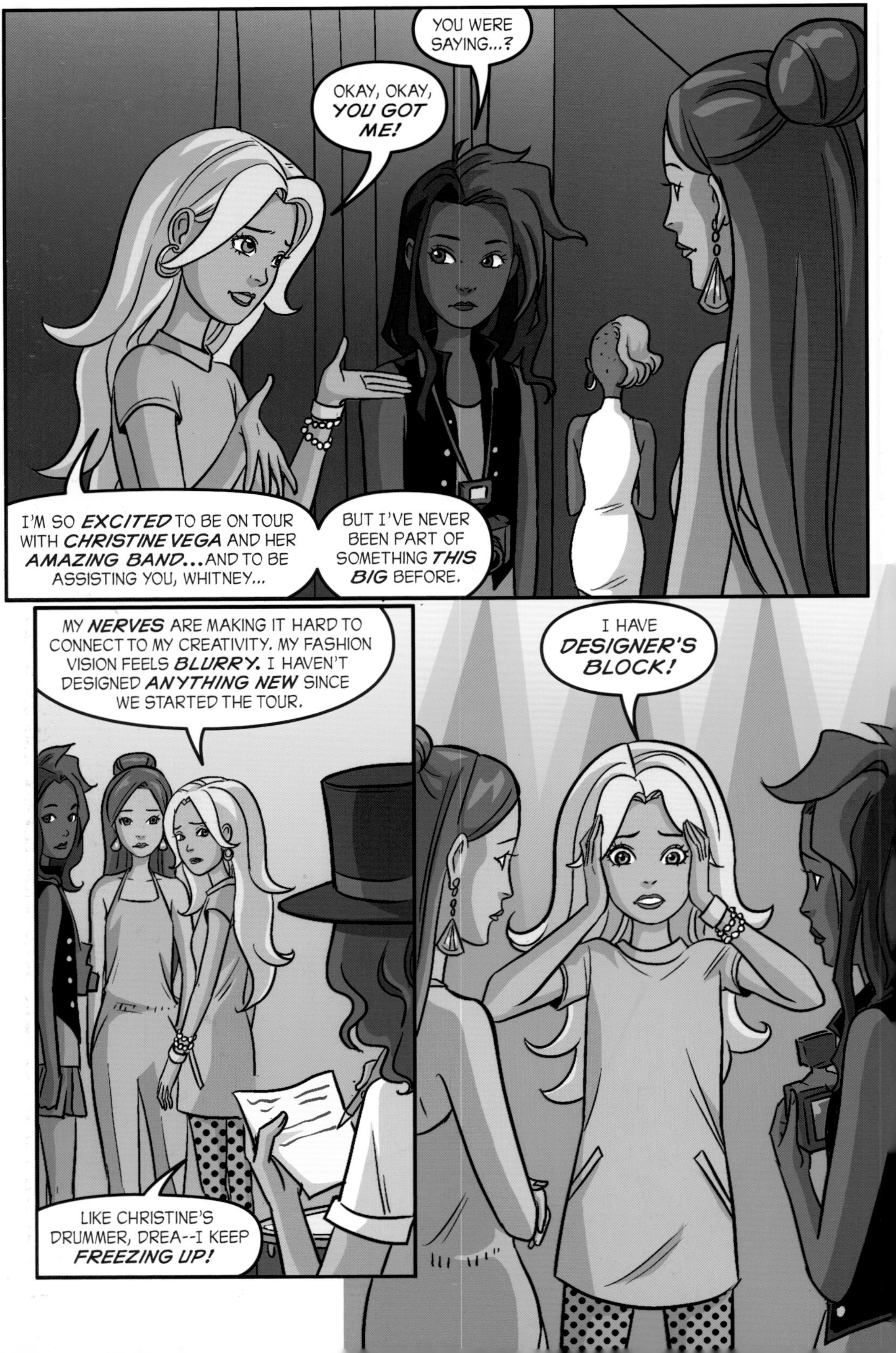

I'M SO EXCITED TO BE ON TOUR WITH CHRISTINE VEGA AND HER AMAZING BAND...AND TO BE ASSISTING YOU, WHITNEY...
BUT I'VE NEVER BEEN PART OF SOMETHING THIS BIG BEFORE.
YOU WERE SAYING...?
OKAY, OKAY, YOU GOT ME!
MY NERVES ARE MAKING IT HARD TO CONNECT TO MY CREATIVITY. MY FASHION VISION FEELS BLURRY. I HAVEN'T DESIGNED ANYTHING NEW SINCE WE STARTED THE TOUR.
LIKE CHRISTINE'S DRUMMER, DREA--I KEEP FREEZING UP!
I HAVE DESIGNER'S BLOCK!

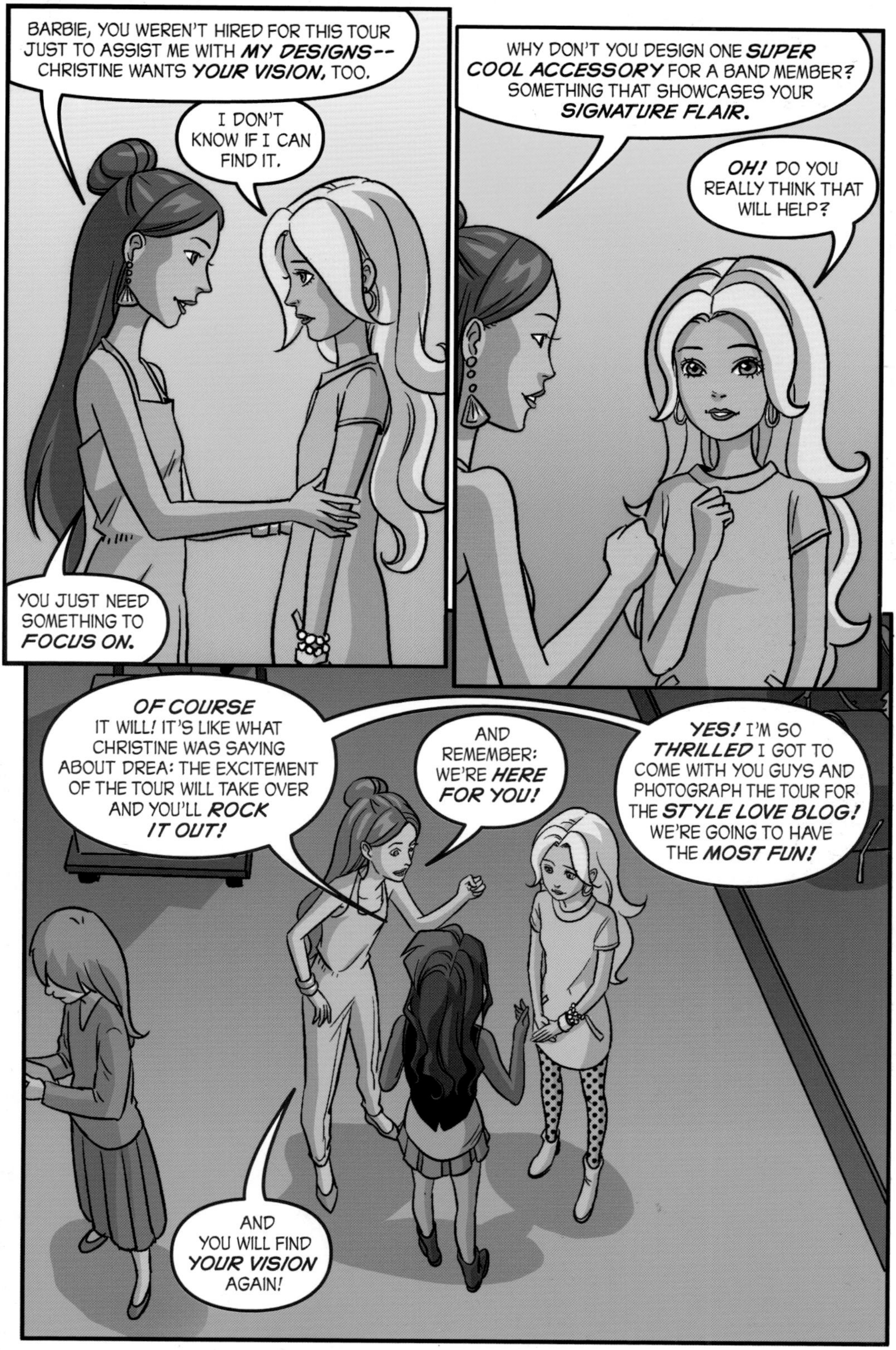
BARBIE, YOU WEREN'T HIRED FOR THIS TOUR JUST TO ASSIST ME WITH MY DESIGNS-- CHRISTINE WANTS YOUR VISION, TOO.
I DON'T KNOW IF I CAN FIND IT.
YOU JUST NEED SOMETHING TO FOCUS ON.
WHY DON'T YOU DESIGN ONE SUPER COOL ACCESSORY FOR A BAND MEMBER? SOMETHING THAT SHOWCASES YOUR SIGNATURE FLAIR.
OH! DO YOU REALLY THINK THAT WILL HELP?
OF COURSE IT WILL! IT'S LIKE WHAT CHRISTINE WAS SAYING ABOUT DREA: THE EXCITEMENT OF THE TOUR WILL TAKE OVER AND YOU'LL ROCK IT OUT!
AND REMEMBER: WE'RE HERE FOR YOU!
YES! I'M SO THRILLED I GOT TO COME WITH YOU GUYS AND PHOTOGRAPH THE TOUR FOR THE STYLE LOVE BLOG! WE'RE GOING TO HAVE THE MOST FUN!
AND YOU WILL FIND YOUR VISION AGAIN!

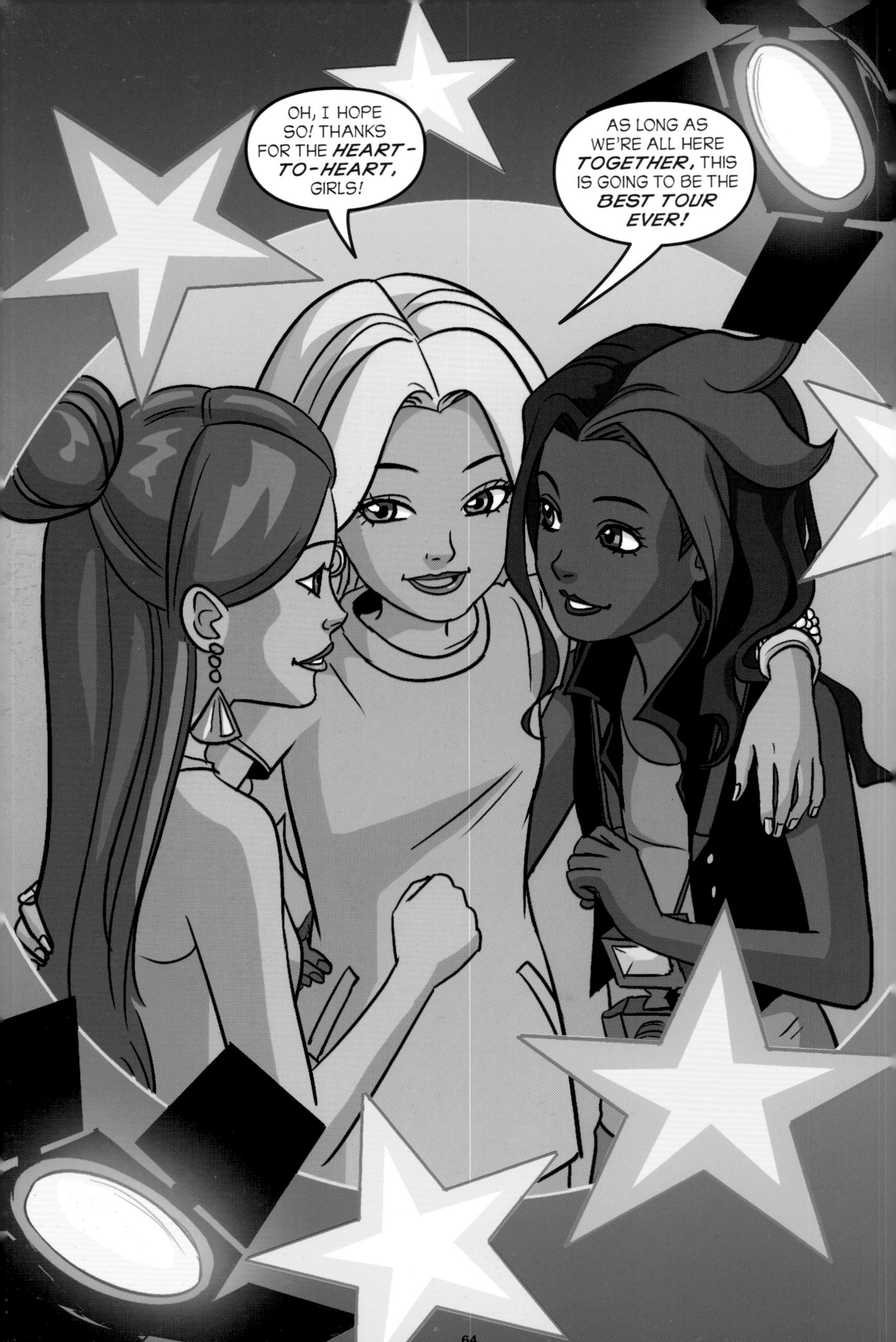
OH, I HOPE SO! THANKS FOR THE HEART-TO-HEART, GIRLS!
AS LONG AS WE'RE ALL HERE TOGETHER, THIS IS GOING TO BE THE BEST TOUR EVER!

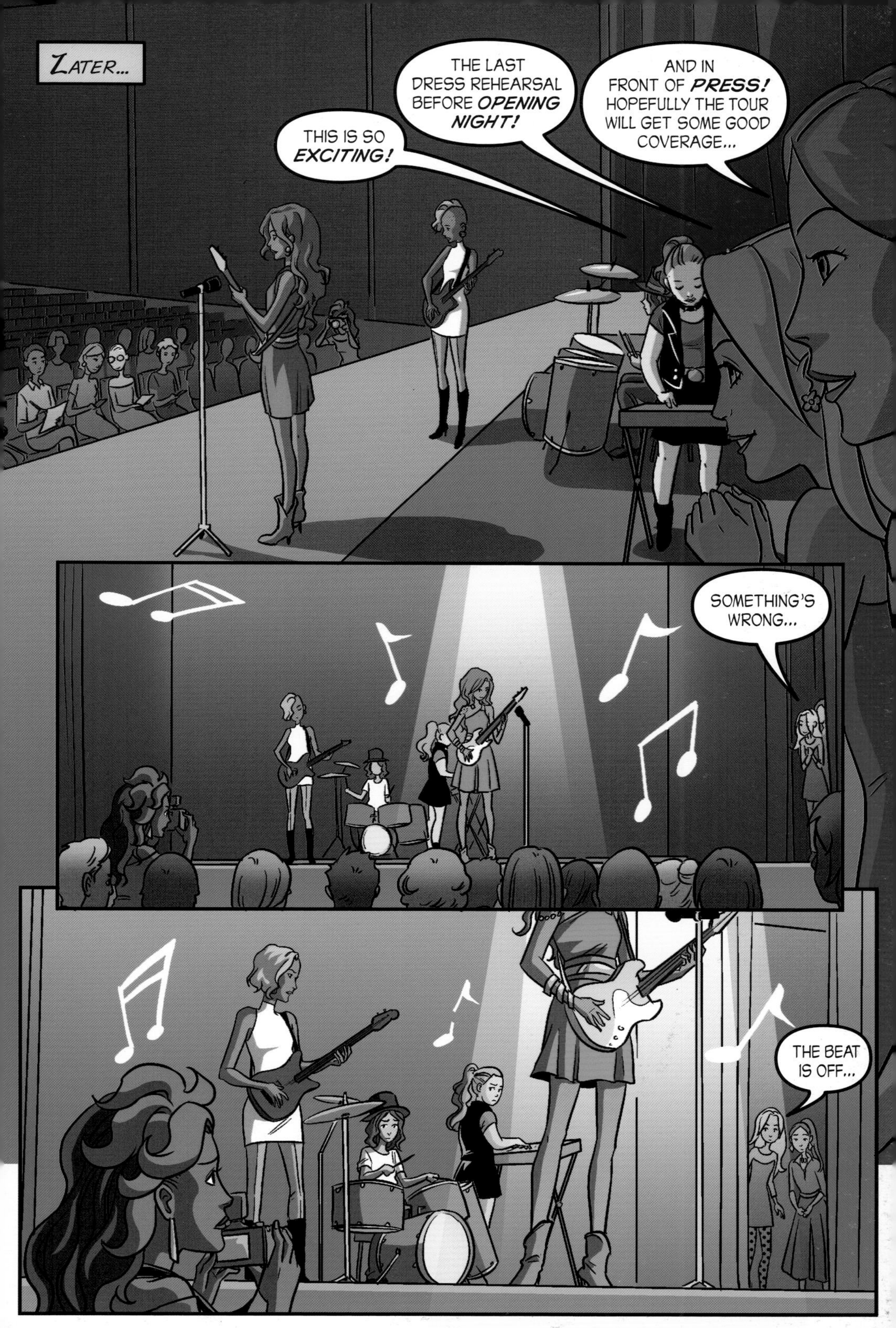
LATER...
THIS IS SO EXCITING!
THE LAST DRESS REHEARSAL BEFORE OPENING NIGHT!
AND IN FRONT OF PRESS! HOPEFULLY THE TOUR WILL GET SOME GOOD COVERAGE...
SOMETHING'S WRONG...
THE BEAT IS OFF...

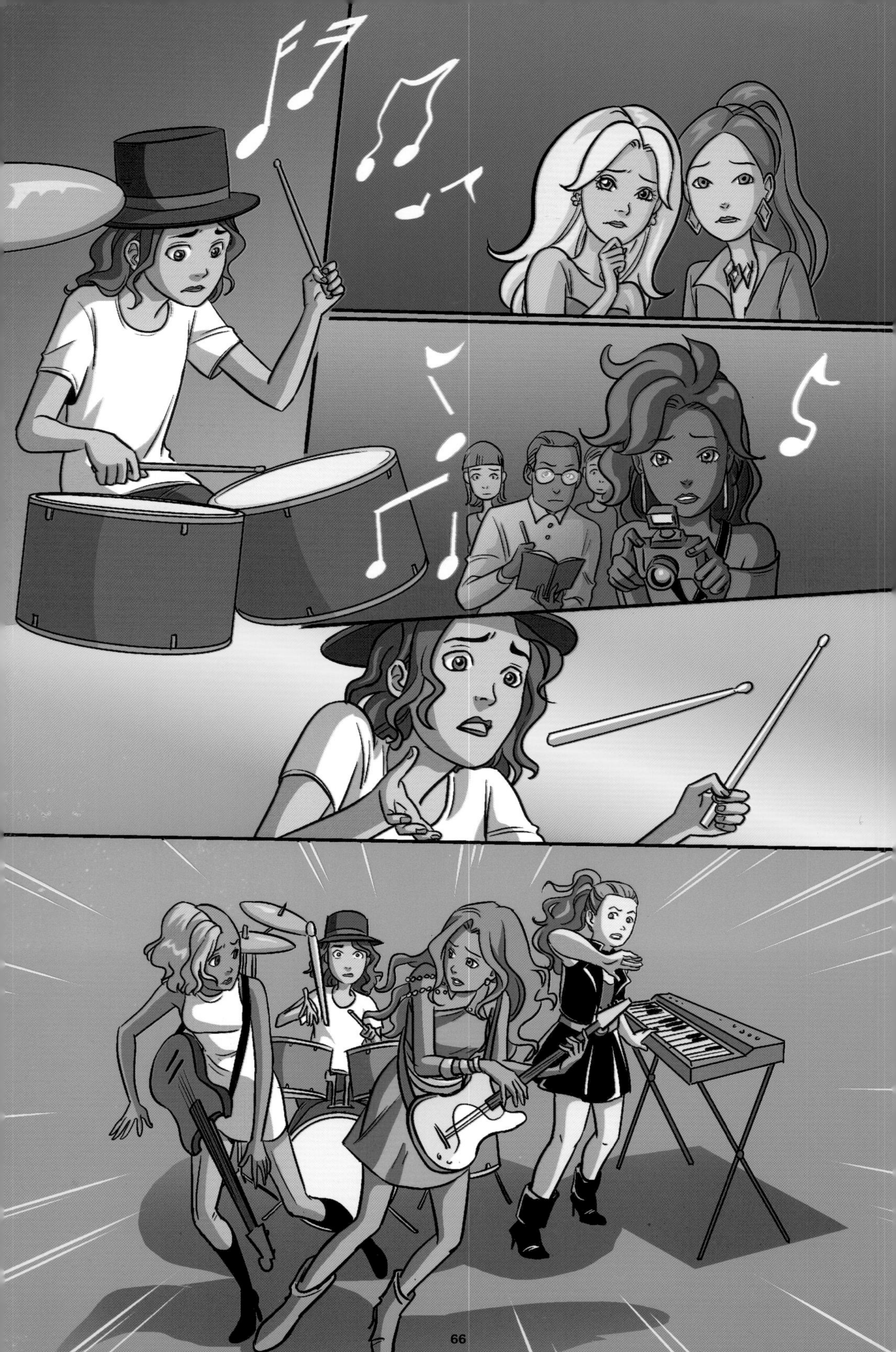

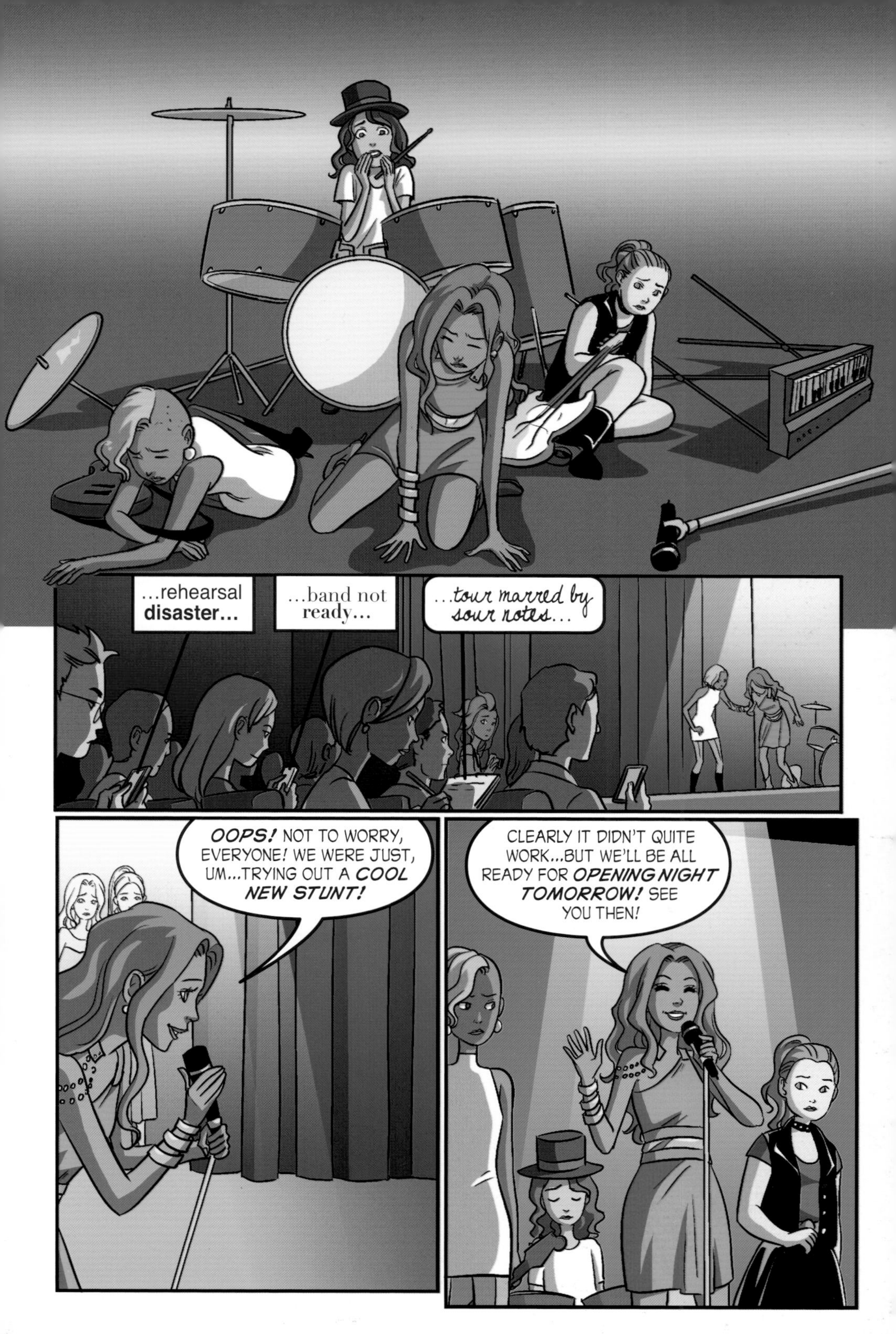

...rehearsal disaster...
...band not ready...
...tour marred by sour notes...
OOPS! NOT TO WORRY, EVERYONE! WE WERE JUST, UM...TRYING OUT A COOL NEW STUNT!
CLEARLY IT DIDN'T QUITE WORK...BUT WE'LL BE ALL READY FOR OPENING NIGHT TOMORROW! SEE YOU THEN!

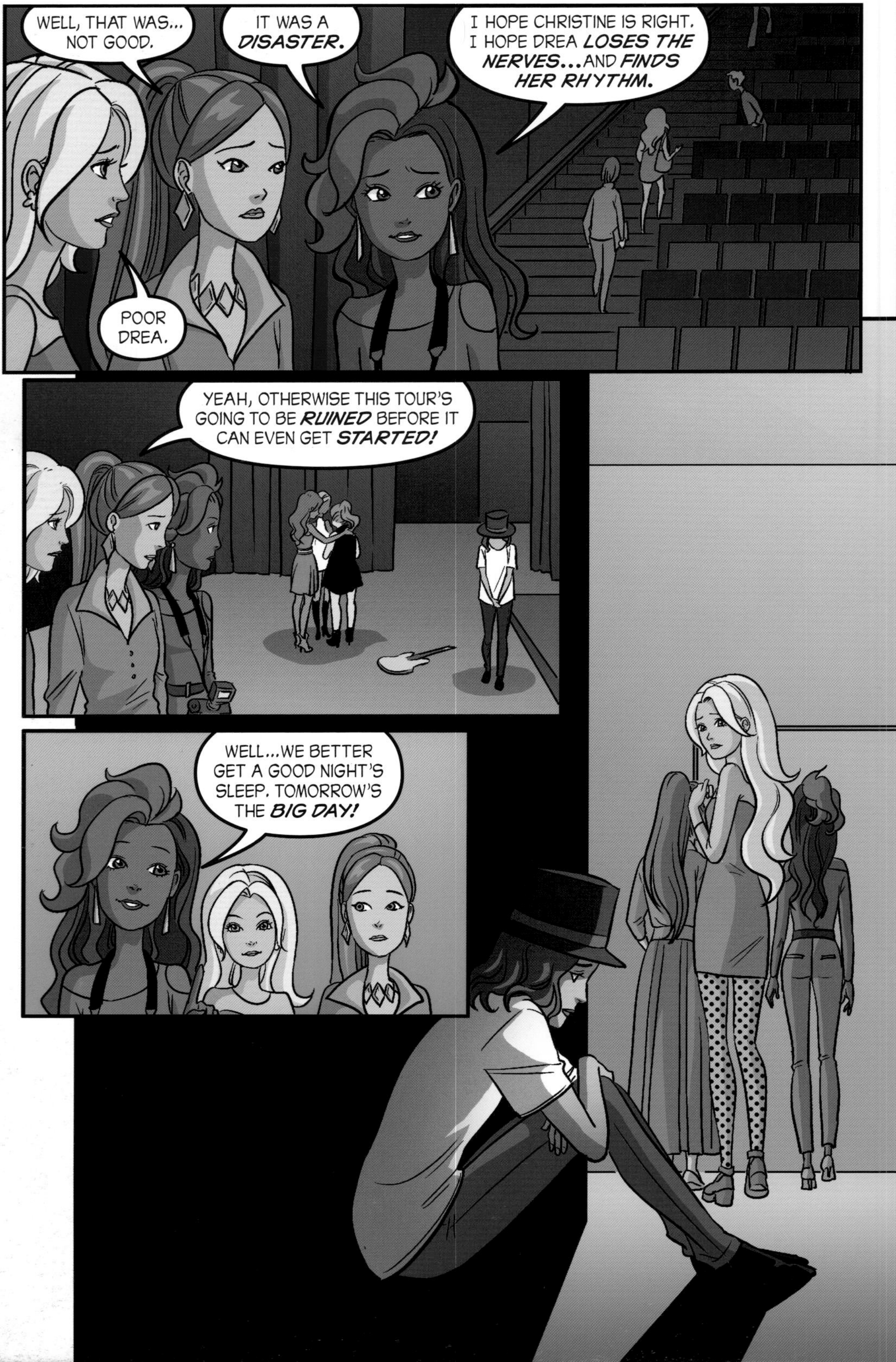
WELL, THAT WAS... NOT GOOD.
POOR DREA.
IT WAS A DISASTER.
I HOPE CHRISTINE IS RIGHT. I HOPE DREA LOSES THE NERVES...AND FINDS HER RHYTHM.
YEAH, OTHERWISE THIS TOUR'S GOING TO BE RUINED BEFORE IT CAN EVEN GET STARTED!
WELL...WE BETTER GET A GOOD NIGHT'S SLEEP. TOMORROW'S THE BIG DAY!

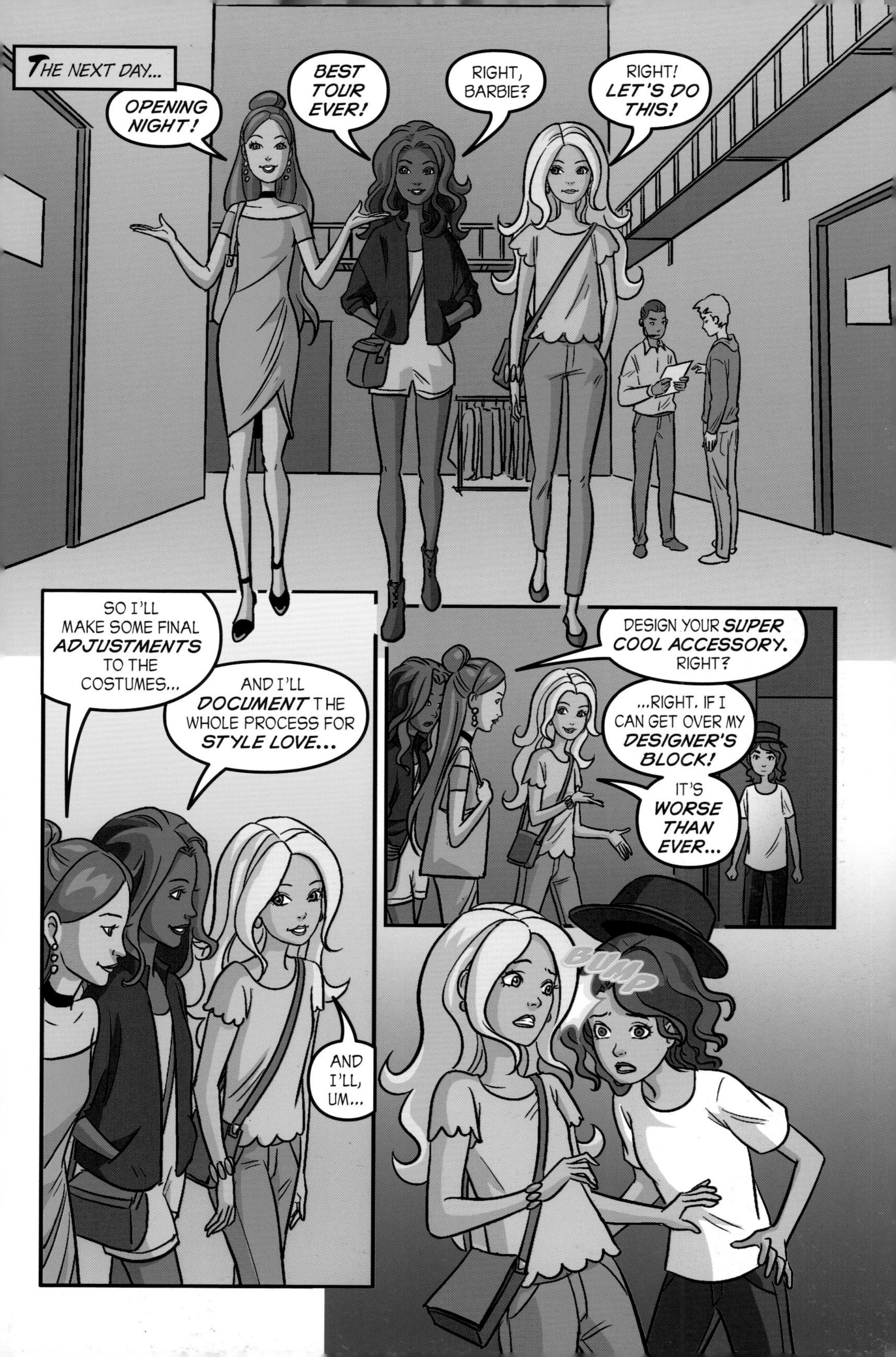
THE NEXT DAY...
OPENING NIGHT!
BEST TOUR EVER!
RIGHT, BARBIE?
RIGHT! LET'S DO THIS!
SO I'LL MAKE SOME FINAL ADJUSTMENTS TO THE COSTUMES...
AND I'LL DOCUMENT THE WHOLE PROCESS FOR STYLE LOVE...
AND I'LL, UM...
DESIGN YOUR SUPER COOL ACCESSORY. RIGHT?
...RIGHT. IF I CAN GET OVER MY DESIGNER'S BLOCK!
IT'S WORSE THAN EVER...
BUMP

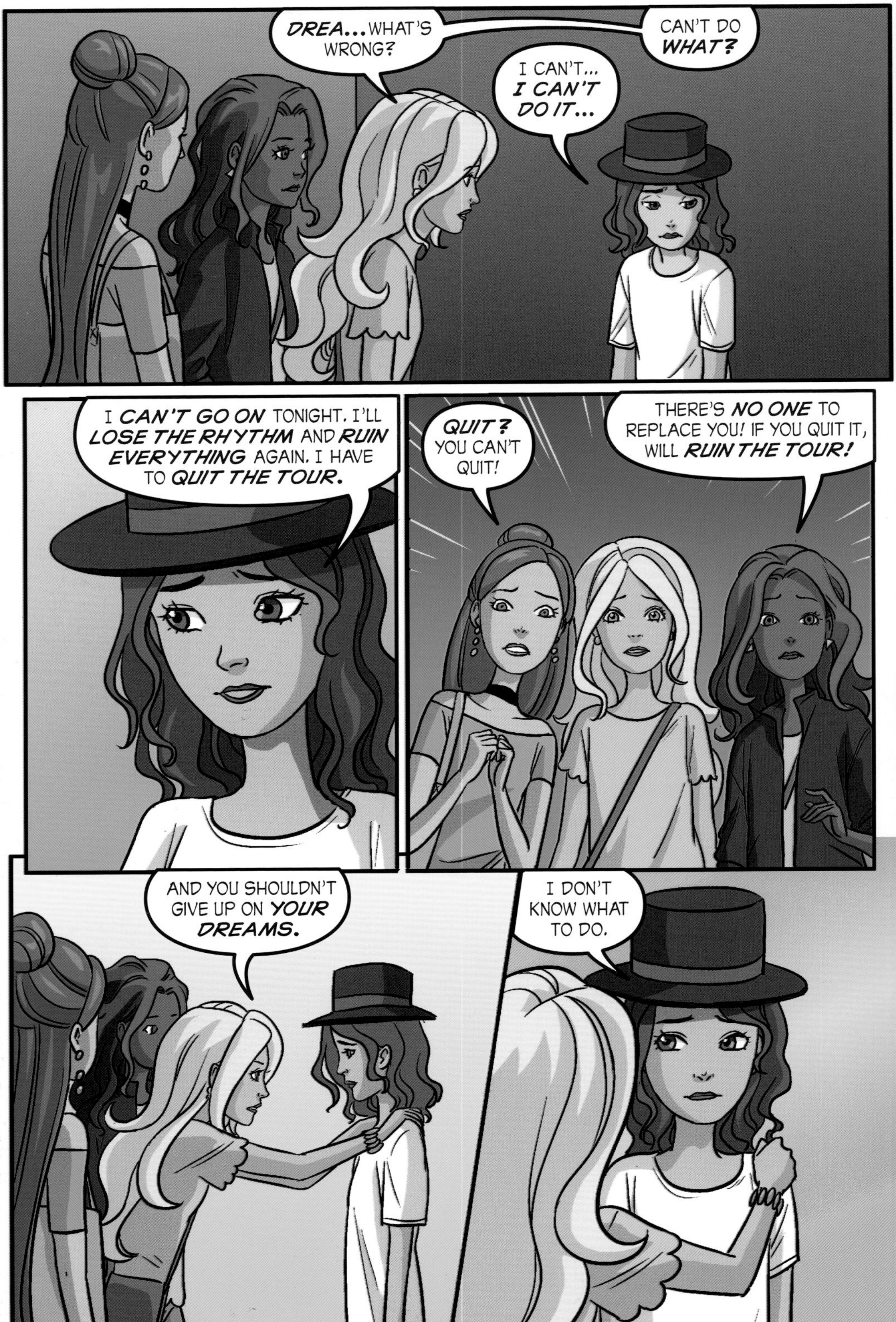
DREA...WHAT'S WRONG?
I CAN'T... I CAN'T DO IT...
CAN'T DO WHAT?
I CAN'T GO ON TONIGHT. I'LL LOSE THE RHYTHM AND RUIN EVERYTHING AGAIN. I HAVE TO QUIT THE TOUR.
QUIT? YOU CAN'T QUIT!
THERE'S NO ONE TO REPLACE YOU! IF YOU QUIT IT, WILL RUIN THE TOUR!
AND YOU SHOULDN'T GIVE UP ON YOUR DREAMS.
I DON'T KNOW WHAT TO DO.

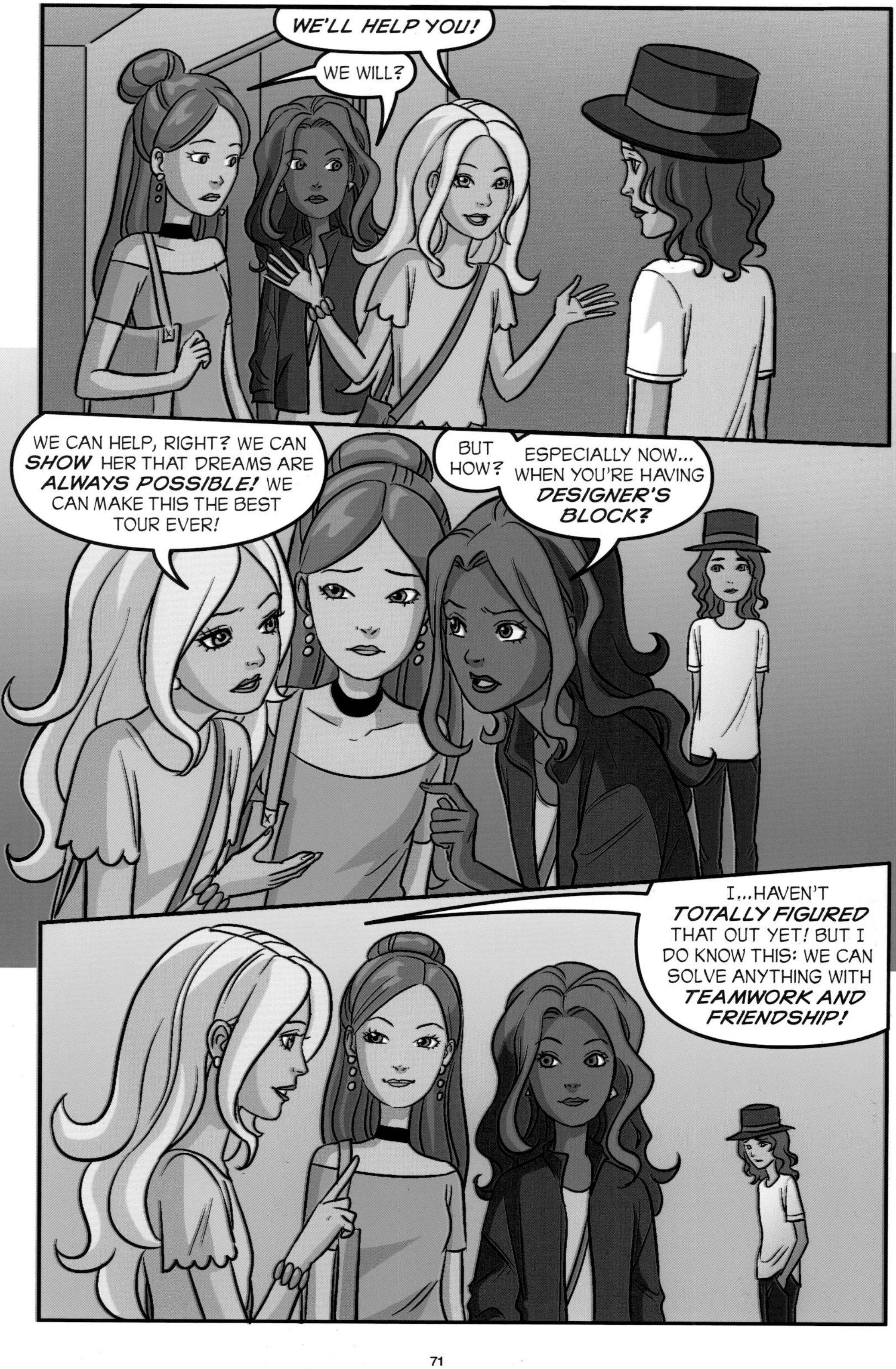

WE'LL HELP YOU!
WE WILL?
WE CAN HELP, RIGHT? WE CAN SHOW HER THAT DREAMS ARE ALWAYS POSSIBLE! WE CAN MAKE THIS THE BEST TOUR EVER!
BUT HOW?
ESPECIALLY NOW... WHEN YOU'RE HAVING DESIGNER'S BLOCK?
I...HAVEN'T TOTALLY FIGURED THAT OUT YET! BUT I DO KNOW THIS: WE CAN SOLVE ANYTHING WITH TEAMWORK AND FRIENDSHIP!

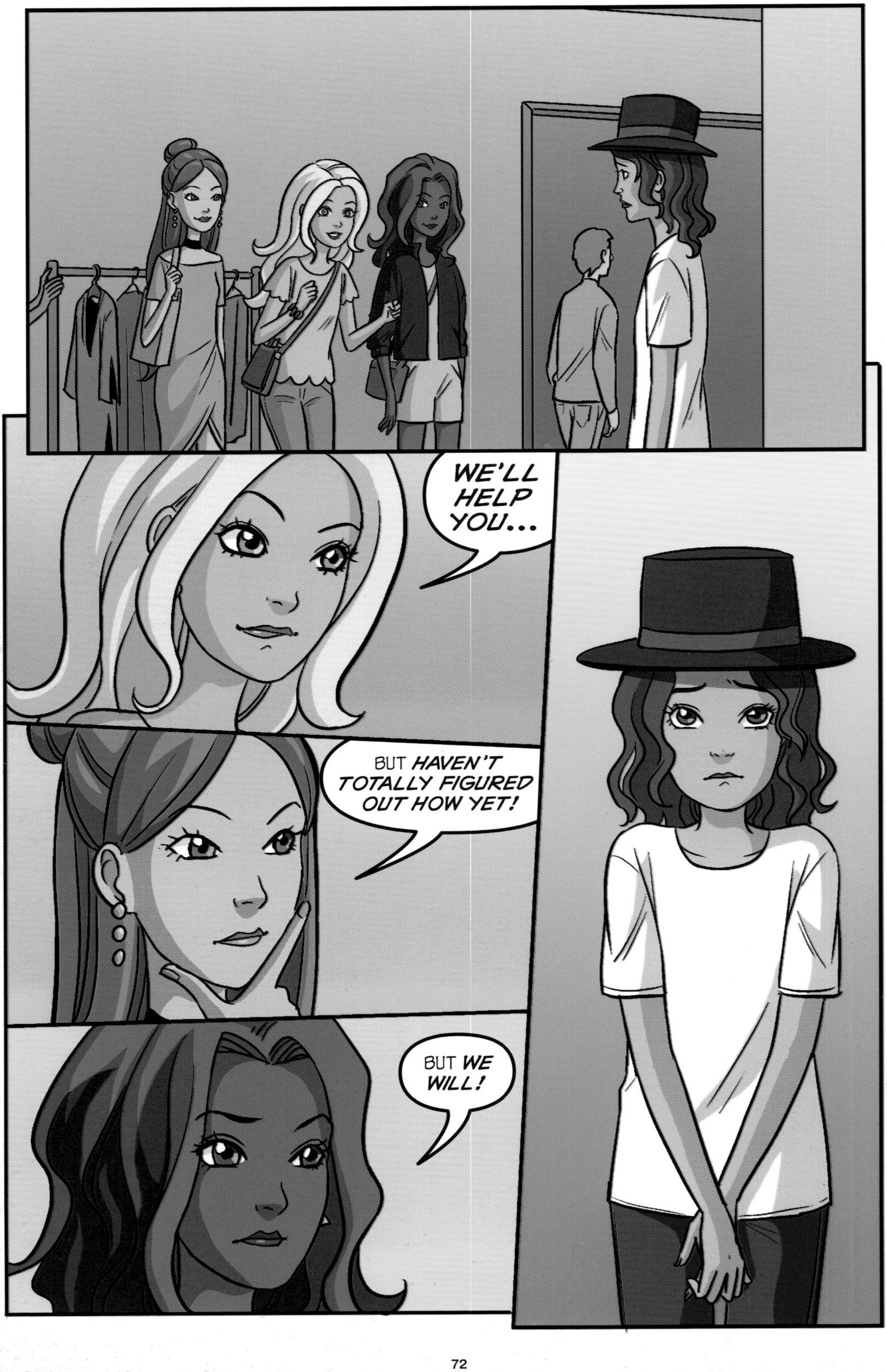
WE'LL HELP YOU...
BUT HAVEN'T TOTALLY FIGURED OUT HOW YET!
BUT WE WILL!

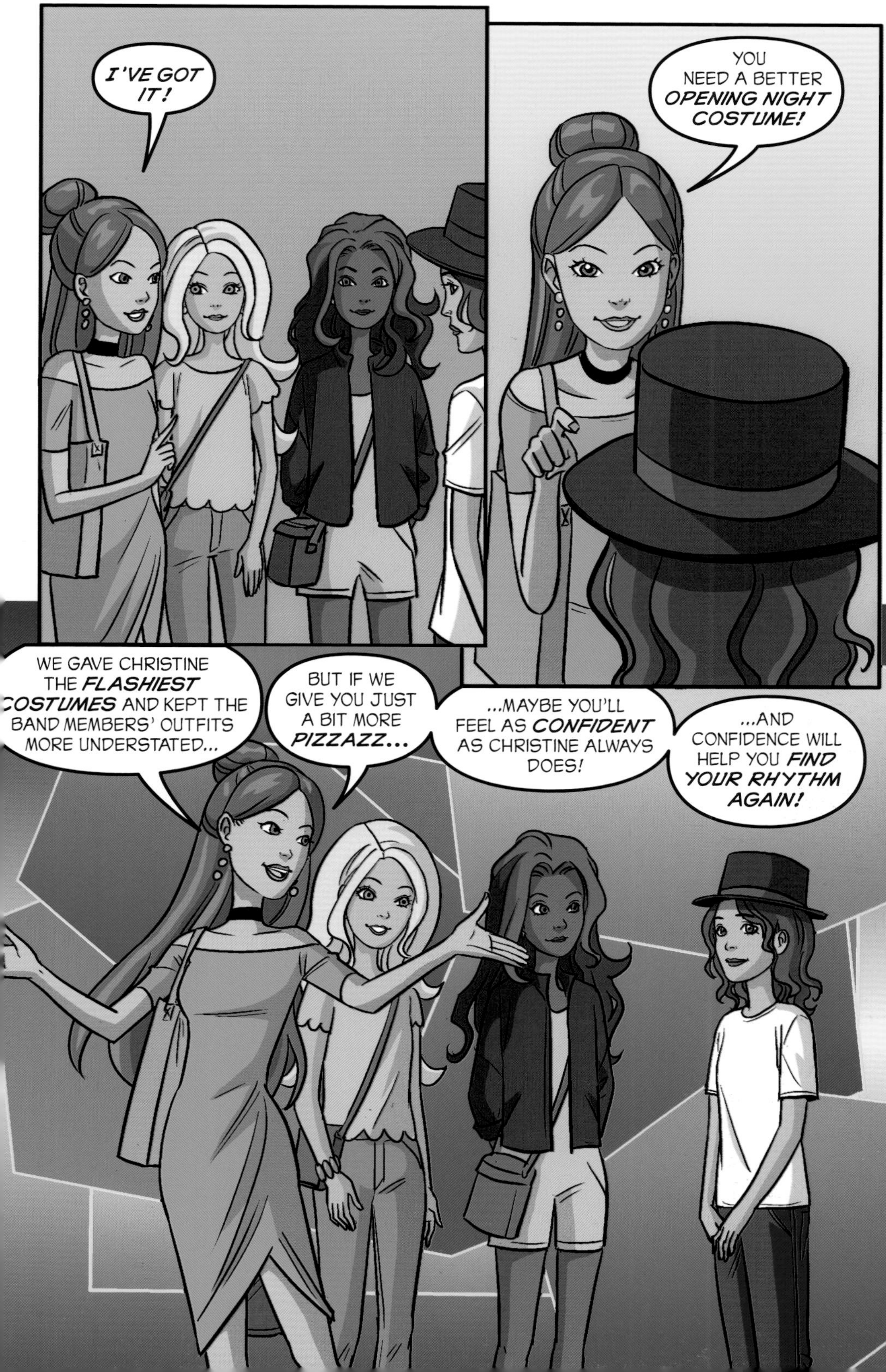
I'VE GOT IT!
YOU NEED A BETTER OPENING NIGHT COSTUME!
WE GAVE CHRISTINE THE FLASHIEST COSTUMES AND KEPT THE BAND MEMBERS' OUTFITS MORE UNDERSTATED...
BUT IF WE GIVE YOU JUST A BIT MORE PIZZAZZ...
...MAYBE YOU'LL FEEL AS CONFIDENT AS CHRISTINE ALWAYS DOES!
...AND CONFIDENCE WILL HELP YOU FIND YOUR RHYTHM AGAIN!

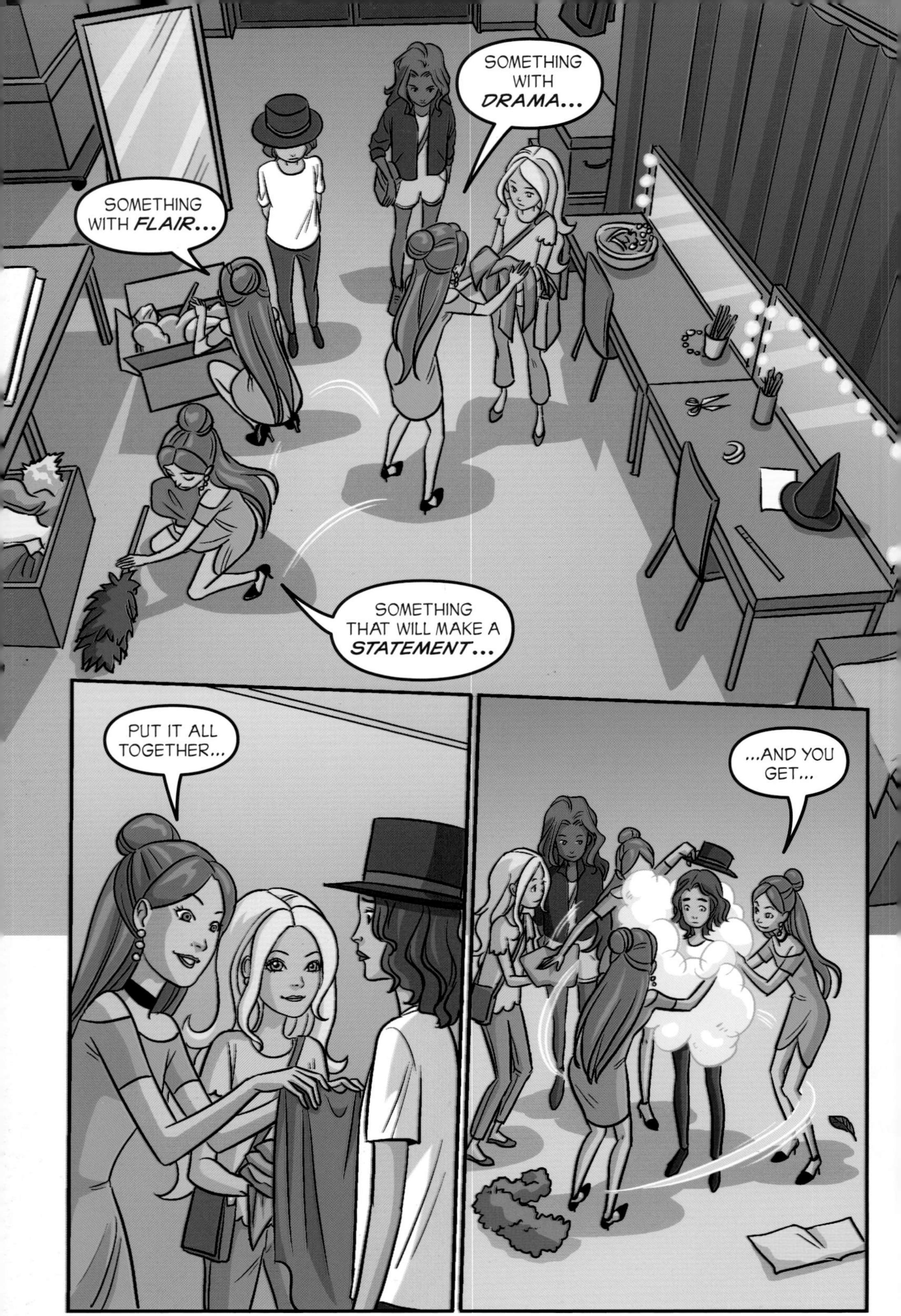
SOMETHING WITH FLAIR...
SOMETHING WITH DRAMA...
SOMETHING THAT WILL MAKE A STATEMENT...
PUT IT ALL TOGETHER...
...AND YOU GET...

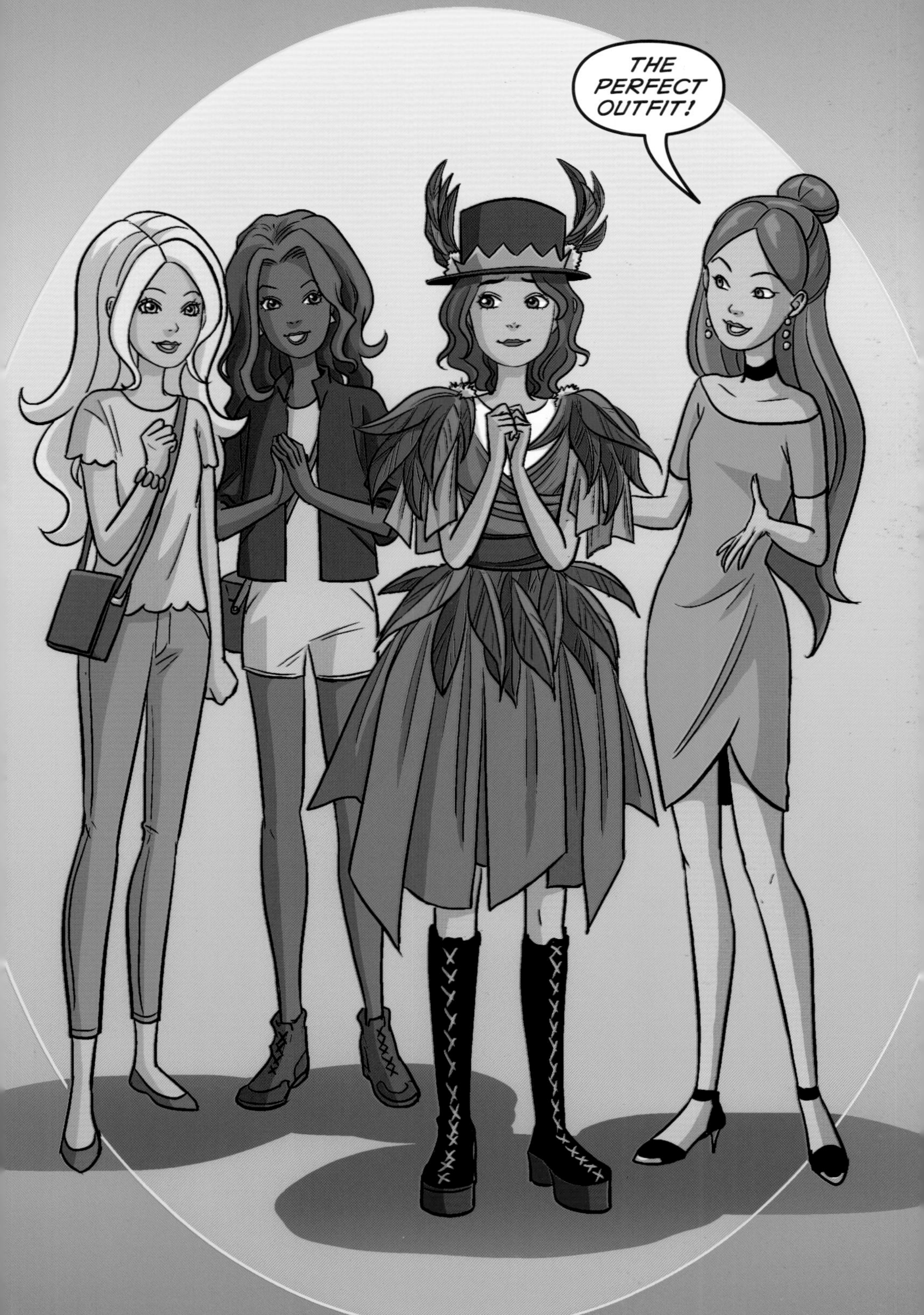
THE PERFECT OUTFIT!

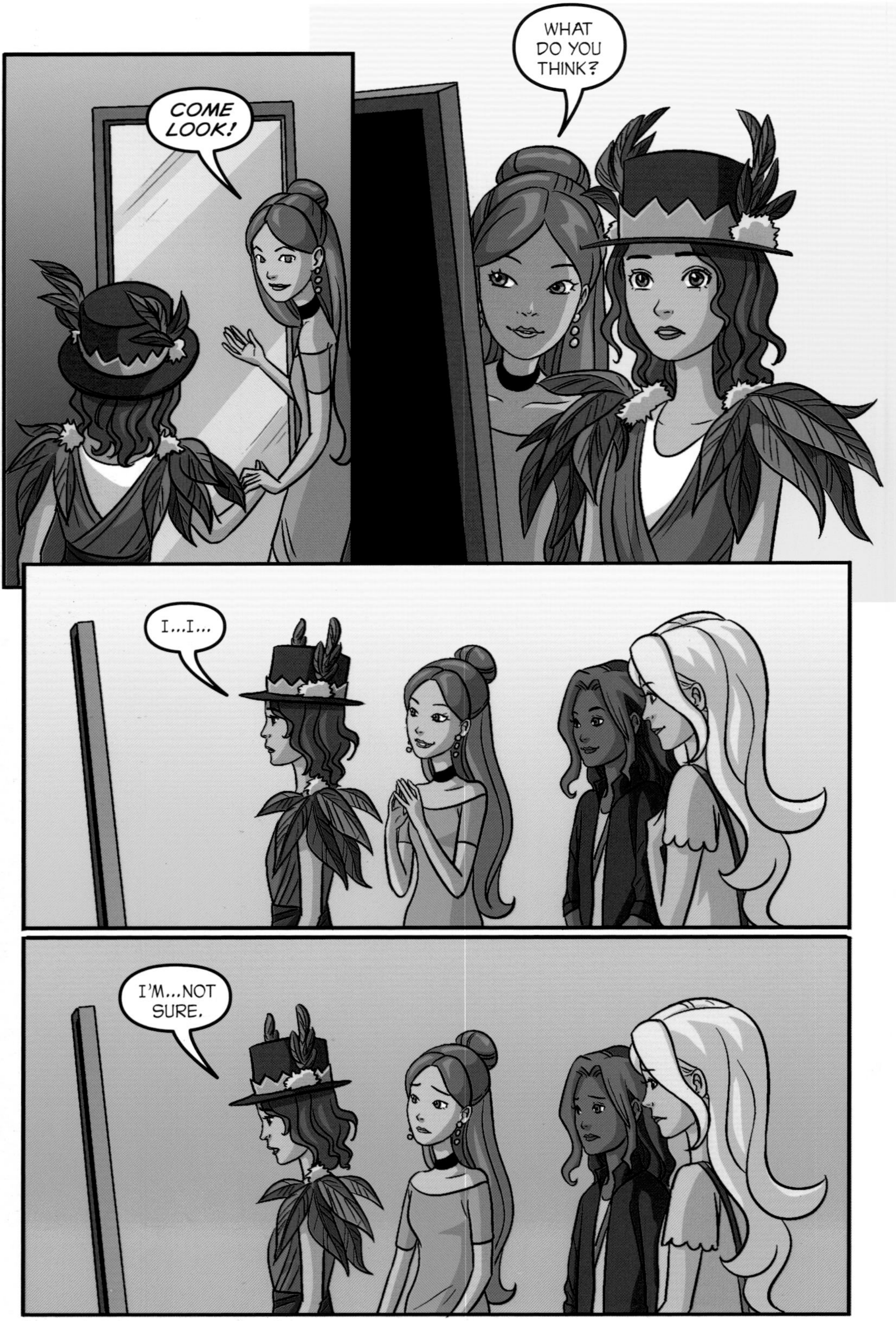
COME LOOK!
WHAT DO YOU THINK?
I...I...
I'M...NOT SURE.

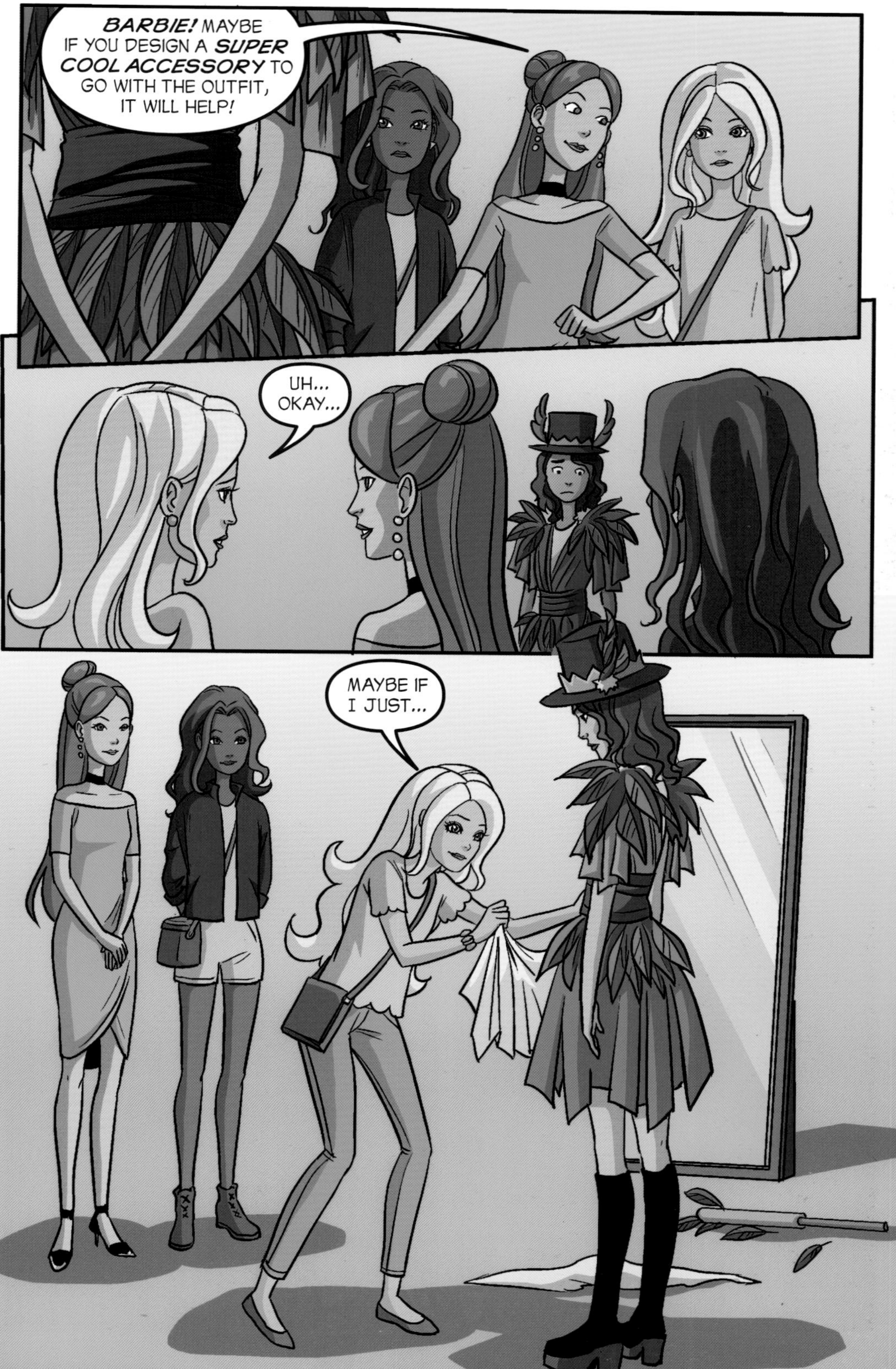
BARBIE! MAYBE IF YOU DESIGN A SUPER COOL ACCESSORY TO GO WITH THE OUTFIT, IT WILL HELP!
UH... OKAY...
MAYBE IF I JUST...

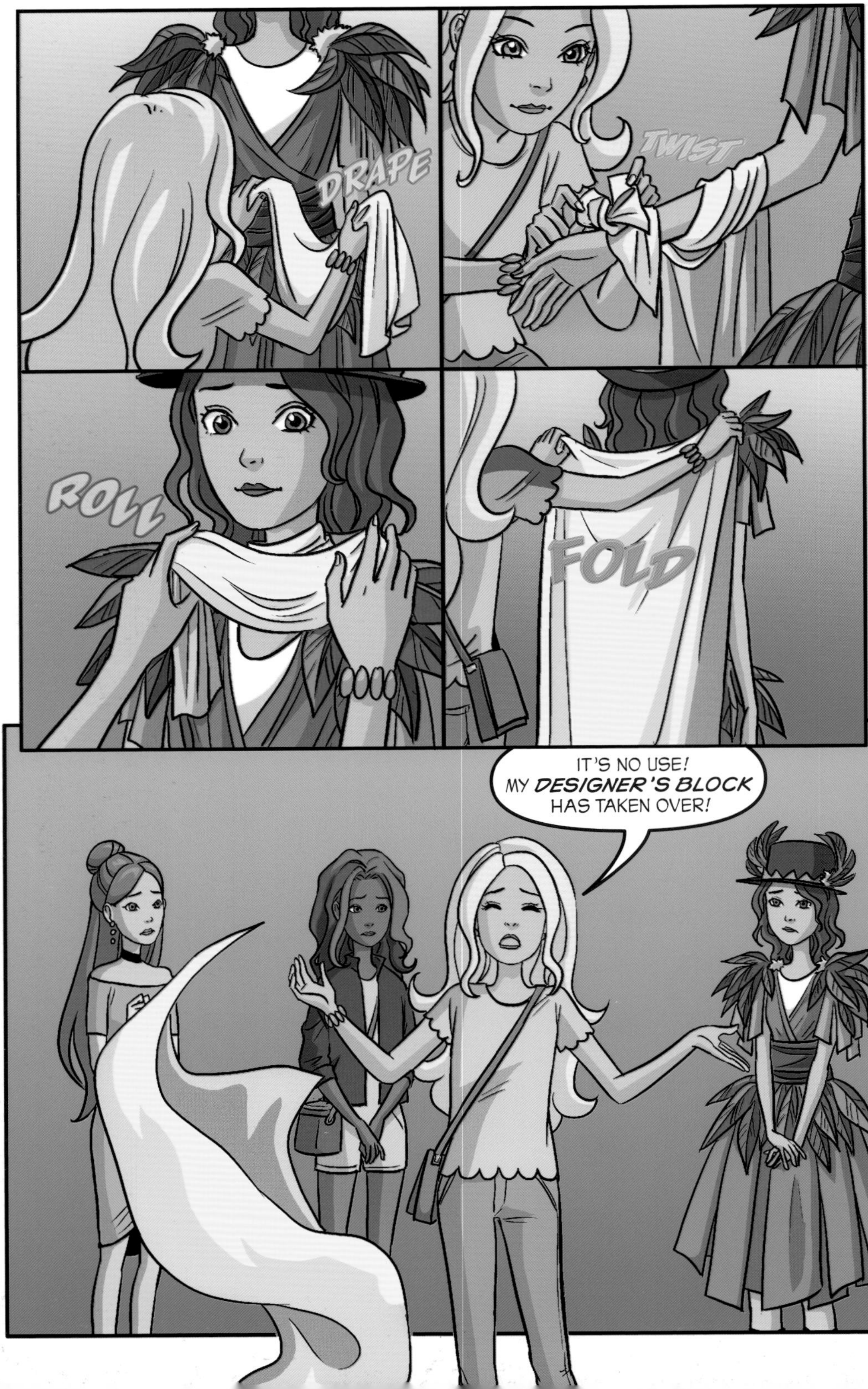
DRAPE
TWIST
ROLL
FOLD
IT'S NO USE! MY *DESIGNER'S BLOCK* HAS TAKEN OVER!

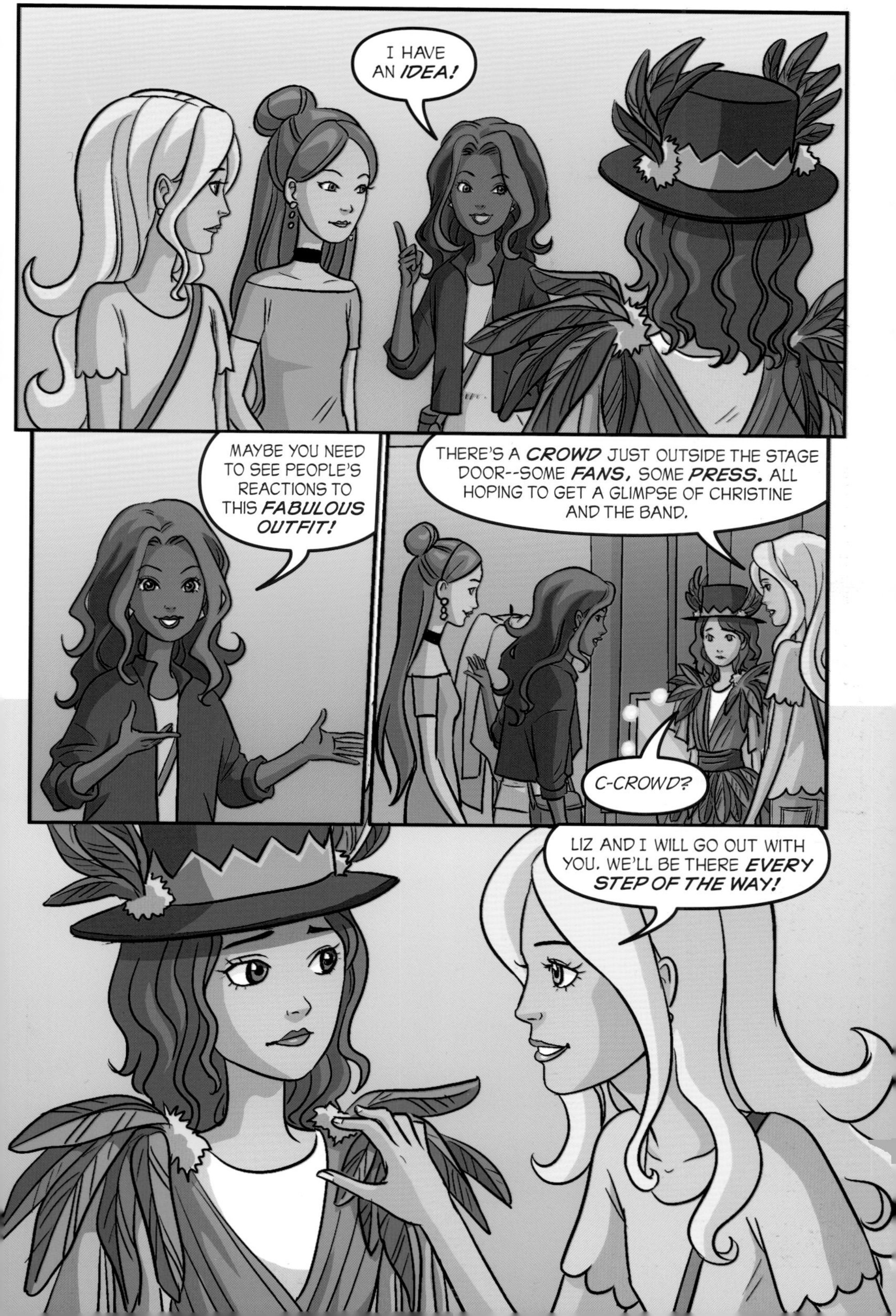
I HAVE AN *IDEA!*
MAYBE YOU NEED TO SEE PEOPLE'S REACTIONS TO THIS ***FABULOUS OUTFIT!***
THERE'S A ***CROWD*** JUST OUTSIDE THE STAGE DOOR--SOME ***FANS,*** SOME ***PRESS.*** ALL HOPING TO GET A GLIMPSE OF CHRISTINE AND THE BAND.
C-CROWD?
LIZ AND I WILL GO OUT WITH YOU. WE'LL BE THERE ***EVERY STEP OF THE WAY!***

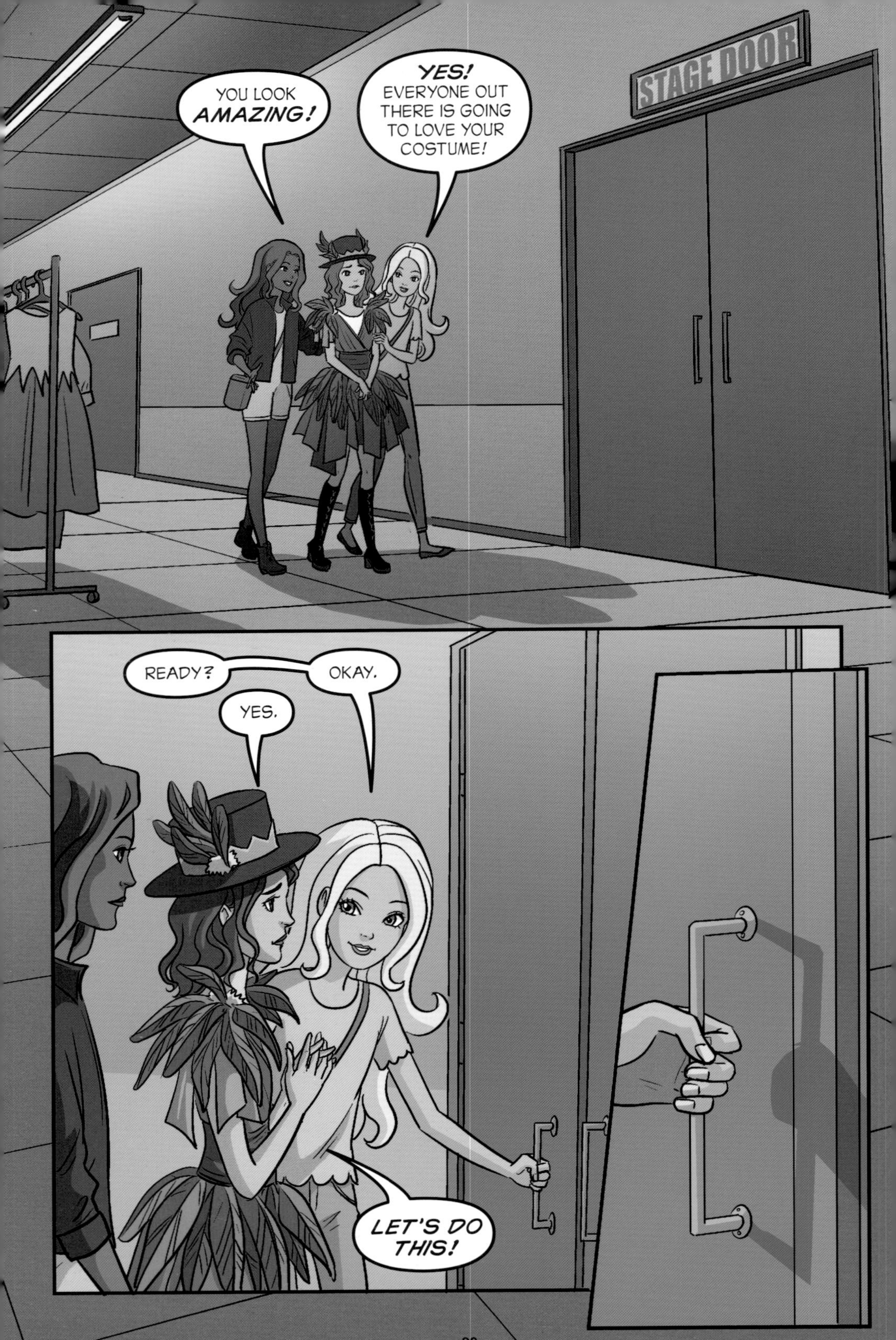
YOU LOOK AMAZING!
YES! EVERYONE OUT THERE IS GOING TO LOVE YOUR COSTUME!
STAGE DOOR
READY?
OKAY.
YES.
LET'S DO THIS!

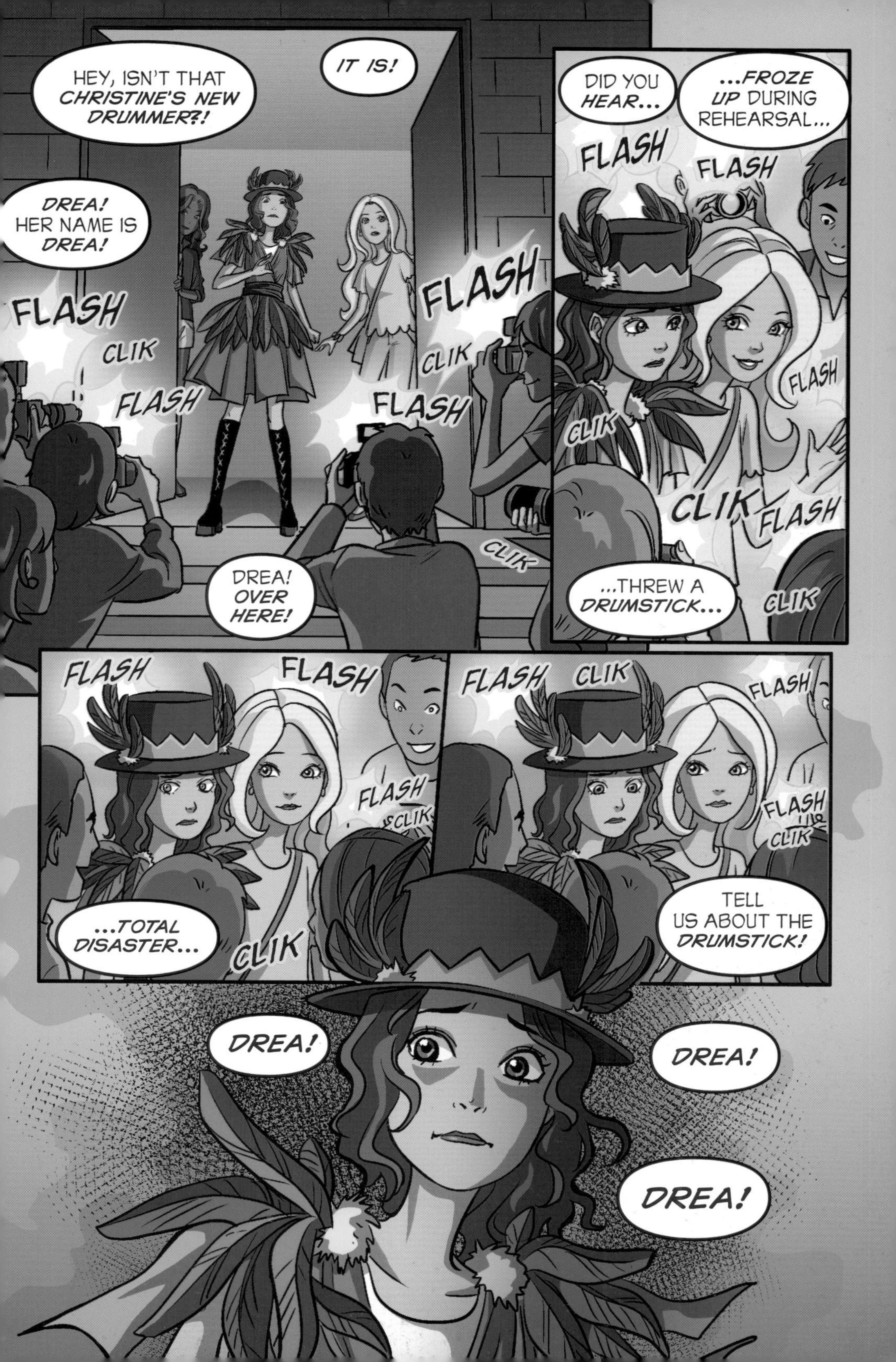

HEY, ISN'T THAT CHRISTINE'S NEW DRUMMER?!
IT IS!
DREA! HER NAME IS DREA!
FLASH
CLIK
FLASH
FLASH
CLIK
FLASH
DREA! OVER HERE!
CLIK
DID YOU HEAR...
...FROZE UP DURING REHEARSAL...
FLASH
FLASH
FLASH
CLIK
CLIK
FLASH
...THREW A DRUMSTICK...
CLIK
FLASH
FLASH
FLASH
CLIK
...TOTAL DISASTER...
CLIK
FLASH
CLIK
FLASH
FLASH
CLIK
TELL US ABOUT THE DRUMSTICK!
DREA!
DREA!
DREA!

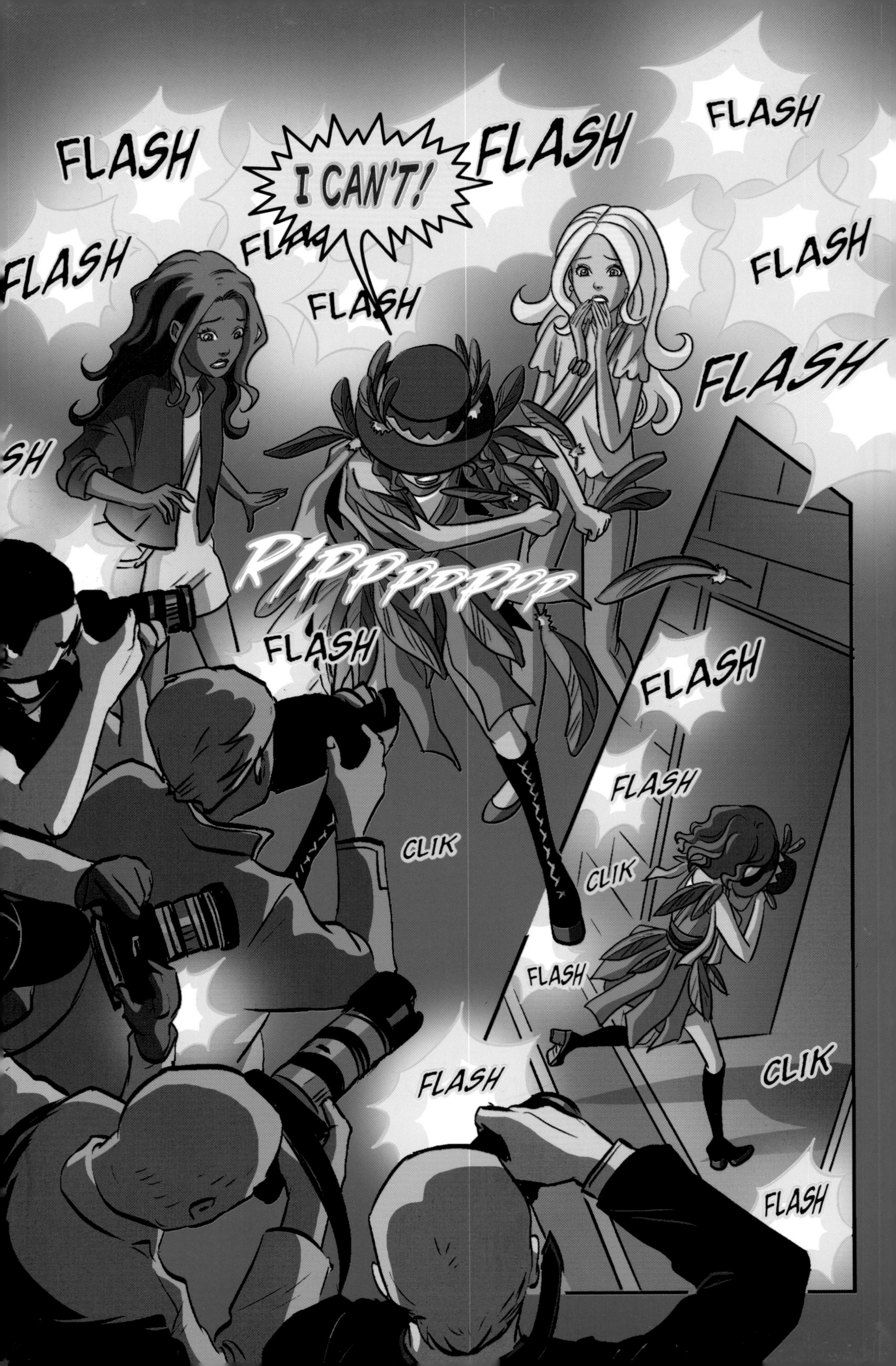
FLASH
I CAN'T!
FLASH
FLASH
FLASH
FLASH
FLASH
FLASH
FLASH
RIPPPPPPPP
FLASH
FLASH
FLASH
CLIK
CLIK
FLASH
FLASH
CLIK
FLASH

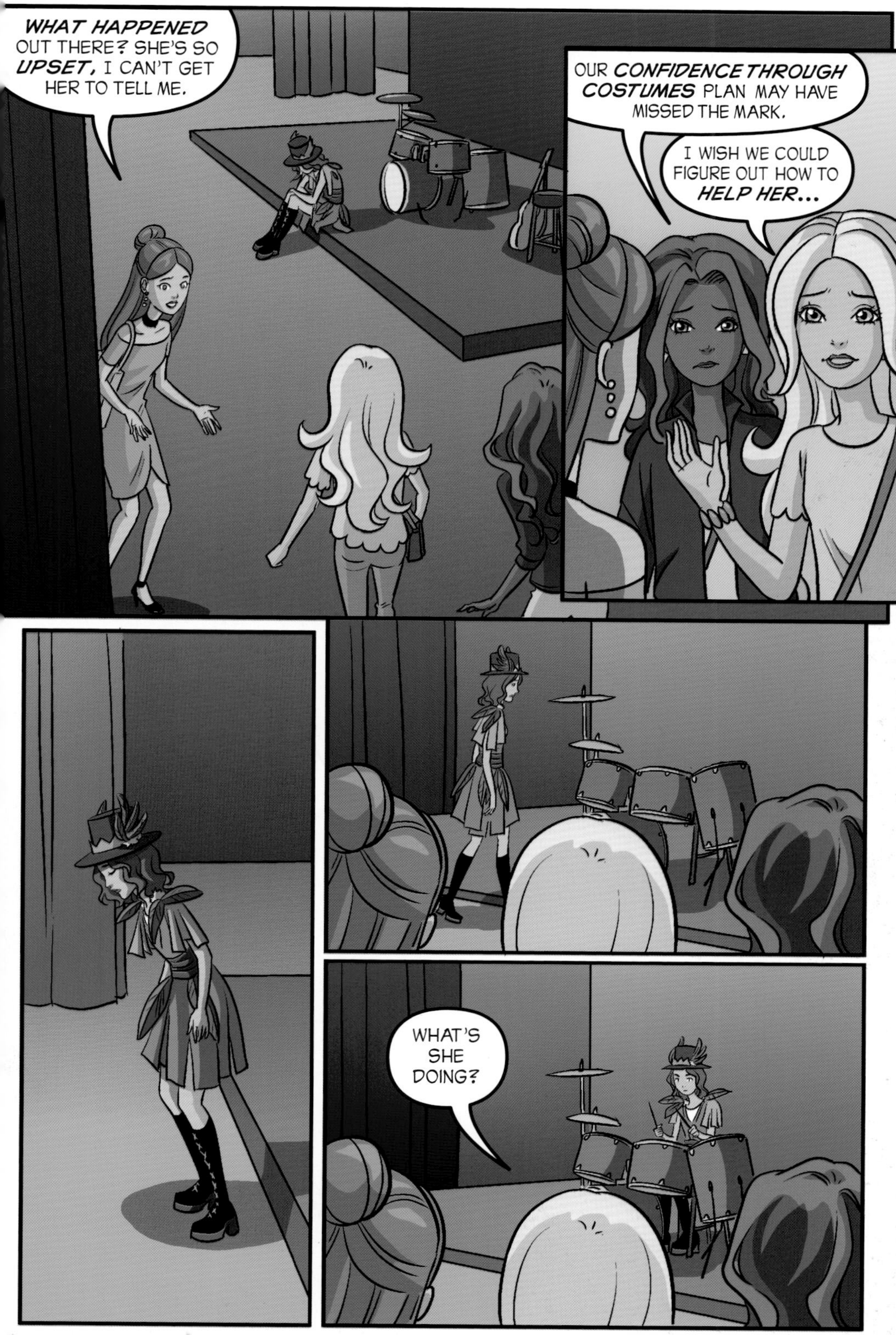
WHAT HAPPENED OUT THERE? SHE'S SO UPSET, I CAN'T GET HER TO TELL ME.
OUR CONFIDENCE THROUGH COSTUMES PLAN MAY HAVE MISSED THE MARK.
I WISH WE COULD FIGURE OUT HOW TO HELP HER...
WHAT'S SHE DOING?

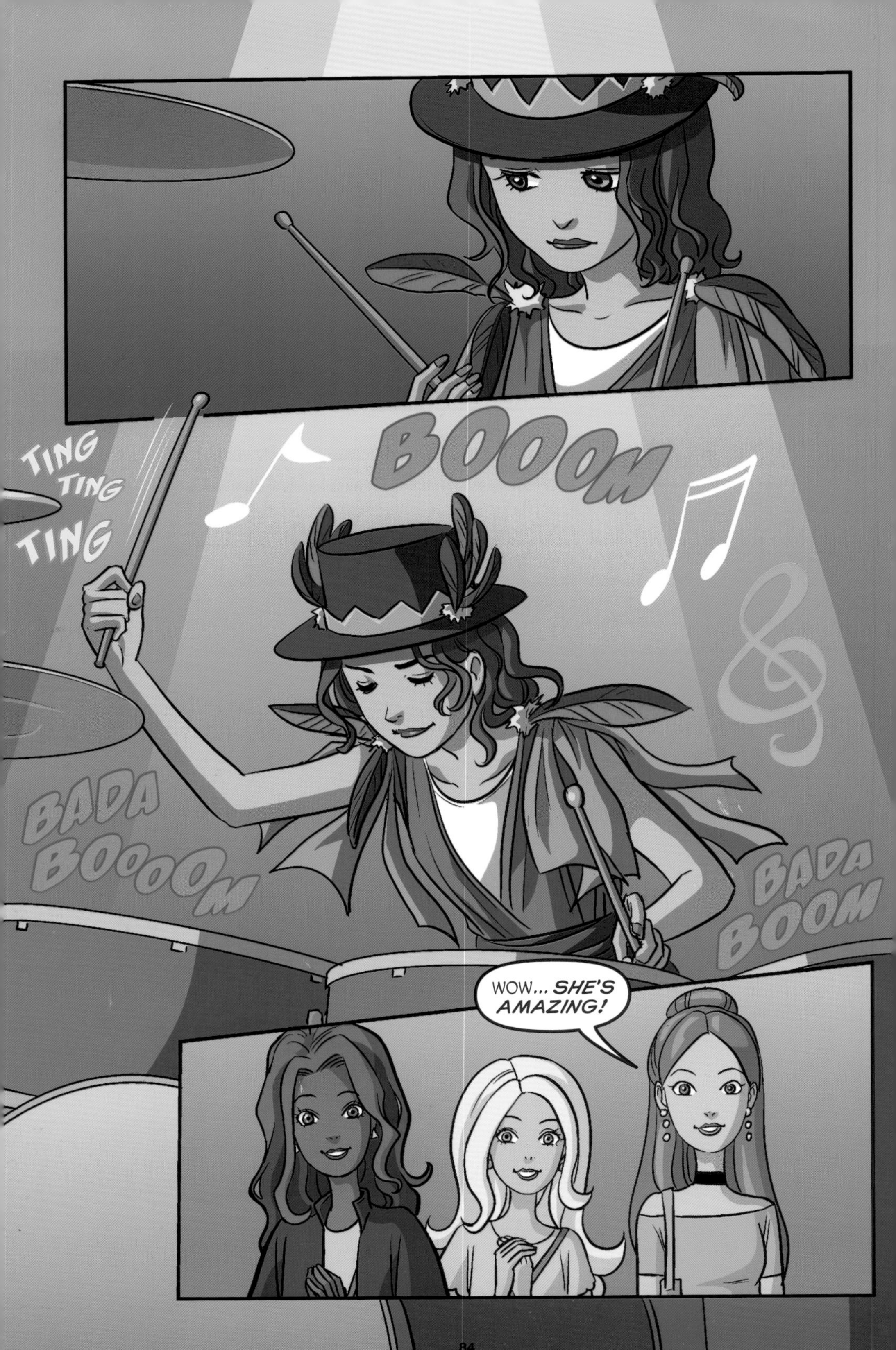
TING
TING
TING
BOOOM
BADA
BOOOOM
BADA
BOOM
WOW... SHE'S AMAZING!

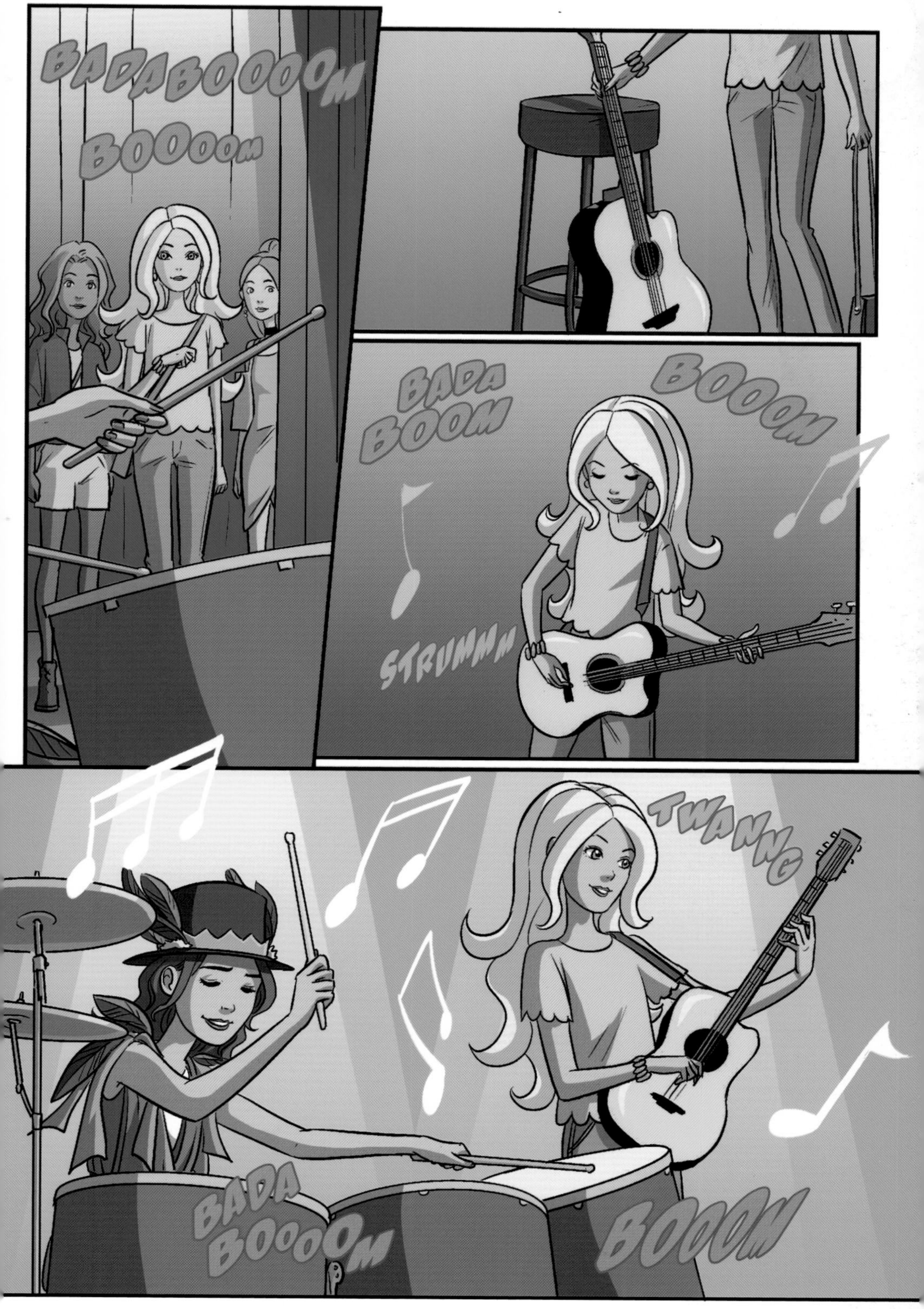
BADABOOOOM
BOOoom
BADA BOOM
BOOOM
STRUMMM
TWANNG
BADA BOOOOM
BOOOM

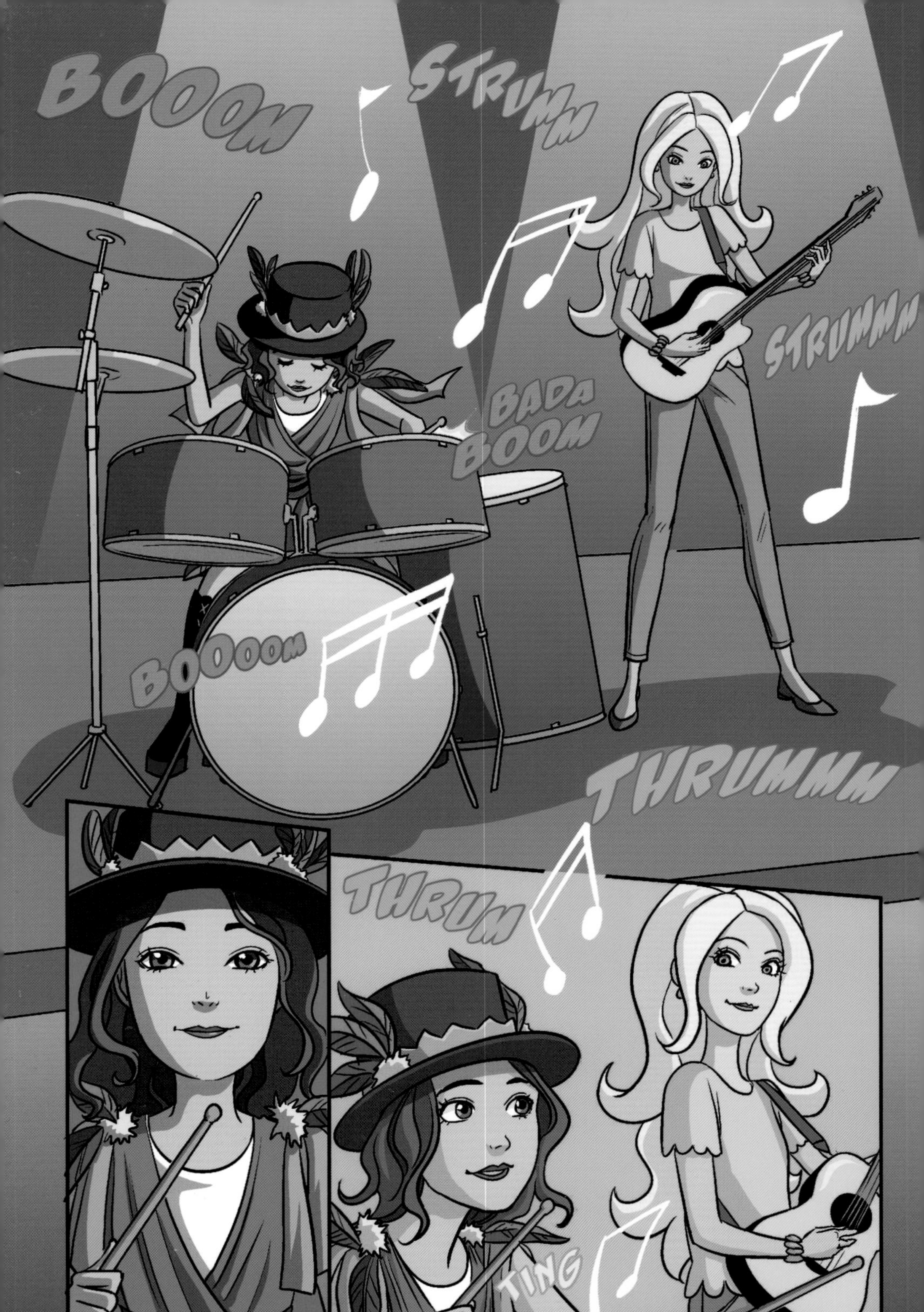
BOOOM
STRUMMM
BADA BOOM
STRUMMM
BOOoom
THRUMMM
THRUM
TING

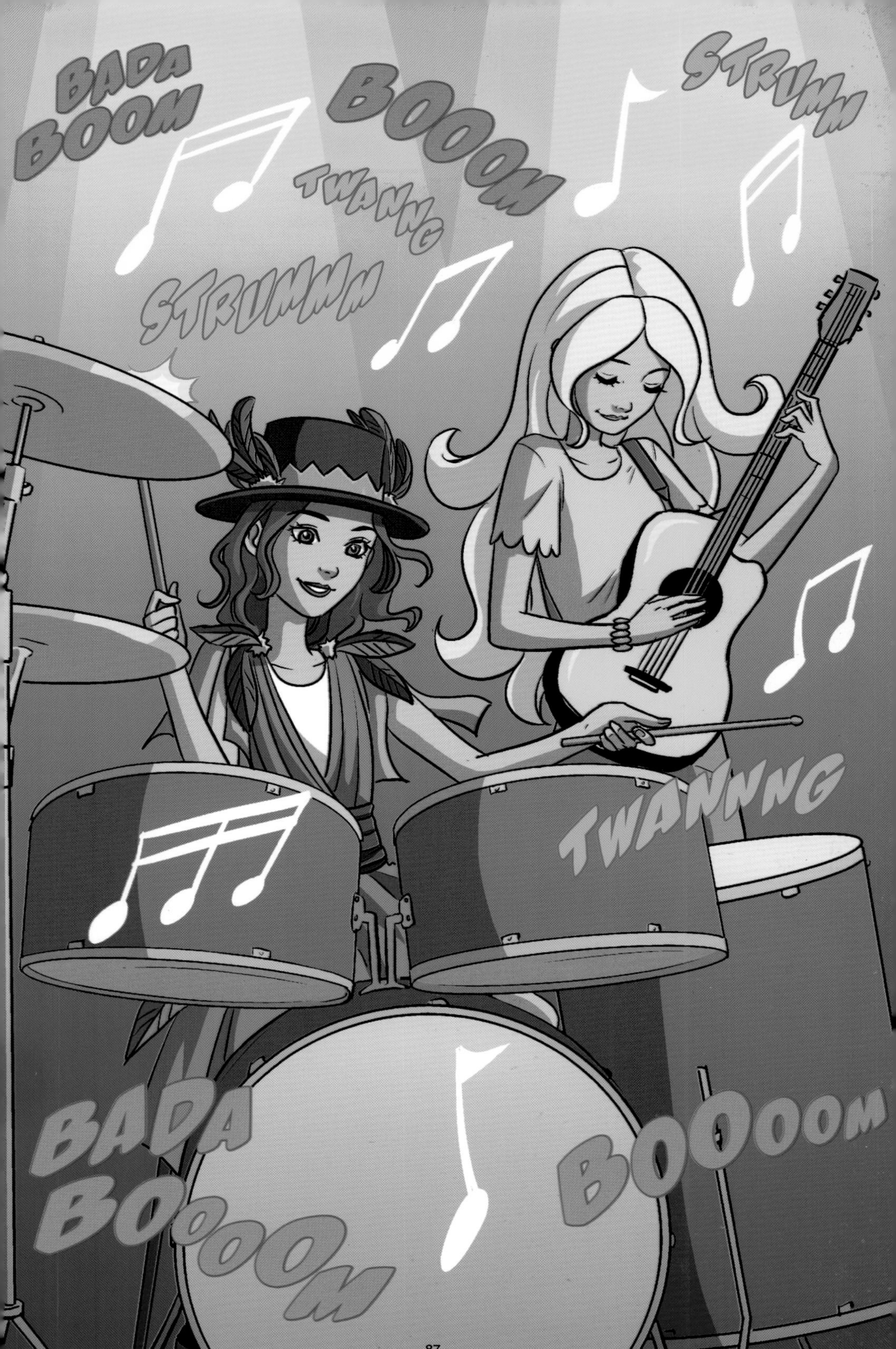
BADA BOOM
BOOOOM
TWANNG
STRUMMM
STRUMM
TWANNNG
BADA BOOOOM
BOOOOOM

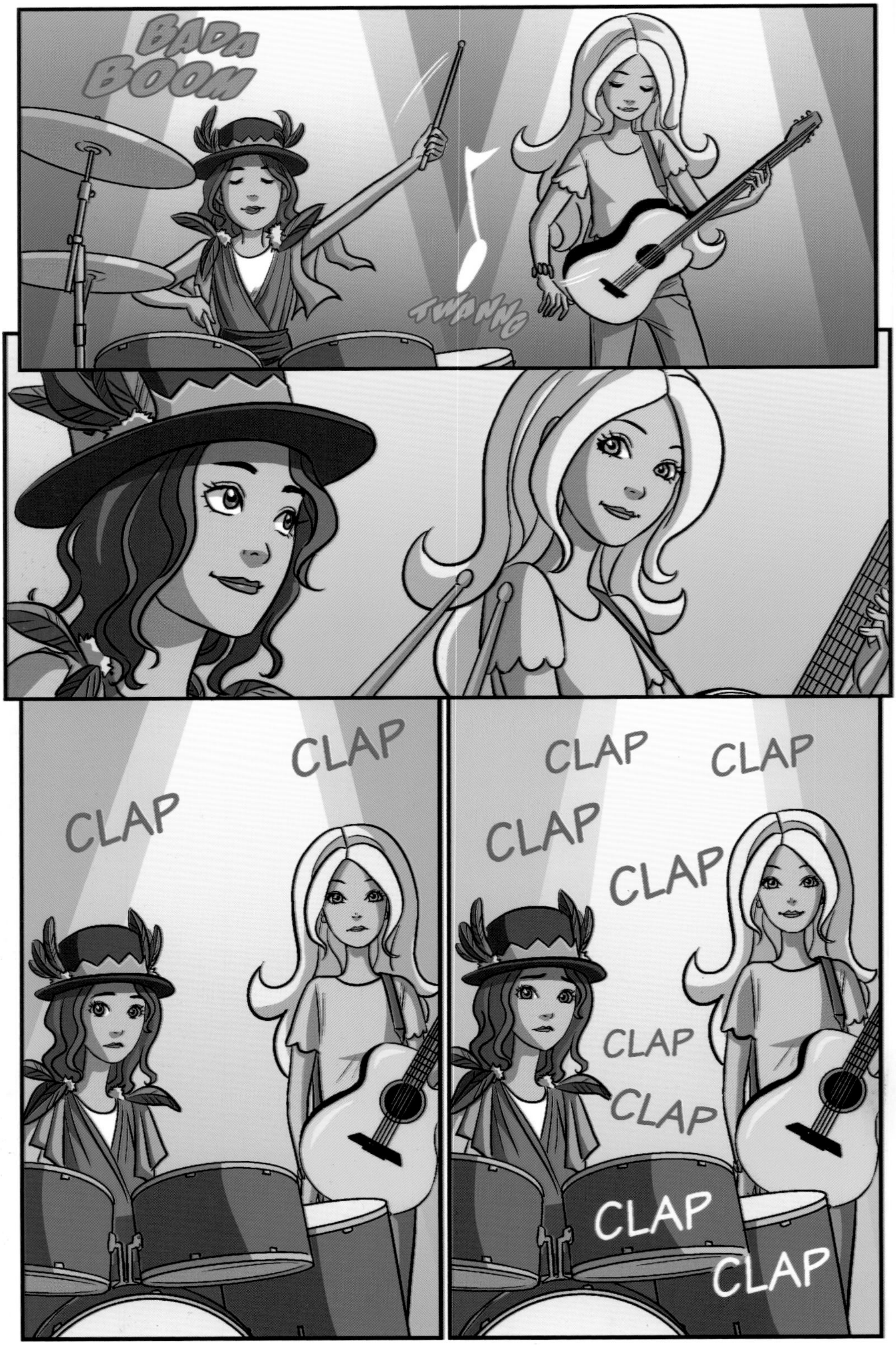
BADA
BOOM
TWANNG
CLAP
CLAP
CLAP
CLAP
CLAP
CLAP
CLAP
CLAP
CLAP
CLAP

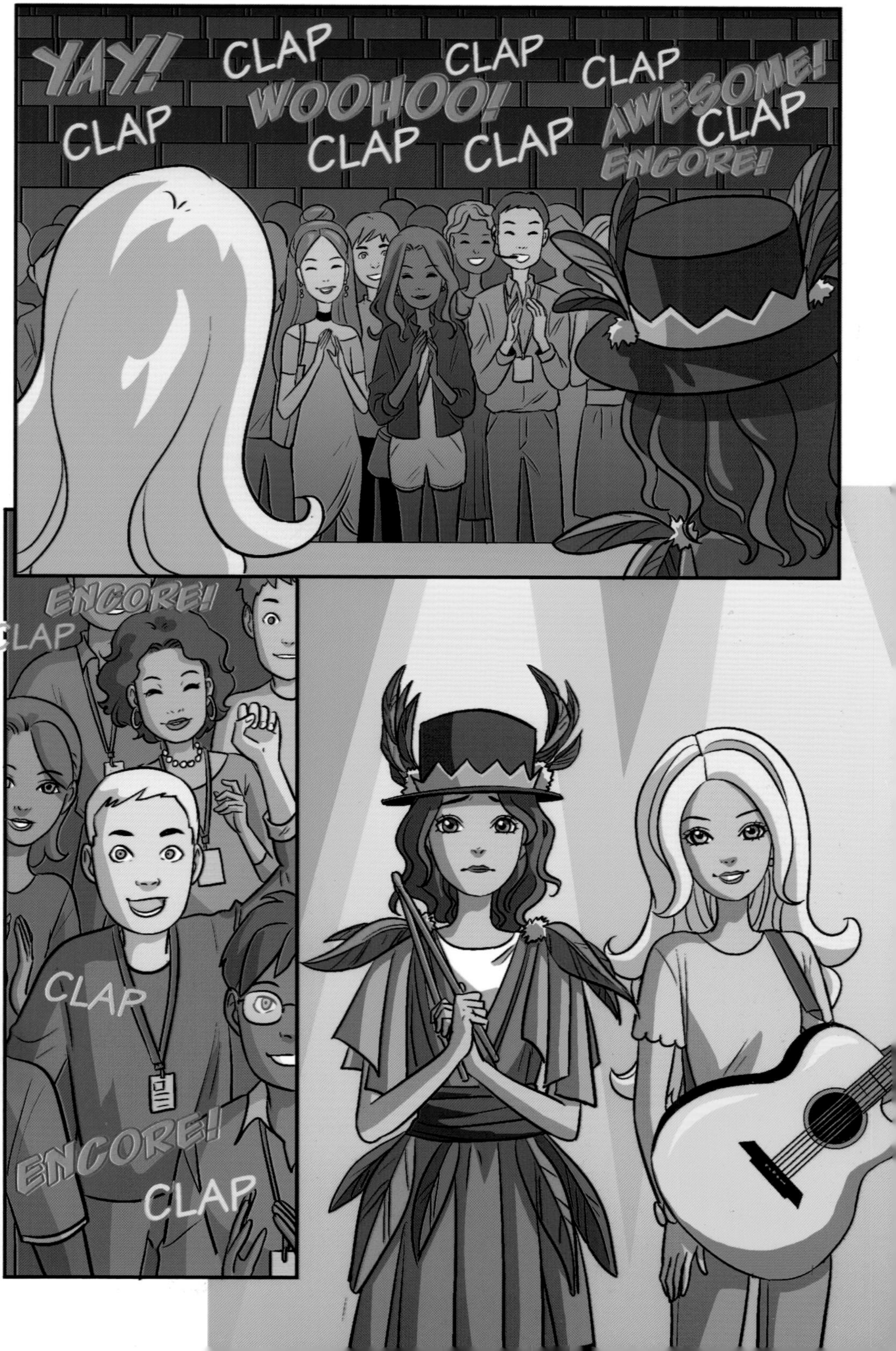
YAY!
CLAP
CLAP
WOOHOO!
CLAP
CLAP
CLAP
CLAP
AWESOME!
CLAP
ENCORE!
ENCORE!
CLAP
CLAP
ENCORE!
CLAP

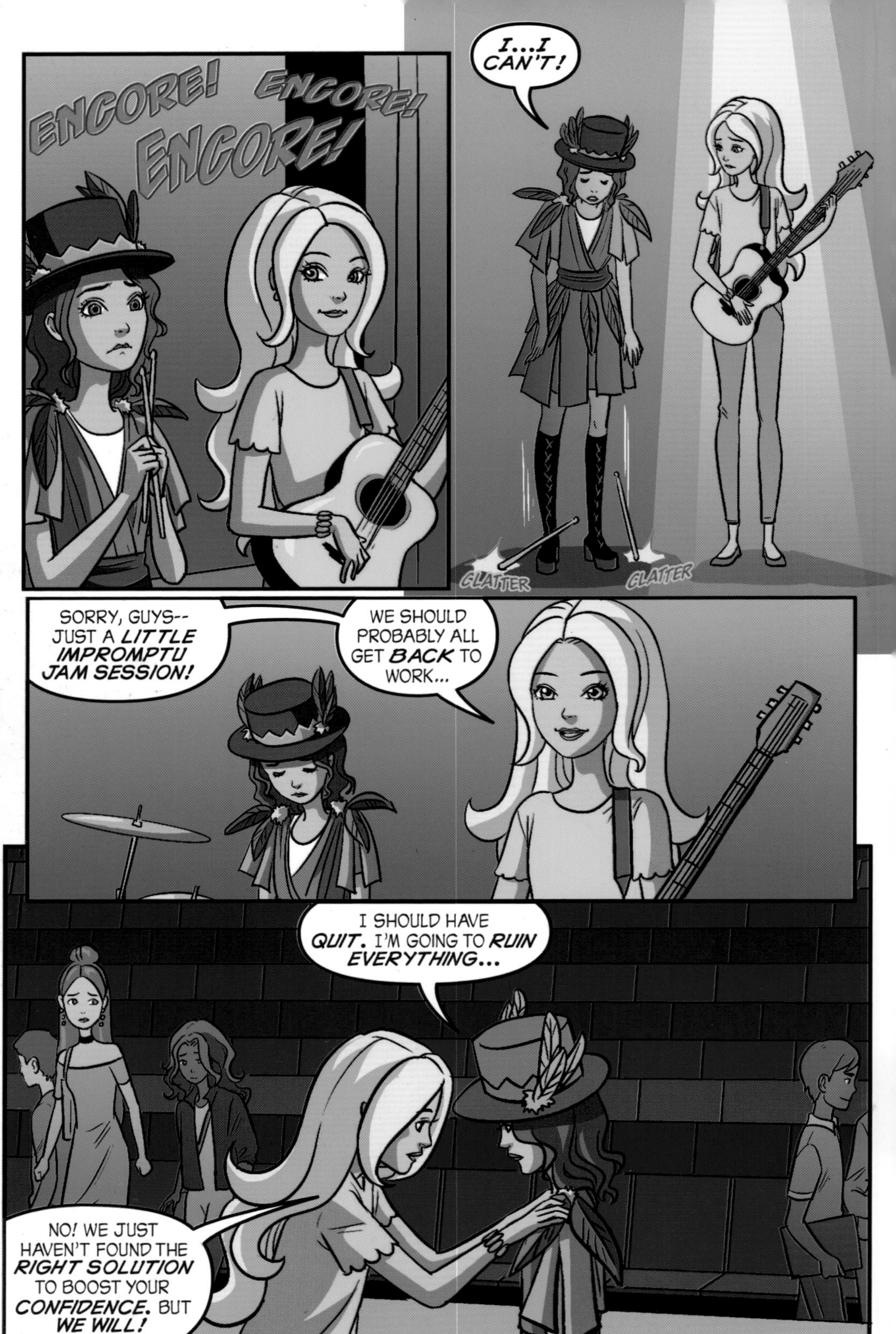
ENCORE! ENCORE! ENCORE!
I...I CAN'T!
CLATTER
CLATTER
SORRY, GUYS-- JUST A *LITTLE IMPROMPTU JAM SESSION!*
WE SHOULD PROBABLY ALL GET *BACK* TO WORK...
I SHOULD HAVE *QUIT.* I'M GOING TO *RUIN EVERYTHING...*
NO! WE JUST HAVEN'T FOUND THE *RIGHT SOLUTION* TO BOOST YOUR *CONFIDENCE.* BUT *WE WILL!*

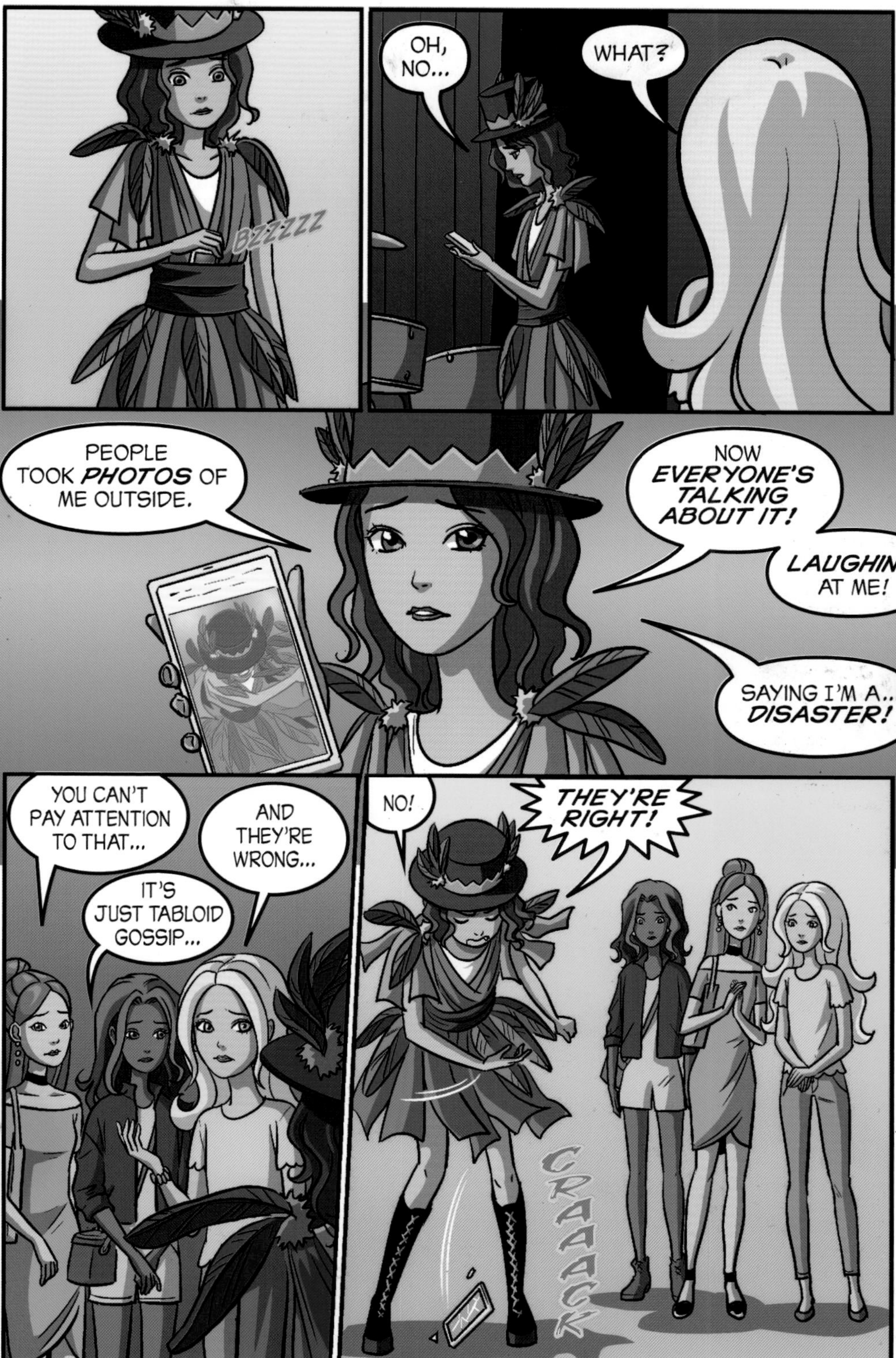
BZZZZZ
OH, NO...
WHAT?
PEOPLE TOOK PHOTOS OF ME OUTSIDE.
NOW EVERYONE'S TALKING ABOUT IT!
LAUGHING AT ME!
SAYING I'M A... DISASTER!
YOU CAN'T PAY ATTENTION TO THAT...
IT'S JUST TABLOID GOSSIP...
AND THEY'RE WRONG...
NO!
THEY'RE RIGHT!
CRAAACK

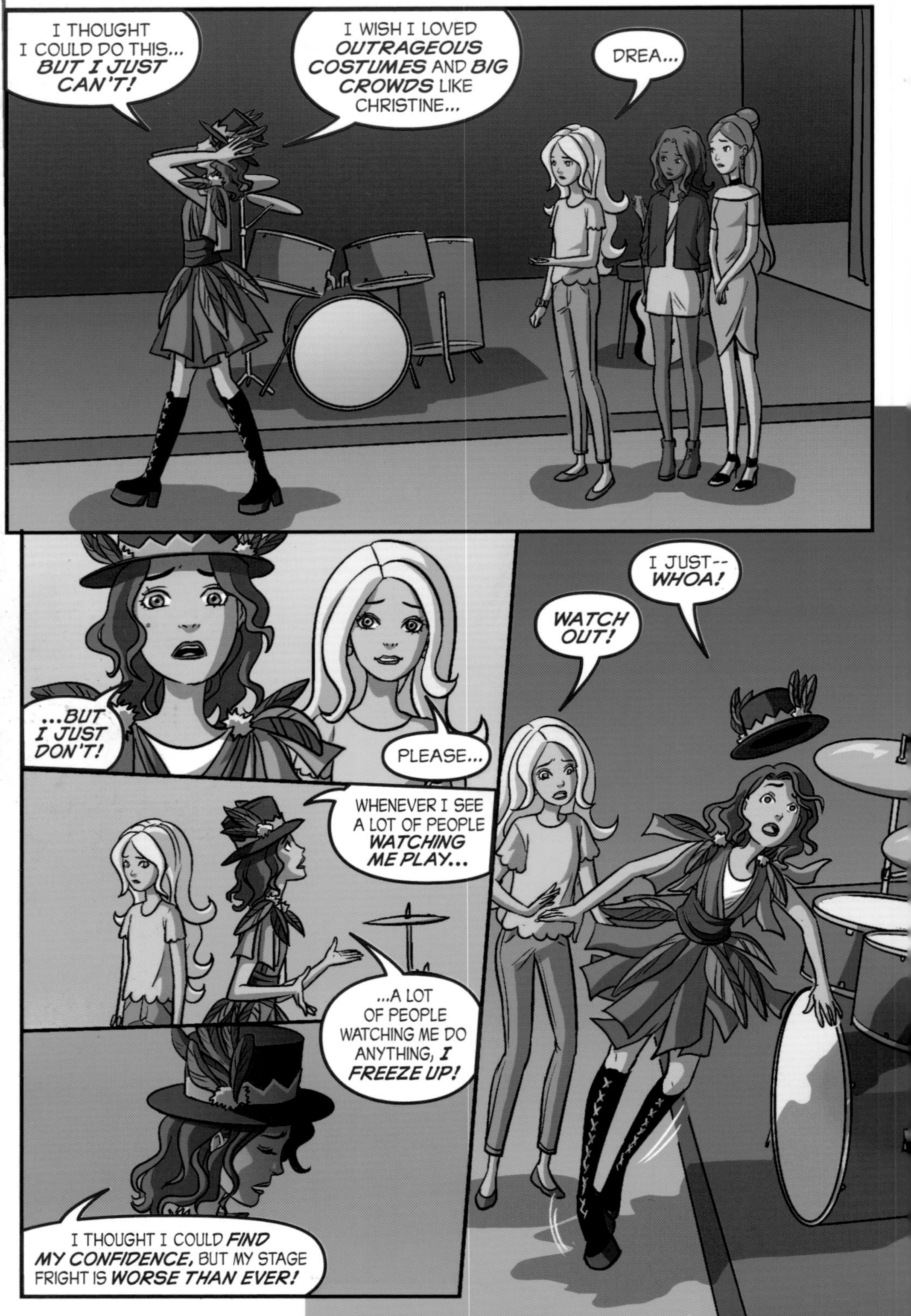
I THOUGHT I COULD DO THIS... BUT I JUST CAN'T!
I WISH I LOVED OUTRAGEOUS COSTUMES AND BIG CROWDS LIKE CHRISTINE...
DREA...
...BUT I JUST DON'T!
PLEASE...
WHENEVER I SEE A LOT OF PEOPLE WATCHING ME PLAY...
...A LOT OF PEOPLE WATCHING ME DO ANYTHING, I FREEZE UP!
I THOUGHT I COULD FIND MY CONFIDENCE, BUT MY STAGE FRIGHT IS WORSE THAN EVER!
I JUST-- WHOA!
WATCH OUT!

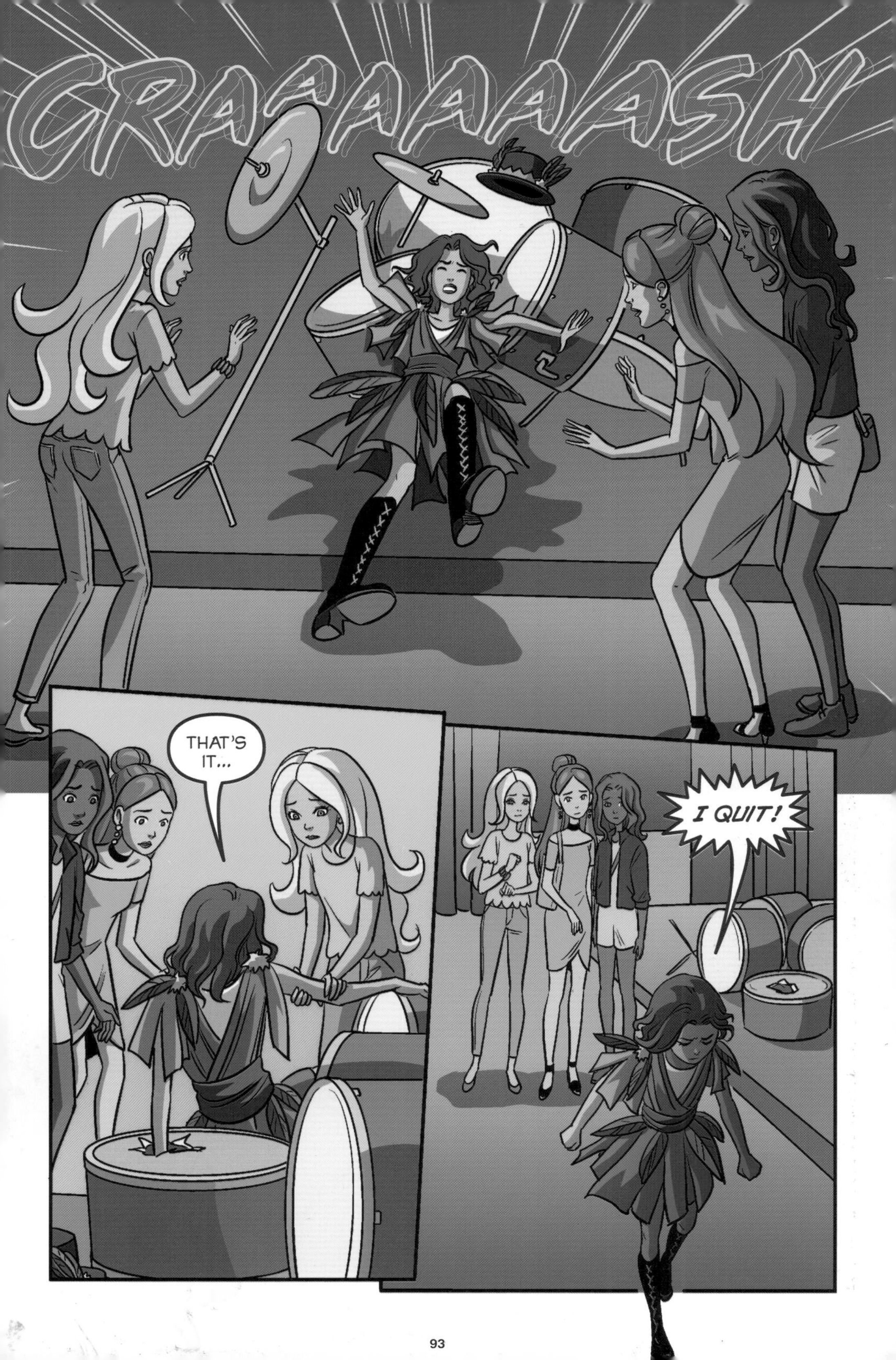
GRAAAAASH
THAT'S IT...
I QUIT!

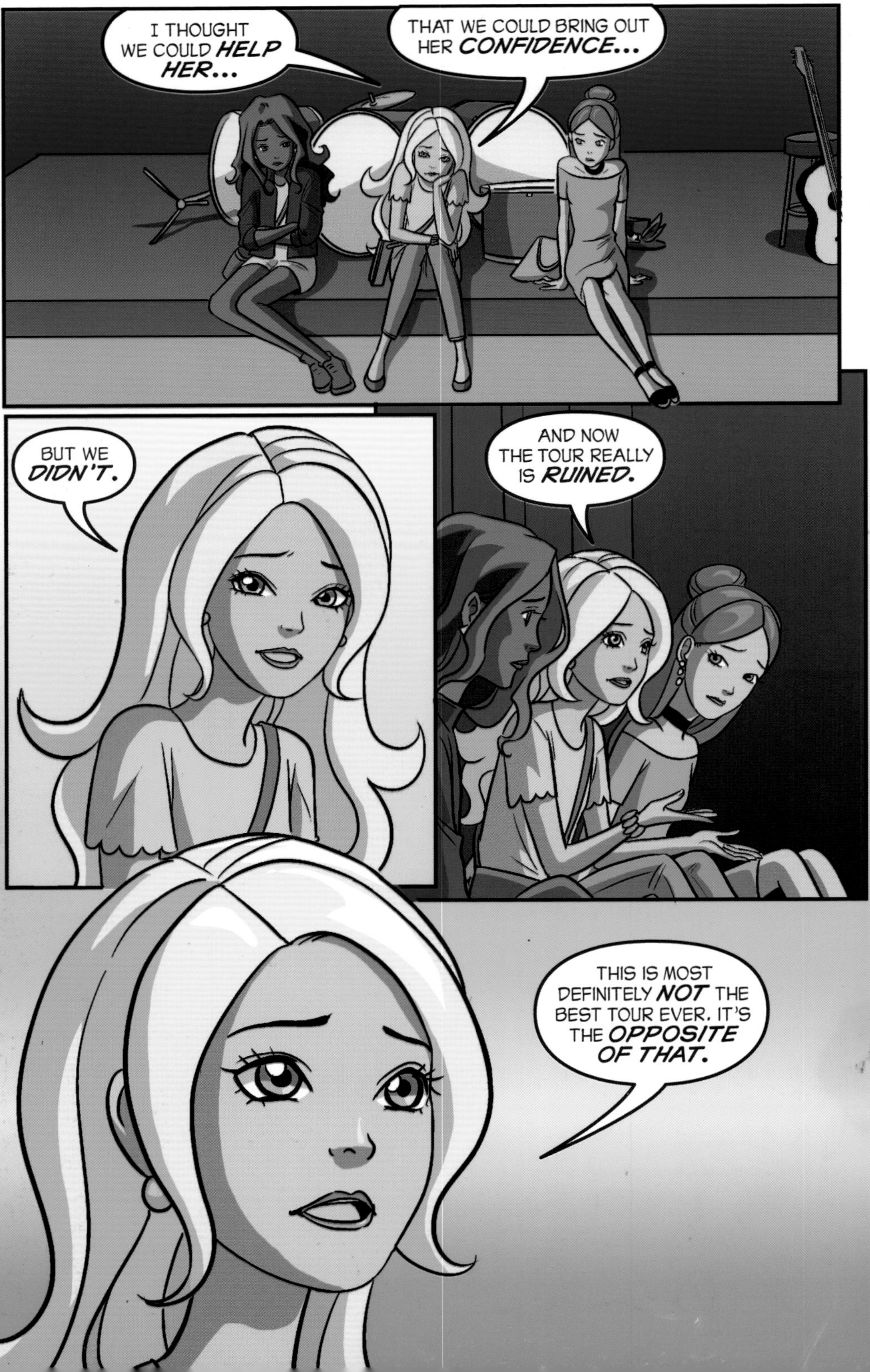
I THOUGHT WE COULD HELP HER...
THAT WE COULD BRING OUT HER CONFIDENCE...
BUT WE DIDN'T.
AND NOW THE TOUR REALLY IS RUINED.
THIS IS MOST DEFINITELY NOT THE BEST TOUR EVER. IT'S THE OPPOSITE OF THAT.

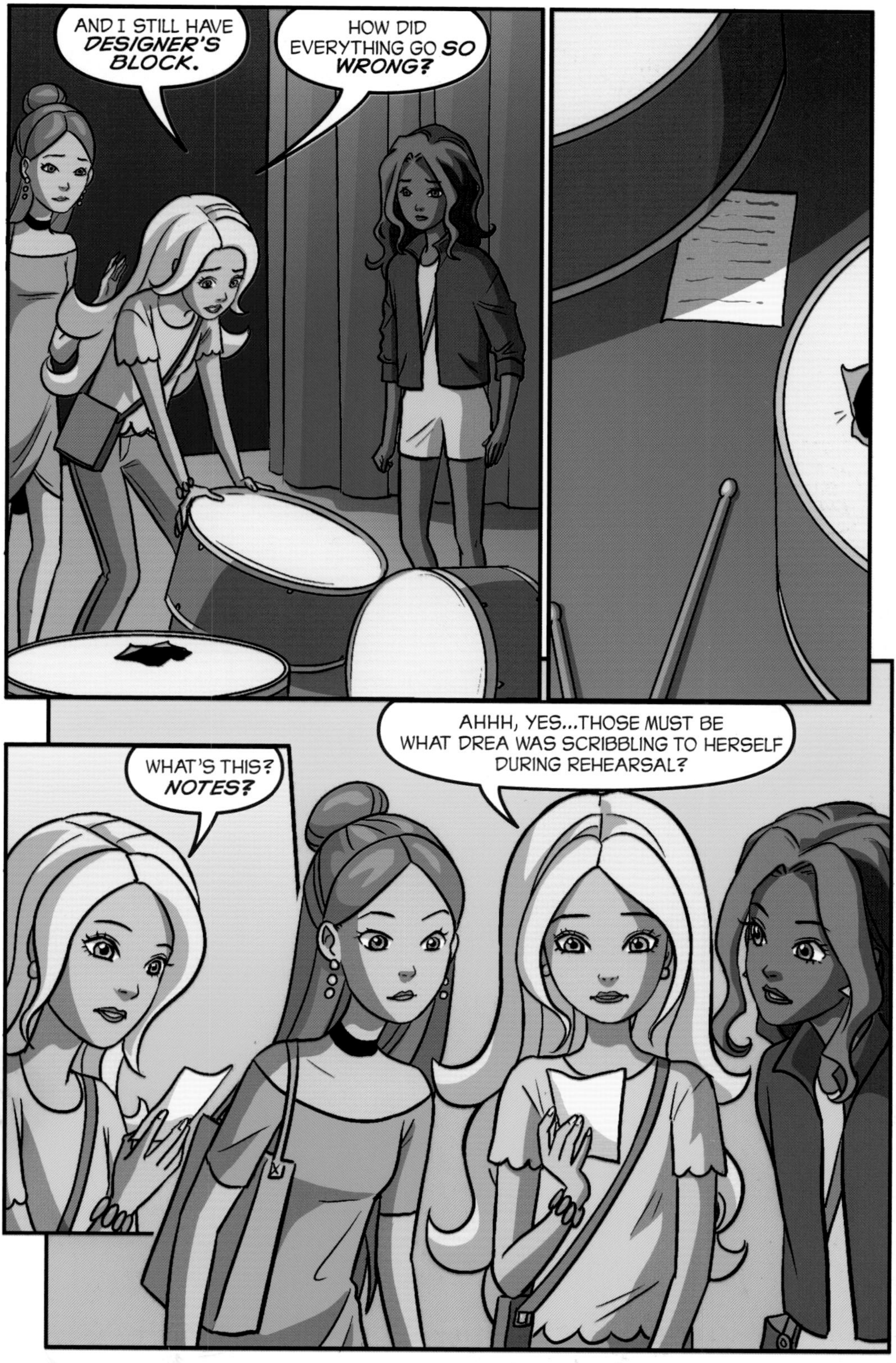
AND I STILL HAVE *DESIGNER'S BLOCK.*
HOW DID EVERYTHING GO ***SO WRONG?***
WHAT'S THIS? ***NOTES?***
AHHH, YES...THOSE MUST BE WHAT DREA WAS SCRIBBLING TO HERSELF DURING REHEARSAL?

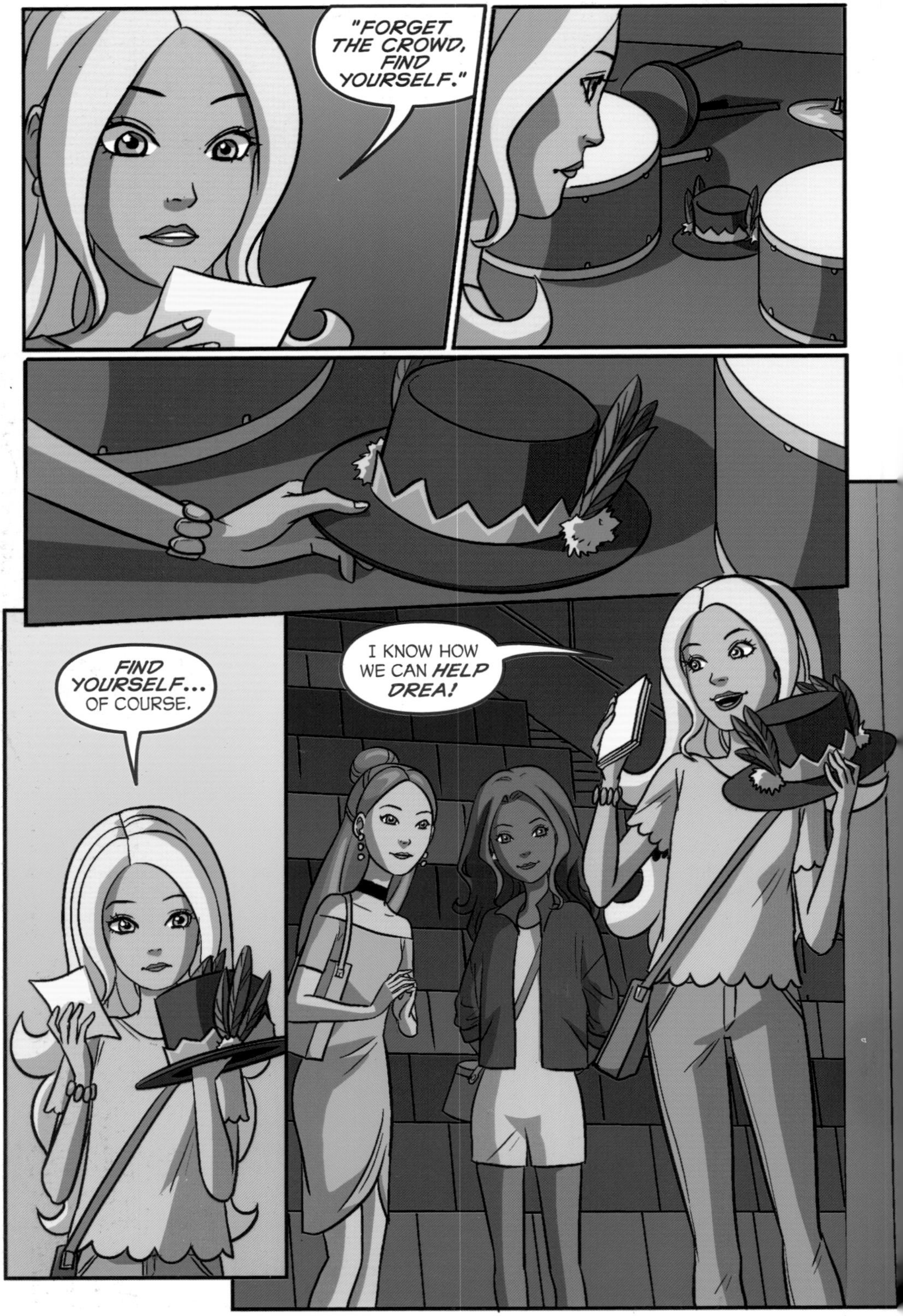
"FORGET THE CROWD, FIND YOURSELF."
FIND YOURSELF... OF COURSE.
I KNOW HOW WE CAN HELP DREA!

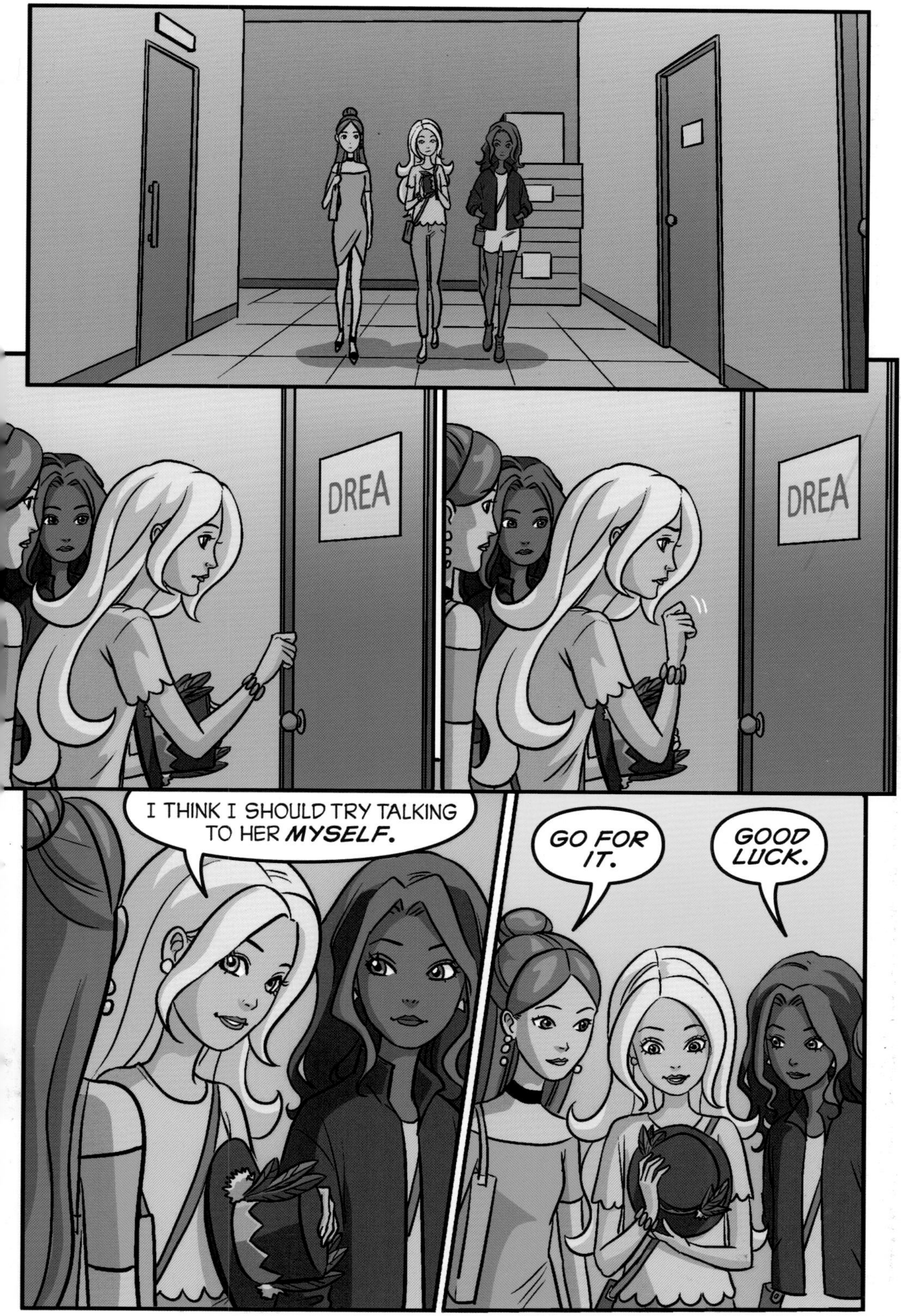
DREA
DREA
I THINK I SHOULD TRY TALKING TO HER MYSELF.
GO FOR IT.
GOOD LUCK.

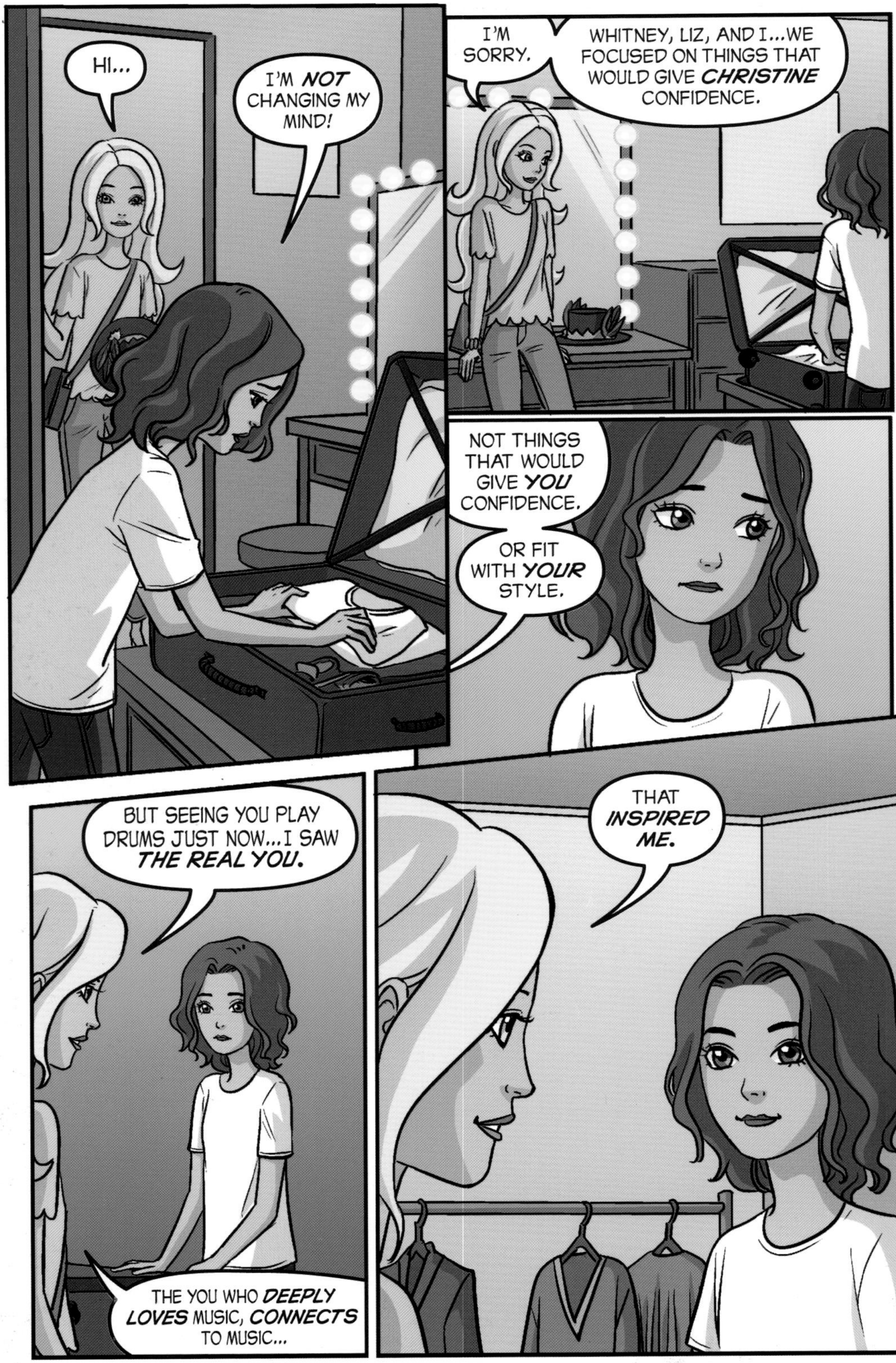
HI...
I'M *NOT* CHANGING MY MIND!
I'M SORRY.
WHITNEY, LIZ, AND I...WE FOCUSED ON THINGS THAT WOULD GIVE *CHRISTINE* CONFIDENCE.
NOT THINGS THAT WOULD GIVE *YOU* CONFIDENCE.
OR FIT WITH *YOUR* STYLE.
BUT SEEING YOU PLAY DRUMS JUST NOW...I SAW *THE REAL YOU.*
THE YOU WHO *DEEPLY LOVES* MUSIC, *CONNECTS* TO MUSIC...
THAT *INSPIRED ME.*

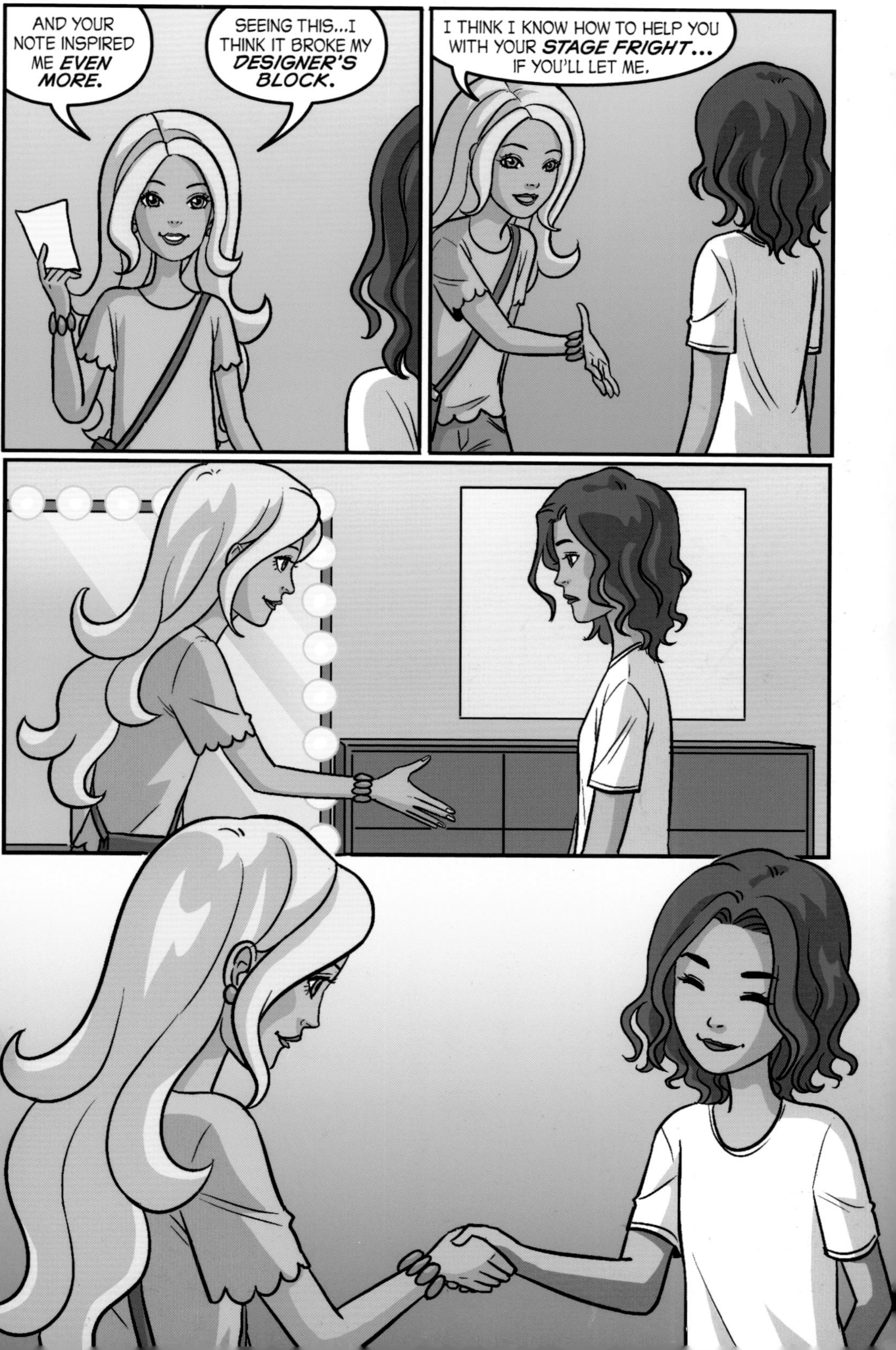
AND YOUR NOTE INSPIRED ME *EVEN MORE.*
SEEING THIS...I THINK IT BROKE MY ***DESIGNER'S BLOCK.***
I THINK I KNOW HOW TO HELP YOU WITH YOUR ***STAGE FRIGHT...*** IF YOU'LL LET ME.

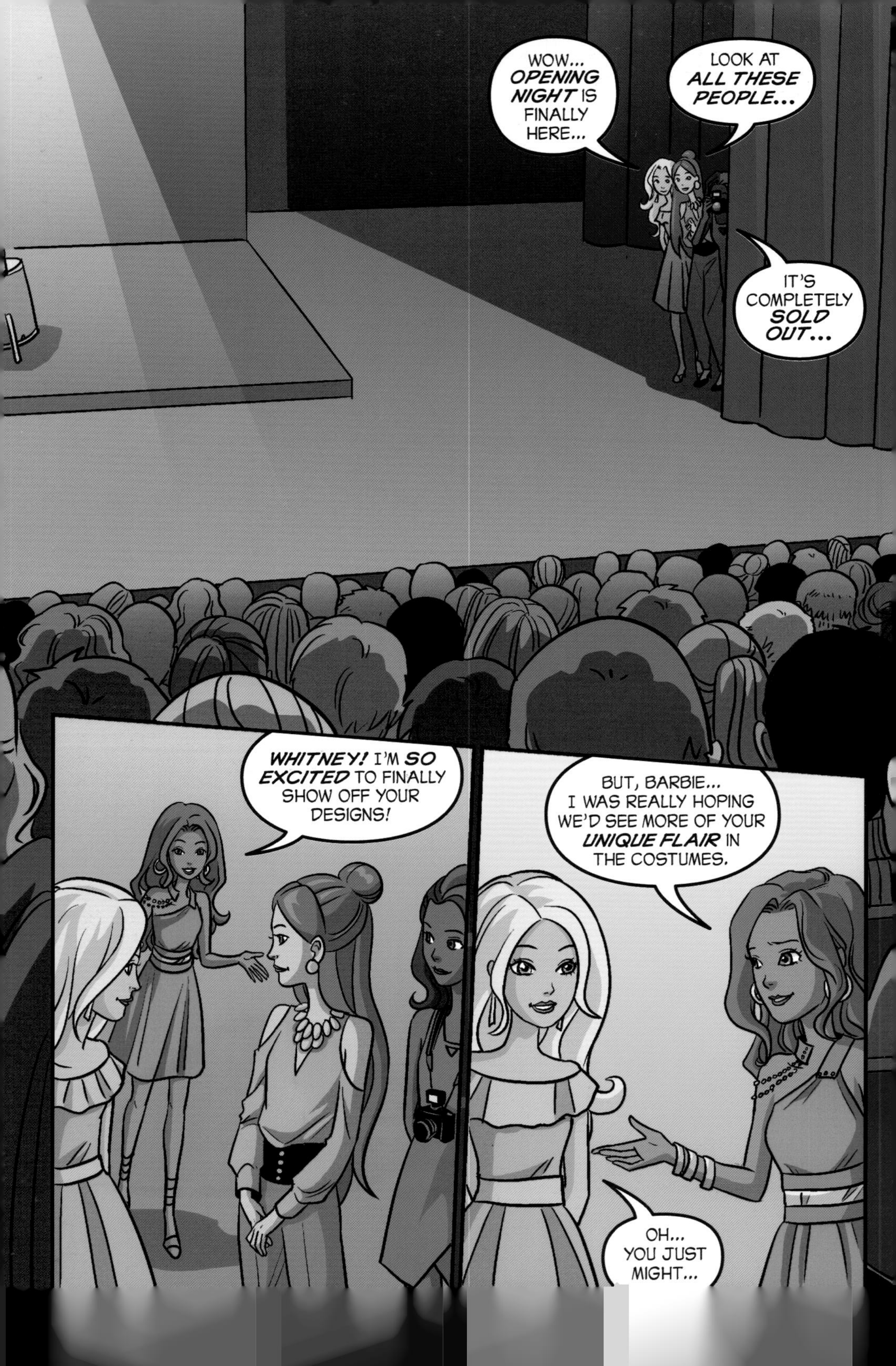
WOW... OPENING NIGHT IS FINALLY HERE...
LOOK AT ALL THESE PEOPLE...
IT'S COMPLETELY SOLD OUT...
WHITNEY! I'M SO EXCITED TO FINALLY SHOW OFF YOUR DESIGNS!
BUT, BARBIE... I WAS REALLY HOPING WE'D SEE MORE OF YOUR UNIQUE FLAIR IN THE COSTUMES.
OH... YOU JUST MIGHT...

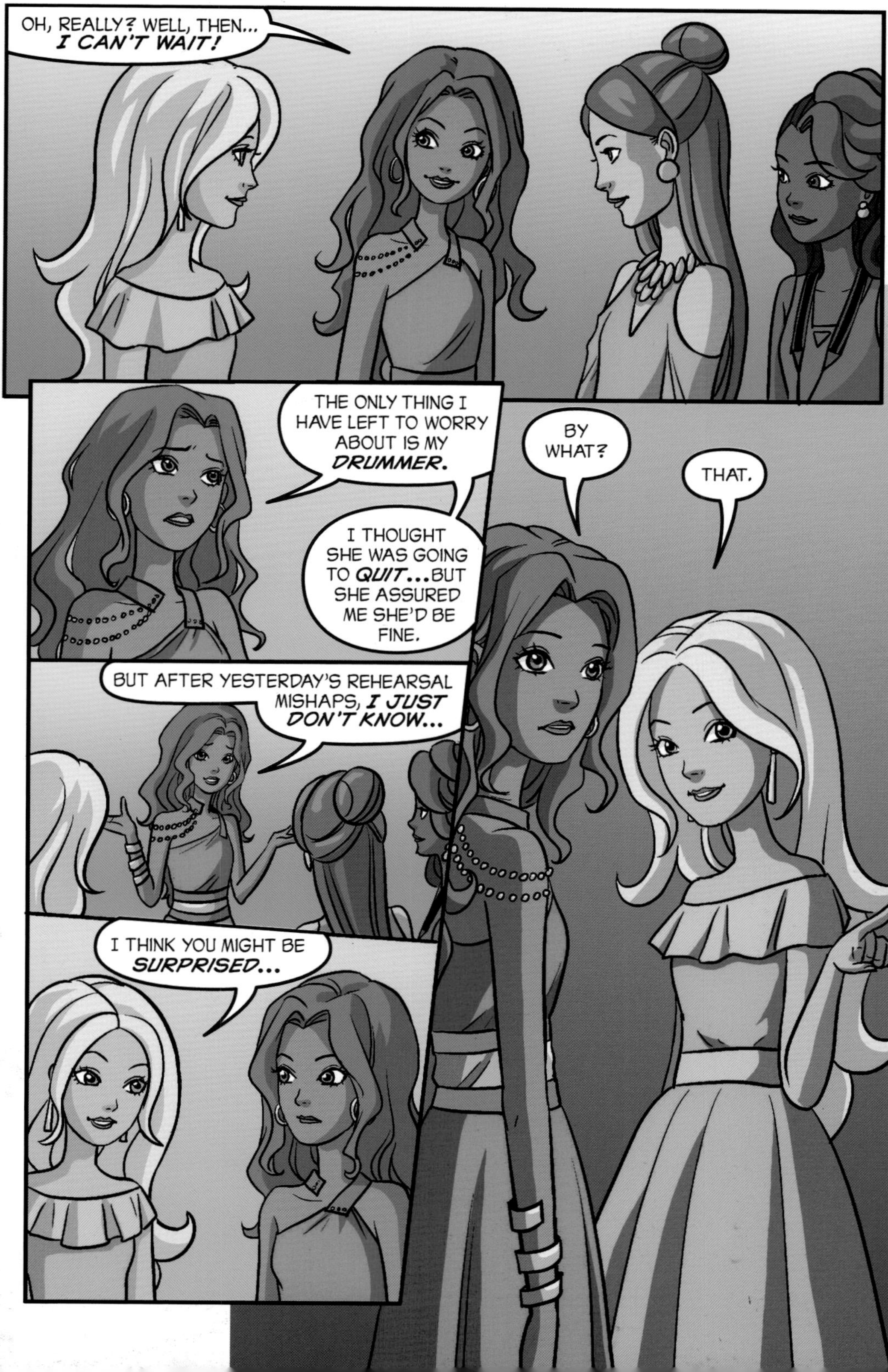
OH, REALLY? WELL, THEN... I CAN'T WAIT!
THE ONLY THING I HAVE LEFT TO WORRY ABOUT IS MY DRUMMER.
I THOUGHT SHE WAS GOING TO QUIT...BUT SHE ASSURED ME SHE'D BE FINE.
BUT AFTER YESTERDAY'S REHEARSAL MISHAPS, I JUST DON'T KNOW...
I THINK YOU MIGHT BE SURPRISED...
BY WHAT?
THAT.

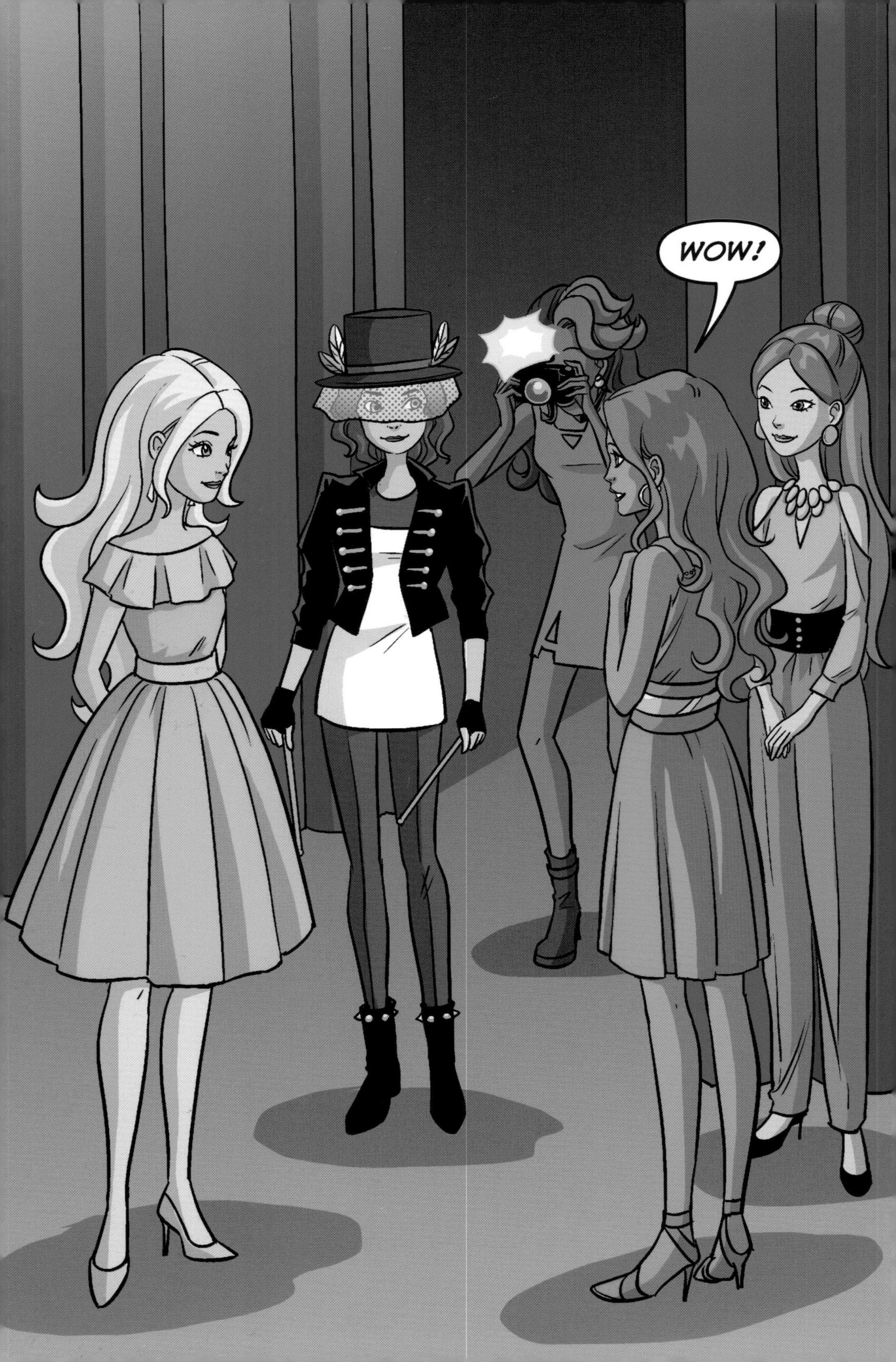
WOW!

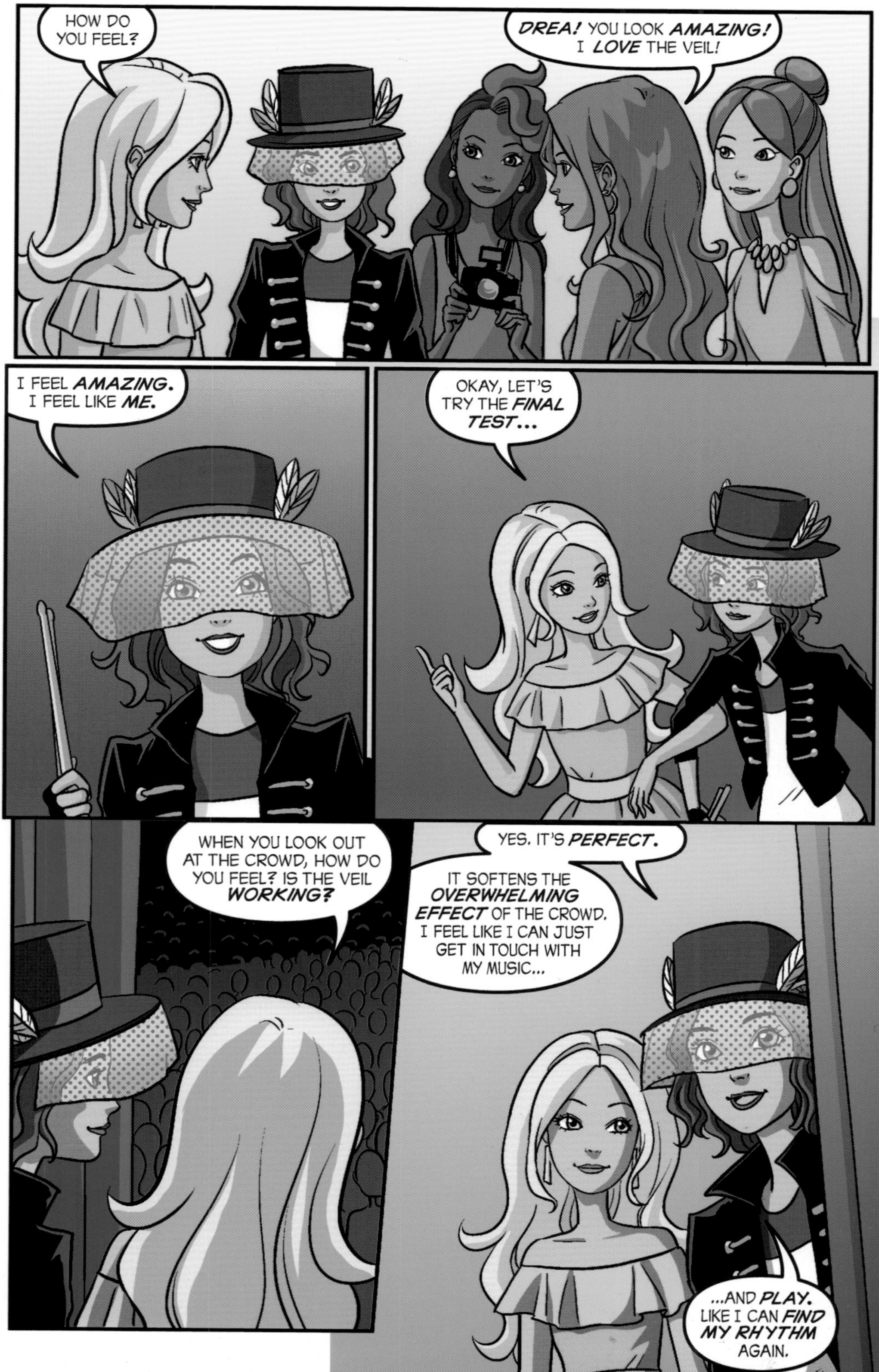
HOW DO YOU FEEL?
DREA! YOU LOOK AMAZING! I LOVE THE VEIL!
I FEEL AMAZING. I FEEL LIKE ME.
OKAY, LET'S TRY THE FINAL TEST...
WHEN YOU LOOK OUT AT THE CROWD, HOW DO YOU FEEL? IS THE VEIL WORKING?
YES. IT'S PERFECT.
IT SOFTENS THE OVERWHELMING EFFECT OF THE CROWD. I FEEL LIKE I CAN JUST GET IN TOUCH WITH MY MUSIC...
...AND PLAY. LIKE I CAN FIND MY RHYTHM AGAIN.

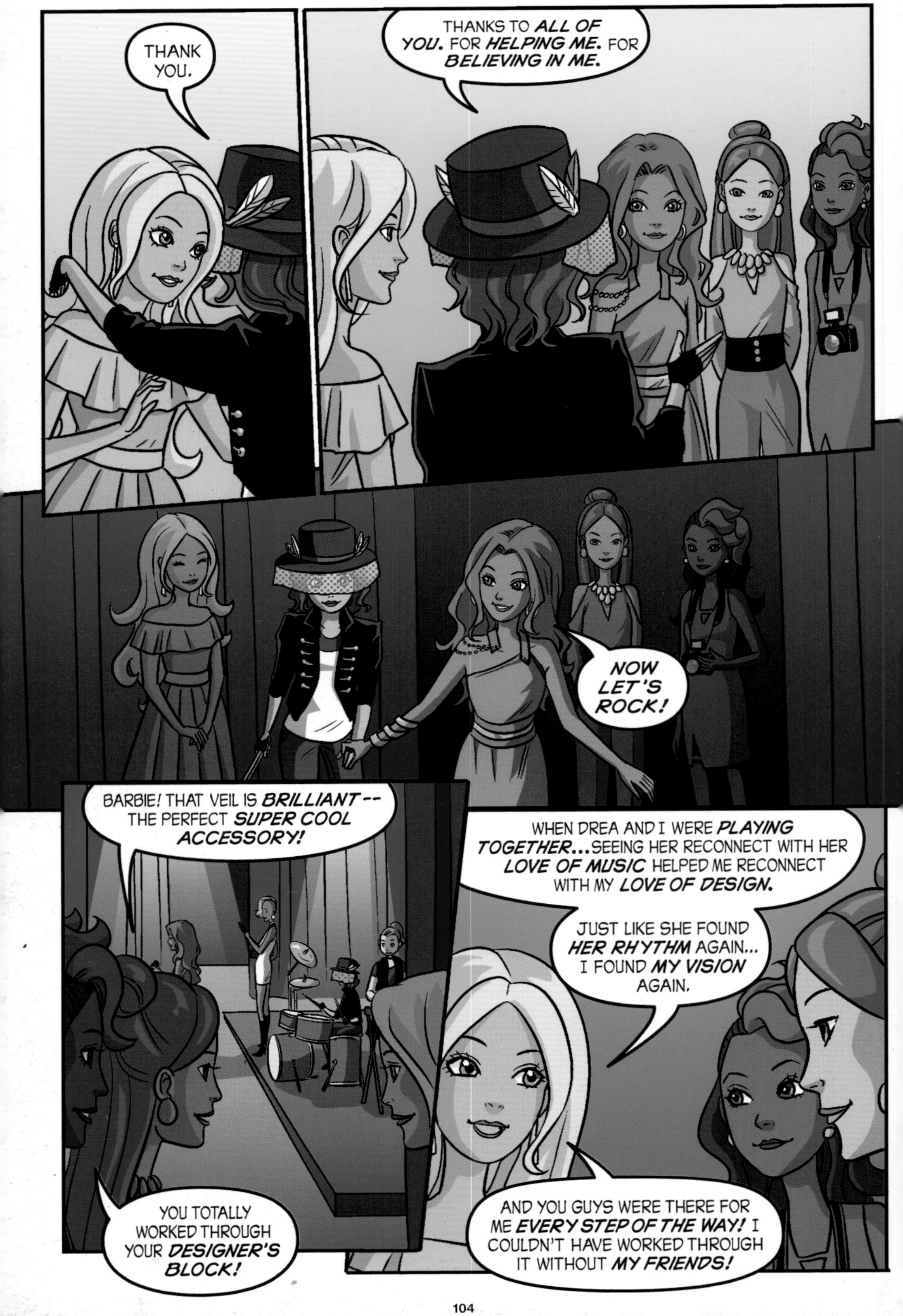
THANK YOU.
THANKS TO ALL OF YOU. FOR HELPING ME. FOR BELIEVING IN ME.
NOW LET'S ROCK!
BARBIE! THAT VEIL IS BRILLIANT -- THE PERFECT SUPER COOL ACCESSORY!
YOU TOTALLY WORKED THROUGH YOUR DESIGNER'S BLOCK!
WHEN DREA AND I WERE PLAYING TOGETHER...SEEING HER RECONNECT WITH HER LOVE OF MUSIC HELPED ME RECONNECT WITH MY LOVE OF DESIGN.
JUST LIKE SHE FOUND HER RHYTHM AGAIN... I FOUND MY VISION AGAIN.
AND YOU GUYS WERE THERE FOR ME EVERY STEP OF THE WAY! I COULDN'T HAVE WORKED THROUGH IT WITHOUT MY FRIENDS!

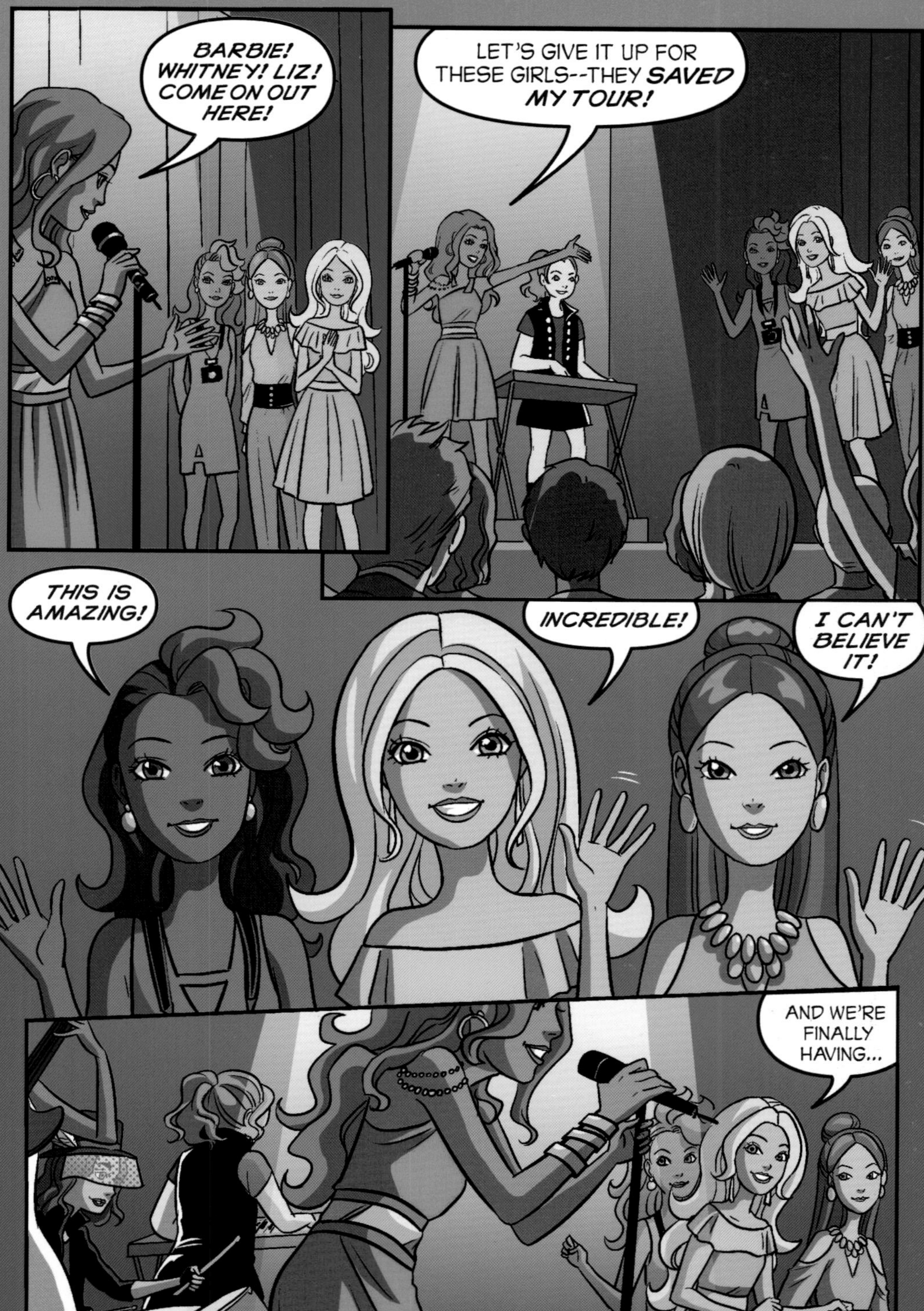
BARBIE! WHITNEY! LIZ! COME ON OUT HERE!
LET'S GIVE IT UP FOR THESE GIRLS--THEY SAVED MY TOUR!
THIS IS AMAZING!
INCREDIBLE!
I CAN'T BELIEVE IT!
AND WE'RE FINALLY HAVING...

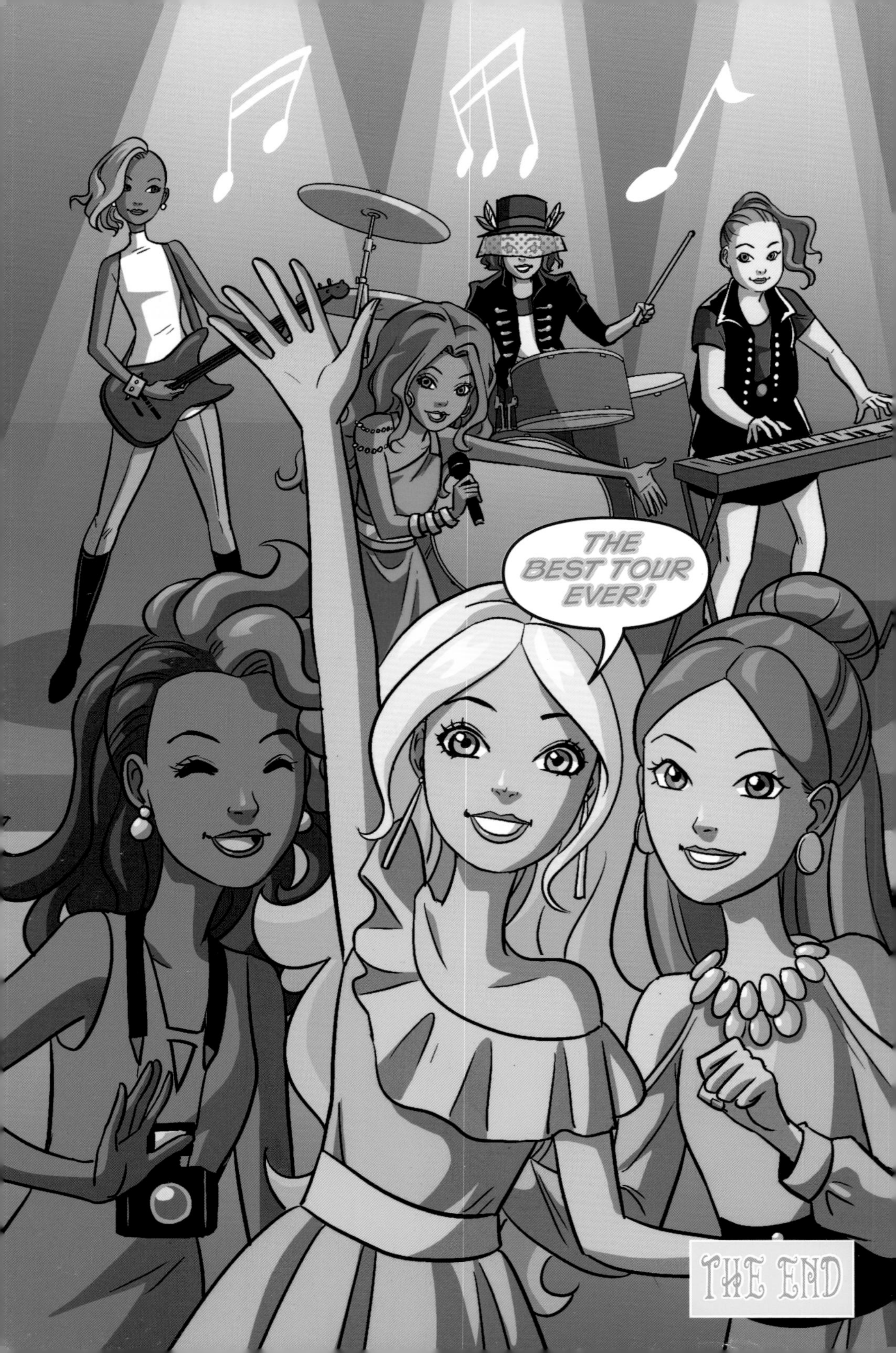
THE BEST TOUR EVER!
THE END

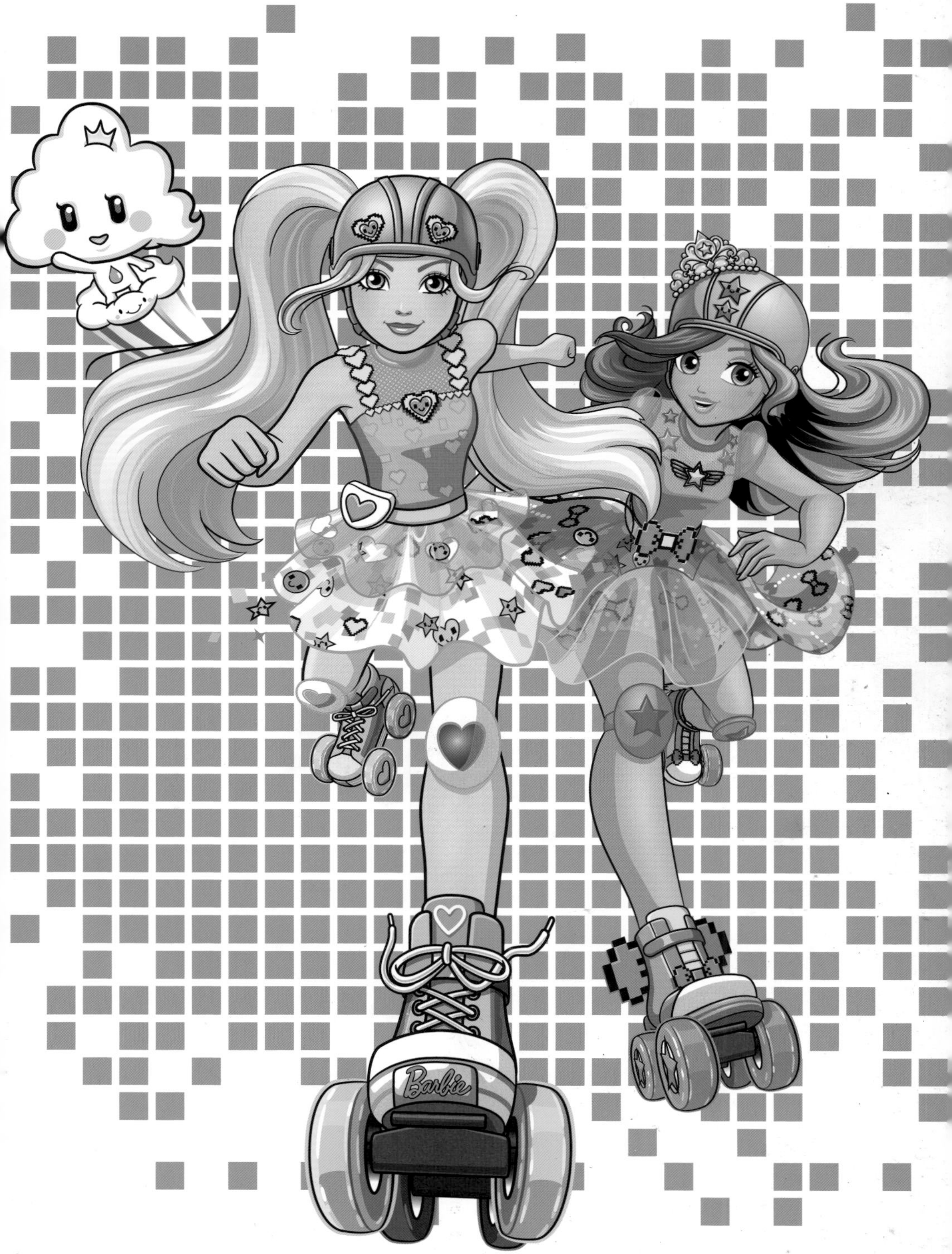

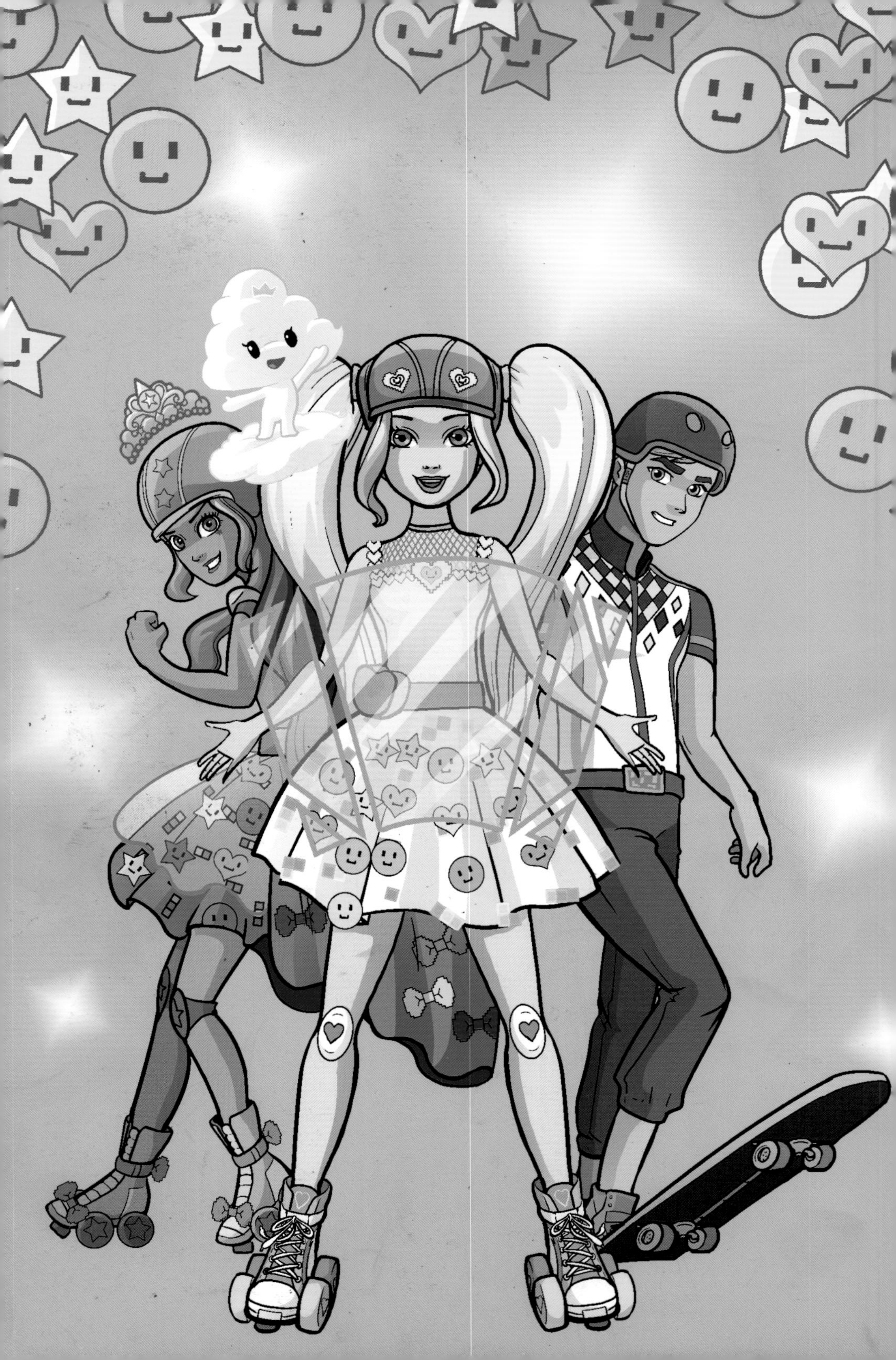

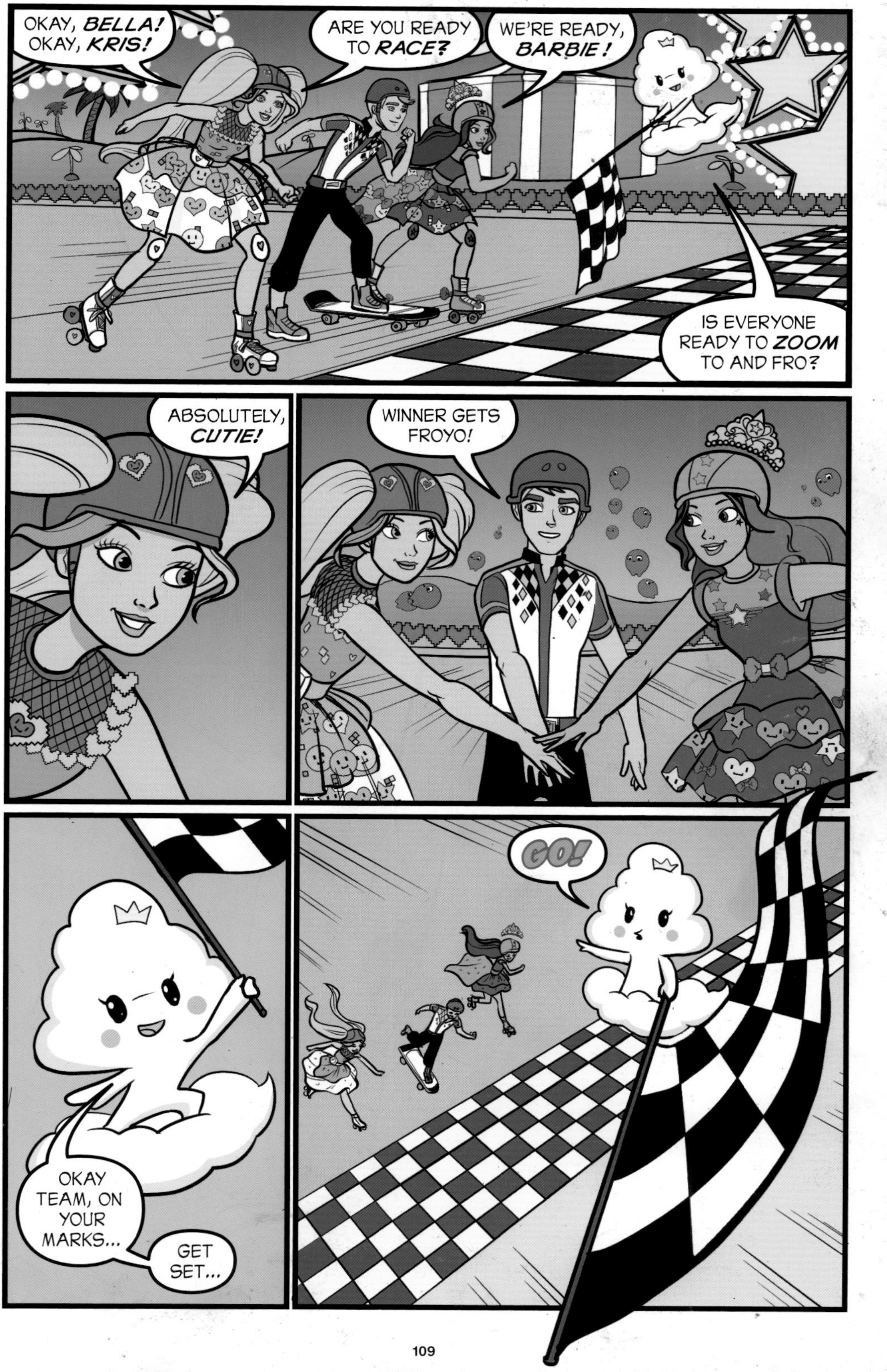

OKAY, BELLA! OKAY, KRIS!
ARE YOU READY TO RACE?
WE'RE READY, BARBIE!
IS EVERYONE READY TO ZOOM TO AND FRO?
ABSOLUTELY, CUTIE!
WINNER GETS FROYO!
OKAY TEAM, ON YOUR MARKS...
GET SET...
GO!

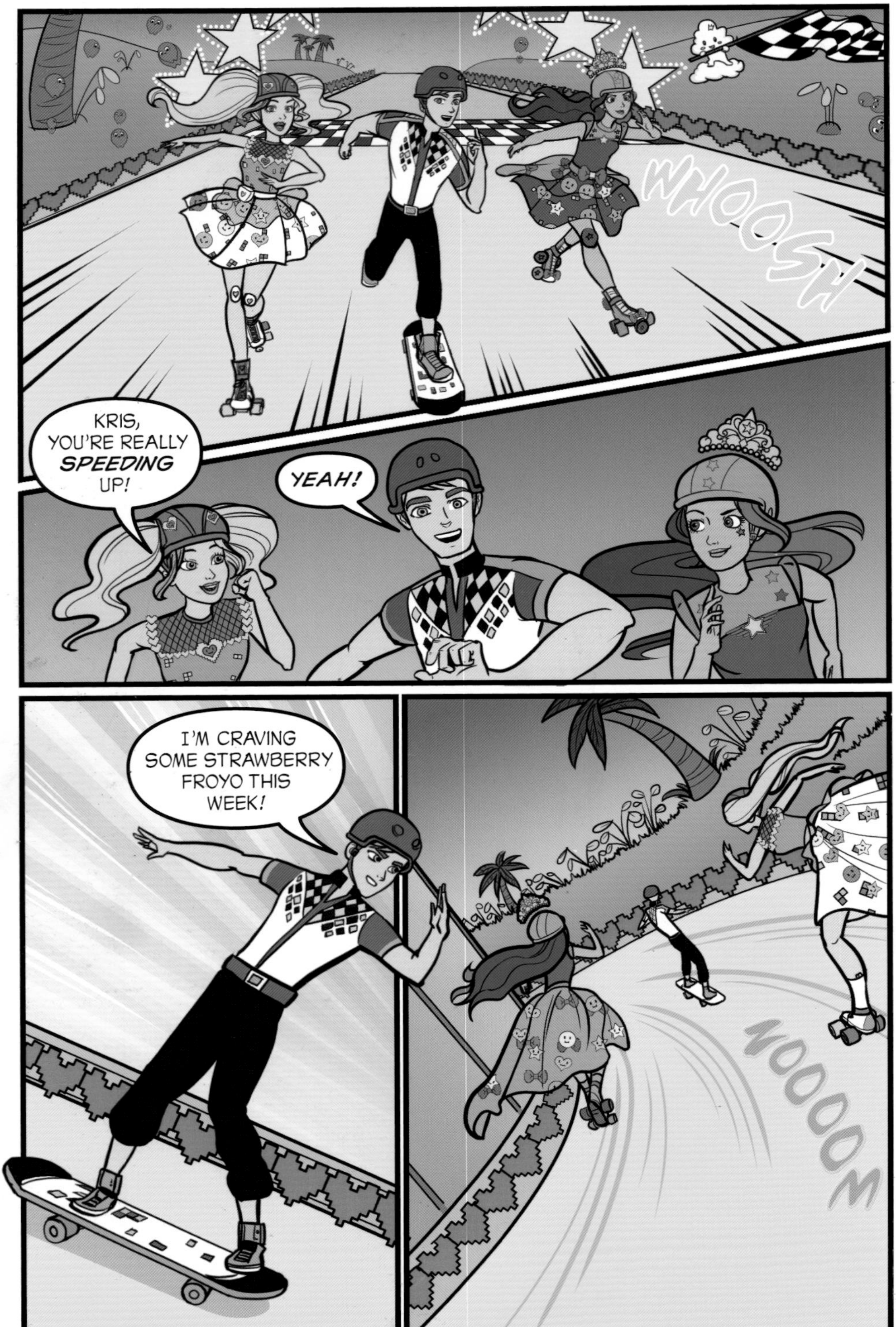
WHOOSH
KRIS, YOU'RE REALLY *SPEEDING* UP!
YEAH!
I'M CRAVING SOME STRAWBERRY FROYO THIS WEEK!
VROOOOOM

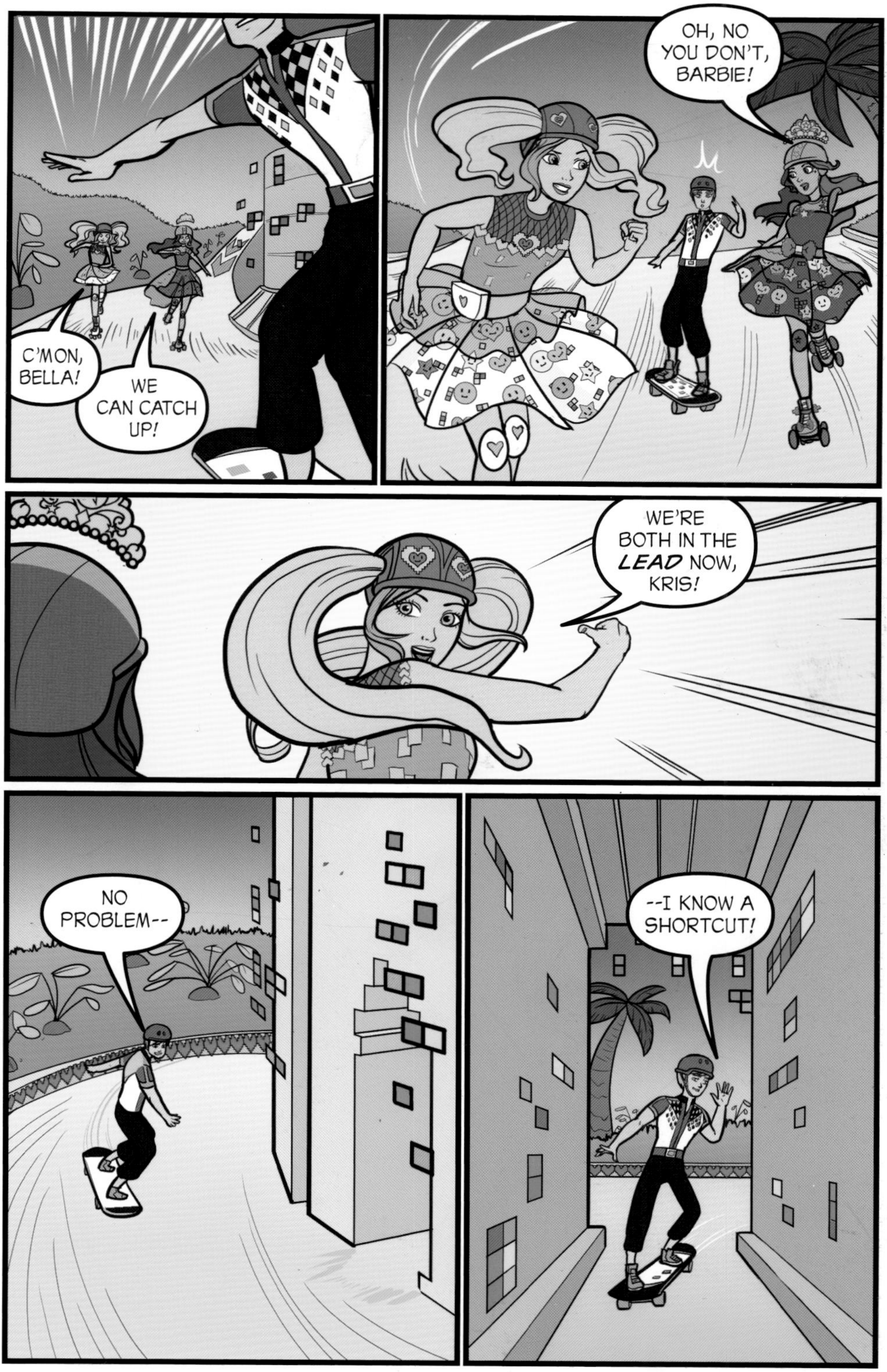
C'MON, BELLA!
WE CAN CATCH UP!
OH, NO YOU DON'T, BARBIE!
WE'RE BOTH IN THE LEAD NOW, KRIS!
NO PROBLEM--
--I KNOW A SHORTCUT!

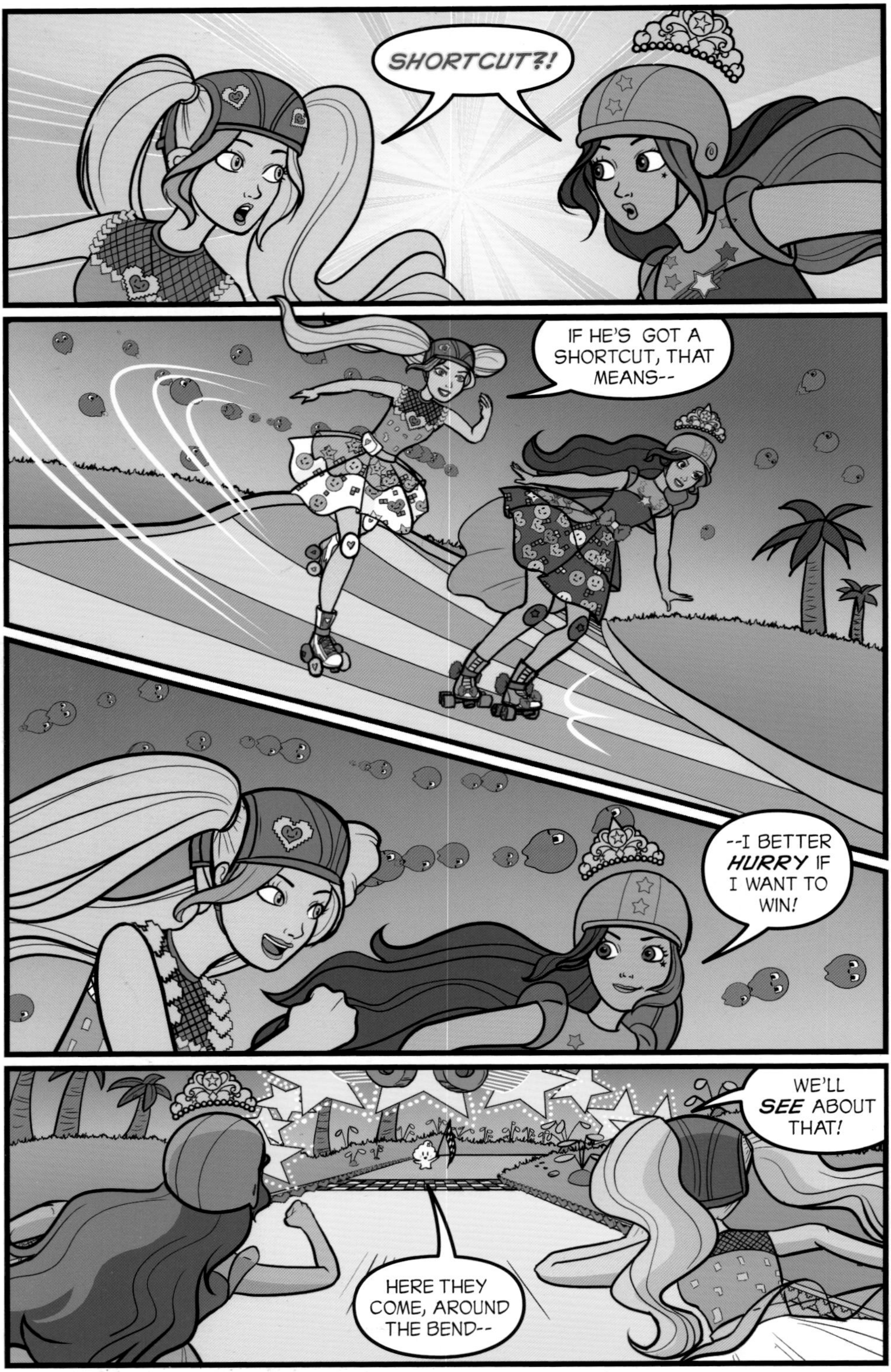
SHORTCUT?!
IF HE'S GOT A SHORTCUT, THAT MEANS--
--I BETTER *HURRY* IF I WANT TO WIN!
WE'LL *SEE* ABOUT THAT!
HERE THEY COME, AROUND THE BEND--

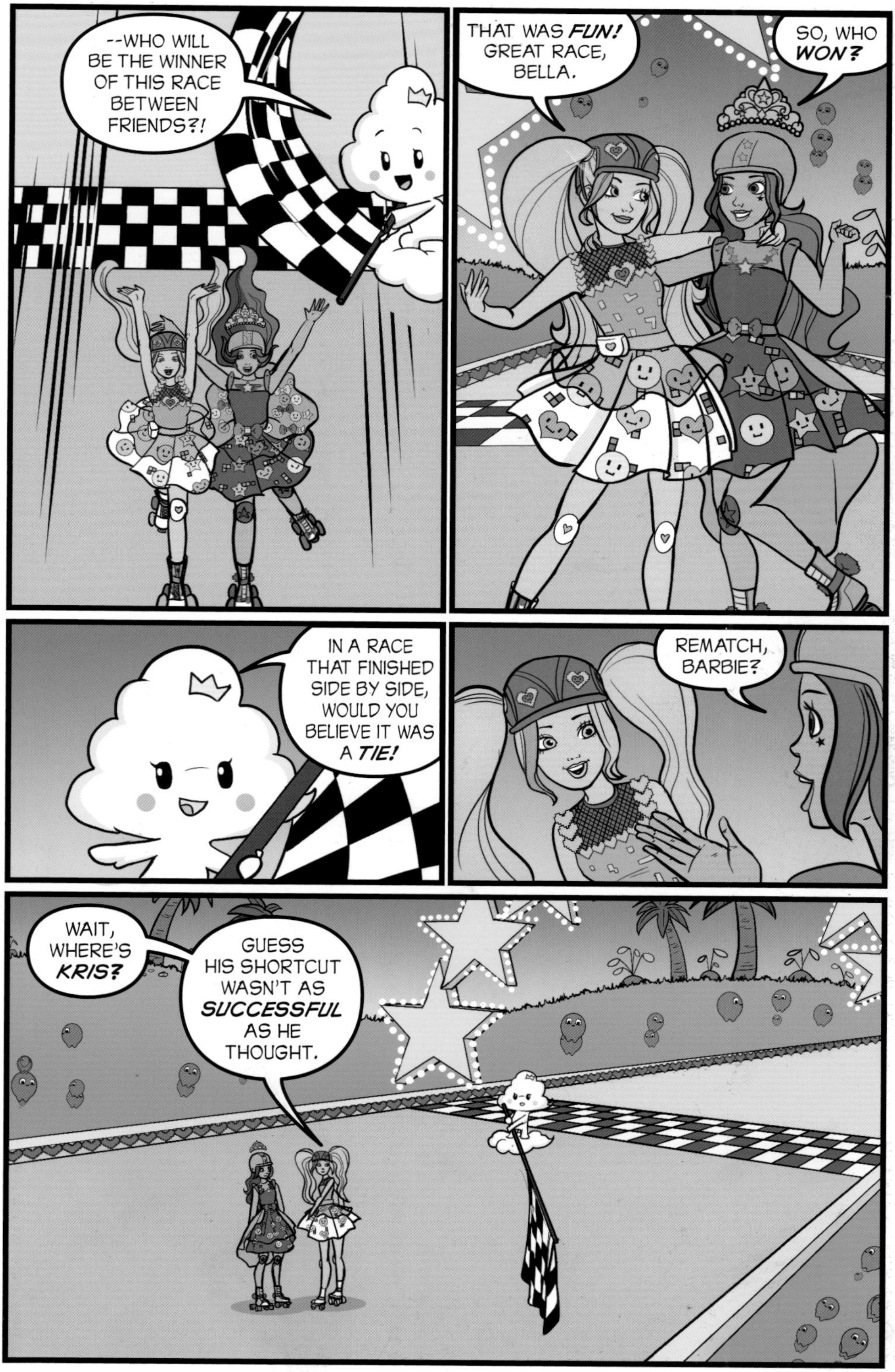
--WHO WILL BE THE WINNER OF THIS RACE BETWEEN FRIENDS?!
THAT WAS FUN! GREAT RACE, BELLA.
SO, WHO WON?
IN A RACE THAT FINISHED SIDE BY SIDE, WOULD YOU BELIEVE IT WAS A TIE!
REMATCH, BARBIE?
WAIT, WHERE'S KRIS?
GUESS HIS SHORTCUT WASN'T AS SUCCESSFUL AS HE THOUGHT.

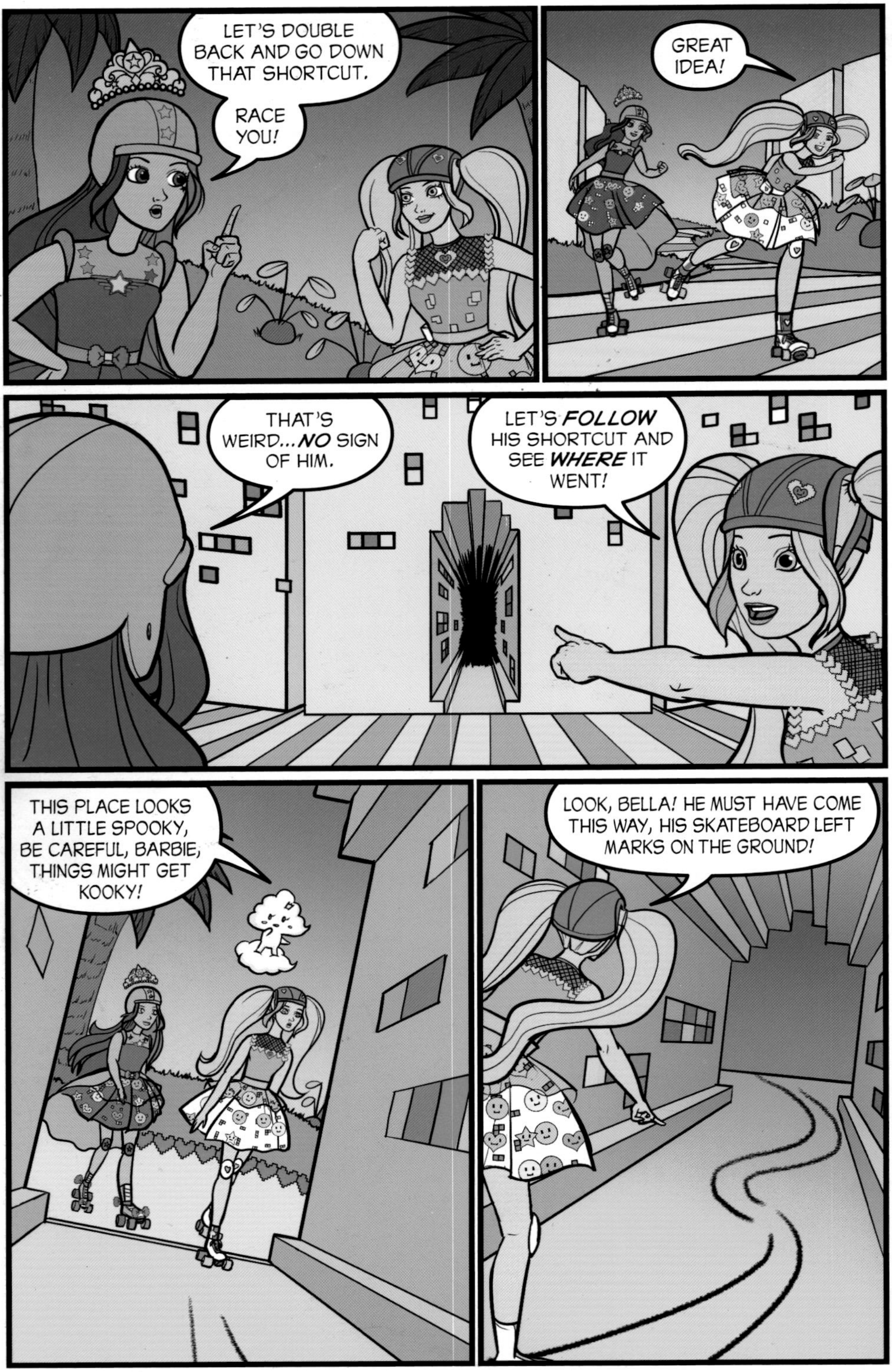
LET'S DOUBLE BACK AND GO DOWN THAT SHORTCUT.
RACE YOU!
GREAT IDEA!
THAT'S WEIRD...NO SIGN OF HIM.
LET'S FOLLOW HIS SHORTCUT AND SEE WHERE IT WENT!
THIS PLACE LOOKS A LITTLE SPOOKY, BE CAREFUL, BARBIE, THINGS MIGHT GET KOOKY!
LOOK, BELLA! HE MUST HAVE COME THIS WAY, HIS SKATEBOARD LEFT MARKS ON THE GROUND!

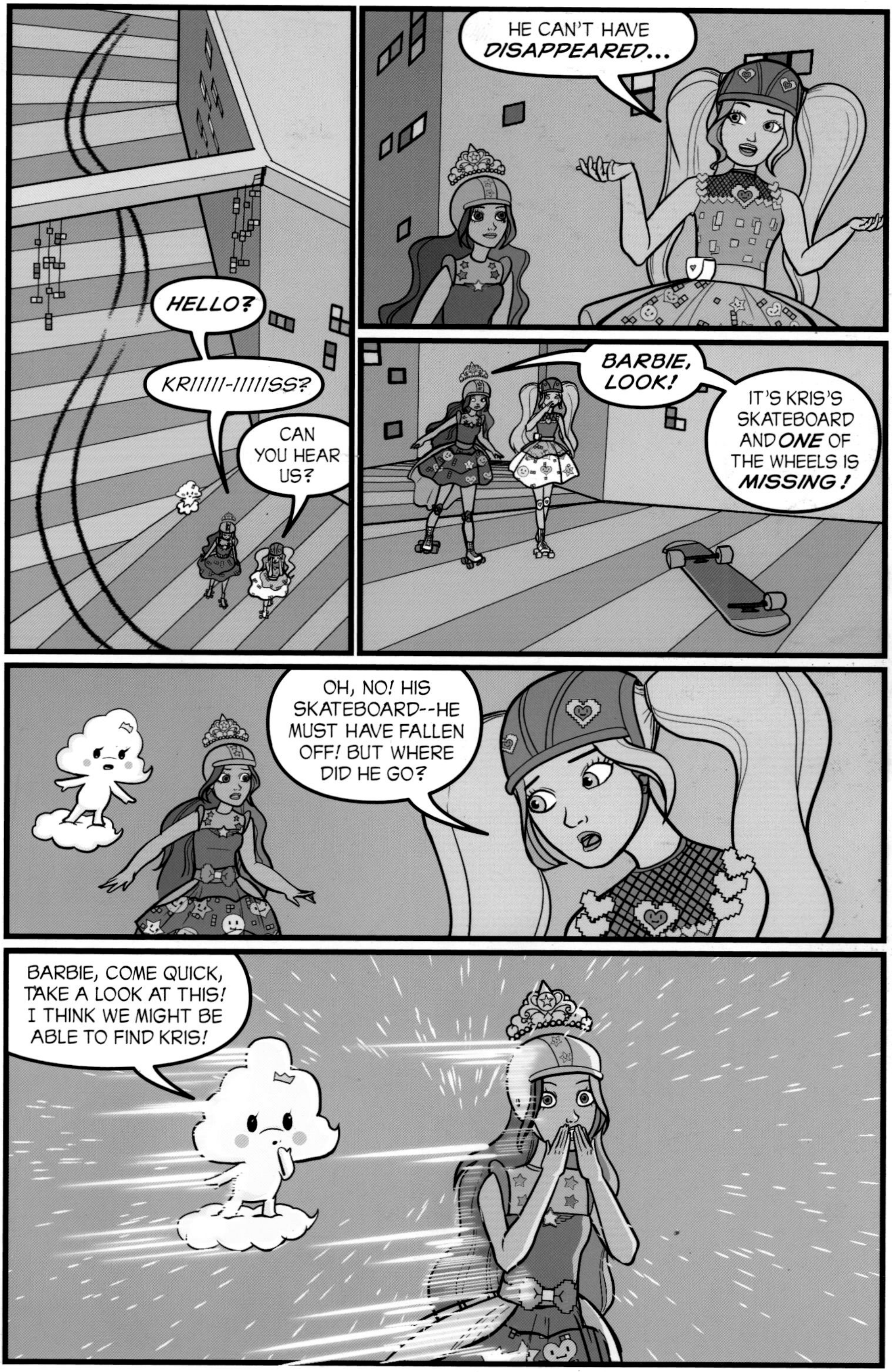
HELLO?
KRIIIII-IIIIISS?
CAN YOU HEAR US?
HE CAN'T HAVE *DISAPPEARED...*
BARBIE, LOOK!
IT'S KRIS'S SKATEBOARD AND *ONE* OF THE WHEELS IS *MISSING!*
OH, NO! HIS SKATEBOARD--HE MUST HAVE FALLEN OFF! BUT WHERE DID HE GO?
BARBIE, COME QUICK, TAKE A LOOK AT THIS! I THINK WE MIGHT BE ABLE TO FIND KRIS!

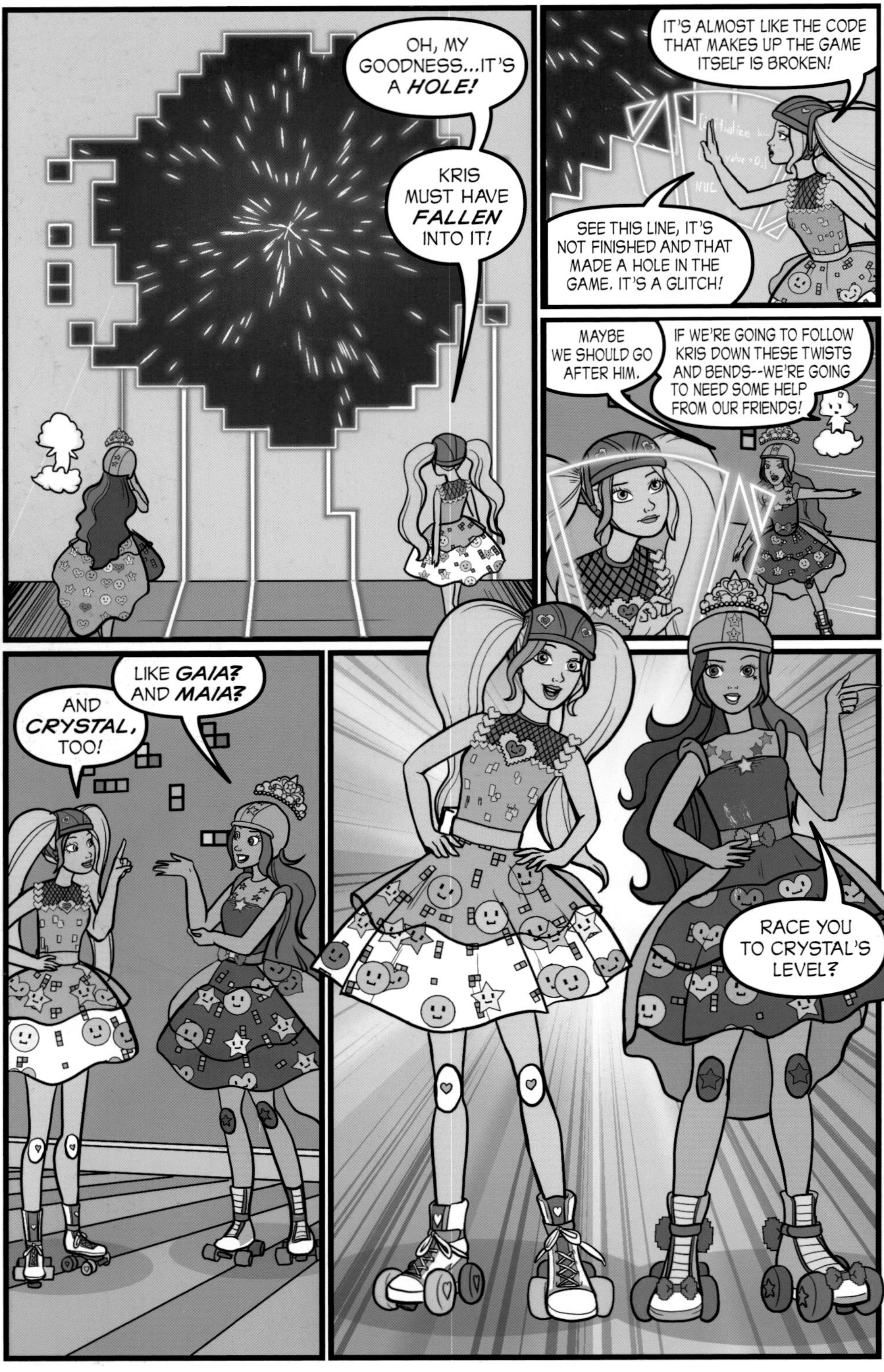
OH, MY GOODNESS...IT'S A *HOLE!*
KRIS MUST HAVE *FALLEN* INTO IT!
IT'S ALMOST LIKE THE CODE THAT MAKES UP THE GAME ITSELF IS BROKEN!
SEE THIS LINE, IT'S NOT FINISHED AND THAT MADE A HOLE IN THE GAME. IT'S A GLITCH!
MAYBE WE SHOULD GO AFTER HIM.
IF WE'RE GOING TO FOLLOW KRIS DOWN THESE TWISTS AND BENDS--WE'RE GOING TO NEED SOME HELP FROM OUR FRIENDS!
LIKE *GAIA?* AND *MAIA?*
AND *CRYSTAL,* TOO!
RACE YOU TO CRYSTAL'S LEVEL?

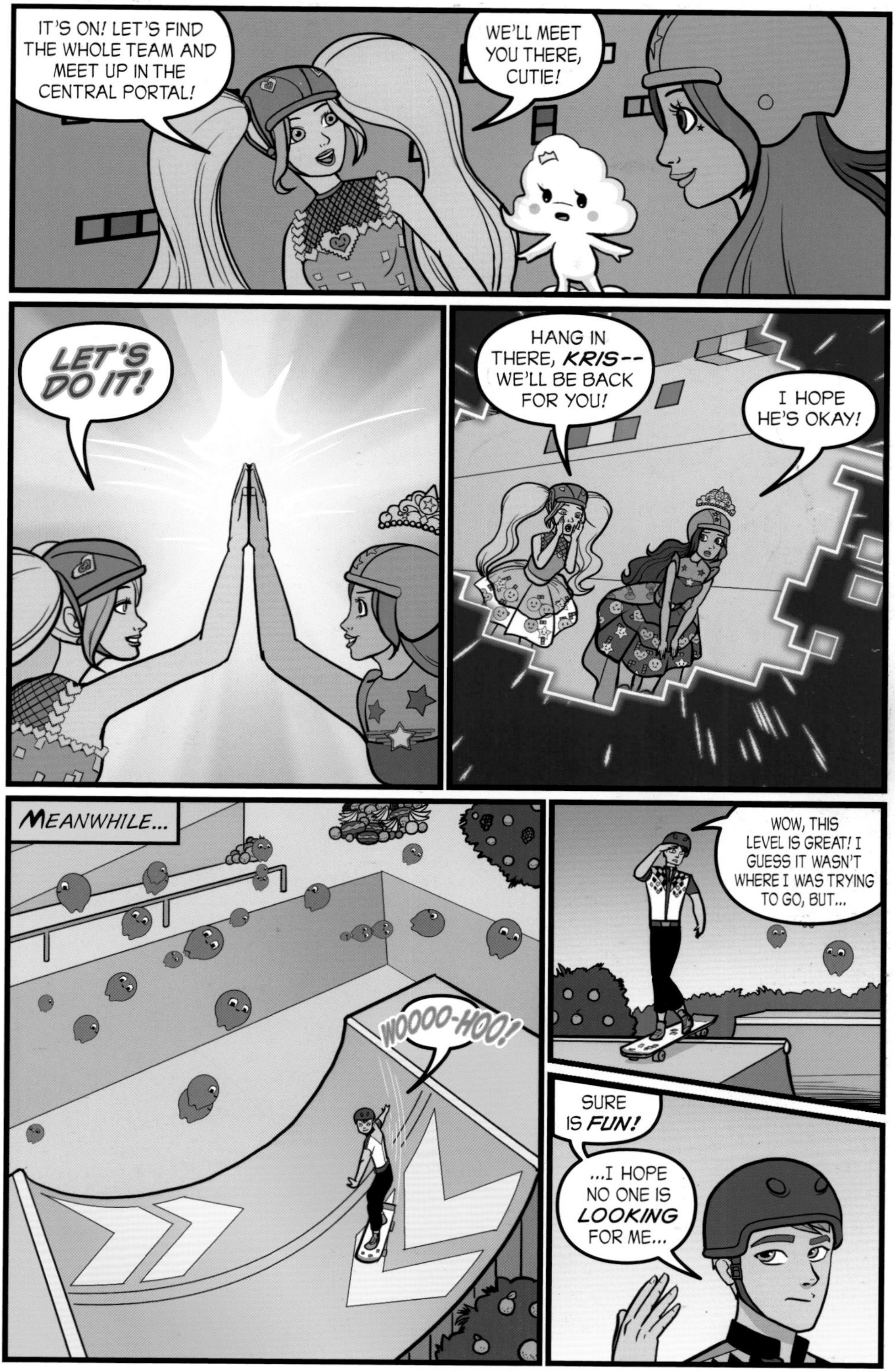
IT'S ON! LET'S FIND THE WHOLE TEAM AND MEET UP IN THE CENTRAL PORTAL!
WE'LL MEET YOU THERE, CUTIE!
LET'S DO IT!
HANG IN THERE, KRIS-- WE'LL BE BACK FOR YOU!
I HOPE HE'S OKAY!
MEANWHILE...
WOOOO-HOO!
WOW, THIS LEVEL IS GREAT! I GUESS IT WASN'T WHERE I WAS TRYING TO GO, BUT...
SURE IS FUN!
...I HOPE NO ONE IS LOOKING FOR ME...

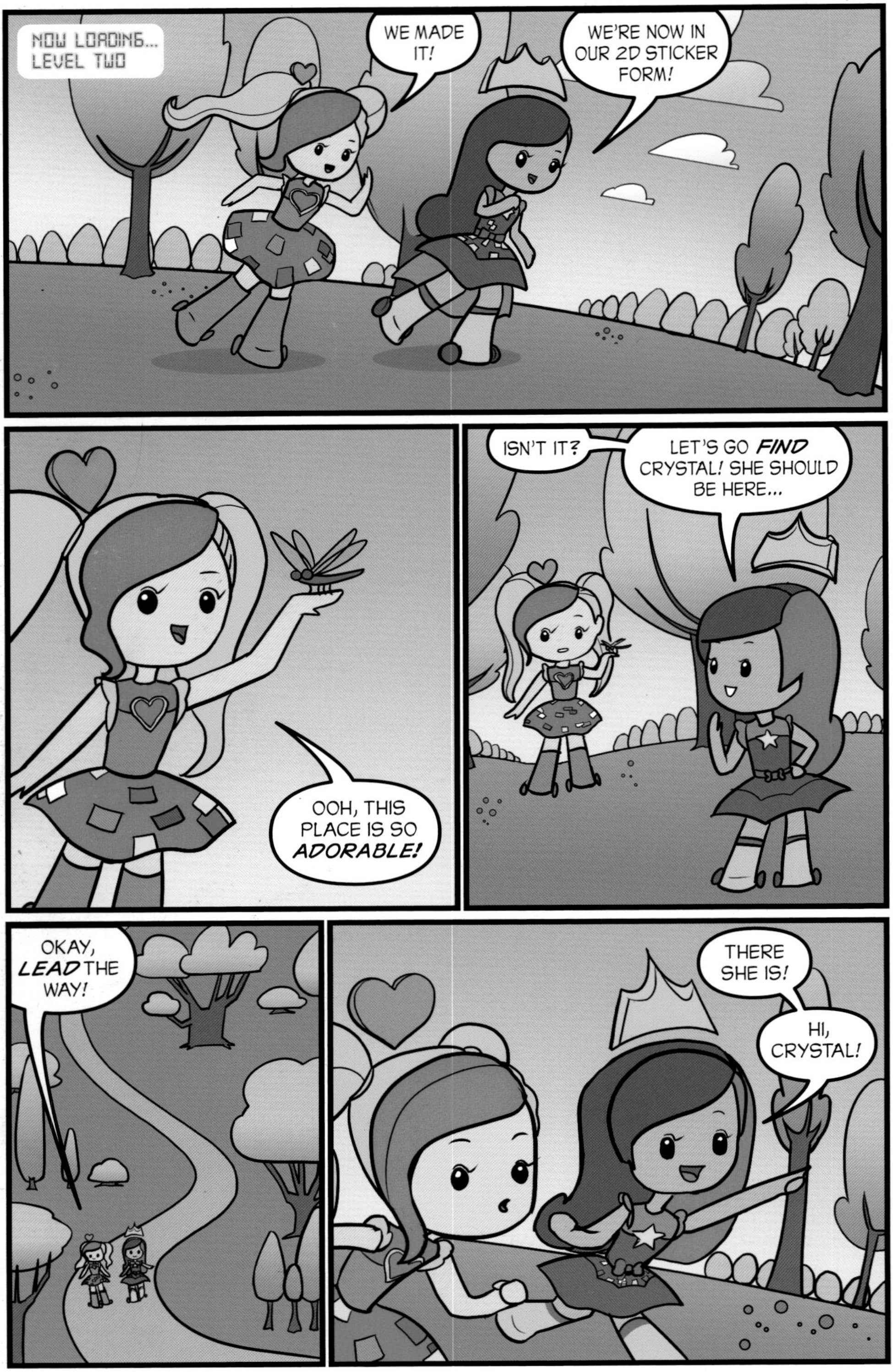
NOW LOADING...
LEVEL TWO
WE MADE IT!
WE'RE NOW IN OUR 2D STICKER FORM!
OOH, THIS PLACE IS SO ADORABLE!
ISN'T IT?
LET'S GO FIND CRYSTAL! SHE SHOULD BE HERE...
OKAY, LEAD THE WAY!
THERE SHE IS!
HI, CRYSTAL!

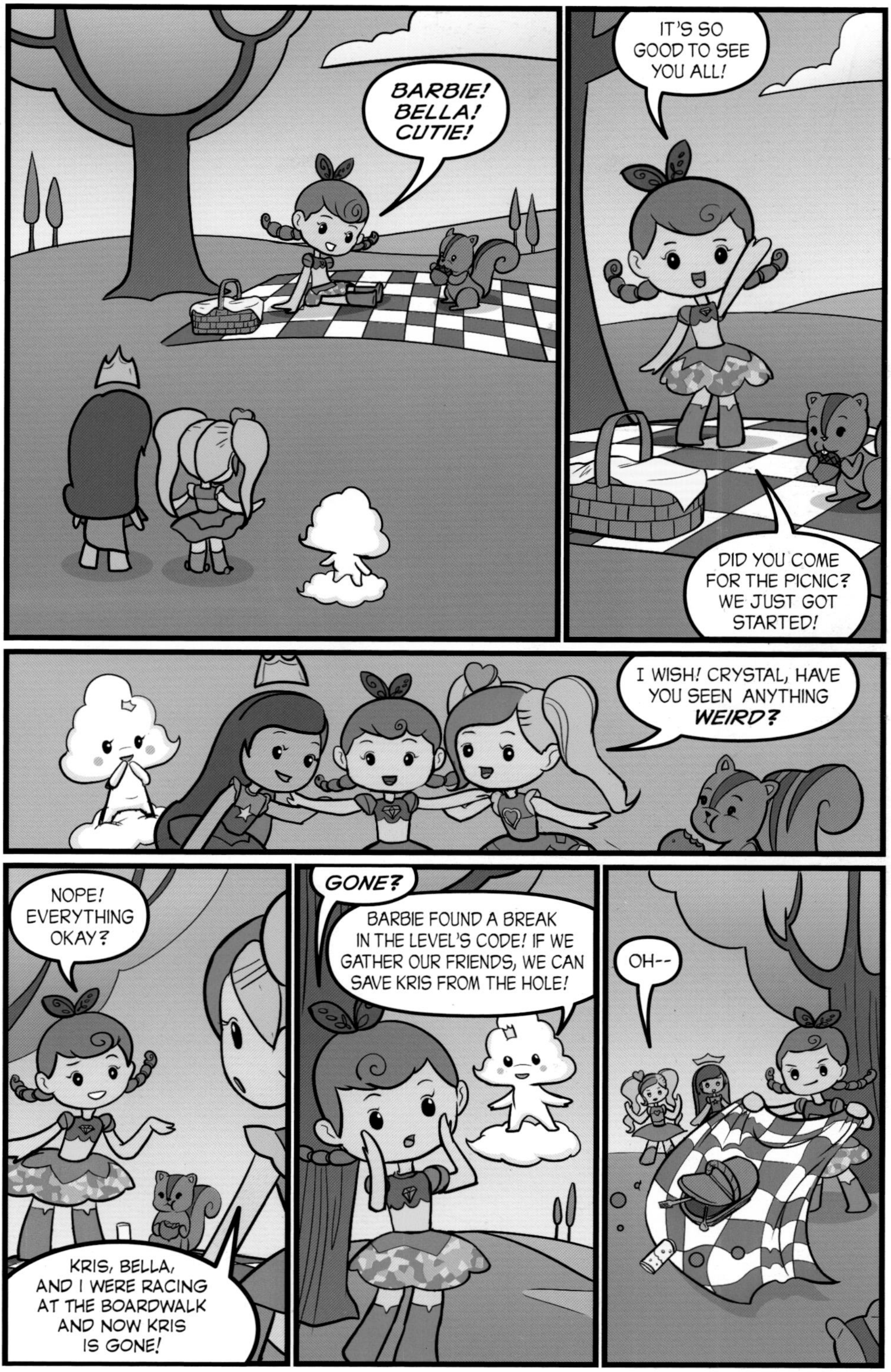
BARBIE! BELLA! CUTIE!
IT'S SO GOOD TO SEE YOU ALL!
DID YOU COME FOR THE PICNIC? WE JUST GOT STARTED!
I WISH! CRYSTAL, HAVE YOU SEEN ANYTHING WEIRD?
NOPE! EVERYTHING OKAY?
KRIS, BELLA, AND I WERE RACING AT THE BOARDWALK AND NOW KRIS IS GONE!
GONE?
BARBIE FOUND A BREAK IN THE LEVEL'S CODE! IF WE GATHER OUR FRIENDS, WE CAN SAVE KRIS FROM THE HOLE!
OH--

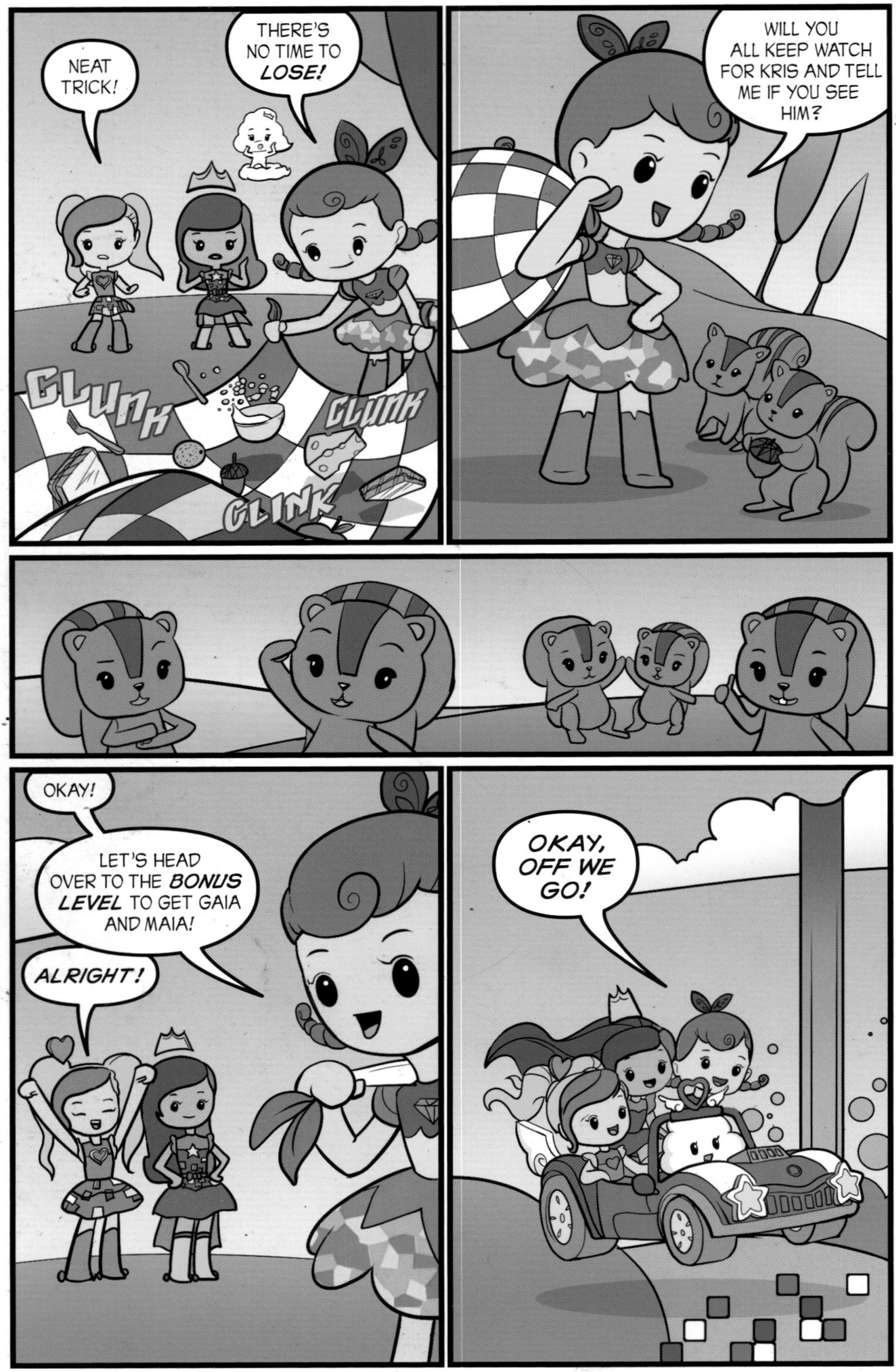

NEAT TRICK!
THERE'S NO TIME TO LOSE!
CLUNK
CLUNK
CLINK
WILL YOU ALL KEEP WATCH FOR KRIS AND TELL ME IF YOU SEE HIM?
OKAY!
LET'S HEAD OVER TO THE BONUS LEVEL TO GET GAIA AND MAIA!
ALRIGHT!
OKAY, OFF WE GO!

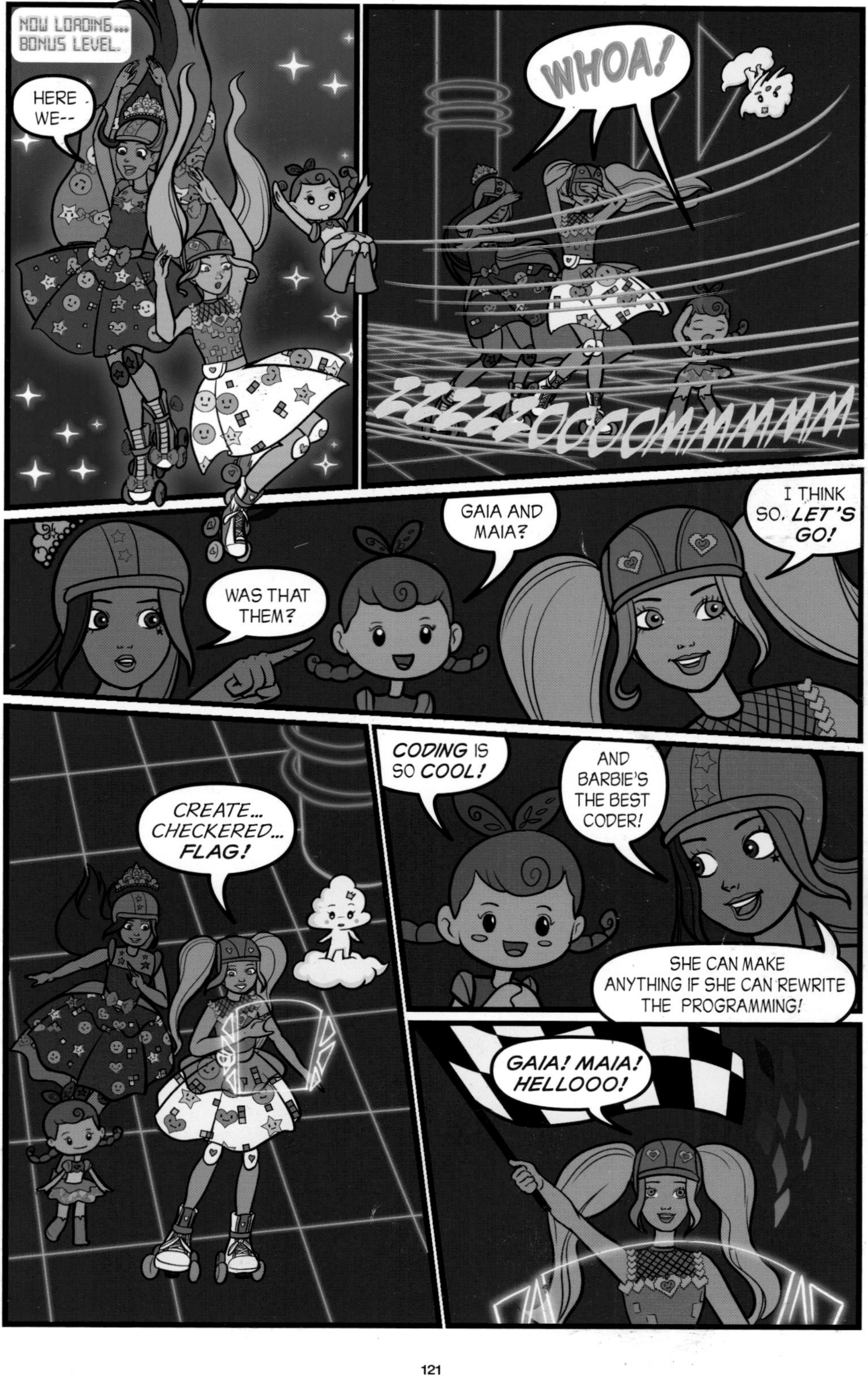
NOW LOADING... BONUS LEVEL.
HERE WE--
WHOA!
ZZZZZOOOOMMMMM
WAS THAT THEM?
GAIA AND MAIA?
I THINK SO. LET'S GO!
CREATE... CHECKERED... FLAG!
CODING IS SO COOL!
AND BARBIE'S THE BEST CODER!
SHE CAN MAKE ANYTHING IF SHE CAN REWRITE THE PROGRAMMING!
GAIA! MAIA! HELLOOO!

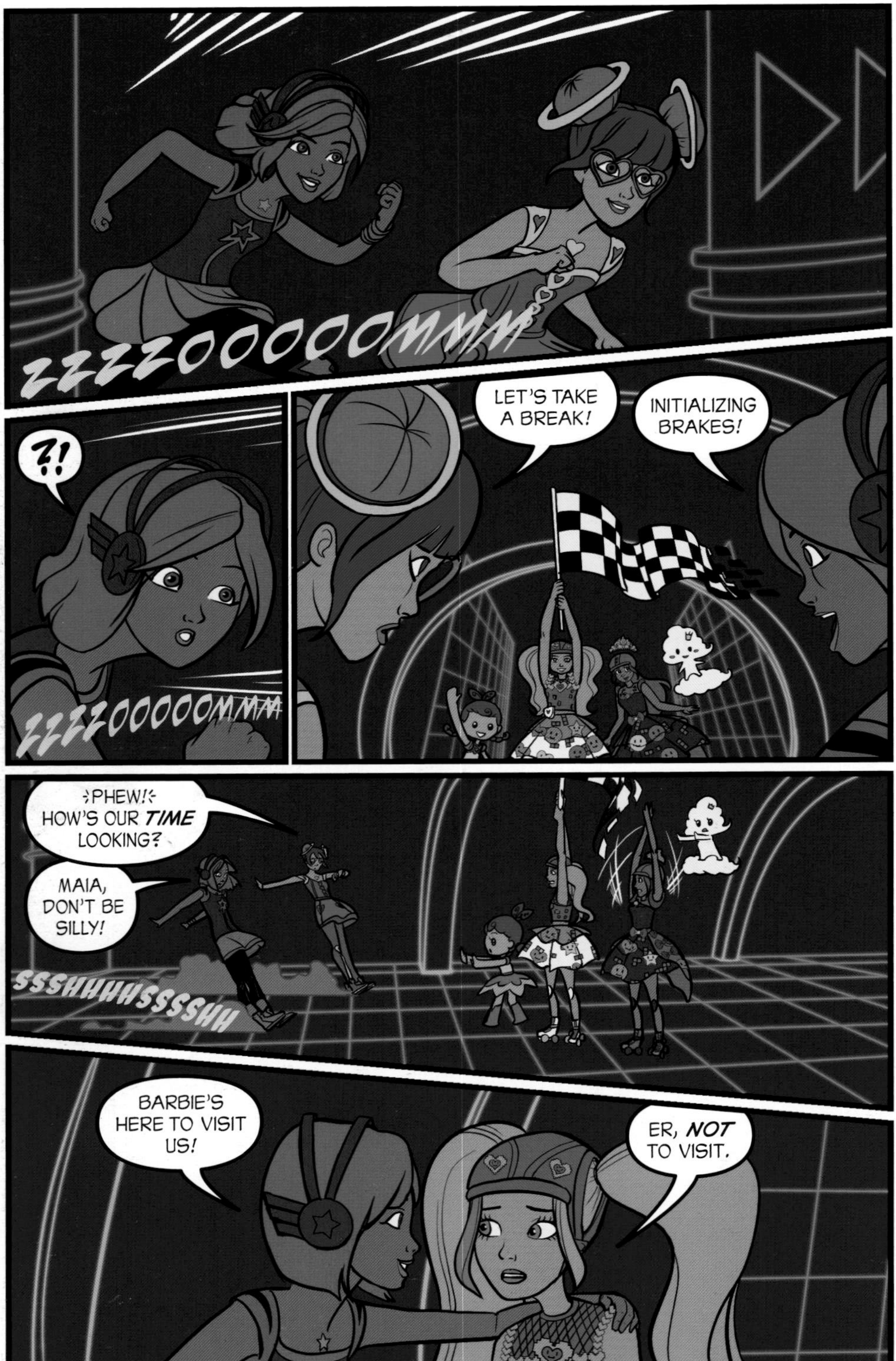
ZZZZOOOOOOMMM
?!
ZZZZOOOOOMMM
LET'S TAKE A BREAK!
INITIALIZING BRAKES!
PHEW! HOW'S OUR *TIME* LOOKING?
MAIA, DON'T BE SILLY!
SSSHHHHSSSSHH
BARBIE'S HERE TO VISIT US!
ER, ***NOT*** TO VISIT.

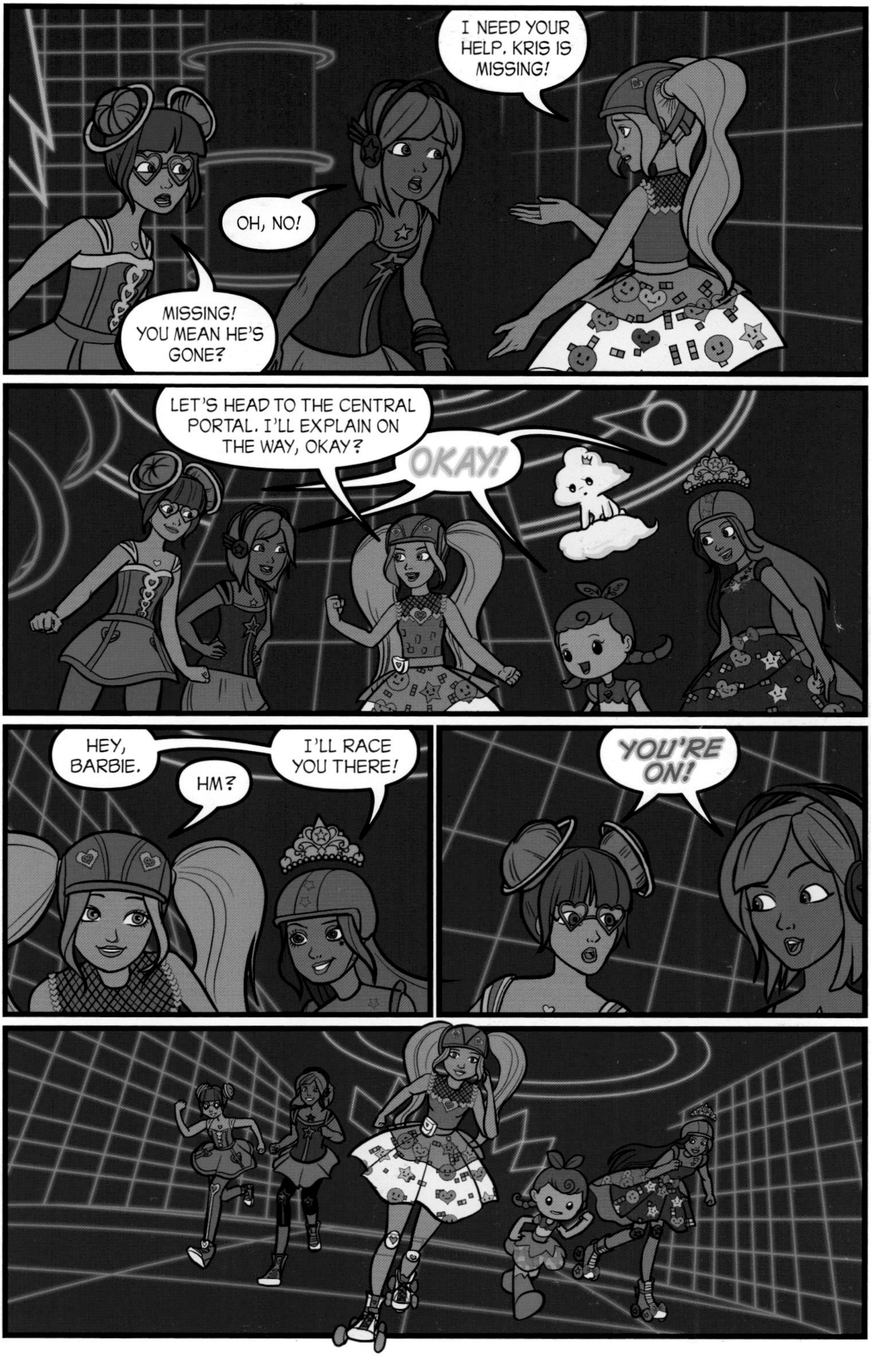
I NEED YOUR HELP. KRIS IS MISSING!
OH, NO!
MISSING! YOU MEAN HE'S GONE?
LET'S HEAD TO THE CENTRAL PORTAL. I'LL EXPLAIN ON THE WAY, OKAY?
OKAY!
HEY, BARBIE.
HM?
I'LL RACE YOU THERE!
YOU'RE ON!

CENTRAL PORTAL. THE TEAM'S SECRET HEADQUARTERS.

OKAY, TEAM, PIPE IN WITH YOUR IDEAS!

CAN YOU CODE A PROJECTION OF THE BOARDWALK, SO WE CAN SEE IT?

AND MAYBE SOME SNACKS?

DONE AND... *DONE!*

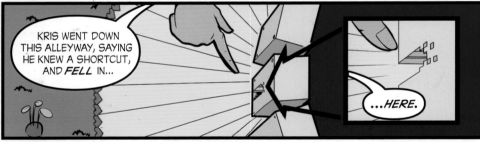

KRIS WENT DOWN THIS ALLEYWAY, SAYING HE KNEW A SHORTCUT, AND *FELL* IN...

...HERE.

KRIS KNEW ABOUT THE SHORTCUT, BUT DID HE KNOW ABOUT THE HOLE?

THAT'S A GOOD POINT. BELLA?

GOSH, I DON'T THINK SO.

IF IT HADN'T BEEN THERE, HE WOULD HAVE COME OUT BY WHERE OUR RACE ENDS. I DON'T THINK HE WAS *TRYING* TO GO THERE.

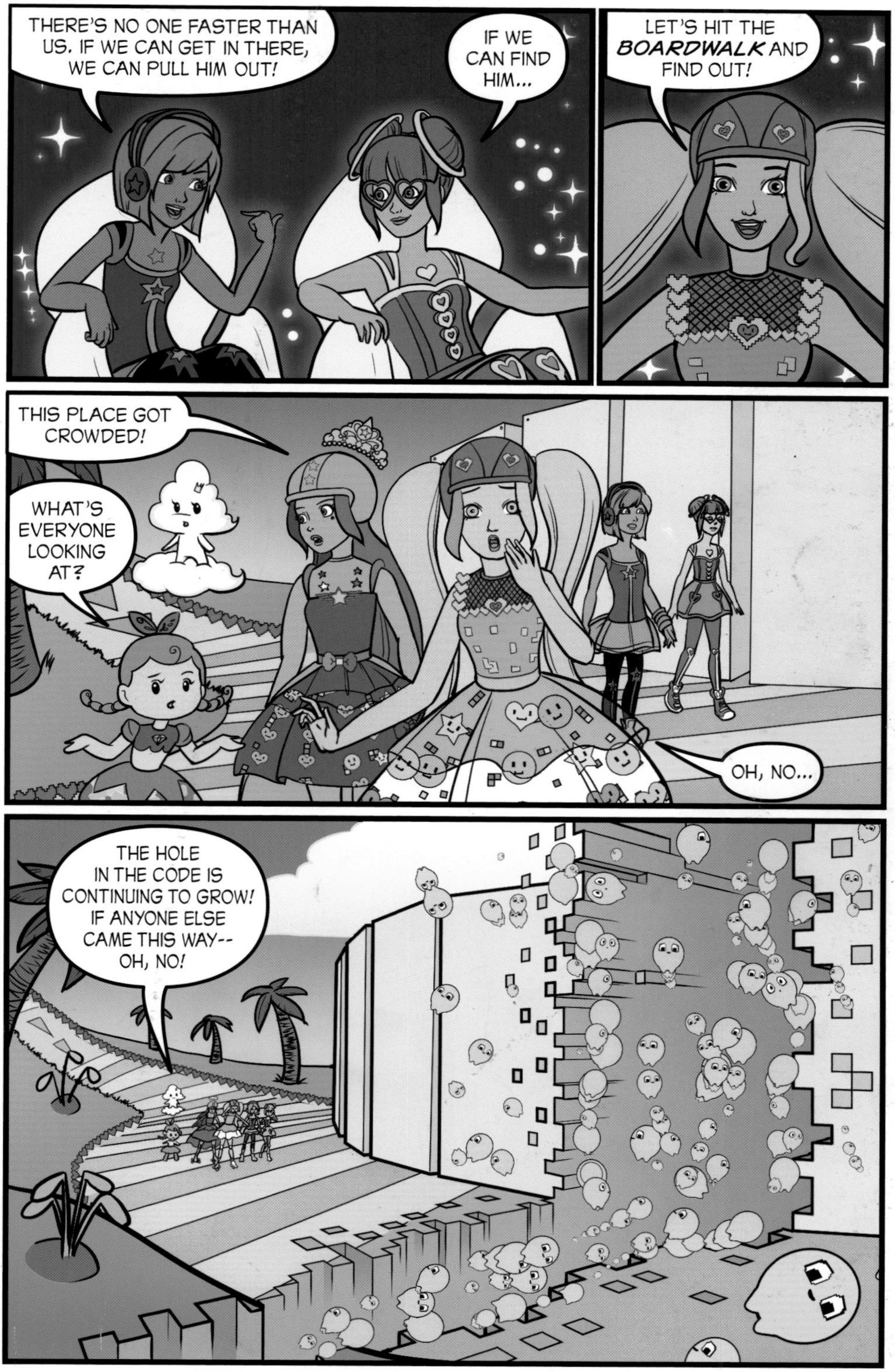
THERE'S NO ONE FASTER THAN US. IF WE CAN GET IN THERE, WE CAN PULL HIM OUT!
IF WE CAN FIND HIM...
LET'S HIT THE *BOARDWALK* AND FIND OUT!
THIS PLACE GOT CROWDED!
WHAT'S EVERYONE LOOKING AT?
OH, NO...
THE HOLE IN THE CODE IS CONTINUING TO GROW! IF ANYONE ELSE CAME THIS WAY-- OH, NO!

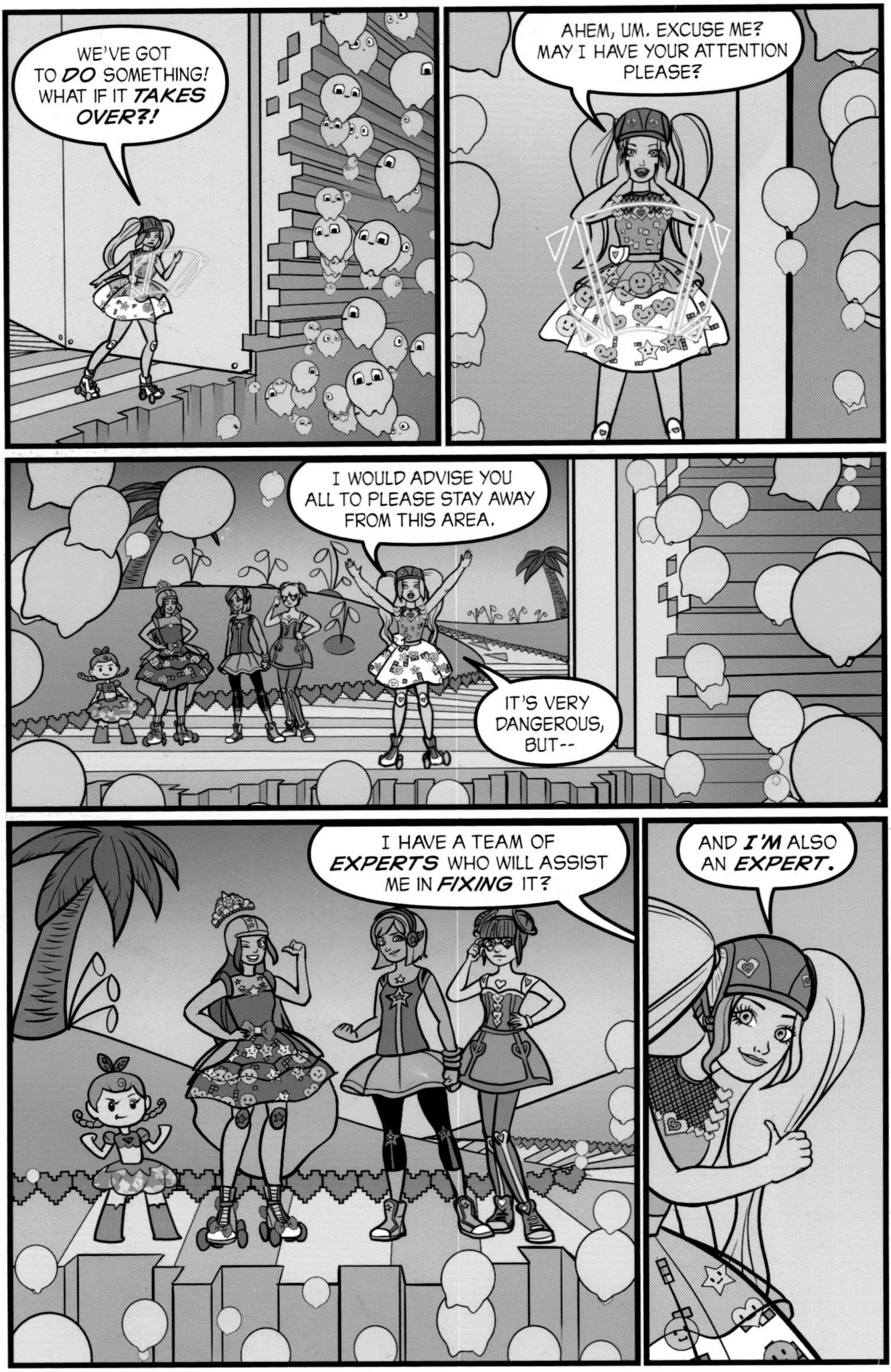
WE'VE GOT TO ***DO*** SOMETHING! WHAT IF IT ***TAKES OVER?!***
AHEM, UM. EXCUSE ME? MAY I HAVE YOUR ATTENTION PLEASE?
I WOULD ADVISE YOU ALL TO PLEASE STAY AWAY FROM THIS AREA.
IT'S VERY DANGEROUS, BUT--
I HAVE A TEAM OF ***EXPERTS*** WHO WILL ASSIST ME IN ***FIXING*** IT?
AND ***I'M*** ALSO AN ***EXPERT.***

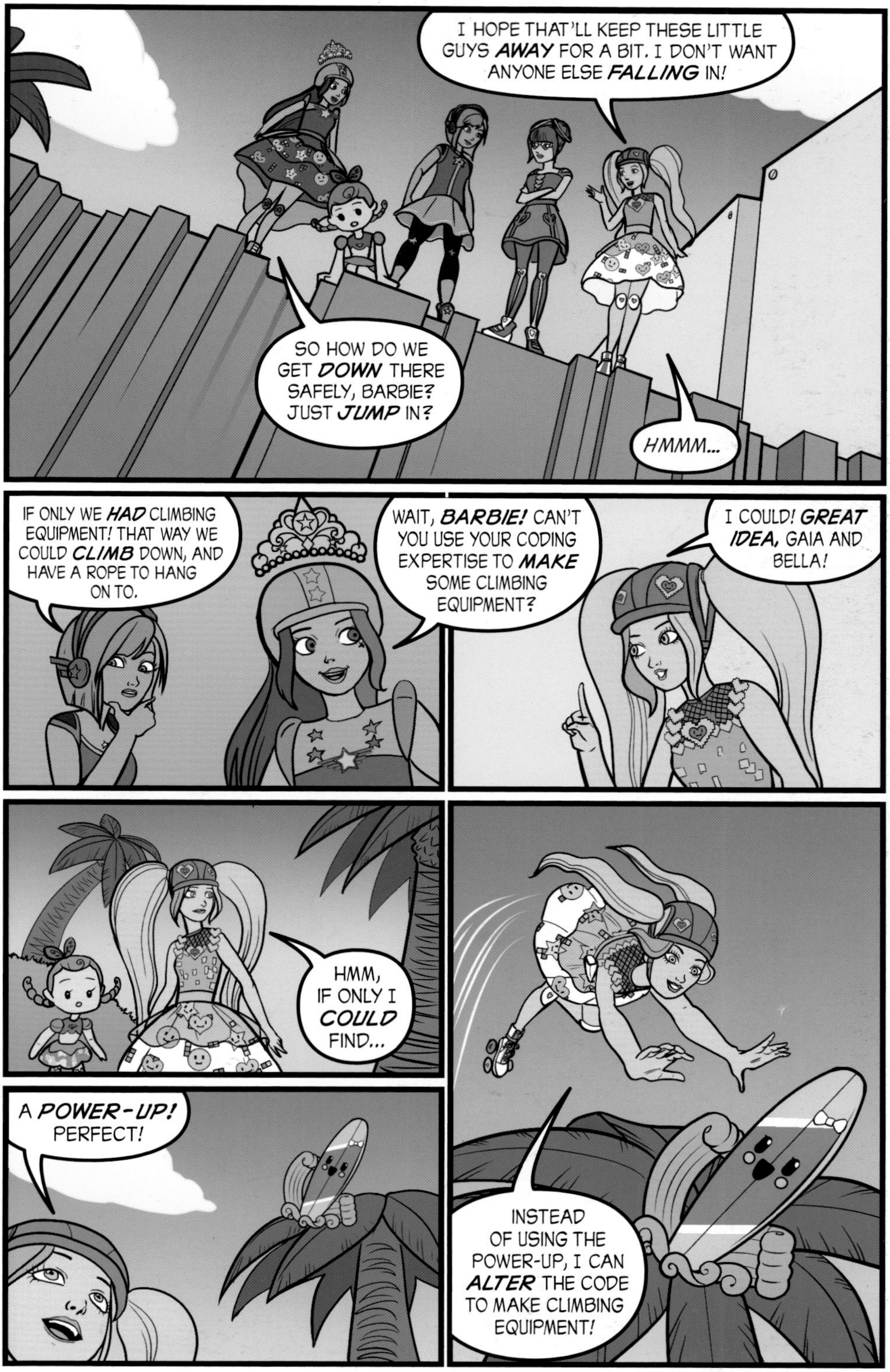
I HOPE THAT'LL KEEP THESE LITTLE GUYS AWAY FOR A BIT. I DON'T WANT ANYONE ELSE FALLING IN!
SO HOW DO WE GET DOWN THERE SAFELY, BARBIE? JUST JUMP IN?
HMMM...
IF ONLY WE HAD CLIMBING EQUIPMENT! THAT WAY WE COULD CLIMB DOWN, AND HAVE A ROPE TO HANG ON TO.
WAIT, BARBIE! CAN'T YOU USE YOUR CODING EXPERTISE TO MAKE SOME CLIMBING EQUIPMENT?
I COULD! GREAT IDEA, GAIA AND BELLA!
HMM, IF ONLY I COULD FIND...
A POWER-UP! PERFECT!
INSTEAD OF USING THE POWER-UP, I CAN ALTER THE CODE TO MAKE CLIMBING EQUIPMENT!

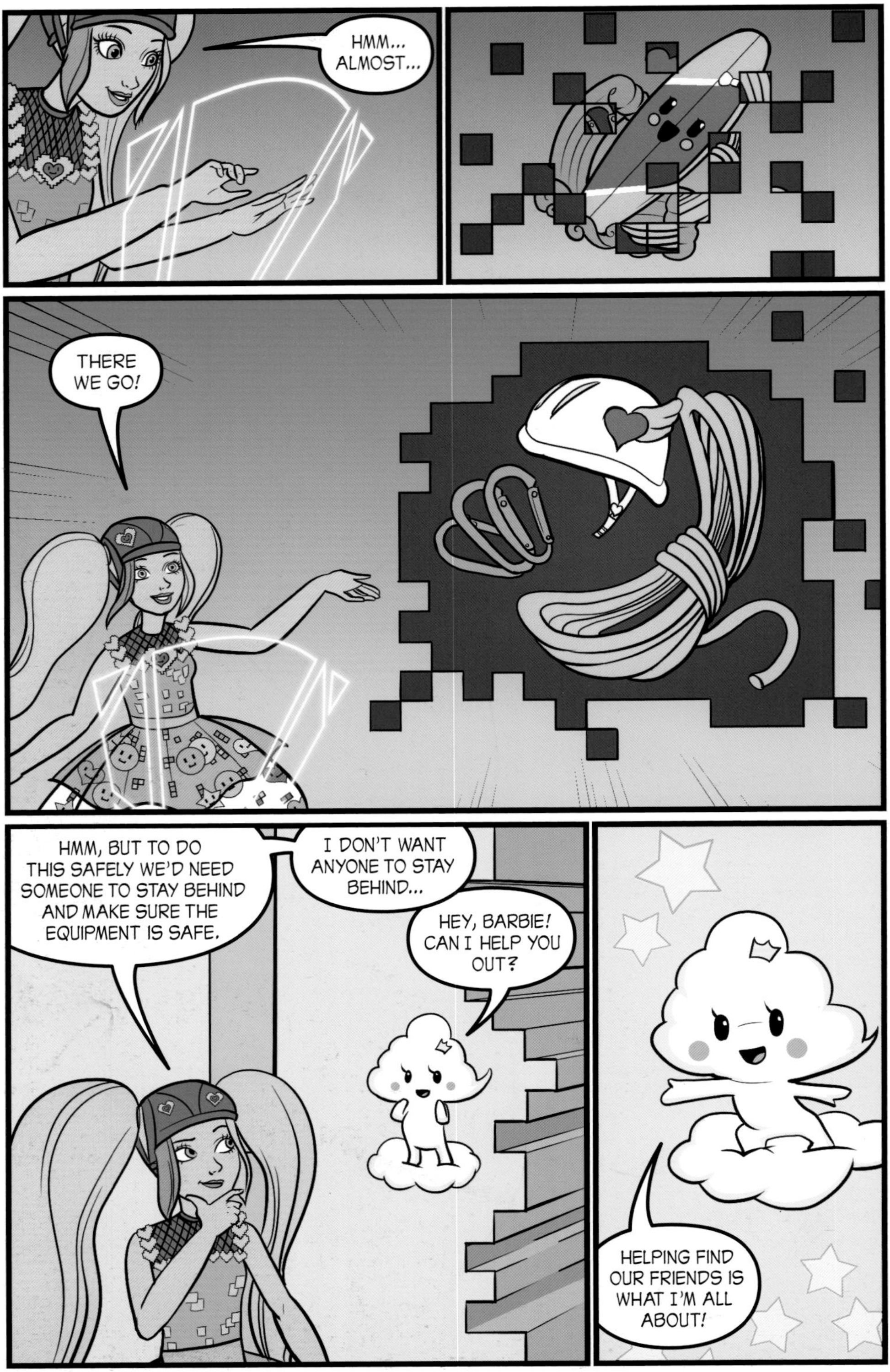
HMM... ALMOST...
THERE WE GO!
HMM, BUT TO DO THIS SAFELY WE'D NEED SOMEONE TO STAY BEHIND AND MAKE SURE THE EQUIPMENT IS SAFE.
I DON'T WANT ANYONE TO STAY BEHIND...
HEY, BARBIE! CAN I HELP YOU OUT?
HELPING FIND OUR FRIENDS IS WHAT I'M ALL ABOUT!

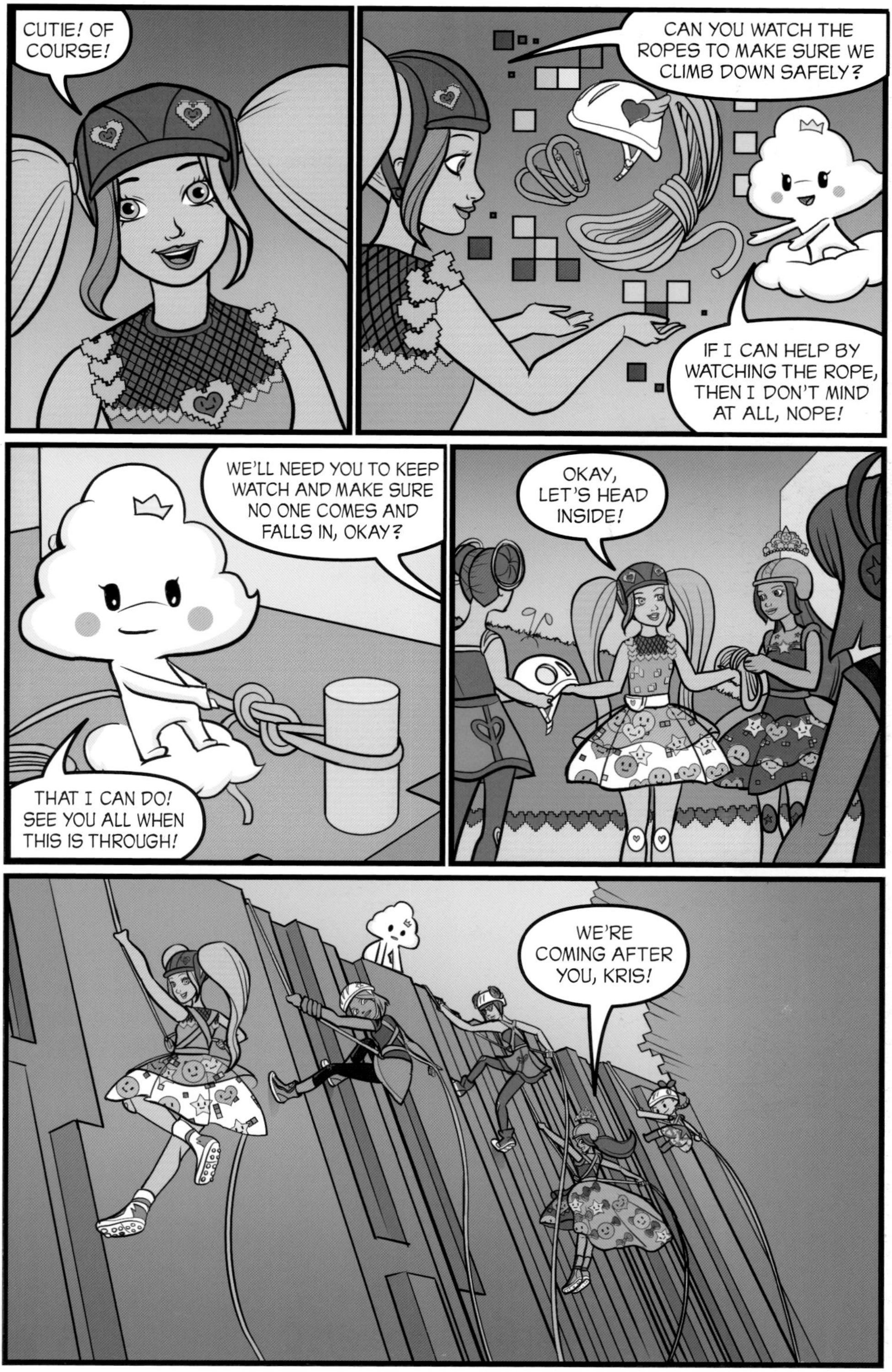
CUTIE! OF COURSE!
CAN YOU WATCH THE ROPES TO MAKE SURE WE CLIMB DOWN SAFELY?
IF I CAN HELP BY WATCHING THE ROPE, THEN I DON'T MIND AT ALL, NOPE!
WE'LL NEED YOU TO KEEP WATCH AND MAKE SURE NO ONE COMES AND FALLS IN, OKAY?
THAT I CAN DO! SEE YOU ALL WHEN THIS IS THROUGH!
OKAY, LET'S HEAD INSIDE!
WE'RE COMING AFTER YOU, KRIS!

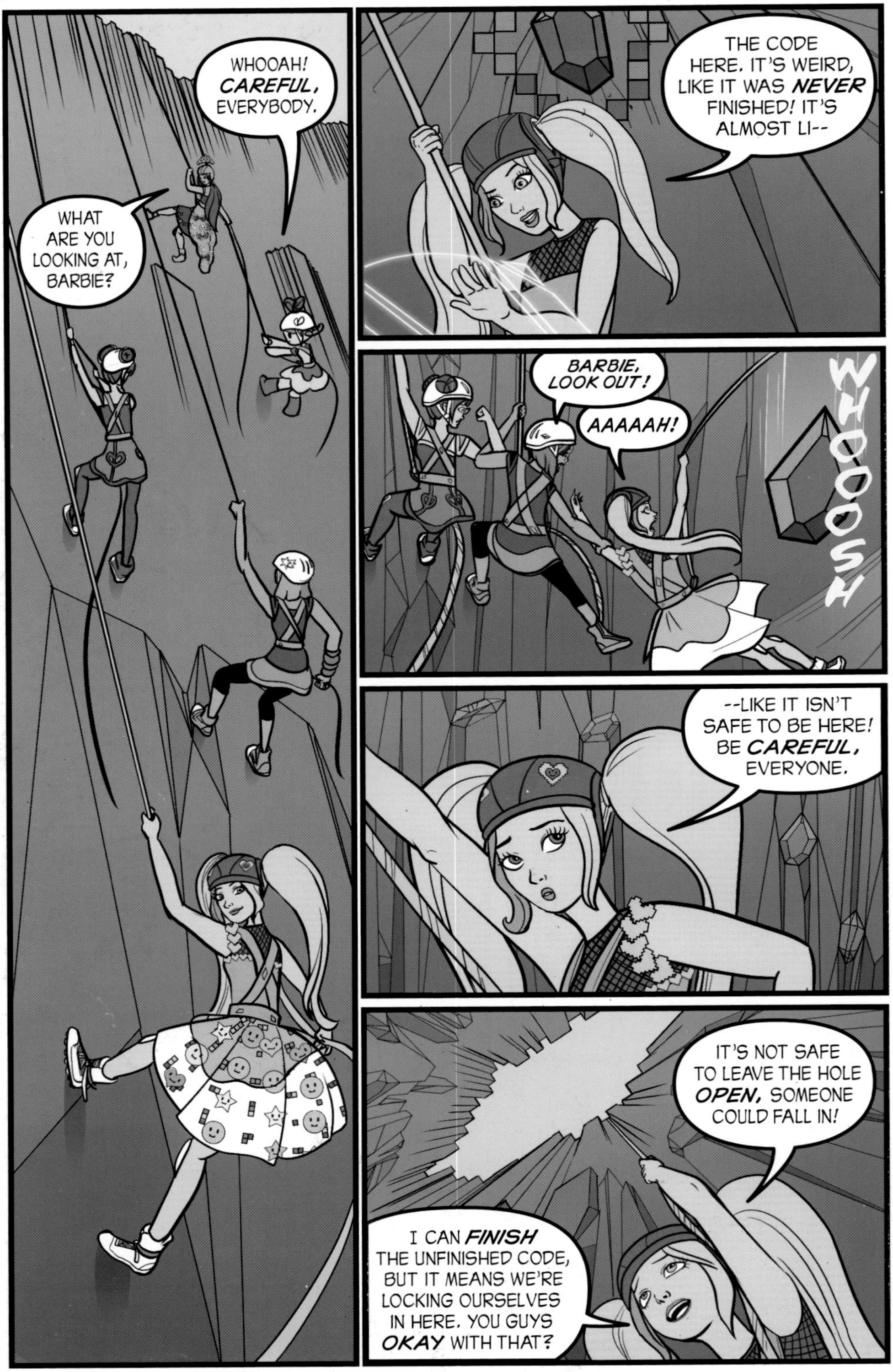
WHOOAH! *CAREFUL,* EVERYBODY.
WHAT ARE YOU LOOKING AT, BARBIE?
THE CODE HERE. IT'S WEIRD, LIKE IT WAS *NEVER* FINISHED! IT'S ALMOST LI--
BARBIE, LOOK OUT!
AAAAAH!
WHOOOOSH
--LIKE IT ISN'T SAFE TO BE HERE! BE *CAREFUL,* EVERYONE.
IT'S NOT SAFE TO LEAVE THE HOLE *OPEN,* SOMEONE COULD FALL IN!
I CAN *FINISH* THE UNFINISHED CODE, BUT IT MEANS WE'RE LOCKING OURSELVES IN HERE. YOU GUYS *OKAY* WITH THAT?

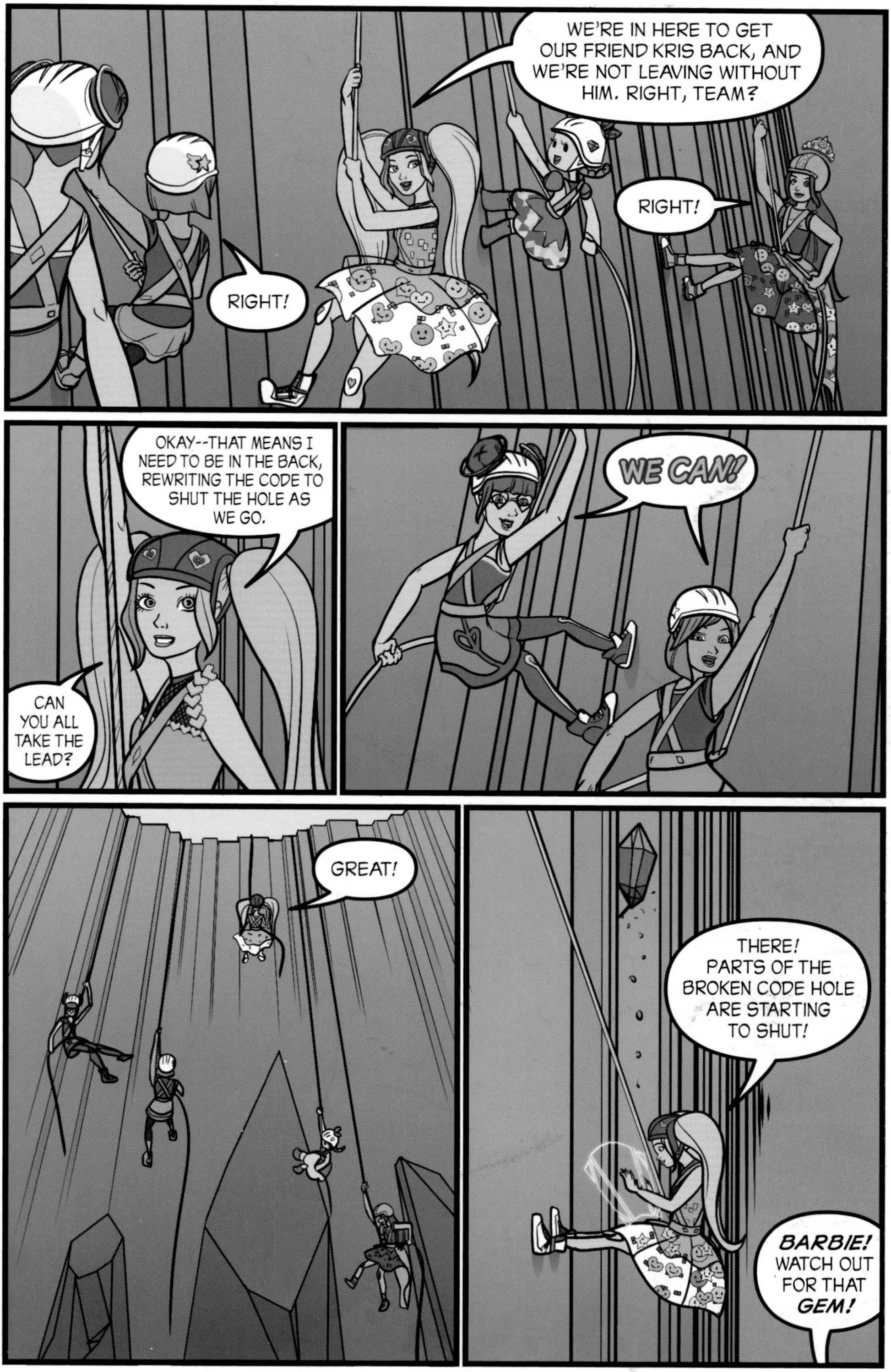
WE'RE IN HERE TO GET OUR FRIEND KRIS BACK, AND WE'RE NOT LEAVING WITHOUT HIM. RIGHT, TEAM?
RIGHT!
RIGHT!
OKAY--THAT MEANS I NEED TO BE IN THE BACK, REWRITING THE CODE TO SHUT THE HOLE AS WE GO.
CAN YOU ALL TAKE THE LEAD?
WE CAN!
GREAT!
THERE! PARTS OF THE BROKEN CODE HOLE ARE STARTING TO SHUT!
BARBIE! WATCH OUT FOR THAT GEM!

GEM?
TRY JELLY INSTEAD!
WHOA!
POWER UP!
NICE!
HERE YOU GO! USE THE SPHERE POWER-UPS TO STOP THE GEM BEFORE THEY GET TO YOU!
BOOP
BOOP
BOOP

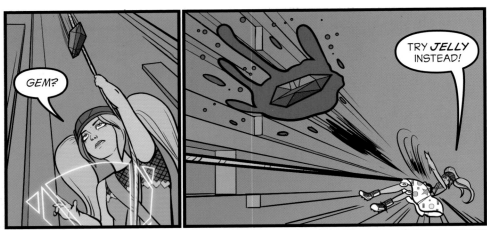

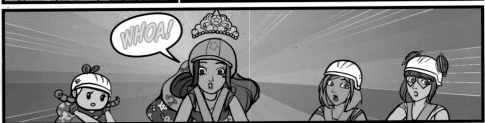

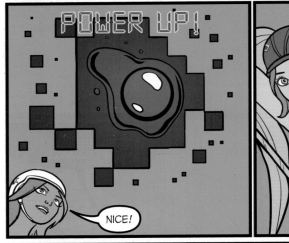

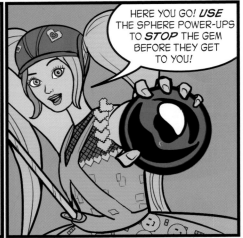

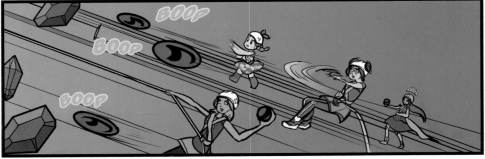

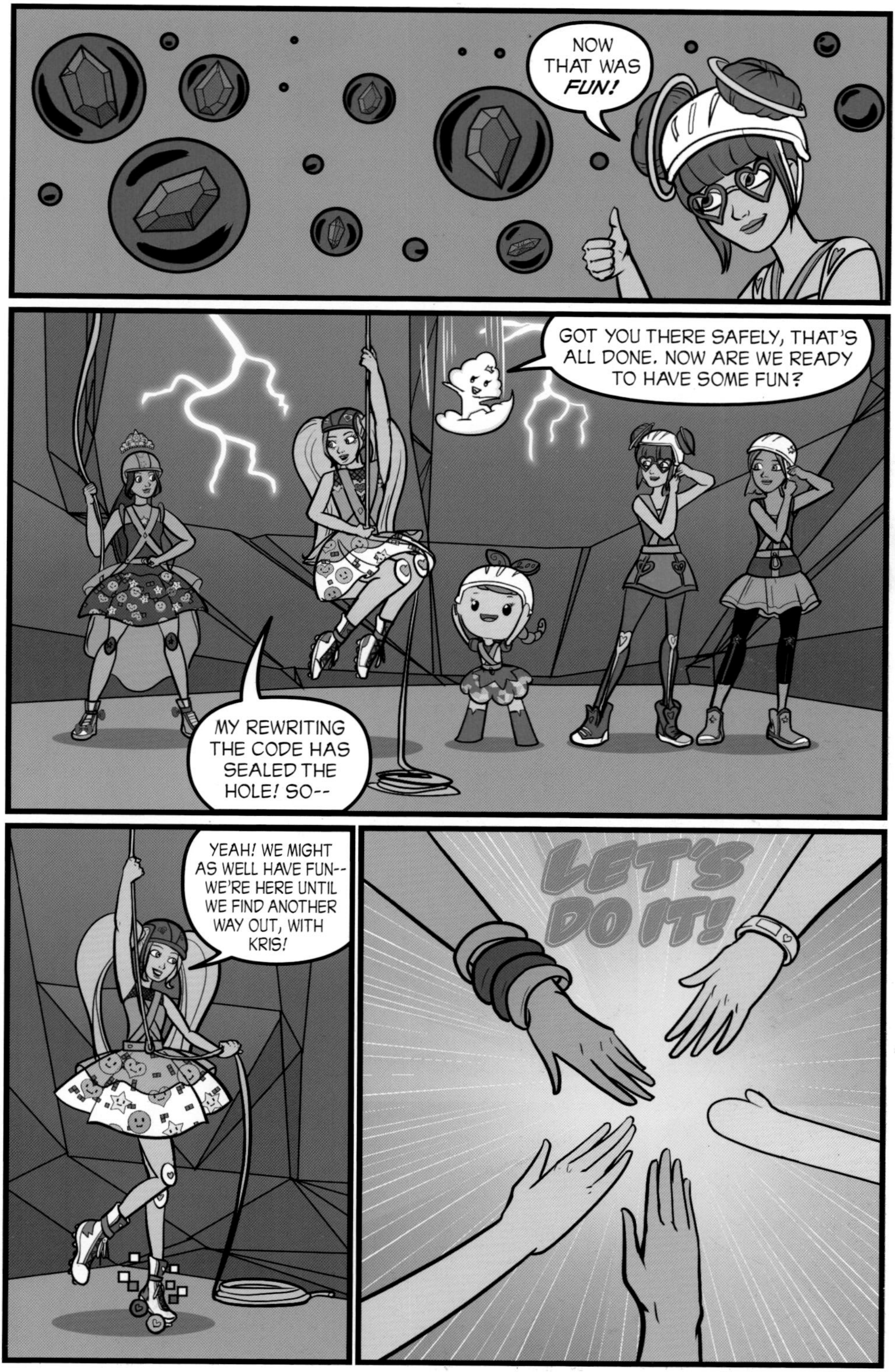
NOW THAT WAS *FUN!*
GOT YOU THERE SAFELY, THAT'S ALL DONE. NOW ARE WE READY TO HAVE SOME FUN?
MY REWRITING THE CODE HAS SEALED THE HOLE! SO--
YEAH! WE MIGHT AS WELL HAVE FUN-- WE'RE HERE UNTIL WE FIND ANOTHER WAY OUT, WITH KRIS!
LET'S DO IT!

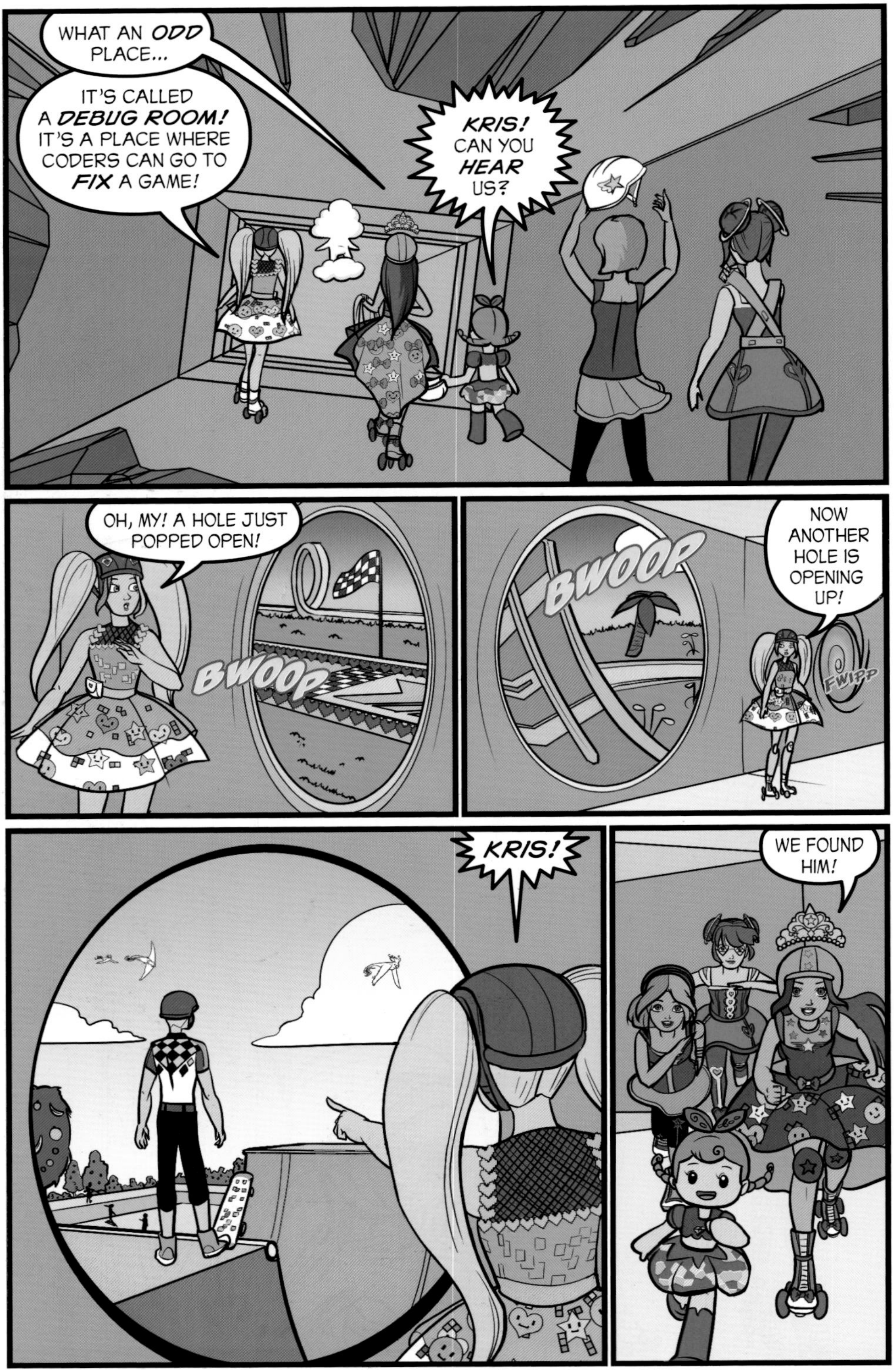
WHAT AN ODD PLACE...
IT'S CALLED A DEBUG ROOM! IT'S A PLACE WHERE CODERS CAN GO TO FIX A GAME!
KRIS! CAN YOU HEAR US?
OH, MY! A HOLE JUST POPPED OPEN!
BWOOP
BWOOP
NOW ANOTHER HOLE IS OPENING UP!
FWIPP
KRIS!
WE FOUND HIM!

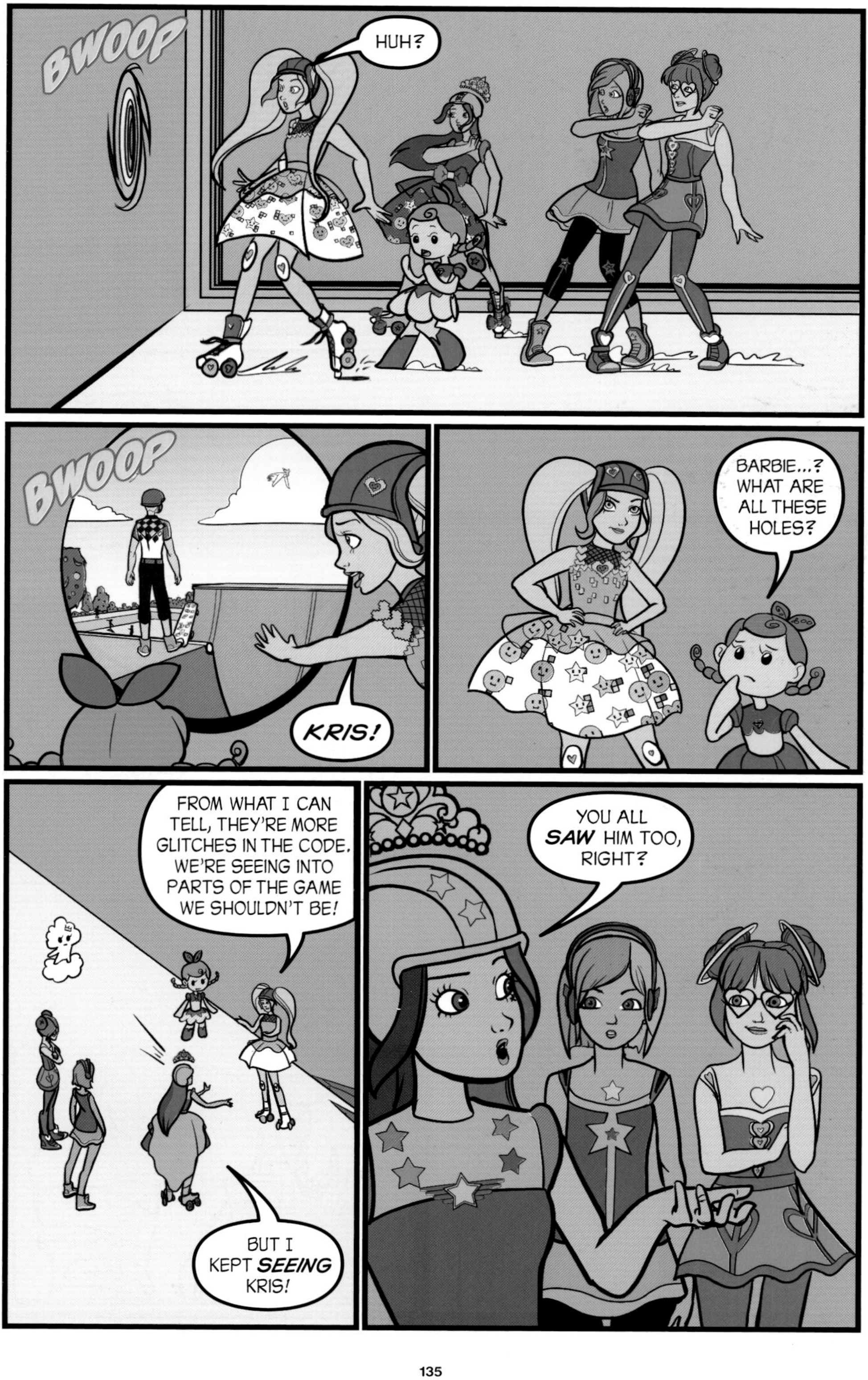
BWOOP
HUH?
BWOOP
KRIS!
BARBIE...? WHAT ARE ALL THESE HOLES?
FROM WHAT I CAN TELL, THEY'RE MORE GLITCHES IN THE CODE. WE'RE SEEING INTO PARTS OF THE GAME WE SHOULDN'T BE!
BUT I KEPT *SEEING* KRIS!
YOU ALL *SAW* HIM TOO, RIGHT?

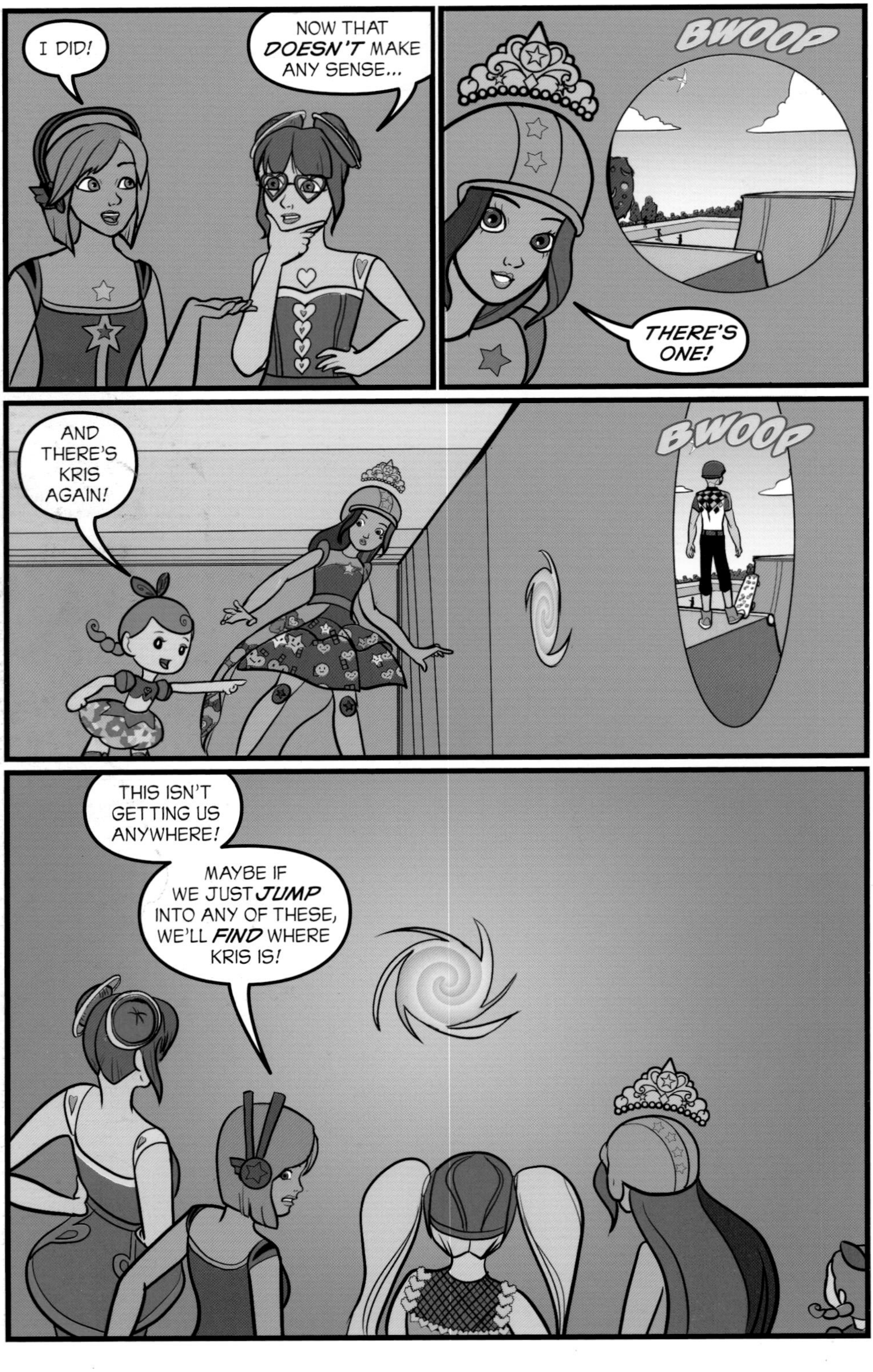
I DID!
NOW THAT DOESN'T MAKE ANY SENSE...
BWOOP
THERE'S ONE!
AND THERE'S KRIS AGAIN!
BWOOP
THIS ISN'T GETTING US ANYWHERE!
MAYBE IF WE JUST JUMP INTO ANY OF THESE, WE'LL FIND WHERE KRIS IS!

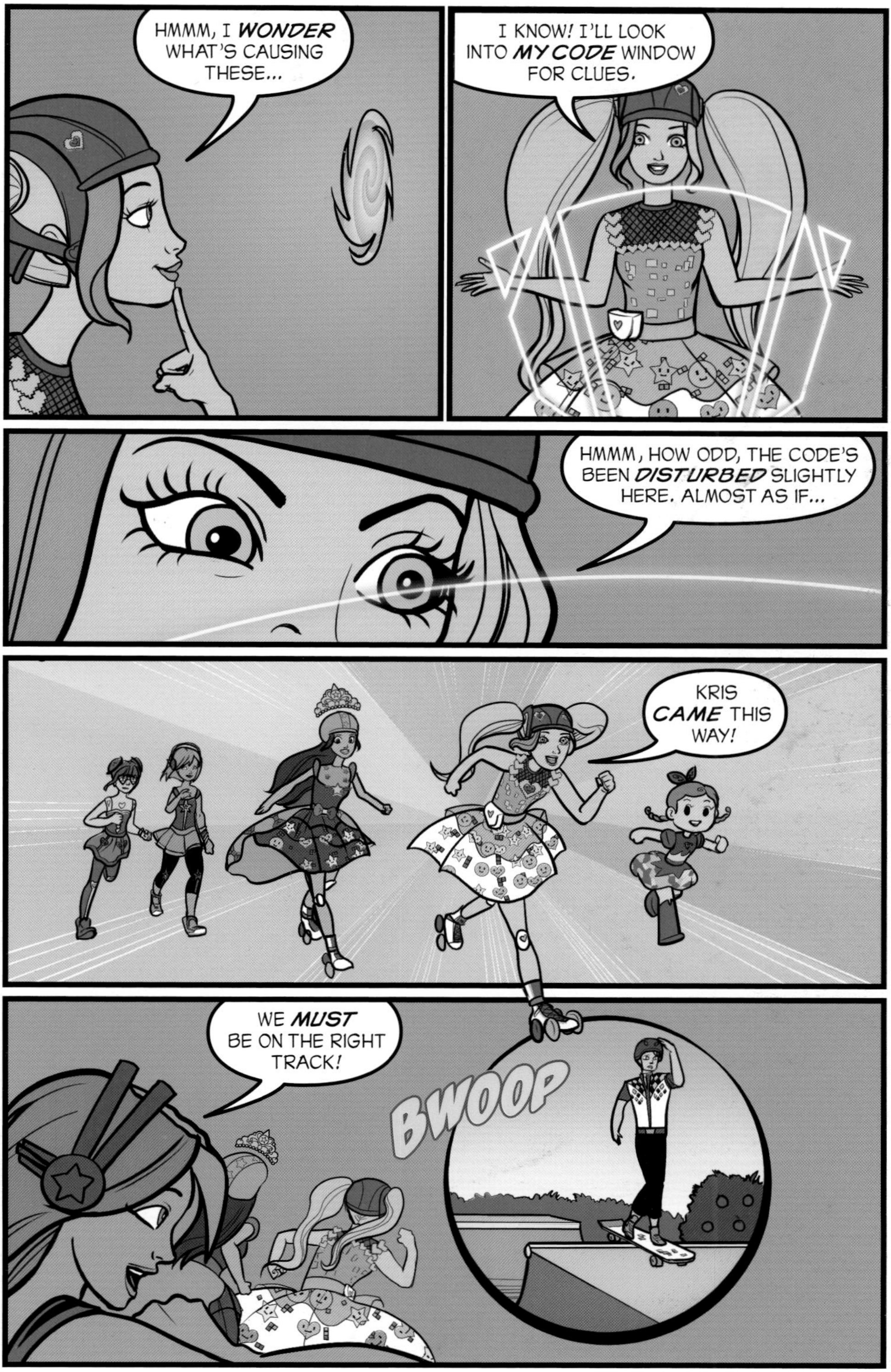
HMMM, I WONDER WHAT'S CAUSING THESE...
I KNOW! I'LL LOOK INTO MY CODE WINDOW FOR CLUES.
HMMM, HOW ODD, THE CODE'S BEEN DISTURBED SLIGHTLY HERE. ALMOST AS IF...
KRIS CAME THIS WAY!
WE MUST BE ON THE RIGHT TRACK!
BWOOP

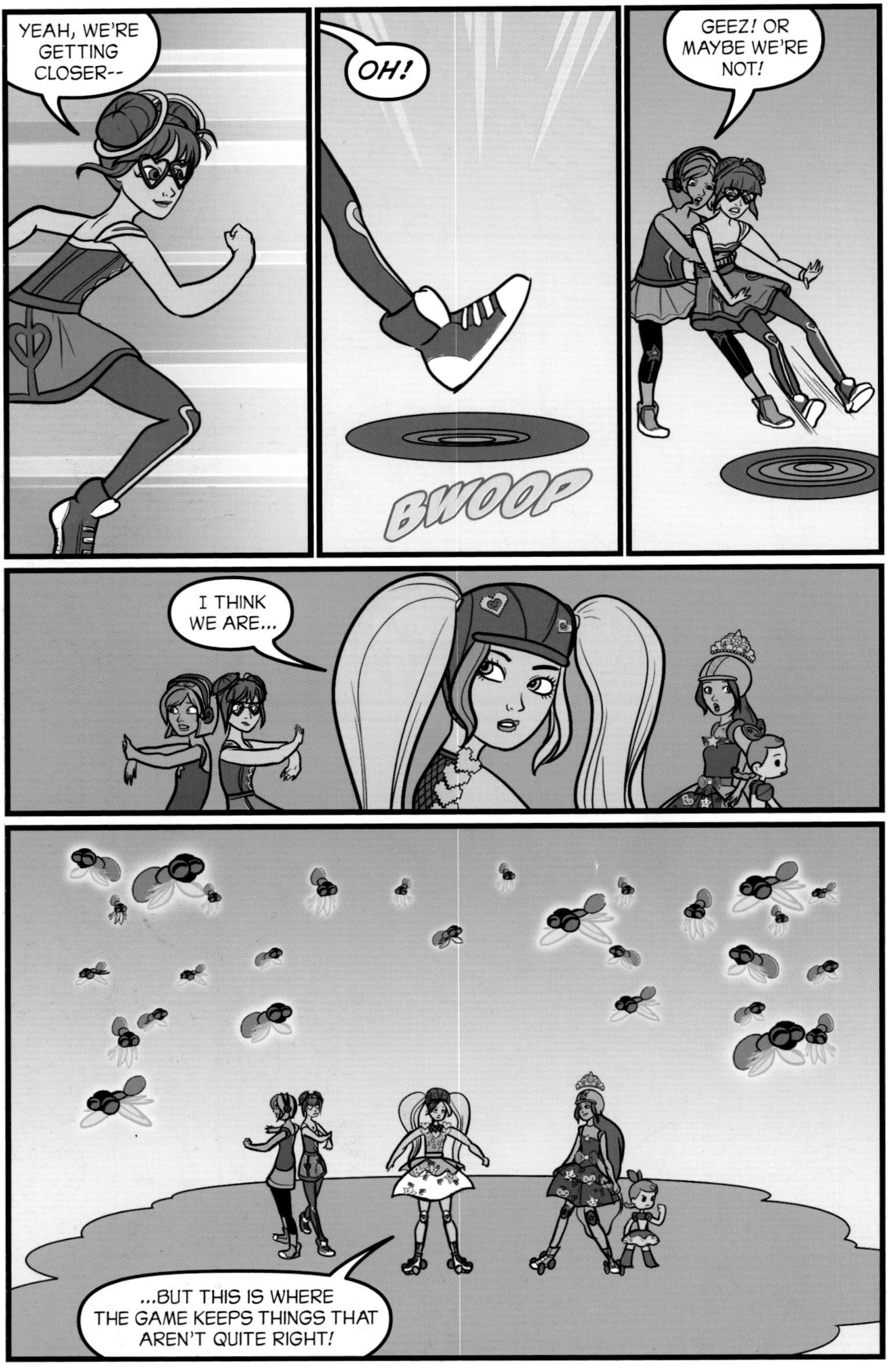
YEAH, WE'RE GETTING CLOSER--
OH!
BWOOP
GEEZ! OR MAYBE WE'RE NOT!
I THINK WE ARE...
...BUT THIS IS WHERE THE GAME KEEPS THINGS THAT AREN'T QUITE RIGHT!

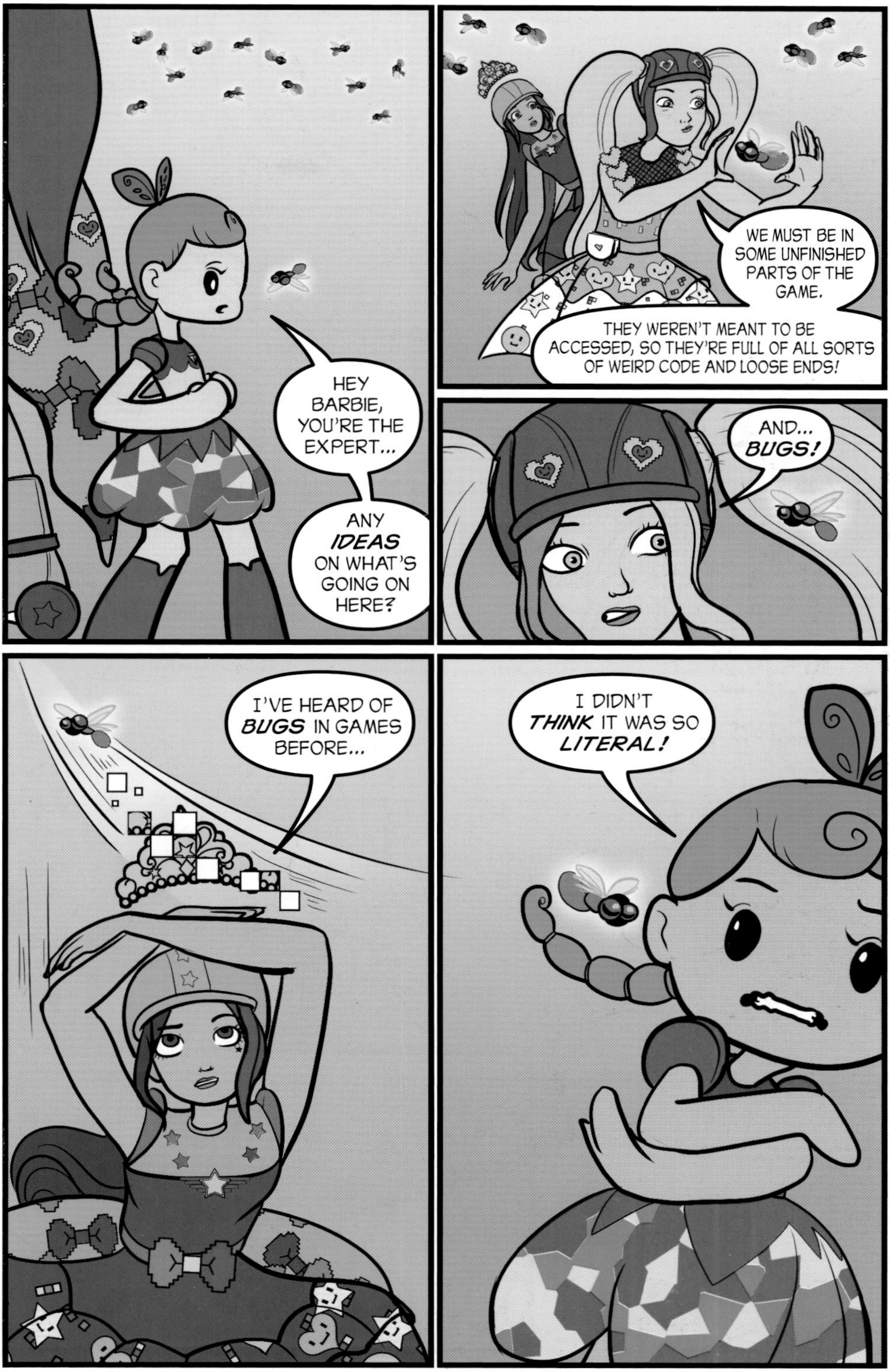
HEY BARBIE, YOU'RE THE EXPERT...
ANY *IDEAS* ON WHAT'S GOING ON HERE?
WE MUST BE IN SOME UNFINISHED PARTS OF THE GAME.
THEY WEREN'T MEANT TO BE ACCESSED, SO THEY'RE FULL OF ALL SORTS OF WEIRD CODE AND LOOSE ENDS!
AND... *BUGS!*
I'VE HEARD OF *BUGS* IN GAMES BEFORE...
I DIDN'T *THINK* IT WAS SO *LITERAL!*

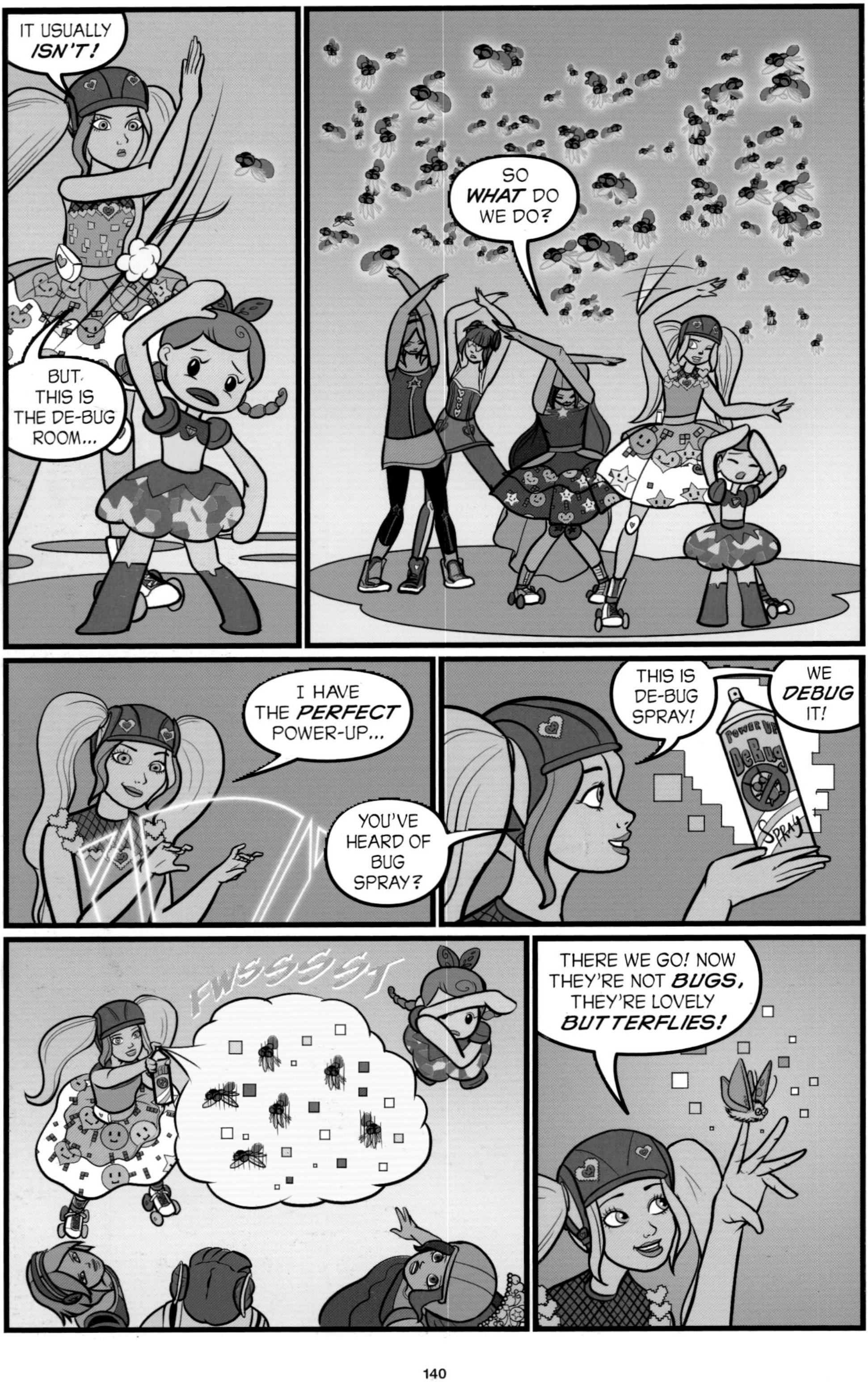
IT USUALLY ISN'T!
BUT THIS IS THE DE-BUG ROOM...
SO WHAT DO WE DO?
I HAVE THE PERFECT POWER-UP...
YOU'VE HEARD OF BUG SPRAY?
THIS IS DE-BUG SPRAY!
WE DEBUG IT!
POWER UP DEBUG SPRAY
FWSSSST
THERE WE GO! NOW THEY'RE NOT BUGS, THEY'RE LOVELY BUTTERFLIES!

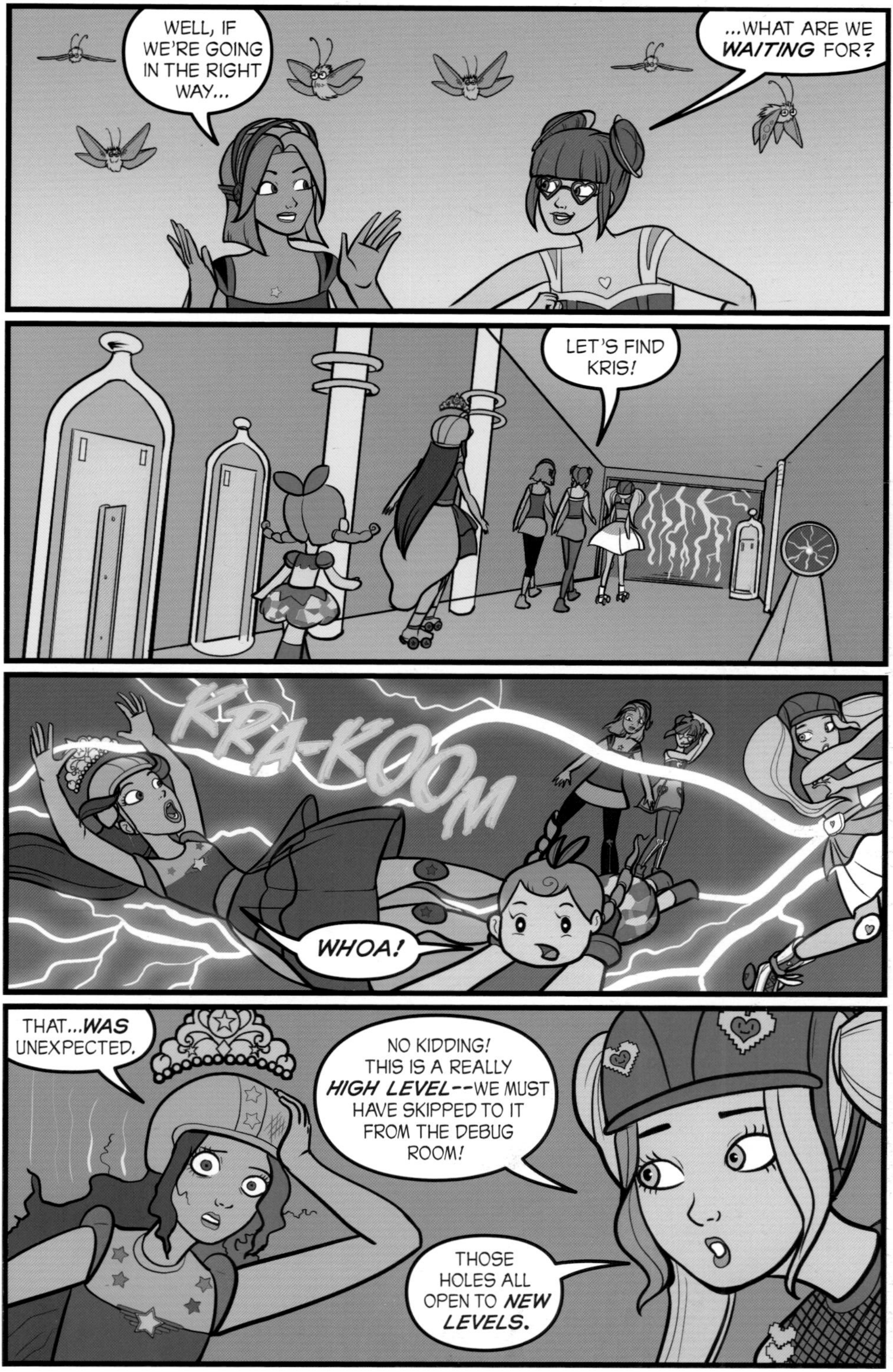
WELL, IF WE'RE GOING IN THE RIGHT WAY...
...WHAT ARE WE *WAITING* FOR?
LET'S FIND KRIS!
KRA-KOOM
WHOA!
THAT...*WAS* UNEXPECTED.
NO KIDDING! THIS IS A REALLY *HIGH LEVEL*--WE MUST HAVE SKIPPED TO IT FROM THE DEBUG ROOM!
THOSE HOLES ALL OPEN TO *NEW LEVELS*.

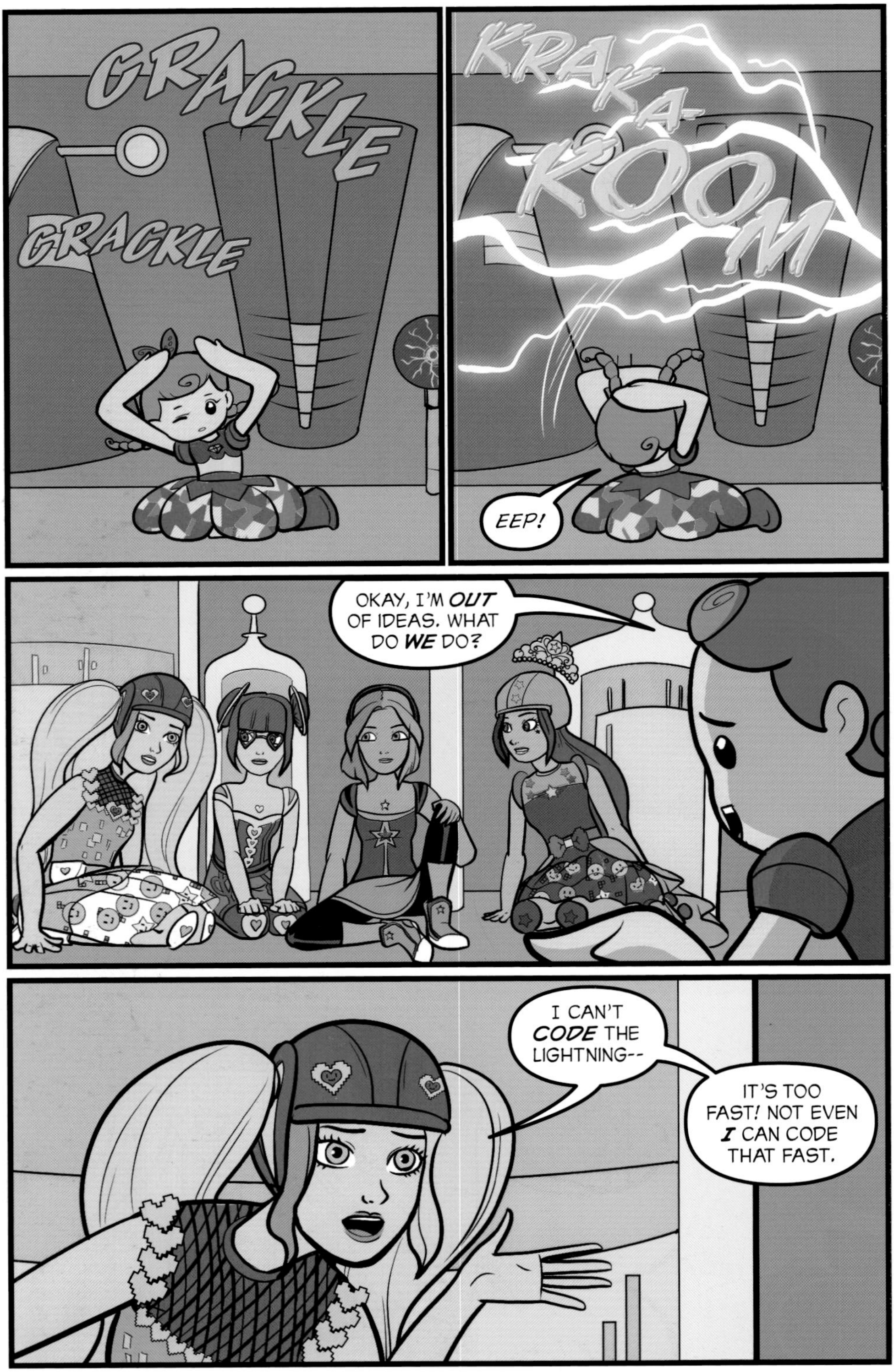
CRACKLE
CRACKLE
KRAKA-KOOM
EEP!
OKAY, I'M OUT OF IDEAS. WHAT DO WE DO?
I CAN'T CODE THE LIGHTNING--
IT'S TOO FAST! NOT EVEN I CAN CODE THAT FAST.

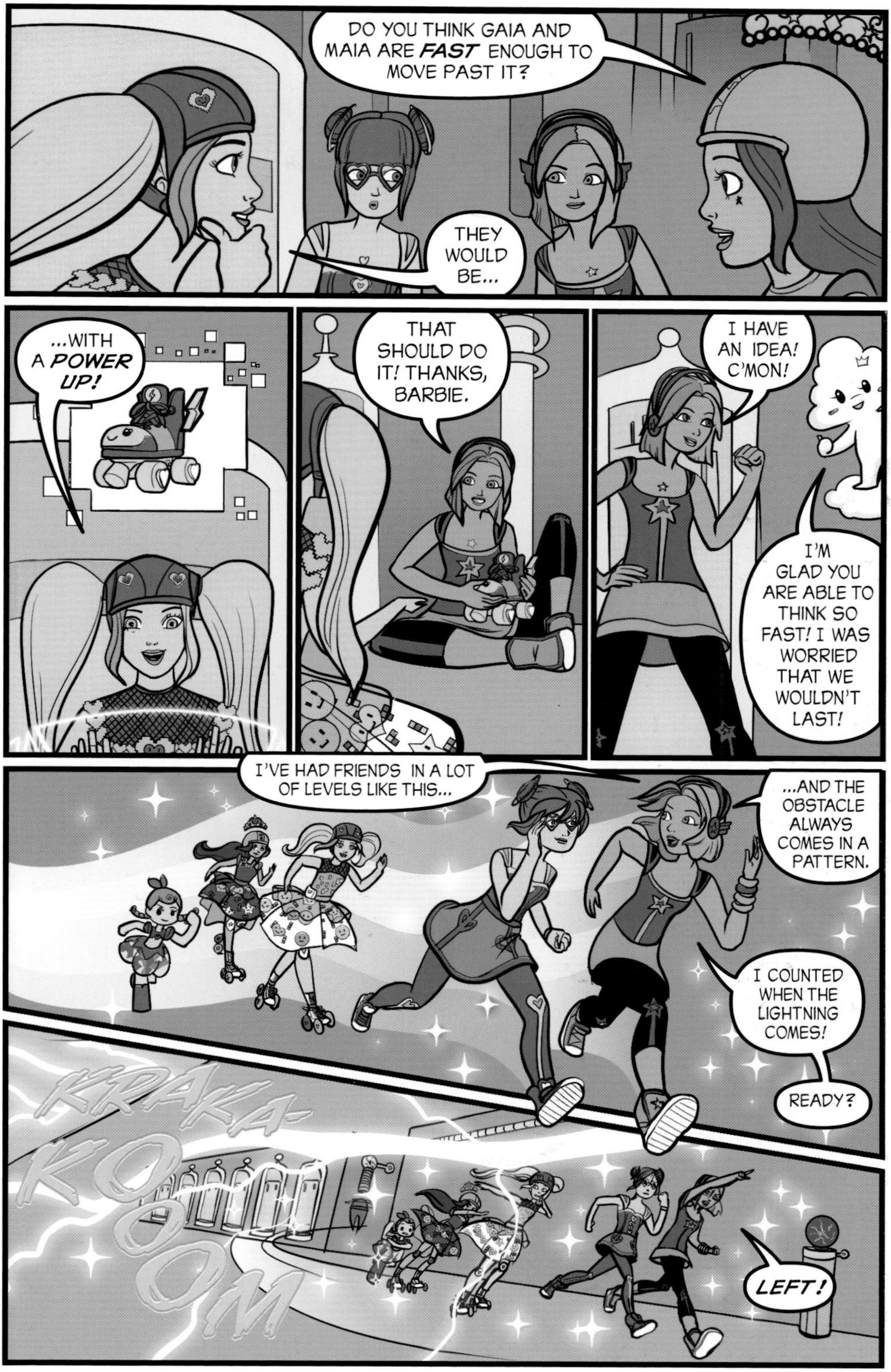
DO YOU THINK GAIA AND MAIA ARE *FAST* ENOUGH TO MOVE PAST IT?
THEY WOULD BE...
...WITH A *POWER UP!*
THAT SHOULD DO IT! THANKS, BARBIE.
I HAVE AN IDEA! C'MON!
I'M GLAD YOU ARE ABLE TO THINK SO FAST! I WAS WORRIED THAT WE WOULDN'T LAST!
I'VE HAD FRIENDS IN A LOT OF LEVELS LIKE THIS...
...AND THE OBSTACLE ALWAYS COMES IN A PATTERN.
I COUNTED WHEN THE LIGHTNING COMES!
READY?
KRAKA-KOOOM
LEFT!

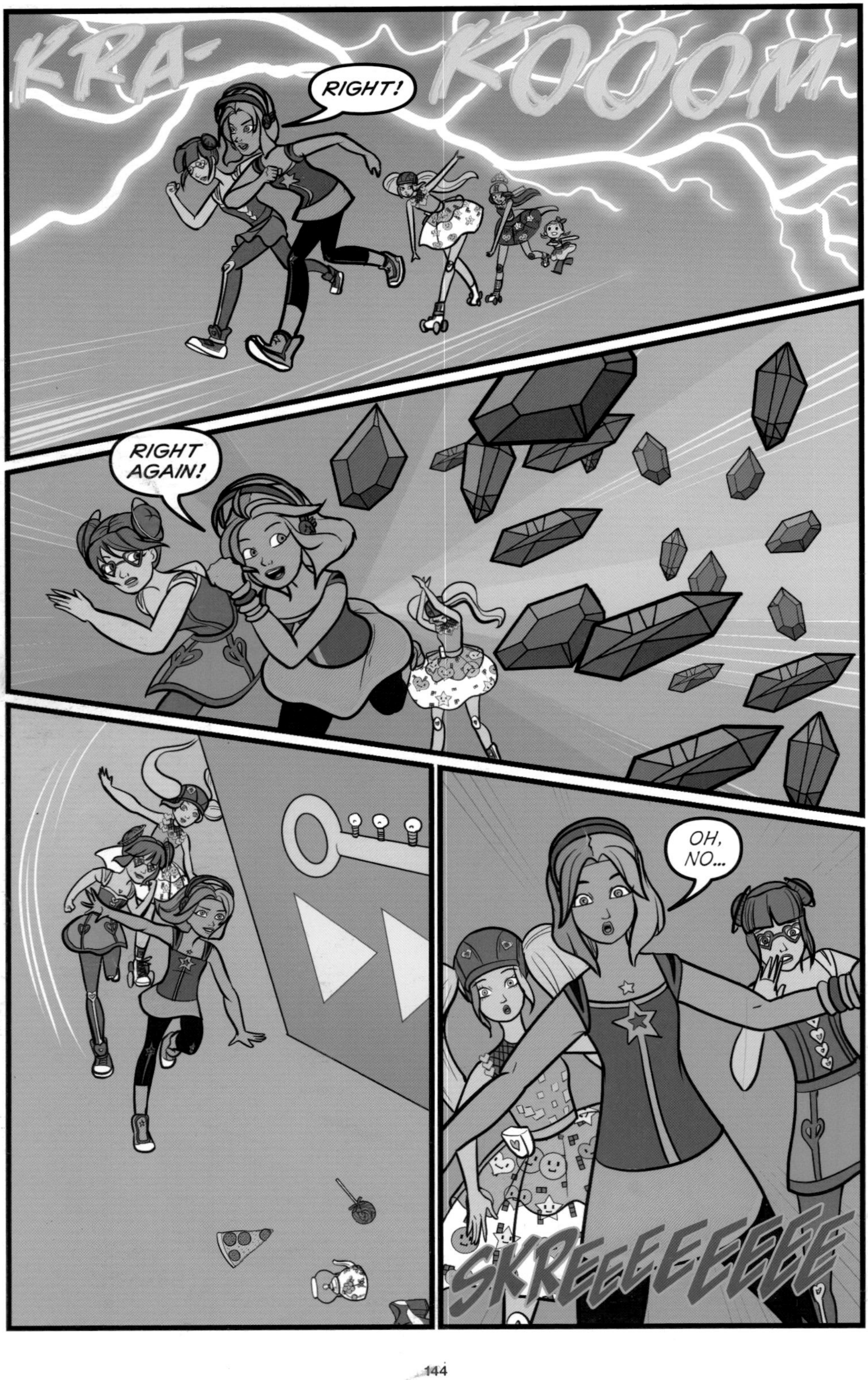
KRA-KOOOM
RIGHT!
RIGHT AGAIN!
OH, NO...
SKREEEEEEEE

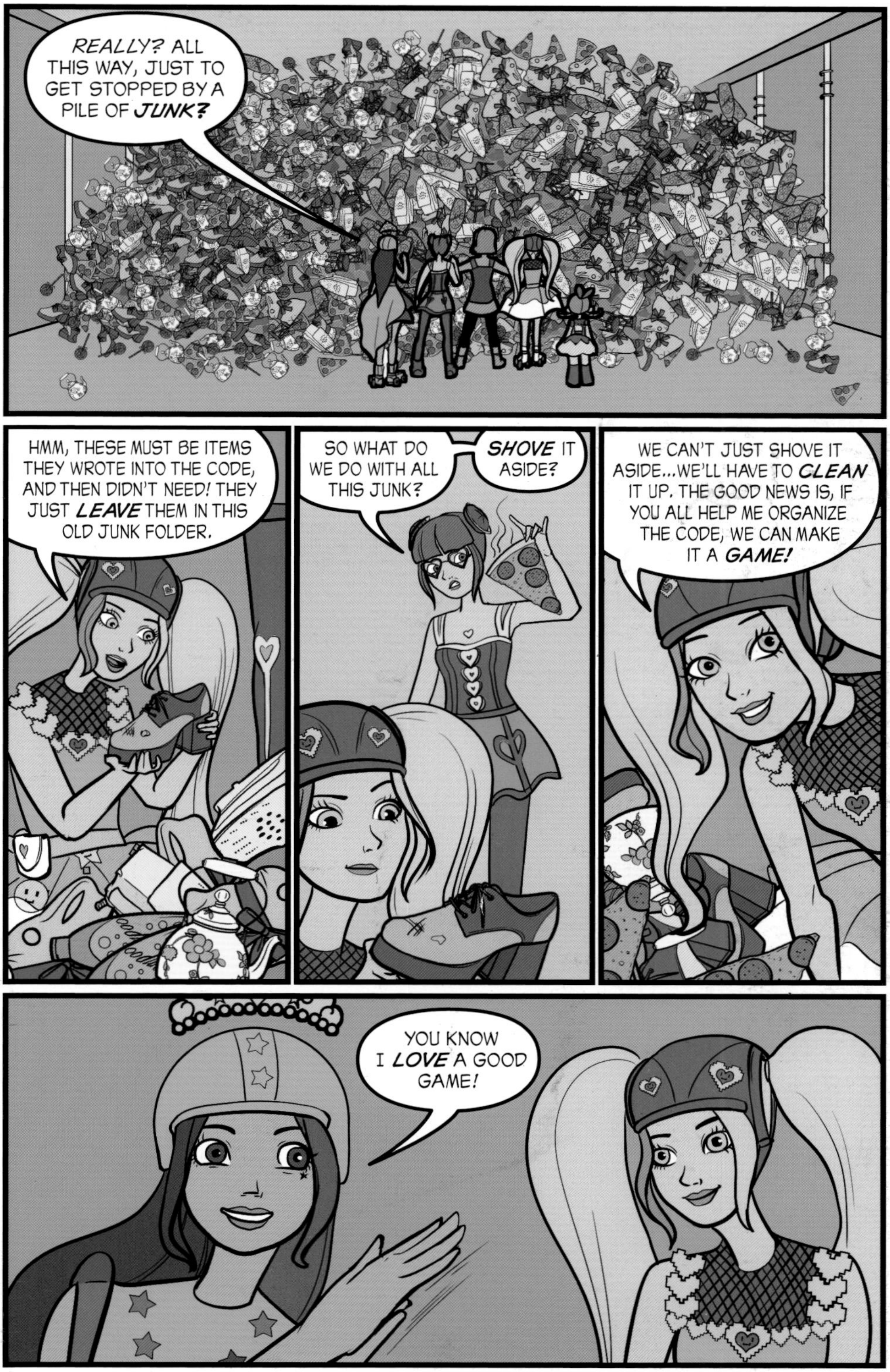
REALLY? ALL THIS WAY, JUST TO GET STOPPED BY A PILE OF JUNK?
HMM, THESE MUST BE ITEMS THEY WROTE INTO THE CODE, AND THEN DIDN'T NEED! THEY JUST LEAVE THEM IN THIS OLD JUNK FOLDER.
SO WHAT DO WE DO WITH ALL THIS JUNK?
SHOVE IT ASIDE?
WE CAN'T JUST SHOVE IT ASIDE...WE'LL HAVE TO CLEAN IT UP. THE GOOD NEWS IS, IF YOU ALL HELP ME ORGANIZE THE CODE, WE CAN MAKE IT A GAME!
YOU KNOW I LOVE A GOOD GAME!

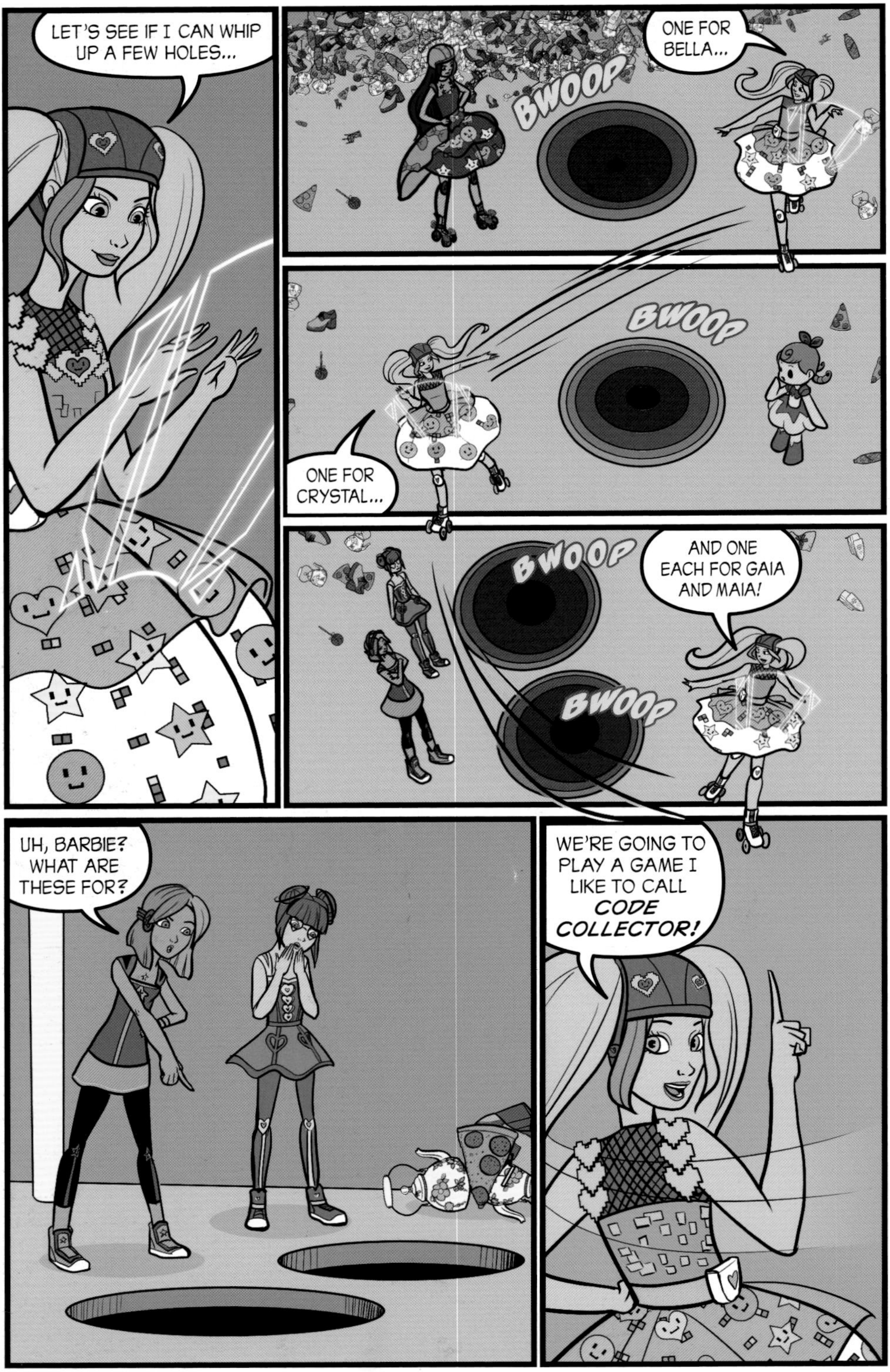
LET'S SEE IF I CAN WHIP UP A FEW HOLES...
ONE FOR BELLA...
BWOOP
BWOOP
ONE FOR CRYSTAL...
BWOOP
AND ONE EACH FOR GAIA AND MAIA!
BWOOP
UH, BARBIE? WHAT ARE THESE FOR?
WE'RE GOING TO PLAY A GAME I LIKE TO CALL *CODE COLLECTOR!*

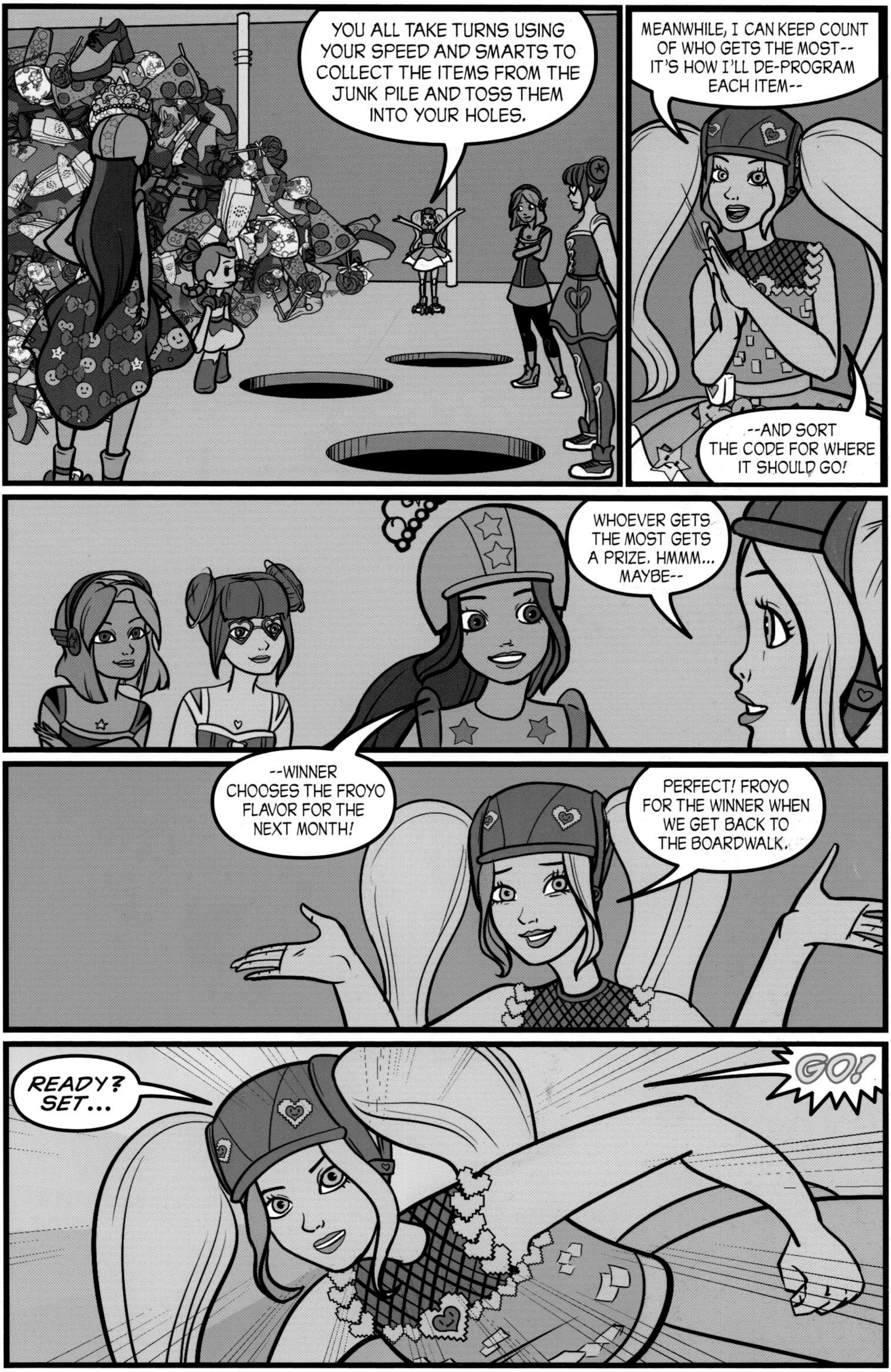

YOU ALL TAKE TURNS USING YOUR SPEED AND SMARTS TO COLLECT THE ITEMS FROM THE JUNK PILE AND TOSS THEM INTO YOUR HOLES.
MEANWHILE, I CAN KEEP COUNT OF WHO GETS THE MOST-- IT'S HOW I'LL DE-PROGRAM EACH ITEM--
--AND SORT THE CODE FOR WHERE IT SHOULD GO!
WHOEVER GETS THE MOST GETS A PRIZE. HMMM... MAYBE--
--WINNER CHOOSES THE FROYO FLAVOR FOR THE NEXT MONTH!
PERFECT! FROYO FOR THE WINNER WHEN WE GET BACK TO THE BOARDWALK.
READY? SET...
GO!

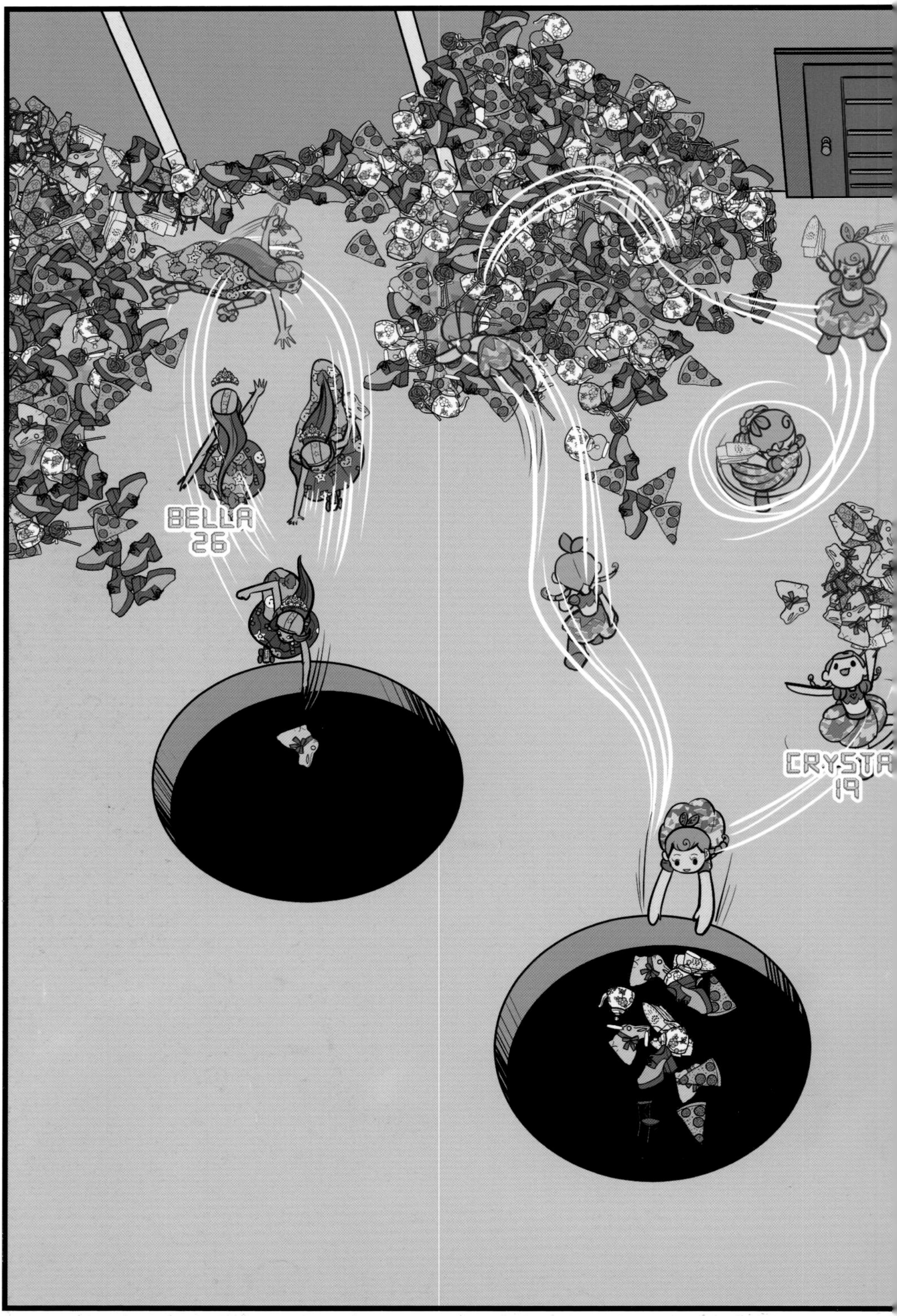
BELLA
26
CRYSTA
19

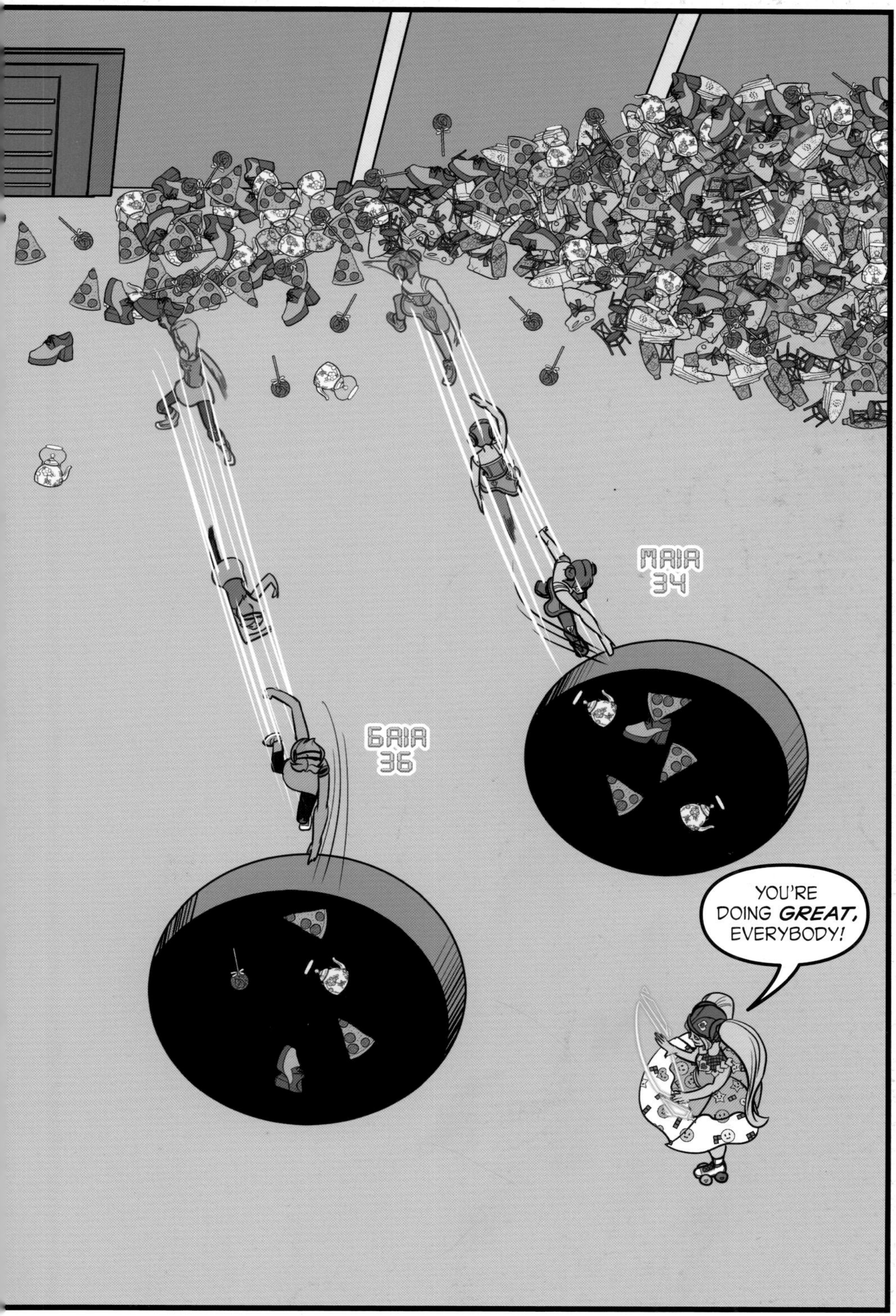
MAIA
34
GAIA
36
YOU'RE DOING **GREAT,** EVERYBODY!

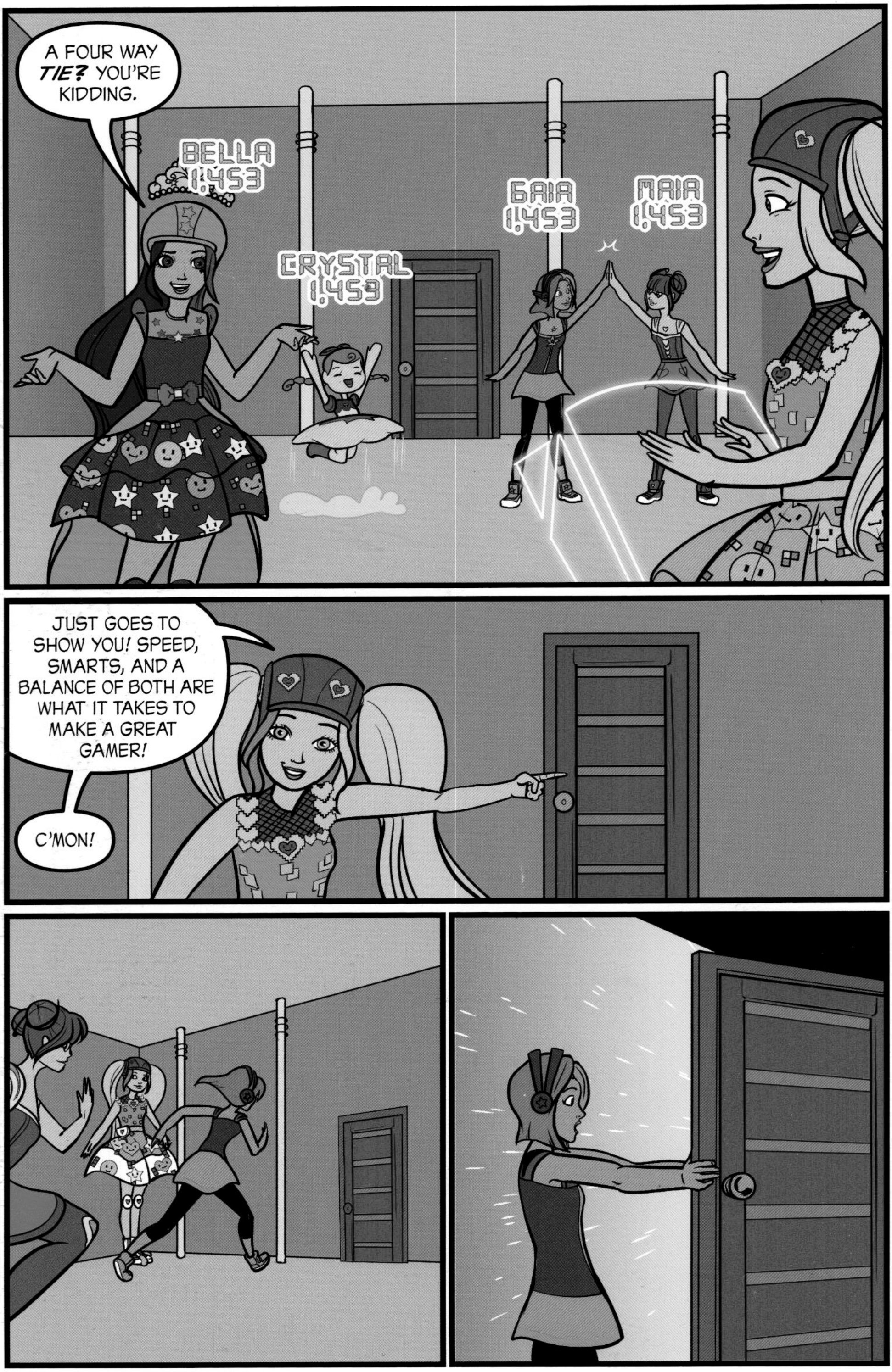
A FOUR WAY *TIE?* YOU'RE KIDDING.
BELLA 1.453
CRYSTAL 1.453
GAIA 1.453
MAIA 1.453
JUST GOES TO SHOW YOU! SPEED, SMARTS, AND A BALANCE OF BOTH ARE WHAT IT TAKES TO MAKE A GREAT GAMER!
C'MON!

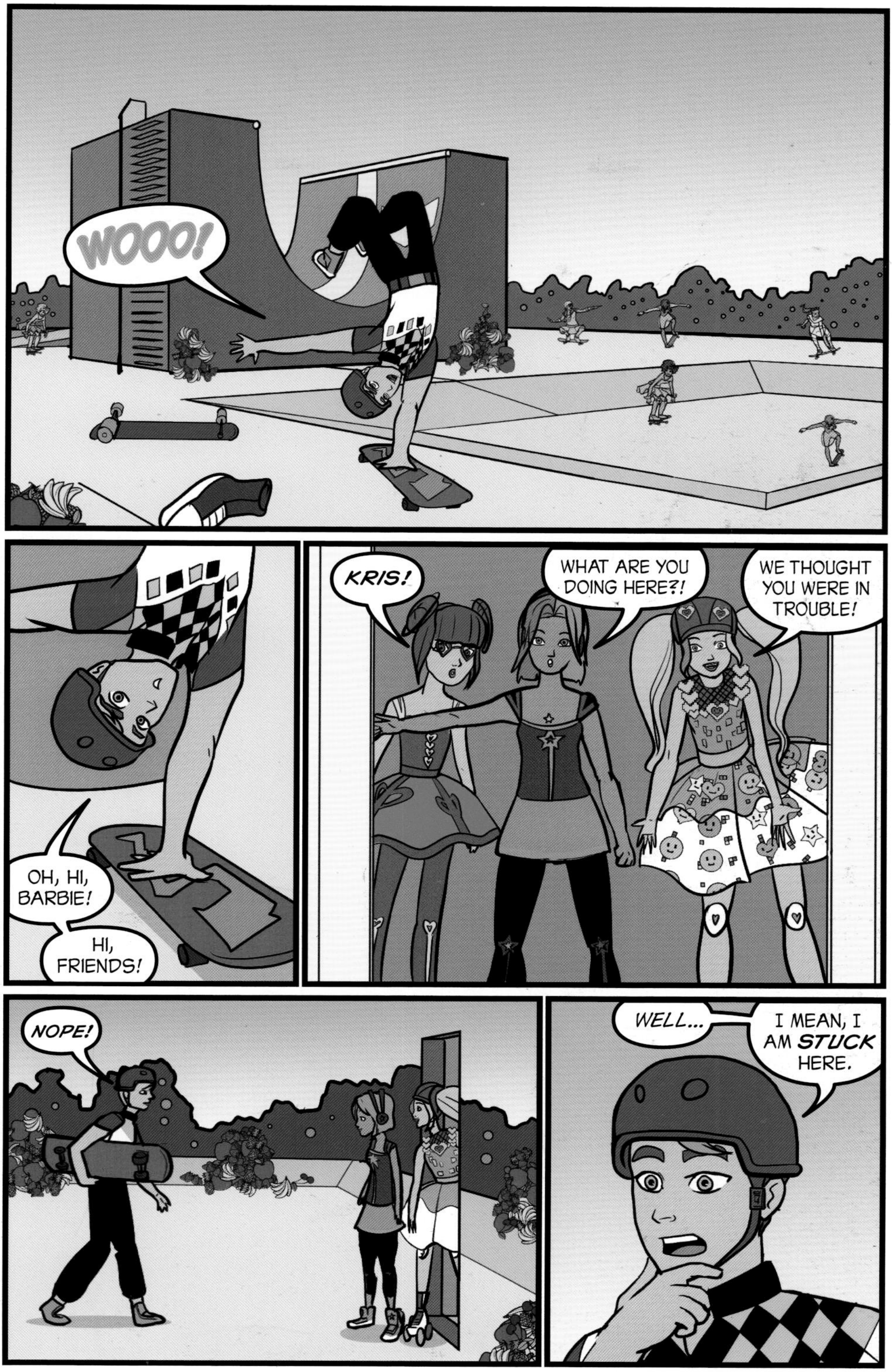
WOOO!
KRIS!
WHAT ARE YOU DOING HERE?!
WE THOUGHT YOU WERE IN TROUBLE!
OH, HI, BARBIE!
HI, FRIENDS!
NOPE!
WELL...
I MEAN, I AM STUCK HERE.

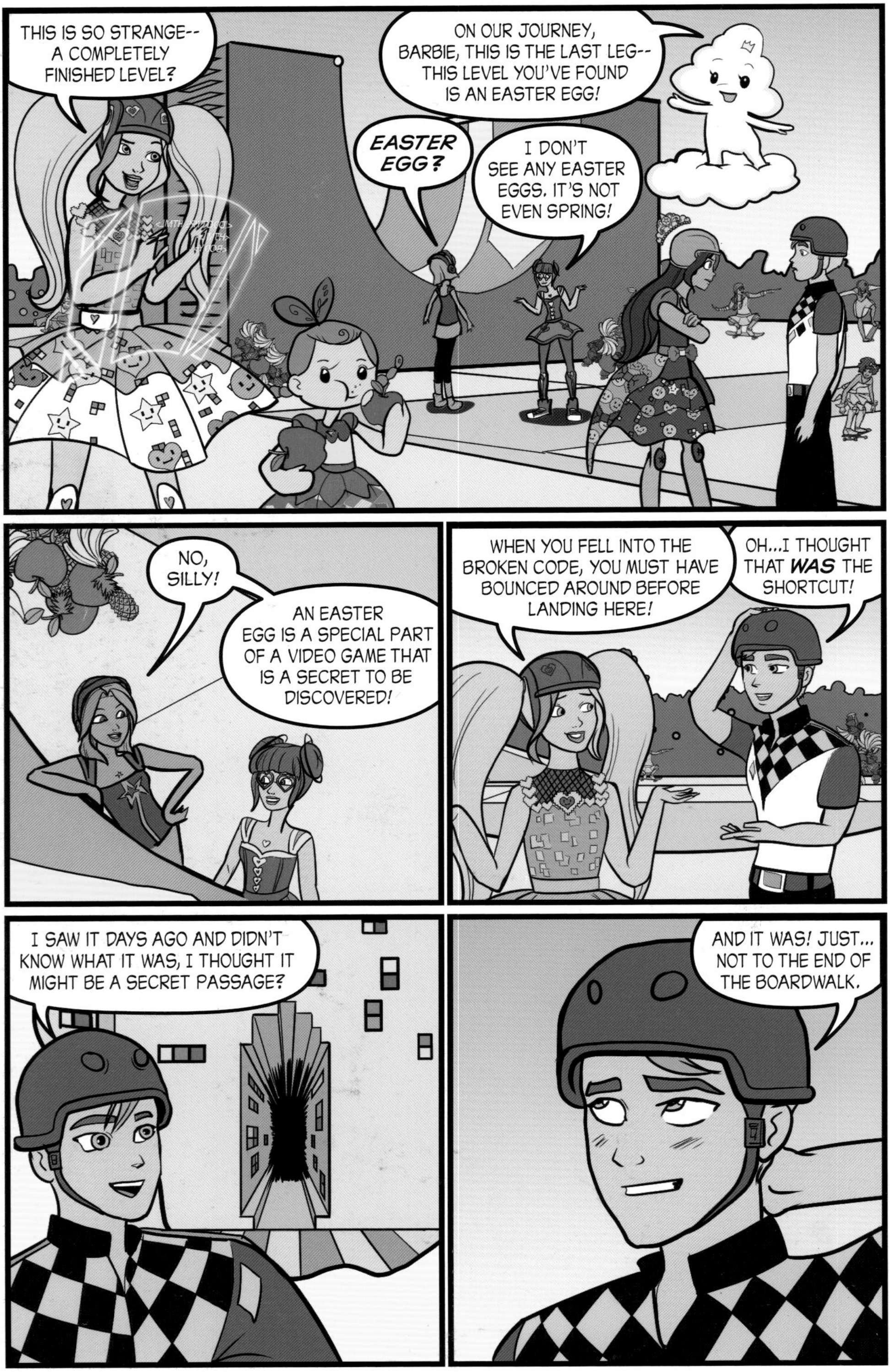
THIS IS SO STRANGE-- A COMPLETELY FINISHED LEVEL?
ON OUR JOURNEY, BARBIE, THIS IS THE LAST LEG-- THIS LEVEL YOU'VE FOUND IS AN EASTER EGG!
EASTER EGG?
I DON'T SEE ANY EASTER EGGS. IT'S NOT EVEN SPRING!
NO, SILLY!
AN EASTER EGG IS A SPECIAL PART OF A VIDEO GAME THAT IS A SECRET TO BE DISCOVERED!
WHEN YOU FELL INTO THE BROKEN CODE, YOU MUST HAVE BOUNCED AROUND BEFORE LANDING HERE!
OH...I THOUGHT THAT **WAS** THE SHORTCUT!
I SAW IT DAYS AGO AND DIDN'T KNOW WHAT IT WAS, I THOUGHT IT MIGHT BE A SECRET PASSAGE?
AND IT WAS! JUST... NOT TO THE END OF THE BOARDWALK.

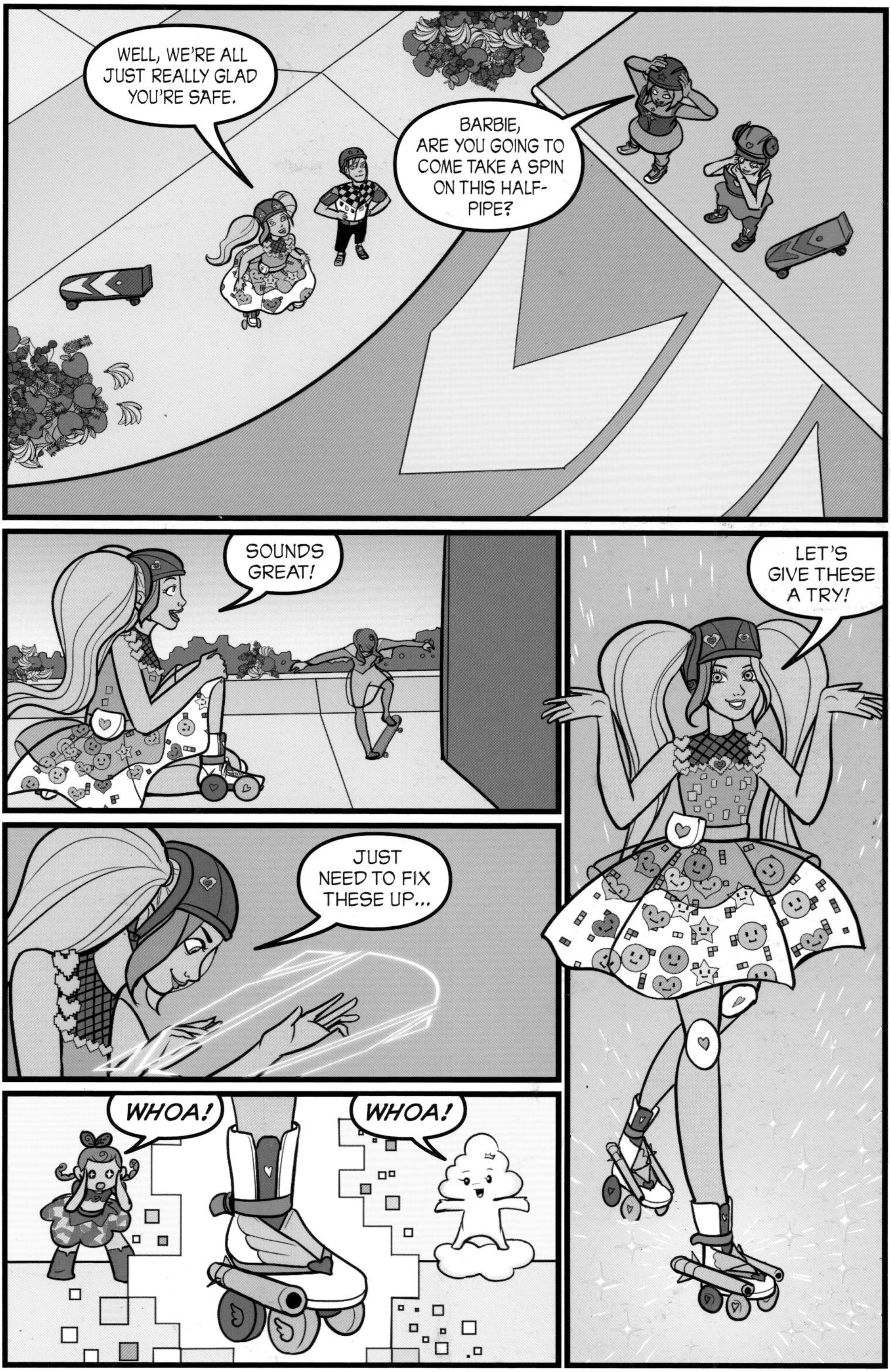

WELL, WE'RE ALL JUST REALLY GLAD YOU'RE SAFE.
BARBIE, ARE YOU GOING TO COME TAKE A SPIN ON THIS HALF-PIPE?
SOUNDS GREAT!
JUST NEED TO FIX THESE UP...
WHOA!
WHOA!
LET'S GIVE THESE A TRY!

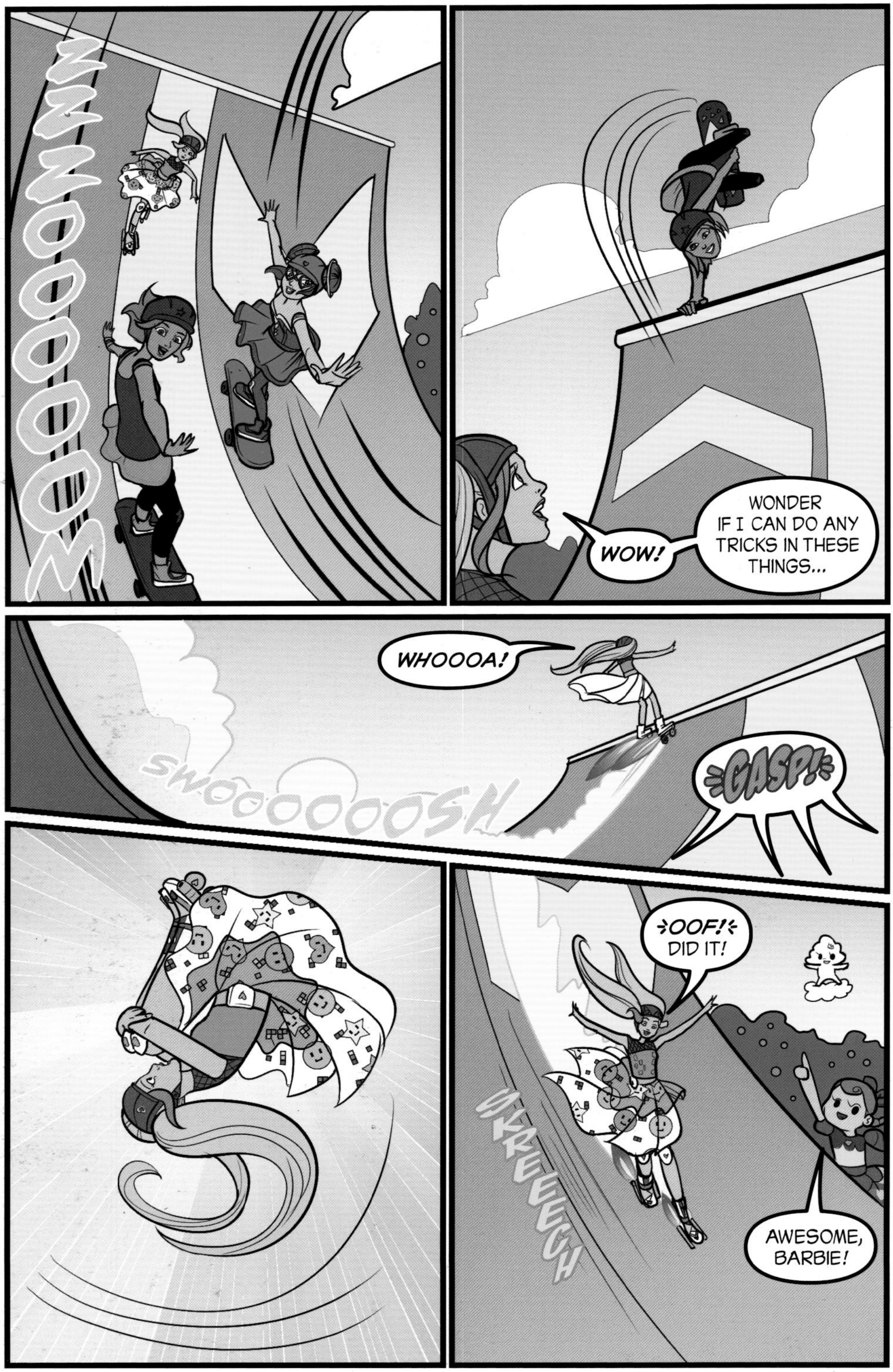
ZZOOOOOOOOOOM
WOW!
WONDER IF I CAN DO ANY TRICKS IN THESE THINGS...
WHOOOA!
SWOOOOOOOSH
GASP!
OOF! DID IT!
SKREEECH
AWESOME, BARBIE!

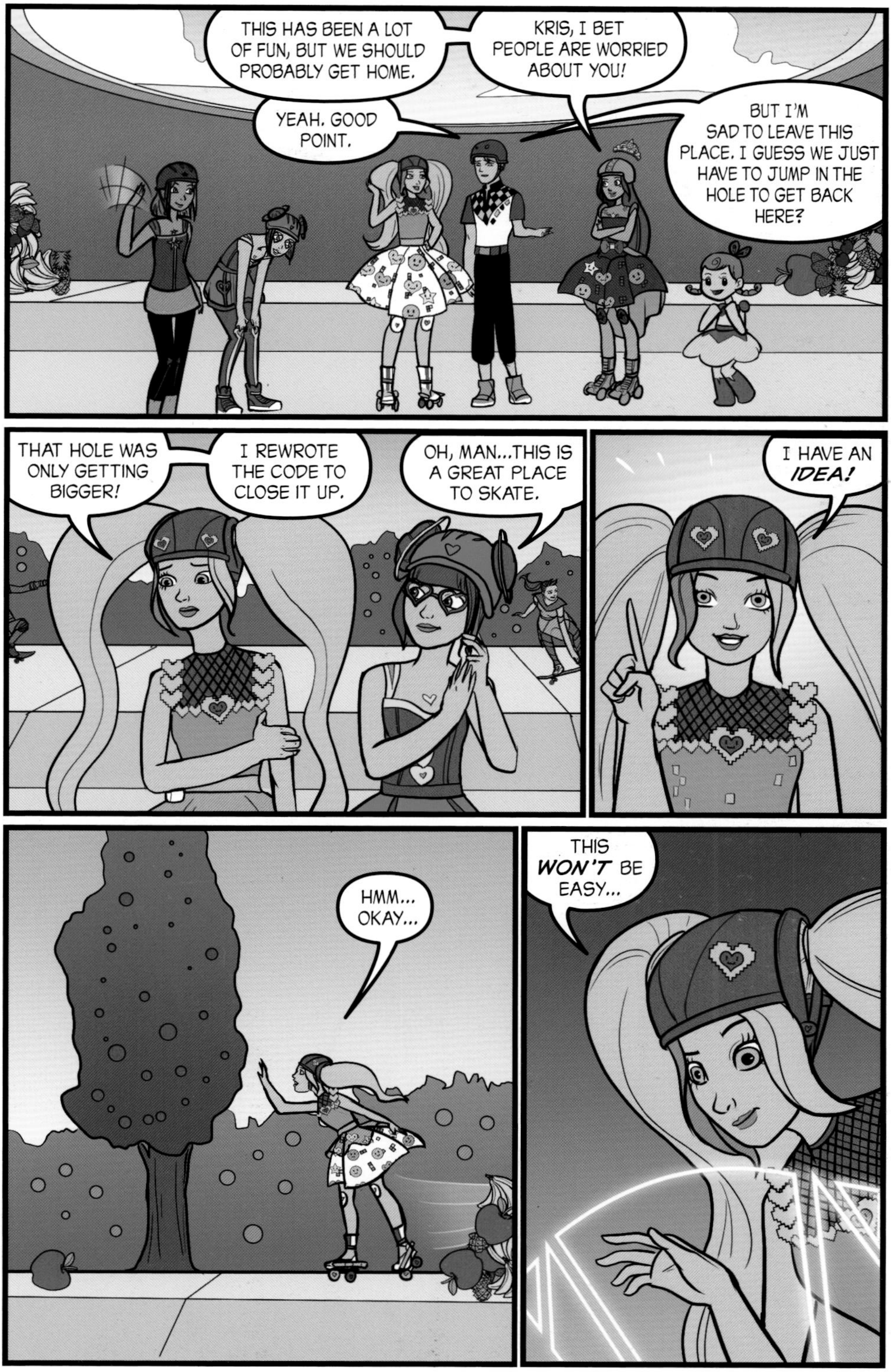

THIS HAS BEEN A LOT OF FUN, BUT WE SHOULD PROBABLY GET HOME.
KRIS, I BET PEOPLE ARE WORRIED ABOUT YOU!
YEAH. GOOD POINT.
BUT I'M SAD TO LEAVE THIS PLACE. I GUESS WE JUST HAVE TO JUMP IN THE HOLE TO GET BACK HERE?
THAT HOLE WAS ONLY GETTING BIGGER!
I REWROTE THE CODE TO CLOSE IT UP.
OH, MAN...THIS IS A GREAT PLACE TO SKATE.
I HAVE AN IDEA!
HMM... OKAY...
THIS WON'T BE EASY...

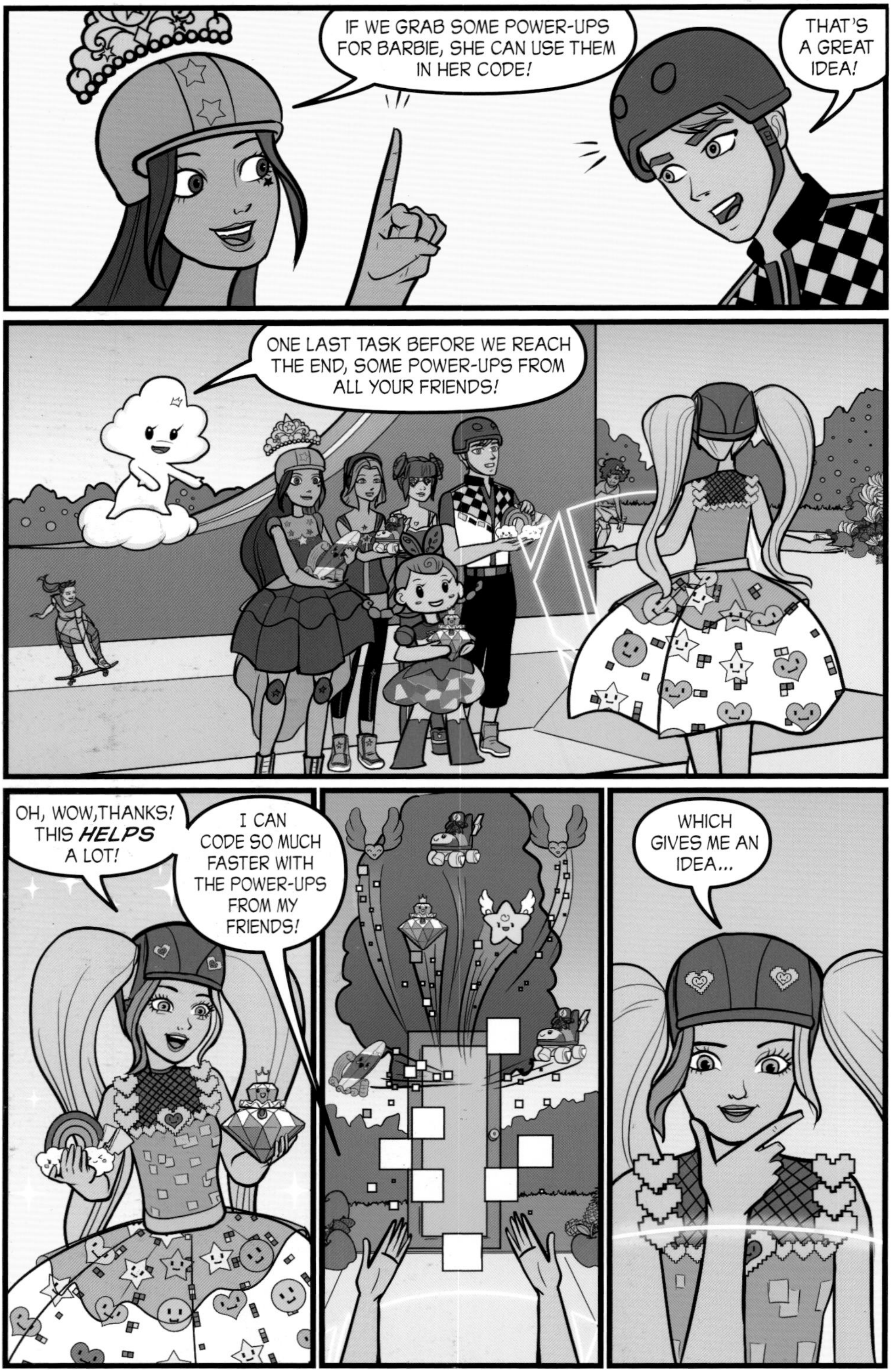

IF WE GRAB SOME POWER-UPS FOR BARBIE, SHE CAN USE THEM IN HER CODE!
THAT'S A GREAT IDEA!
ONE LAST TASK BEFORE WE REACH THE END, SOME POWER-UPS FROM ALL YOUR FRIENDS!
OH, WOW,THANKS! THIS *HELPS* A LOT!
I CAN CODE SO MUCH FASTER WITH THE POWER-UPS FROM MY FRIENDS!
WHICH GIVES ME AN IDEA...

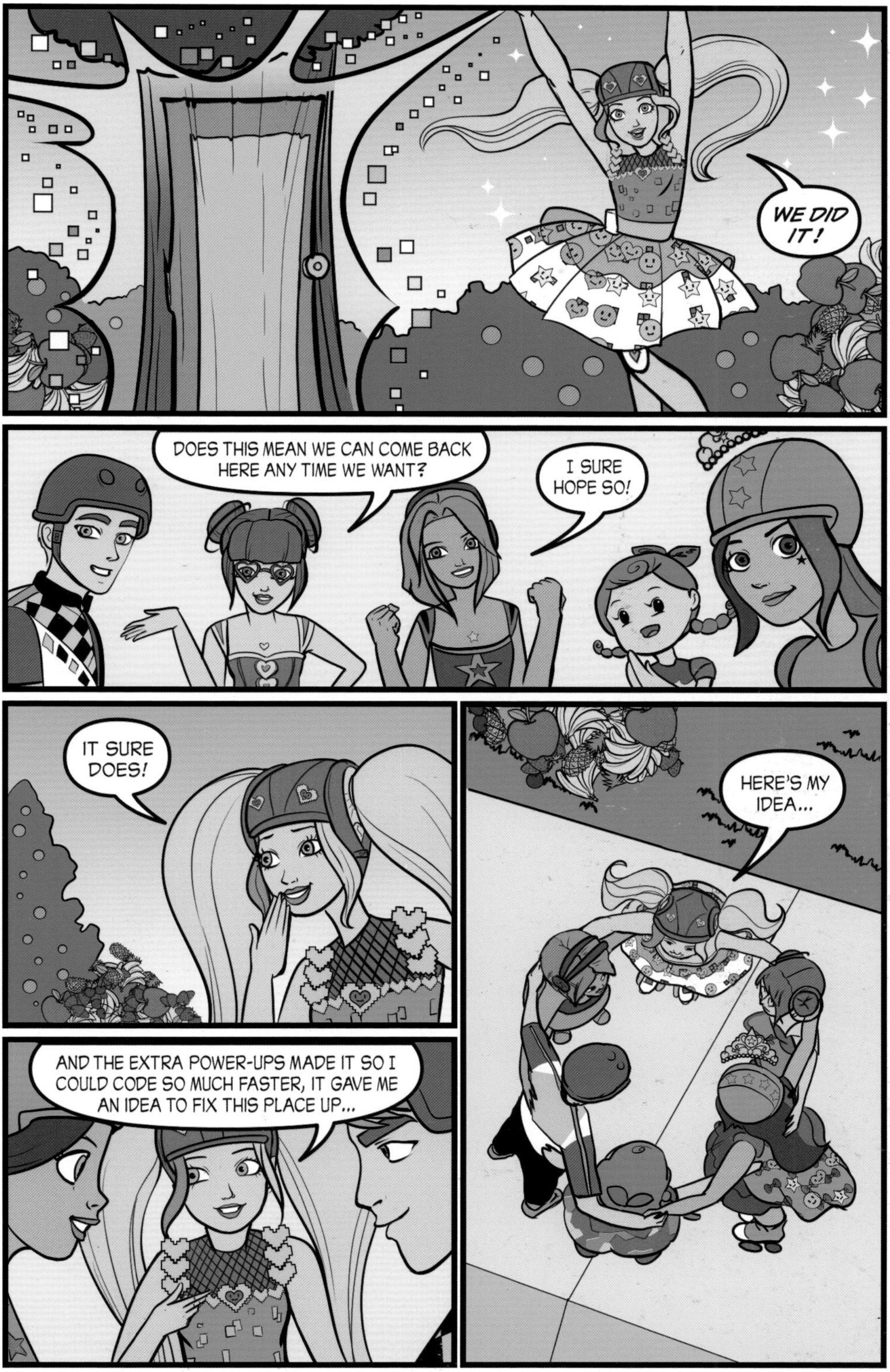
WE DID IT!
DOES THIS MEAN WE CAN COME BACK HERE ANY TIME WE WANT?
I SURE HOPE SO!
IT SURE DOES!
AND THE EXTRA POWER-UPS MADE IT SO I COULD CODE SO MUCH FASTER, IT GAVE ME AN IDEA TO FIX THIS PLACE UP...
HERE'S MY IDEA...

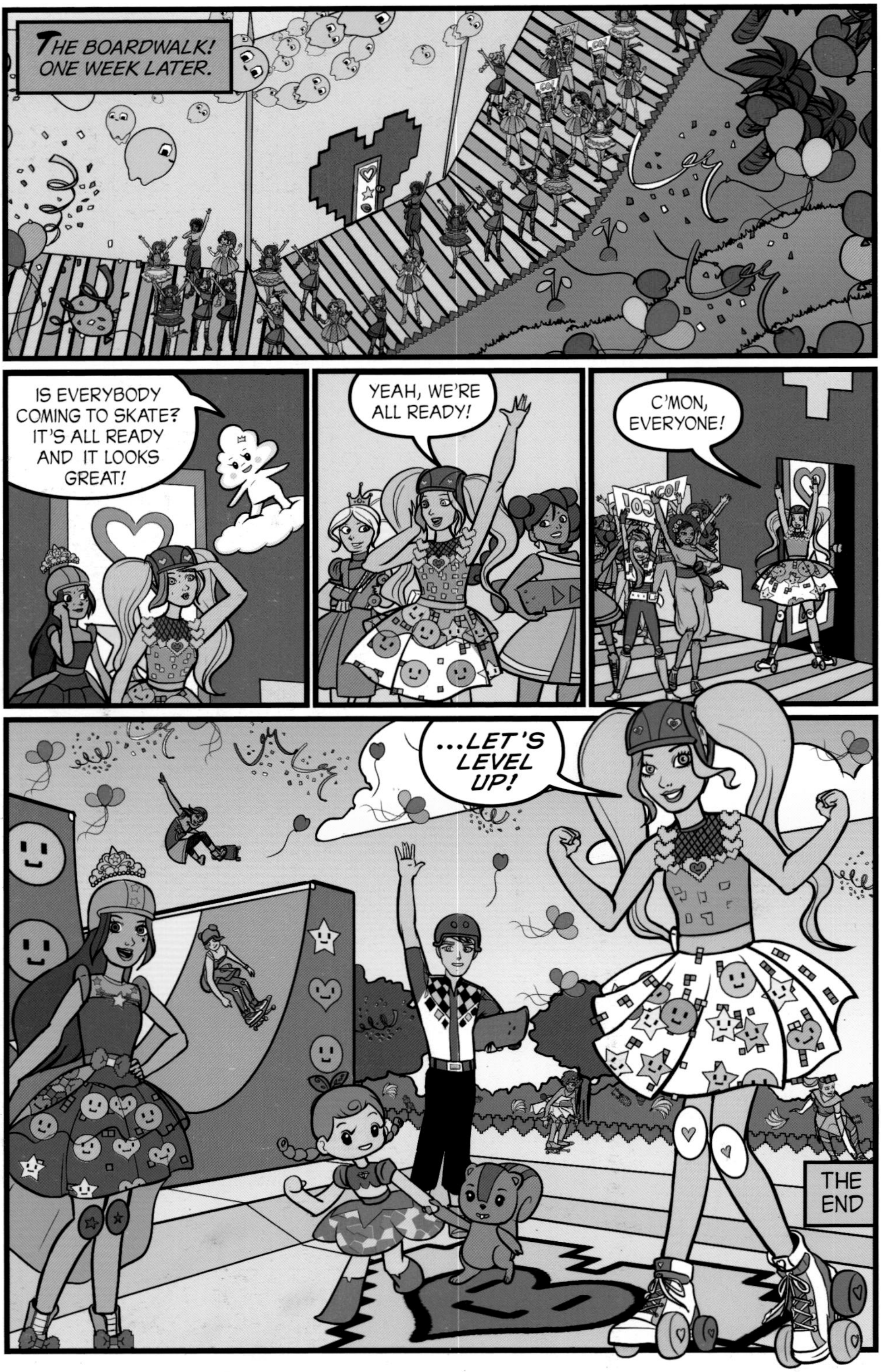
THE BOARDWALK! ONE WEEK LATER.
IS EVERYBODY COMING TO SKATE? IT'S ALL READY AND IT LOOKS GREAT!
YEAH, WE'RE ALL READY!
C'MON, EVERYONE!
...LET'S LEVEL UP!
THE END

WATCH OUT FOR PAPERCUTZ™

Welcome to the fun-filled, fantastic first BARBIE 3 IN 1 graphic novel from Papercutz, those fashionable folks dedicated to publishing great graphic novels for all ages. I'm Jim Salicrup, Editor-in-Chief and a big-time Barbie fan. The idea behind this new BARBIE 3 IN 1 graphic novel is really simple—three Barbie graphic novels in one:

The first two are BARBIE FASHION SUPERSTAR and BARBIE BIG DREAMS, BEST FRIENDS in which Barbie decides to become a fashion designer. This exciting career ultimately leads to Barbie designing an onstage costume for one of the world's biggest pop stars. But when Barbie experiences designer's block and can't get into the stitch of things, helping out a shy drummer may surprisingly get her back on track.

The third graphic novel is BARBIE VIDEO GAME HERO. Barbie races through the video game world alongside her friends, Bella, Kris, and Cutie. But when Kris suddenly disappears, Barbie and Bella discover a hole in the game's code. They will need to team-up with the rest of their video game friends to find Kris, protect the game, and fix some major bugs along the way.

A fashion designer…a video game coder…All these graphic novels simply prove what Barbie says—"You can be anything!" Or as Ruth Handler, the creator of Barbie has said, "My whole philosophy of Barbie was that, through the doll, the little girl could be anything she wanted to be. Barbie always represented the fact that a woman has choices. The purpose of BARBIE is to inspire the limitless potential in every girl.

For more news about upcoming BARBIE graphic novels and other great series be sure to visit us at Papercutz.com.

Thanks,

Jim

STAY IN TOUCH!

EMAIL: salicrup@papercutz.com
WEB: papercutz.com
INSTAGRAM: @papercutzgn
TWITTER: @papercutzgn
FACEBOOK: PAPERCUTZGRAPHICNOVELS
FANMAIL: Papercutz, 160 Broadway, Suite 700
East Wing, New York, NY 10038